DANCING
WITH THE
DARK

DANCING WITH THE DARK

TRUE Encounters with the Paranormal
by Masters of the Macabre

EDITED BY STEPHEN JONES

CARROLL & GRAF PUBLISHERS, INC.
NEW YORK

Collection and introduction copyright © 1997 by Stephen Jones

First Carroll & Graf edition 1999

Carroll & Graf Publishers, Inc.
19 West 21st Street
New York, NY 10010-6805

Library of Congress Cataloging-in-Publication Data is available.
ISBN: 0-7867-0620-1

Manufactured in the United States of America

For Mandy,
who can always lift my spirits

Contents

STEPHEN JONES

Introduction: Dancing With the Dark

Stephen Jones (b. 1953) was born in London. He is the winner of two World Fantasy Awards, two Horror Writers Association Bram Stoker Awards and the International Horror Critics Guild Award, as well as being a ten-times recipient of the British Fantasy Award and a Hugo Award nominee. A genre movie publicist and consultant (the first three *Hellraiser* movies, *Night Life* (a.k.a. *Grave Misdemeanours*), *Nightbreed*, BBC TV's *Horror Café*, *Split Second*, *Mind Ripper*, *Last Gasp* etc.), he is the co-editor of *Horror: 100 Best Books*, *The Best Horror From Fantasy Tales*, *Gaslight & Ghosts*, *Now We Are Sick*, *H. P. Lovecraft's Book of Horror*, *The Anthology of Fantasy & the Supernatural* and the *Best New Horror*, *Dark Terrors*, *Dark Voices* and *Fantasy Tales* series. He has written *The Illustrated Vampire Movie Guide*, *The Illustrated Dinosaur Movie Guide*, *The Illustrated Frankenstein Movie Guide* and *The Illustrated Werewolf Movie Guide*, and compiled *The Mammoth Book of Terror*, *The Mammoth Book of Vampires*, *The Mammoth Book of Zombies*, *The Mammoth Book of Werewolves*, *The Mammoth Book of Frankenstein*, *The Mammoth Book of Dracula*, *Shadows Over Innsmouth*, *Exorcisms and Ecstasies by Karl Edward Wagner*, *The Vampire Stories of R. Chetwynd-Hayes*, *James Herbert: By Horror Haunted*, *Clive Barker's A–Z of Horror*, *Clive Barker's Shadows in Eden*, *Clive Barker's The Nightbreed Chronicles* and *The Hellraiser Chronicles*.

> There are more things in heaven and earth, Horatio,
> Than are dreamt of in your philosophy.
>   *Hamlet*, William Shakespeare

I don't know if Shakespeare actually believed in the paranormal, but he certainly included many aspects of the supernatural in his plays. From the Ghost of *Hamlet*, through the witches of *Macbeth* to the fairies of *A Midsummer Night's Dream*, he created powerful drama from the mythology of horror and folk tales.

So, too, have the many contributors to this present volume. After all, that's how most of them make (or, in a few cases, made) their living. They are all professional story tellers, working with the fabric of their imaginations to create visions which aspire to raise our eyes to the stars or squeeze them closed in sheer terror.

'Where do you get your ideas?' is probably the one question that most authors – particularly those who work in the horror, fantasy or science fiction fields – are asked more often than any other. The answer can be found in many of the accounts that comprise this volume, as more than seventy of the world's most successful and well-known exponents of the magical and the macabre, along with the rising stars of horror fiction and film, recount their real-life encounters with the supernatural and the unexplainable.

When I was originally approached with the concept for this book I was somewhat dubious. Would there be enough writers who had actually experienced paranormal events to fill an entire volume? And, if so, would they be willing to share their encounters with others?

I was genuinely delighted at just how many did respond to my solicitations, and the range of experiences they had to relate. Compiling this book has been a fascinating exercise, and I was particularly surprised to discover a correlation between certain events – where a specific incident closely mirrored another in the book, or when writers on opposite sides of the world described surprisingly similar phenomena.

Of course, not everyone whom I approached had an encounter to relate. For example, Peter Straub wanted to contribute something but explained that he was 'sadly short of ghostly, psychic or other bizarre experiences', while the inimitable Harlan Ellison revealed in no uncertain terms just what he thought about people who claimed to have had confrontations with the paranormal.

And what of my own experiences? In many ways I am probably well suited to compile a volume such as this. I have always wanted to believe in the paranormal, but I continue to remain something of sceptic. I have worked in the horror and dark fantasy fiction genres for more than a quarter of a century and, like many people, I am a big fan of such television shows as *The X Files*. Even when I was much younger, I was captivated by those Erich von Daniken books purporting to offer proof of alien visitations to Earth. I would dearly love to be convinced that there really are phantoms, fairies and creatures of the night; that black panthers prowl the English moors and prehistoric monsters inhabit the world's deepest lakes; that the Bermuda Triangle, lost Atlantis and alien abductions actually exist.

But, truth to tell, I have never yet experienced a genuine supernatural event. Perhaps that is why I still enjoy so much reading the fiction and watching the movies.

Like many others, I have experienced disturbing dreams, strange coincidences, moments of synchronicity or the feeling of *déjà-vu*. There was a mist-shrouded valley at twilight that inspired an irrational hysteria in myself and fellow-schoolboys on a walking tour of Wales; my schoolfriends and I experimented with a Ouija board in the presence of a Roman Catholic priest with startling results; there are ornaments that still hurl themselves off the bookshelves in my living-room and lights which appear to turn themselves on around the house without the aid of any human agency; and

I have had the impression several times of a ghostly woman and her pet – a cat, I think – who have visited me when I have been severely ill, and the fever has always broken soon after their visit . . .

Yet if you were to ask me whether I have ever experienced any paranormal phenomena that I can actually *prove*, then the answer would have to be, regrettably, no . . .

However, I know most of the contributors to this book – either as friends and colleagues or by reputation – and I implicitly believe and trust the integrity of the accounts they have chronicled herein.

So perhaps Shakespeare was correct after all. If you continue to keep an open mind then I trust that, like me, the following essays and anecdotes will go some way towards convincing you that maybe, after all, there *are* more things in heaven and earth than any of us can possibly dream of . . .

As someone who has always dreamed of dancing with the dark, I for one certainly hope so.

London
January 1997

JOAN AIKEN

My Feelings About Ghosts

Joan Delano Aiken (b. 1924) was born in a haunted house in Rye, Sussex, and has always had a passion for ghost stories. She began working for BBC Radio in 1944 and later in the United London office as the Features Editor of *Argosy* magazine and as a copywriter in an advertising agency. She took up full-time writing in 1962, since when she has produced an impressive number of fantasies, ghost stories and mysteries for children and adults, including *The Wolves of Willoughby Chase* (filmed in 1988), *Black Hearts Over Battersea* and *The Cockatrice Boys*. Her short fiction has been collected in such volumes as *All You've Ever Wanted, A Small Pinch of Weather, The Windscreen Weepers, The Green Flash, A Bundle of Nerves, A Touch of Chill, A Whisper in the Night, A Goose on Your Grave* and *A Fit of Shivers*, amongst others. She has also written several historical romances and sequels to works by Jane Austen. The daughter of writer Conrad Aiken, she is married to the American landscape painter Julius Goldstein. They divide their time between Petworth, West Sussex, and New York.

Born in a haunted house – Jeake's House, in Rye – and living in another – The Hermitage, in Petworth – I feel it unfair that neither of the spectral occupants, Samuel Jeake in the first and a black monk in the second, has ever seen fit to make himself known to me in person. Or, not quite.

When I was a child, the presence of Samuel Jeake, a

seventeenth-century astrologer, could sometimes be felt about the draughty, high-ceilinged rooms of the house he had built: vases inexplicably fell off mantelpieces, my father's typewriter could be heard to chatter to itself at night; and it certainly did take a terrific effort of will for me to cross the big dark double room which was my father's study, in order to get to my own bedroom on the far side of it, last thing at night. After our family quitted the house in 1948 I have heard stories about it: one of the later owners was working in an upstairs room which he used as his office (incidentally, the room where I was born) when he heard a step go past him up the stair next to his open door. Knowing that, apart from himself, the house was supposed to be empty, he promptly phoned the police, who came at once, but found nobody on the upper floor. The intruder could not possibly have left for there was only one way down. 'It will be the ghost,' said the police. 'We're quite used to that. Rye is full of them.' (Incidentally, Jeake's House is now a B&B.)

What are ghostly happenings? Why do they happen?

Wires get crossed, perhaps. The boss of a friend of ours left his office early one day and went home, calling at a fish-and-chip shop on the way. Close to the fish-and-chippery was a phone box and, as he passed it, the phone rang. He picked up the receiver. It was his own secretary, at the office, telling him about an urgent job. By mistake, instead of his home number, she had dialled his National Insurance number next to it on the index card ... which happened to be the number of the call-box ...

My present house, The Hermitage, is, as I said, supposed to be haunted by a black monk. Neighbours have seen him on the path beyond our garden wall, but I haven't been so lucky. We bought the house as a total ruin, which had stood empty for twelve years, and spent a year completely renovating it, from the hole in the roof to the swamp in the cellar. The builder's workmen were not too keen on some parts of it, particularly two little attic rooms which I had made into one and use as my study. After the job was finished, I made an appearance on a local television programme and talked about the problems of converting a listed building. A couple of weeks later I was stopped in the street in Chichester by a woman who said, 'Saw you on TV! My sister used to clean for the lady who lived in that house before you. She said she often used to see the Black Monk. He'd come in one door and go out through another.' Unfortunately, in our building operations we had blocked up several doors and opened others in different places. It may be that we disrupted the Black Monk's one-way system; at all events, he has never appeared.

What I *did* think I saw, for several years after we moved in, was a female figure in the garden. After twelve years' disuse this was in a terrible state, overgrown with brambles, nettles, ivy, bindweed and wild hop. As I doggedly scythed and hacked and mowed through the wilderness, I would quite often think I saw this distant figure watching my efforts with a kind of amused, pitying contempt. 'Was she a very expert gardener?' I asked a neighbour's husband who had once known the former occupants. He laughed. 'Not she!' he said. 'All she liked was birds. They would never have a phone in the house, in case it scared the birds. After her husband died, she wouldn't sleep alone in the house. Went down every night to sleep at the Swan Hotel. But she used to come back every day and sit on a bench in the garden. One night she never came back to the Swan, and next day they found her sitting on the bench, dead.'

My neighbour went on to tell various tales of the couple's ineptitude about the garden, how the husband had once started sawing off the branch against which his ladder was propped, and had been interrupted by a caller just in time. I am a fairly inefficient gardener myself, and it occurred to me that the wife might be watching hopefully to see if I committed any such cack-handed act. I have not seen her so often of late; perhaps she has given up on that and gone to occupy herself elsewhere. When my mother died, Martin

Armstrong, my stepfather, said that he felt her presence
about the house for a week or so; then, he supposed, she got
her bearings and took off.

Martin, one of the most rational and sceptical people I
have ever met, had had several ghostly experiences. When
young, he lived in a haunted pele tower in the village of
Corbridge. Heavy breathing could be heard in one room;
not only humans but also the family parrot were made
nervous by this sound. And in his grandparents' house there
was a corner where, sometimes, an invisible presence made
the family dog growl and bristle. But Martin's best ghostly
happening was in a train between Winchelsea and Hastings,
where he suddenly realized that he was facing a rather nasty
little boy in an Eton jacket who was sitting *six inches above
the seat*. Very slowly the black-and-red pattern of the
upholstery began to appear through the boy, who then
vanished. Martin came to the conclusion that the boy, a
ghost, must have been sitting on the lap of some person who
was still alive.

Martin himself wrote several very hair-raising ghost stories. My favourite, 'The Pipe-Smoker', takes place in the
sitting-room of the cottage where I lived from age five on,
and where my brother David still lives. The cottage is very
old, but never, to us, felt in the least haunted; the sitting-
room, however, downstairs and back, was a modern addition
built by the old lady who sold the house to Martin. It had a
bow window divided into five lights, and at night, if the
curtains were not drawn, you could, by standing in the
middle of the room, see five reflections of yourself. Martin,
who smoked Players Navy Cut cigarettes in those days, wrote
a story about a man, looking up as he lit a cigarette, to see
that four of his reflections had done likewise but the fifth
had defiantly lit a pipe ... I won't spoil the story for possible
future readers by giving away the dénouement, but it was
very mysterious and unexpected, and made a deep
impression on me when I first came across it.

Now it occurs to me to wonder if we make stories up and then wait for them to happen? After his own death, Martin himself was seen in his study, the room directly above the five-windowed sitting-room. 'I'd rather not sleep in that room again, if you don't mind,' a visitor told my brother. 'The old gentleman comes in and potters about . . .'

Perhaps my ex-neighbour, out in the garden, is waiting for me to go out and sit down beside her on the bench. I rather like to think so. Sometime I will write that story . . .

SARAH ASH

Timeswitch

———————————•-•-•———————————

Sarah Ash (b. 1950) was born in Bath, Somerset. She trained
as a musician and studied composition at Cambridge, since
when she has taught music and collaborated on several
theatre pieces for young performers, including *Space Out!*, a
1960s space opera based on the legend of Psyche. She made
her short fiction début in *Far Point IV* in 1992, and her
stories have subsequently appeared in *Interzone* and *Best New
Horror 4*. Her first novel, *Moths to a Flame*, appeared in 1995
and was followed a year later by *Songspinners*.

———————————•-•-•———————————

*Open the front door of No. 3, The Circus, Bath, and for a
moment you stand, blinking, on the threshold of the eighteenth
century. Marble pillars, walls a delicate shade of Georgian
green, an elegant sweep of staircase of glistening polished wood
. . . Yet behind this gracious façade lies concealed the world of
the servant, the service stair of 104 stone steps from the
basement to the attic. And in the dusty basement, a locked door
encrusted with cobwebs, rumoured to lead to the under-cellar,
a vast unlit labyrinth which stretches beneath The Circus . . .*

I was nine when Miss Wharton invited me to tea to see her
dolls.

Her dolls – exquisite china dolls – dated from her
childhood in the Victorian reign. She had other treasures

too: inlaid Italian cabinets with secret compartments which flew open when concealed springs were activated; samplers; delicate painted fans, feather fans, carved ivory fans ... On the walls hug dark-daubed oil paintings in gilded frames; she had studied painting in Paris, she told me.

I have long since forgotten what the eccentric elderly lady who lived in the basement and the bookish little girl who lived in the attic flat of the Circus house found to talk about. Except one thing, which slipped so innocently into our conversation that at first I was not sure I had heard right. 'It' was often to be discovered in this very room ... sometimes she sensed 'it' passing through, at other times 'it' moved up and down the passageway outside. Once she had even come upon 'it' in that very chair beside me – I remember staring transfixed at the antique chair as if her 'visitor' might have left some visible trace.

Slowly I began to realize: 'it' was no living companion, but a *ghost*.

A shadow slips across the hallway ... a trick of the light?

I left her flat, constantly glancing behind me as I climbed the 104 stairs to our flat, conscious of a chill draught that seemed to issue from behind the cobwebbed locked door to the under-cellar.

My mother briskly dismissed my story of ghosts and hauntings; Miss Wharton was probably lonely and had invented a companion for herself.

A shadow flickers – a wind-twitched candleshadow – on the edge of the eye's seeing ...

But now I sensed I was no longer alone when I climbed the stairs. Between each bare landing hung large mirrors which reflected the staircase behind me; and when it grew dark, there were timeswitches to press to illumine the stairwell. Winter afternoons were the worst. My great terror was that the timeswitch would go out half-way between landings, plunging me into dusty twilight: trapped between past and present.

Once – only once – I saw something.

A shadow.

A moving shadow, nothing more.

Yet that shadow left me with a lingering taint of darkness. I felt the echoes of some past unrecorded tragedy that still resonated in the dusty stairwell concealed behind the Georgian elegance . . .

A year or so later we moved away. The morning I saw the Pickfords van arriving, I felt as if a suffocating shroud had lifted from my shoulders. I almost danced on my way to school.

I still revisit No. 3, The Circus.

In dreams.

It is no longer a place of childhood terror but the house of my imagination, full of strange and wonderful rooms in which mysteries reveal themselves. A power-house for a writer. I suppose I owe a debt of gratitude to Miss Wharton and her invitation to afternoon tea.

But it would take more than a cup of tea to persuade me to return to the basement on a twilight winter's afternoon. I fear I'm not as fit as I was at nine to race the timeswitches and stay one step ahead of the dark.

MIKE ASHLEY

The Rustle in the Grass

———————————•►•———————————

Mike Ashley (b. 1948) was born in Middlesex, and now lives in Kent, where he has worked for Kent County Council for more than thirty years. In his spare time he is a contributor to a wide range of encyclopedias and periodicals and is the author and editor of numerous research books and anthologies in the related fields of science fiction, fantasy, crime and horror. Among his many anthologies are *Mystery and Horror, Algernon Blackwood: Tales of the Supernatural, The Mammoth Book of Short Horror Novels, The Magic Mirror: Lost Supernatural and Mystery Stories by Algernon Blackwood, When Spirits Talk, The Camelot Chronicles, The Merlin Chronicles, The Chronicles of the Holy Grail, Fantasy Stories, Ghost Stories, The Mammoth Book of Fairy Stories, The Mammoth Book of Sherlock Holmes Stories* and *The Chronicles of the Knights of the Round Table.* His non-fiction titles include the four-volume *History of the Science Fiction Magazine, Who's Who in Horror and Fantasy Fiction, Fantasy Reader's Guide to Ramsey Campbell, Monthly Terrors: An Index to the Weird Fantasy Magazines* (with Frank Parnell), *Science Fiction, Fantasy, and Weird Fiction Magazines* (with Marshall Tymn), the Bram Stoker Award-winning *Supernatural Index: An Index to Horror and Fantasy Anthologies* (with William G. Contento) and *The Starlight Man: The Biography of Algernon Blackwood.*

———————————•►•———————————

I suppose we all have strange experiences now and again that we can't entirely explain, but they are not of sufficient interest to dwell upon and usually they are forgotten after a while. I've had my share of these experiences, few worthy of discussion, but there was one occasion when my scalp did begin to prickle and that *frisson* of fear sparked down my spine, because this odd little experience was more charged than the others and remains firmly impressed on my mind.

It began simply enough. It must have been around 1975 or 1976, as we still lived in Sittingbourne then, and we had our pet German shepherd dog, Raz. Every night I'd take him out for his walk, usually around eleven. This one night, though, we were later, certainly after midnight.

It had been raining, and although that had passed and it was a warm, muggy night, everywhere was still saturated. Our routes varied, but one of the shorter ones took me along the side of the main railway line that runs from London down to the Kentish coastal resorts of Herne Bay and Margate.

The last train used to pass through at about 12.45 a.m. and, sure enough, as Raz and I reached the short cul-de-sac which ran alongside the track, I could hear the distant whining sound that an oncoming train makes along the rails. I need to describe this cul-de-sac. As you entered it, the side to the right had houses along it – bungalows, I seem to recall – with unfenced gardens. There were street-lights, which were still on. To the left was a reasonably wide verge that ran up to a heavy-duty wire-netting fence fixed to concrete posts – the type that are cranked over at the top and armed with barbed wire to stop people getting on to the line. This verge was generally left unattended and over the years, besides the grass – which at this time of year had grown quite high, almost like hay – there was all manner of shrubbery and undergrowth which had built up, though none of it so thick that it obscured the fence or the track. Raz would often sniff around all this with canine delight.

On this night, sometime after the train had passed, I became aware that Raz had stopped sniffing and was looking rather intently at some spot deep in the undergrowth. I was interested, since I thought perhaps he had disturbed something like a hedgehog or maybe a rat. It was deathly quiet by now, but I could hear some faint rustling in the grass, certainly nothing loud. It was the kind of noise you hear when a blackbird is rooting around dead leaves for grubs.

I peered closely but could see nothing, nor could I detect any movement in the undergrowth. As I watched, I became aware that Raz's gaze was moving, as if whatever was making the noise was also moving through the long grass. Though I got close to the long grass and looked into it, I could see nothing, nor any sign of movement. I could just hear this rustling.

Then a low growling began. It was Raz. Deep down in his throat he was showing that he didn't like what he was hearing. Gradually the hackles on his back began to rise. I told him to shush, but he wouldn't. Even when I went to stroke and fuss him, his gaze did not move from whatever it was he followed along the grass. He just looked at me, briefly, with a slight whine.

Now some of you may think that perhaps his sensitive hearing was picking up another train coming along the track. That thought also passed through my mind. Certainly I could detect none, and I was sure that there was no later train. In any case, none came along in all that time I was out or by the time I had returned home. More to the point, Raz and I often took this walk and often heard that noise, and he had never reacted to it before.

While I was wondering what it was, something happened that started my skin crawling. Raz's gaze, which had fixedly followed his nose, now began to move across the road. As he did this, so the rustling in the grass stopped. After only a few moments, while I strained to focus on whatever he was seeing, his gaze became riveted in the middle of the road, just a few yards away. There was absolutely nothing there, but whatever Raz was sensing must obviously have stopped.

Then I really got the jitters. Raz began to shrink back. Not cower – he wasn't that kind of dog. But he moved slowly backwards, not just away from whatever it was but almost as if something was coming towards him.

And towards me!

I have to confess that, fascinated though I was, the show of fear in Raz was starting to give me the sweats. He had now slunk back far enough that I had to move with him, as he was still on the lead. Between us and whatever it was, a fairly large puddle reflected one of the street-lights. As I watched, suddenly, the water shimmered. I felt no breeze or any other movement, but something sent a slight ripple over this puddle, just like a vibration.

By then I was convinced there had to be something there. I pulled hard on Raz's lead, but he would not budge forward and, as he had a choke-chain on, I didn't persist. Suddenly Raz yelped and jumped to one side, and again came that growling in his throat. His eyes continued to follow something. It was evident to me that whatever it was was now passing him by and heading down towards the end of the cul-de-sac.

Raz continued to stare intently for a while, and then the hackles gradually dropped, the growling stopped and he looked around at me with almost a 'What was that?' look in his eyes. This time when I spoke to him, he happily shook himself and went back to sniffing the kerbside.

I have no idea what it was, and it never happened again even though we had several other strolls along that stretch of road (although never that late again, as I recall). Since I didn't know anyone who lived in those houses, I never asked them whether they had experienced anything. It was just one of those odd moments when I believe a dog's heightened awareness picked up something the rest of us cannot. Supernatural? Who knows . . .?

PETER ATKINS

Take Care of Grandma

────────────●━●────────────

Peter Atkins (b. 1955) was born in Liverpool and now lives in Los Angeles. After being introduced to Clive Barker by a mutual friend in 1974, he joined Barker's theatre group the Dog Company, and worked with them for the next six years. He was flayed alive in Barker's experimental short film, *The Forbidden*, and trod the boards for another half-decade as composer, musician and singer with a band called The Chase before establishing himself as a screenwriter with *Hellbound: Hellraiser II*, *Hellraiser III: Hell on Earth* and *Hellraiser Bloodline*. His novel *Morningstar* was published in 1992 and was followed by a second, *Big Thunder*, five years later. His short fiction has been published in *Fear*, *Demons and Deviants*, *Best New Horror 4*, *Skull: The Magazine of Dark Fiction* and the *Hellraiser* comic books, while his other credits include two episodes of the *Inside-Out* television series, an episode of HBO's *Perversions of Science*, *Fist of the Northstar*, and *Wishmaster*.

────────────●━●────────────

You know, I've waited all my life for a manifestation or two. I've read all the right books, taken all the right drugs, and surely offended enough people then-living and now-dead to ensure a quick night-time visit from a wrathful revenant.

And what's been the result? Bugger all. The world has remained resolutely solid, all visitors decidedly corporeal. Nothing. Not a shimmer. Not a wail. No cold spots in the house, no unexplained tracks in the unswept floors, no ghastly tread on the midnight staircase.

Ghosts. Screw 'em. If they don't want to play, that's their problem. So I never shook a spectral hand. Big deal.

Because I did see a UFO.

And I did shine an impossible light from my eyes in the middle of the night.

And, when my mother was eight years old, she was supernaturally warned that her grandmother was going to die. And her grandmother did.

It was a very bright afternoon in the summer of 1965. I was nine years old, and so were Kenny Woodman, Alan Leech and Les Thompson. It was maybe ten minutes after four o'clock and we were walking home from the playing field that our school – too poor to have its own – rented from a cricket club about a mile from the red-brick shed that was Heygreen Road County Primary.

It was Les Thompson who saw it first. I'd like to say, for the sake of drama, that it was the gravity of what he was seeing that rendered him speechless, but Les was close-mouthed at the best of times. He simply pointed to an area somewhere above the roofs of the row houses on the other side of the street and all our heads turned to follow the direction of his finger.

The object was triangular and white. But its whiteness was odd – the whiteness not of metal or plastic or of any manufactured material, but the whiteness of clouds. This thing wasn't a cloud, though. Its edges and angles were sharp and precise and it was moving very steadily in a straight line across the sky parallel to the roofs below it.

One point of the triangle was at the top. Near the left-hand side of the straight line that formed its bottom there was a smaller, square area (probably about a tenth of the total mass) that seemed to be open to the sky behind it.

Apart from the thing itself, the sky, blue and cloudless,

was empty. So it was difficult for any of us to judge distance or size. It was either small and very close or huge and very far away. Apart from an initial 'What is it?' or so, I don't remember any of us saying anything. We simply kept walking and kept looking. It was moving in the same direction as us and not much faster. It had gained maybe a block on us when we lost sight of it.

What is interesting is that I mean that quite literally. The object didn't disappear behind a building or a cloud, and nor did it drop out of view below the artificial horizon of the roofs. Instead, it simply ceased to be visible, slowly fading out of view like a process-shot dissolve in a movie.

We got back to school a couple of minutes later and caught our various buses home. I told my mother about what I'd seen and suggested we tell the police. She said that was a very good idea but why didn't we eat first. So I ate. Then I turned on the TV and watched *Johnny Quest* (or that season's equivalent required-viewing-for-nine-year-olds) and later went out to play with Dave Rae and Billy Hogan. I never got around to informing the authorities.

In the winter of 1979 I was living in a one-room flat in the north-London district of Crouch End. I was working with the Dog Company, an avant-garde theatre group whose members also included Clive Barker and Doug Bradley. Having no money whatsoever, we were reliant on the kindness of friends for rehearsal space and were currently using the upstairs room of a health-food restaurant called Earth Exchange, a place that was a fair walk from the district in which we all lived.

Consequently, being on time involved me waking up at eight in the morning, a trick I've never managed to perfect without artificial aid. My alarm clock at the time was an old-fashioned hand-wound thing with no light and which was, to say the least, idiosyncratic.

The way I figured it was that each morning it woke up

first, cast a bleary eye around at the day and then, based on certain factors such as light, temperature and how it damn well felt, made a decision as to whether it should ring or not. I can only assume it had my best interests at heart, but its paternalism meant that I was regularly late for rehearsals.

Normally this didn't matter much. One day, though – and I forget the reason – it was deemed imperative that I be on time. I couldn't afford a new alarm clock – and besides, I rather liked the working arrangement I had with the existing one – so when I went to sleep I tried to impress upon it how important it was that it should ring the next morning. It promised it would.

Now, call me untrusting, but anxiety woke me at some unspecified time the next morning. It was winter and my room was pitch black. I didn't know what time it was, I couldn't see the clock face in the darkness, and my cigarette lighter was nowhere near my bed. I was in a hypnagogic state, neither fully awake nor asleep, so without thinking I turned to look at the clock. A light shone from my eyes, illuminating the dial perfectly. It was only five o'clock and so, relieved, and thinking nothing of what had just happened, I went back to sleep.

The alarm rang on time three hours later and I made the rehearsal.

When my mother was eight years old, she and several of her friends took a glass and some pieces of paper with letters of the alphabet on them, and, with this impromptu Ouija board, made contact with the dead. Apparently, this was a fairly common parlour game for kids in the 1930s.

She can't recall any of the other questions that were asked of whatever spirit they had managed to summon, but she remembers clearly asking if it had any advice for her. The glass spun among the letters and spelled out the message, TAKE CARE OF GRANDMA.

Three days later, her grandmother fell down the stairs, broke her neck and died.

My mother, in case you're wondering, was nowhere near the house at the time.

I don't know how direct an influence these tiny incidents had on my fiction, but I think it's safe to say that they helped convince me subconsciously that we live permanently in the proximity of things beyond the everyday and that, if the veil that keeps them from us can be rent at all, it is rent accidentally and arbitrarily and when we least expect it.

A concomitant conclusion is that any effort deliberately to pierce the veil is somehow doomed to failure. It is in the unguarded moment – when we are cameraless and unprepared – that we may see, however briefly, beyond the fields we know.

CLIVE BARKER

Life After Death

━━━━━━━━━━━━━━━━━━•◆•━━━━━━━━━━━━━━━━━━

Clive Barker (b. 1952) was born in Liverpool and currently lives in Beverly Hills, California. When he was sixteen years old, he was inspired by local author Ramsey Campbell, who was invited to his school to talk to the pupils about writing horror fiction. Barker moved to London when he was twenty-one and began to gain a measure of success writing plays with members of his theatre group, the Dog Company. He made a ground-breaking literary début in 1984 with the simultaneous publication of the first three volumes of *Clive Barker's Books of Blood*. He soon followed them with an ambitious Faustian novel, *The Damnation Game*, and a further trio of *Books of Blood* the following year. His subsequent books have included the bestselling novels *Weaveworld*, *The Hellbound Heart*, *Cabal*, *The Great and Secret Show: The First Book of the Art*, *Imajica*, *The Thief of Always: A Fable*, *Everville: The Second Book of the Art* and *Sacrament*, plus two collections of plays, *Incarnations* and *Forms of Heaven*. In addition to his work as a novelist, short-story writer and illustrator, he also writes, produces and directs for the stage and screen. His films include *Hellraiser* and its sequels, *Nightbreed*, *Lord of Illusions* and the *Candyman* series. Barker revealed his belief in life after death to Douglas E. Winter in a 1985 interview:

━━━━━━━━━━━━━━━━━━•◆•━━━━━━━━━━━━━━━━━━

I don't feel that my taste was shaped by anything in particular that happened in my childhood. I remember strange things from my childhood, but there were no traumas. I was always an imaginative child, and my imagination has a considerable range – from very fanciful, light material to rather darker stuff. I know I had a reputation for being a dreamer; I had imaginary friends, and I liked monsters and drew monsters and so on. But I think lots of kids like monsters.

I believe in life after death. I absolutely assume the continuity, in some form or another, of mind after bodily corruption. I certainly don't believe in any patriarchal god – I don't believe in Yahweh, the vengeful Lord of the Old Testament. But I don't think we live in a universe in which anything's ever lost. Transformed maybe, but never lost. I think that may be the bottom line of any religious belief. And that's probably as far as I'm able to go. But it gets me through the night.

STEPHEN BAXTER

The Cartographer

—————————— • ▬ • ——————————

Stephen Baxter (b. 1957) was born in Liverpool and currently lives in Great Missenden, Buckinghamshire. A 'hard' science fiction writer, he is a trained engineer with degrees from Cambridge and Southampton Universities. He made his fiction début in *Interzone* in 1986, and was a runner-up in the L. Ron Hubbard Writers of the Future contest two years later. *Raft* marked his acclaimed début as a science fiction novelist in 1991, since when he has published *Timelike Infinity, Anti-Ice, Flux, Ring, The Time Ships, Voyage* and *Titan*, while his short fiction has been collected in *Vacuum Diagrams*. *The Time Ships* won the 1996 John W. Campbell Award for Best Novel, along with the BSFA Award for Best Novel of 1995 and the Kurd Lasswitz Award for Best Foreign-Language Novel published in Germany in 1995.

—————————— • ▬ • ——————————

In 1995 I published a science fiction novel called *The Time Ships*. This was a sequel to H. G. Wells's classic novel *The Time Machine*, written in 1895 and researched when Wells was a student at Imperial College, London.

Wells's book stars a gentleman scientist we know only as the Time Traveller, based in Richmond. The Traveller builds the eponymous Time Machine in his conservatory, and sets off into the future. He returns, and treats dinner-party guests to a lurid tale of life in the year AD 802701, and then sets off once more into time – never to return. My book takes up the story of what might have become of the Time Traveller.

One of the more charming aspects of Wells's novel is the glimpse he gives us of the evolution of Richmond through time. When researching my sequel I paid many visits to this beautiful Victorian suburb, trying to see the area through the eyes of Wells and his characters. Wells is not specific, but I eventually concluded that the site of the Traveller's house must have been the Petersham Road, which has good views of the river and the meadows beyond.

Shortly after the hardback publication of *The Time Ships*, I received a puzzling letter from a man I shall refer to as the Cartographer.

The Cartographer described puzzling anomalies in modern maps of Richmond. For example, in a recent *A–Z* map book of London, a building called Gloucester House is shown on the edge of the Courtlands Estate on Sheen Road, a little to the east of Petersham Road. But Gloucester House ceased to exist fifty years earlier, when it was bombed during the Second World War. According to the Cartographer, the misprints also appeared in council maps of the area.

The Cartographer also looked back to Ordnance Survey maps of the borough prepared in 1955, and 'the elevation of Richmond in maps before and after simply can't be reconciled'.

The Cartographer believed that *The Time Machine* held clues as to the cause of these anomalies. The Courtlands Estate was, he said, originally the site of Stawell House, which the Cartographer claimed was 'almost certainly' the site of the Time Traveller's home. The Cartographer believed a deeper mystery was at work here, connected with characters buried in nearby East Sheen Cemetery, which included the occultist Montague Summers.

The Cartographer held discussions with the publishers of the *A–Z* series, who told him that all recent alterations had been submitted by Richmond Council in the year in which the Mayor of Richmond had also held a senior post at Imperial College – where Wells researched his novel.

The Cartographer's letter concluded by saying he could not reveal more at this time, but asking for my future, unspecified help.

A little later I received another letter, from an anonymous source, saying the Cartographer had been found dead on a tube train.

Misprints – or a space–time anomaly, perhaps caused by Victorian time travel experiments?

Wells's great book was, we believe, pure fiction, but a lingering air of uncertainty surrounds it. Perhaps this is because of the devices Wells uses to convince us of his story's veracity – for example the tale is told second-hand, by a member of the famous dinner party.

Likewise, I tried to give my sequel a framework of 'fact'. I included a foreword in which I addressed the reader directly, telling how the novel was based on a manuscript – strangely aged – which I supposedly found in a second-hand book store on the Charing Cross Road.

It has struck me as odd that more than once I have been asked which bookshop, and to produce the original manuscript.

And, inexplicably, my 'fake' foreword has been omitted from the paperback edition of my novel . . .

ROBERT BLOCH

Not Quite So Pragmatic

Robert Bloch (1917–1994) was born in Chicago and later moved to Los Angeles, where he worked as a scriptwriter in movies and television. His interest in the pulp magazine *Weird Tales* led to a correspondence with author H. P. Lovecraft, who advised him to try his own hand at writing fiction. The rest, as they say, is history. Despite having published more than two dozen novels and over four hundred short stories, he will always be identified with his 1959 book *Psycho* and Alfred Hitchcock's subsequent film version. His many novels and collections include *The Opener of the Way, Pleasant Dreams, Yours Truly Jack the Ripper: Tales of Horror, Atoms and Evil, The Skull of the Marquis de Sade and Other Stories, Fear Today Gone Tomorrow, American Gothic, Strange Eons, Such Stuff As Screams Are Made Of, Psycho II, The Night of the Ripper, Lori, Psycho House, The Jekyll Legacy* (with Andre Norton) and *The Early Fears*. In his 1993 'unauthorized autobiography', *Once Around the Bloch*, the award-winning author revealed how, while he and his wife were visiting Boris Karloff during a trip to England in the 1960s, the actor told him a peculiar story. Bloch also explained to critic Douglas E. Winter how his increasing dissatisfaction with psychiatric explanations led to a growing belief in the supernatural:

Shortly before we left for home, the Karloffs invited Elly and me to spend the day with them at their summer cottage near

Liphook. They picked us up at the station and conducted a guided tour of the quaint little English village, with Boris pointing out 'ye olde' this and 'ye olde' that. 'And look,' he exclaimed. 'There's ye olde Woolworth's!'

The remark was typical, as was his warmth and lack of pretension, but for some odd reason Elly was only able to address him as 'Mr Karloff'. Perhaps it was a carryover from childhood trauma after seeing the monster on screen. 'Call me Boris!' he insisted, but, fond of him as she was, to her they remained 'Mr Karloff and Evie'.

While Mr Karloff and I were occupied downstairs, Evie took Elly upstairs for a thorough examination of the premises. Arthritic problems and a touch of acrophobia kept Boris grounded. Following luncheon he and I repaired to the garden, which was bordered by a recently constructed wall. Boris had watched the work in progress and admired the handicraft of the artisan. 'Now that's a real contribution,' he said. 'Long after you and I are dead and forgotten, that wall will still be there.'

Later, *en route* back to the station, the subject of mortality was touched upon again. Driving into town Boris drew our attention to a house as we passed by. 'Something rather odd happened there,' he told us.

'Odd?' I said.

Boris shrugged. 'Let's see what you make of it.'

According to his story the Karloffs were acquainted with friends who knew the woman occupying the house in question. One afternoon they came to call on her and were met at the door by a maid, who invited them into the parlour until the lady of the house came downstairs.

The maid left and the couple sat waiting. Perhaps five minutes passed before their hostess descended the hall staircase and entered the room. Halting there, she stared at them, surprised. 'How did you get in here?' she asked.

'The maid let us in.'

'But I don't have a maid.'

'Then who was that young lady?'

'What young lady? I'm living here alone.'

At least that's what she thought at the time. But her visitors had seen, heard and been admitted to the house by someone else whose appearance both agreed upon.

Only later did they and their hostess discover that a girl answering to her description had met her death in this dwelling.

'A ghost?' I said.

Boris smiled. 'All I can tell you is that since then others have encountered the young lady, sometimes at night and sometimes in broad daylight.'

'You've never seen her?'

His smile broadened. 'I'm not anxious to do so.'

As for me, I have never seen a ghost, though years ago author Charles Higham entertained Elly and me in a home once belonging to playwright Vicki Baum. Her apparition was apparently still in residence, and we definitely felt an inexplicable chill which emanated from upper rooms which should have been sweltering in summer heat, though we heard none of the noises which plagued Charles frequently. He soon sought quieter quarters.

Only in recent years have I ceased being quite so much of a pragmatic, because I have encountered enough incidents of what you might call paranormal inexplicabilities to shake my composure. I now feel that I don't know everything that there is to be known about the world and that the scientists who claim to know by means of mathematics and measurements and the ability to repeat experiments are constantly being confounded as new things come along that force them to revise their so-called 'laws' and expand their horizons. To me, a mechanistic explanation is far too simple.

I have no spiritual view that would coincide with the dogma of any organized religion. But I do believe that most of us are mindful of our own subjective definitions of good and evil. Most people have, even in the absence of a so-called conscience, knowledge of whether they are doing something that is harmful or helpful. I don't know whether any of the conventional legends and mythologies and superstitions coincide with my notion of what constitutes good or evil, although I've read and heard enough about seemingly inexplicable events in which some of these concepts seem personified. Cases of so-called possession, that sort of thing. I am not saying that I am still window-shopping; but I haven't closed my eyes.

RAMSEY CAMPBELL

The Nearest to a Ghost

Ramsey Campbell (b. 1946) was born in Liverpool, where he still lives with his wife Jenny and their two children, Tammy and Matt. After working as a tax officer from 1962 to 1966, and a library assistant, he became a full-time writer. His first book, a collection of stories entitled *The Inhabitant of the Lake and Less Welcome Tenants*, was published by August Derleth's legendary Arkham House imprint in 1964, since when his novels have included *The Doll Who Ate His Mother, The Face That Must Die, The Parasite, The Nameless, Incarnate, The Claw* (a.k.a. *Night of the Claw*), *Obsession, The Hungry Moon, The Influence, Ancient Images, Midnight Sun, The Count of Eleven, The Long Lost, The One Safe Place* and *The House on Nazareth Hill*. His short fiction has been collected in such volumes as *Demons by Daylight, The Height of the Scream, Dark Companions, Scared Stiff, Waking Nightmares, Alone With the Horrors* and *Strange Things and Stranger Places*; and he has edited a number of anthologies including *Superhorror, New Terrors, Uncanny Banquet* and five volumes of the *Best New Horror* series (with Stephen Jones). He has won the World Fantasy Award four times, the British Fantasy Award eight times and the Bram Stoker Award twice. A film reviewer for BBC Radio Merseyside since 1969, he is also President of both the British Fantasy Society and the Society of Fantastic Films.

If you need to believe in ghosts in order to see any, I should
have been overwhelmed by them when I was a child. Much
of my reading conjured them, and worse things, up – the
creature 'with legs as long as a horse's ... but its body no
bigger and its legs no longer than those of a cat' which leaps
through the nursery window in *The Princess and the Goblin*,
the human remains and shapes far less than human which
clambered into my mind out of the tales of M. R. James and
his peers – and while it might be fun to imagine them by
daylight, they grew clearer and more active once I went to
bed. On a more benign level, though not necessarily more
reassuring when remembered while the night-light flickered,
my mother had assured me she'd seen apparitions of favourite relatives. That said, she was equally convinced that BBC
radio broadcasts contained messages intended for her personally – all it took was for a character to have a name or a
life that resembled hers – and so from a very early age I
became sophisticated in sorting out what seemed from what
was real. This sophistication deserted me once I was alone in
bed, however, and it wasn't until my mid-teens that I ceased
to be terrified of the dark – around or at the same time as
my having been educated by Christian Brothers turned me
into an atheist. I can't say which loss of fear caused the
other. I do think that the prospect of encountering a ghost
began to appeal to my imagination only once I was convinced I never would.

Since we all struggle not to turn into our parents, one
reason for my scepticism may have been that my mother
surrounded herself with the supernatural – not just Roman
Catholicism but stuff that Catholics weren't supposed to
believe in in those days, about such things as black cats and
walking under ladders. Her father had died before she got
married, but he still sometimes dealt her a peremptory tap
on the shoulder. Her mother was living with us when she
died, and I was scared of going upstairs while the corpse was
in her bedroom – scared not of anything the body might do,

just of its presence. Soon after the funeral my mother saw the old lady standing in a nightgown at the top of the stairs, and found the nightgown crumpled on the landing when she went up. I wasn't there to see, and, having spent much of my childhood rationalizing her imaginings, I wasn't disposed to believe. By that age I may have been too busy putting the extremes of my imagination into prose form.

I've written about my relationship with my mother elsewhere, in the foreword to *The Face That Must Die* and in a more self-contained version of the piece. Suffice it here to say that she may have had some intermittent sense of her own mental problems, in so far as she often threatened to come back to haunt me if I had her put into any kind of care when she grew old. Desperation at that stage made me abandon her instead, reducing her to a state in which she was taken into hospital to die.

The Saturday after the funeral I drove with her ashes to the family grave in Huddersfield, only to find there was nobody to tell me where the plot was. The single time I'd visited it was for my grandmother's funeral twenty years earlier. I decided to come back on a weekday when there would be someone to consult, and went for a walk before returning to the car. The apparently aimless stroll took me by the shortest possible route to the point where I stopped and found I was standing beside my mother's family plot. As I saw the grave and the headstone were untended I was overwhelmed by a surge of grief which I felt was not my own. It vanished, and gave way to mine, as I scattered her ashes on the grave. Perhaps in some sense she did haunt me after all. Beneath her name on the memorial the inscription reads HOME AT LAST.

If this was a haunting I hadn't sought, the ones I did seek proved less responsive. Not long after I began to review films for BBC Radio Merseyside, my then producer Tony Wolfe decided to involve me in a series investigating the supernatural. *Lands Beyond the Day* was its name – my title, if hardly a reason to boast. Tony met the diocesan exorcist, the Witchfinder General as we nicknamed him; and John Owen (anthologized by August Derleth as Frank Mace) interviewed Singing Sid Ordish, Litherland's leading trumpet medium. My wife and I journeyed to Newton-le-Willows to meet Leonard Jones, a psychometrist who held a kitchen knife of Jenny's and gave her the name of an old relative which she had to phone her mother to learn was accurate – an impressive performance by the psychic but, I thought, too wild a talent to be of much application. Jones also painted psychic paintings reminiscent of the work of Fernand Léger, and in the course of his occult research had fallen foul of a Mancunian coven, after which encounter he'd fallen downstairs. (At least that must have been more dramatic than the plight of the Amityville priest who, having visited the bogus haunted house, seems to have needed only to come down with a virus to convince himself the Devil was after him.)

It remained for *Lands Beyond the Day* to visit a haunted location. This was Everton Library, where the tale went that an attendant had hanged himself some decades earlier. (Hauntings of workplaces generally seem to involve suicides or at least the rumours of them, suggesting that employment isn't always as desirable as it's supposed to be.) Cherry Newton, a friend, and I talked our way with a BBC tape recorder through the library one night – its cellars, its attic full of books, the latter commoner in libraries then than now – and did a good job of scaring each other for the tape. Once, below the street, we heard a cough. I returned the tape to the radio station, and next day it was played back to me. The last few minutes of our commentary had been replaced by silence, broken only by a cough. I confess to finding that pretty scary, but a sceptic who took part in the discussion which brought the series to an end reminded me that the tape had been out of my hands.

I've visited two famously haunted places on my own behalf. Robert Aickman and I were among a party who travelled to Chingle Hall near Preston, where a disabled guide told us some stories but showed us no ghosts. (The artist Martin McKenna and his girlfriend had a more memorable time there recently, when their guide dropped dead before their eyes.) Robert's signature is presumably still in the visitor's book, and that's my scrawl adjacent to it. More disquieting than Chingle Hall is Plas Teg, and it deserves at least a paragraph to itself.

Plas Teg is a Jacobean mansion in north Wales. Perhaps I shouldn't locate it more exactly, since the present owner tells me publicity brings vandals. Its ghosts, according to the booklet she publishes, not to mention the television documentary in which she talked about them to Colin Wilson, are many. Nowadays visitors are given a guided tour, but when we first visited the house one could wander at will through the renovated sections. The first bedroom Jenny entered she immediately emerged from, dismayed by the atmosphere in it, and this room proved to have been used as an execution chamber, not least by Judge Jefferies. Upstairs, the Great Chamber has a witch mark carved within the fireplace, above which is a hideous painting by Snyder, a pupil of Rubens, of the Medusa's head from which crawl insects as well as snakes. A recent canvas which hangs in one of the bedrooms shows a naked male body whose inverted head leans backwards towards the viewer, its face erased, and a study of an inverted head from the neck down beside it, exhibiting distress. I'm at a loss to understand why I find this picture so disturbing.

Whatever time of year it is, several of the upstairs windowsills are strewn with dozens of dead flies for no reason the owner of Plas Teg can explain. While visiting the mansion with artist J. K. Potter and his partner Susanne, we discovered a framed sampler in a basement storeroom. Above the motto on the sampler was the number 777; below, the Seal of Solomon. The motto was Aleister Crowley's: 'Do What Thou Wilt.' I think it safe to say there is something odd about Plas Teg. I should have liked to spend a night, but the owner preferred to do without the publicity, and so I've never stayed in a haunted house.

I don't mind thinking that I live in one, though. Jenny has often sensed a presence in the bedroom next to my workroom on the second floor (third if you're American), and years ago, while staying with us, her sister Penny was convinced our children had come up behind her in the room, when they were really downstairs. Not long after this incident we were burgled. It appeared the criminals had made their way up the house, taking all Jenny's jewellery on the way. Something had frightened them in the bedroom I've referred to, however, because they'd fled so hastily they had left the jewellery there. I may not believe in ghosts, but I'm grateful to them, and not only as a writer.

So I have no more definite ghosts for you – not at the time of writing. In due course I may be one, however, and then I'll know if they exist, though perhaps I won't believe that either, won't know how to distinguish between any afterlife and my last dream. Maybe you, my posthumous reader, can help by trying to invoke me. Maybe by reading this you already have. Is that me behind you? Is that my breath, if lungs less substantial than rotten leaves can breathe, on the back of your neck? Is that shadow that flickers across the page all of my hand that I can summon up? Is that glimpse at the edge of your vision, that object which flutters like a wind-blown scrap of litter caught on a twig, trying to shape itself into my face? Is that sound you almost heard the best such a mouth could produce in the way of a voice? Don't you know how important it is that you understand its message? This may be the nearest to a ghost you've ever been. That's certainly how I feel as I write.

HUGH B. CAVE

Haitian *Mystères*

Hugh Barnett Cave (b. 1910) was born in Chester, but emigrated to America with his family when he was five. He sold his first fiction in 1929 and went on to publish an incredible eight hundred stories in such pulp magazines as *Weird Tales, Strange Tales, Ghost Stories, Black Book Detective Magazine, Spicy Mystery Stories* and the so-called 'shudder pulps', *Horror Stories* and *Terror Tales*. Cave left the field for almost three decades, moving to Haiti and later Jamaica, where he established a coffee plantation and wrote two highly praised travel books, *Haiti: Highroad to Adventure* and *Four Paths to Paradise: A Book About Jamaica*. In 1977, Karl Edward Wagner's Carcosa imprint published a volume of Cave's best horror tales, *Murgunstrumm and Others*, and he returned to the genre with new stories and a string of modern horror novels: *Legion of the Dead, The Nebulon Horror, The Evil, Shades of Evil, Disciples of Dread, The Lower Deep, Lucifer's Eye* and *Forbidden Passage*. More recent volumes include a biography, *Pulp Man's Odyssey: The Hugh B. Cave Story* by Audrey Parente; a personal memoir, *Magazines I Remember*; and several further collections of stories, including *The Corpse Maker, Death Stalks the Night, The Dagger of Tsiang* and *The Door Below*. In 1991 Cave received the Life Achievement Award from the Horror Writers Association.

I spent the best part of five years in Haiti, exploring that Caribbean land of mystery and researching its predominantly peasant voodoo religion. I have used Haiti and voodoo in a number of my novels, and in many shorter works for magazines.

While attending many, many voodoo services, I of course saw the usual things that are written about, many of them rather wildly in Sunday newspaper supplements and supermarket shock sheets. I saw people walking barefoot on beds of fire; lifting white-hot iron bars in their bare hands and striding about with them; dipping their hands in iron pots full of boiling oil as part of *brulé zin* initiation services. And, of course, the many, many 'possessions', some of which I suspected were less real than they appeared to be. (The sexual orgies – no. Biting the heads off live chickens – no. If those things happen in voodoo, I have never seen them, and I have attended voodoo gatherings all over Haiti, from remote mountain villages to the slums of the capital.)

Two things that I witnessed strike me as appropriate material for this volume. The first took place at a service in the southern peninsula town of Petit Goave.

The service in question was a simple one that had to do with farmers and farming, featuring a character called Azaca who, with a peasant's sisal bag over one shoulder, walks about the peristyle scattering seeds to ensure a good crop. I sat on a bench taking notes, and beside me sat a boy of about seven or eight years old with whom I held a conversation in Creole. He had come down from the mountains with his mother, he told me, to attend this service. His name was Ti-Bagay – obviously a nickname, for it means 'Little Thing'.

A middle-aged *houngan* led the service that evening, drawing the usual *vevés* with cornmeal on the peristyle's dirt floor. The three drummers pounded or tapped out the appropriate rhythms. Everything was quite normal. Then to the service, uninvited, came Papa Gedé, the *loa* of death.

Now Gedé is something of a character – not the solemn, serious type one might expect when dealing with death, but one who likes to slap a black top hat on his head, snatch up a drink and go strutting about the peristyle pinching or slapping the bottoms of any females who happen to come within reach. He almost always comes to a service uninvited, but his visits are so frequent – that is to say, he so often 'possesses' someone – that his coming is anticipated and prepared for. On the concrete slab that supports the central post or *poteau mitan* by means of which the spirits attend a service, most *houngans* and *mambos* make sure to have a top hat and bottle waiting for him. In the bottle is what is called a *trompé*, and Gedé's favourite one consists of first-distillation rum, called *clairin*, in which have been steeped the hottest red-hot peppers you will find this side of Hell's fires.

Well now, I was sitting there watching 'Zaca strut about sowing his seeds, and talking to little Ti-Bagay beside me about his life in the mountains, when suddenly the god of death made his appearance at the service. And he did so by possessing the lad beside me!

In the midst of a sentence, Ti-Bagay leaped to his feet and began to whirl and stamp his feet and throw his arms about in a grotesque dance. The dance took him to the *poteau mitan*, where he snatched up a full bottle of Gedé's favourite drink, the raw rum spiked with fiery peppers. Pulling the cork with his teeth, he spat it out, tipped the bottle to his mouth, and drank and drank and drank while strutting about the peristyle as though he owned it. On passing the central post a second time, he snatched up the top hat and slapped it on his head. Then he began reaching out to pinch and slap female bottoms.

When he returned the bottle to the *poteau mitan* it was empty. The dance went on for another five minutes or so, the drums silent and all the sixty or seventy persons present simply staring in what I believe was amazement. Then suddenly my little peasant friend stumbled, fell and, after a twitch or two, lay motionless on the dirt floor.

The *houngan* and others ran to him, gently picked him up and carried him into the *hounfor*, the 'inner sanctum' of voodoo in which the altar and various paraphernalia are found. For some reason I looked at my watch as the *houngan* and his helpers emerged and the service went on.

Less than five minutes later Ti-Bagay walked out of the *hounfor*, came straight across the peristyle to the bench on which I was sitting and took his place beside me again. *And* – this is true, I swear it – resumed talking to me at the exact point where he had been interrupted by the possession, as though nothing had happened. This lad had consumed nearly a quart of raw rum spiked with hot peppers. (I picked up the bottle later, poured the few remaining drops into my hand, touched my tongue to them, and thought for hours that my tongue would never feel right again.) He had been the voodoo god of death for at least fifteen minutes, doing all the things Papa Gedé is known to do. He had lost consciousness and recovered. And he didn't remember anything he had done during that interval. Nor was he the least bit tipsy.

He should have died, a Haitian doctor friend told me later. That much pepper-spiked rum should have killed anyone so young.

Strange things happen in voodoo.

The second incident occurred at a *hounfor* in a slum district of Port-au-Prince, Haiti's capital, where the person in charge was a *mambo*, a priestess, of such repute that, when she died soon afterwards, her funeral was perhaps the most talked-about in Haitian voodoo history. She was called Maman Lorgina and was old when I knew her, and she had given me permission to call upon her on this occasion and take some pictures of her. I did take pictures, by the way, and later used some of them in painting Lorgina's portrait, later used as a cover for *Tome* magazine.

I had been to Lorgina's *hounfor* several times for services, some of which had lasted most of the night, but this time I went in daylight, by appointment. The peristyle was deserted. As I walked across it to the inner sanctum, I was thinking about Ti-Bagay and the god of death. The door to the inner sanctum was closed, and as I lifted a hand to knock, I heard voices from within. Lorgina's was one of them. At least two others were the voices of men.

I waited. I had been in that *hounfor* twice before, to photograph the altar with its row of *govis*. The latter are painted earthenware jugs, about a foot high, that are said to contain the spirits of the dead. Lorgina's people had made and blessed two such jars for me, one in the mostly black of Papa Gedé, the other in the rose and blue of Maîtresse Erzilie Fréda, the *loa* of love.

After perhaps three or four minutes the voices ceased, and I knocked. Maman Lorgina opened the door and bade me enter. I did so and found her alone there, except for some lithographs of Catholic saints on the walls, and the row of *govis* on the altar.

It is said that some *mambos* and *houngans* are able to talk to the spirits in the *govis*. Lorgina had certainly been talking to *someone* in that otherwise empty inner sanctum while I waited outside, and at least two of those conversing with her had had male voices.

But the inner sanctum was empty and there was no other door. No one could have left without my knowing it.

Strange things happen in voodoo. Indeed they do.

R. CHETWYND-HAYES

One-Way Trip

————————•▬•————————

Ronald Chetwynd-Hayes (b. 1919) was born in Isleworth, west London. He has been called 'Britain's prince of chill', and is the author of twelve novels and twenty-four collections of stories, and editor of twenty-three anthologies. His books include *The Unbidden, The Elemental, The Monster Club, Tales from the Dark Lands, The House of Dracula, Dracula's Children, Tales from the Hidden World, Hell is What You Make It, The Psychic Detective* and *Shudders and Shivers,* as well as twelve volumes of *The Fontana Book of Great Ghost Stories* and six volumes of *The Armada Monster Book* series for children. The author of two film novelizations, *Dominique* and *The Awakening* (the latter based on Bram Stoker's *The Jewel of the Seven Stars*), his own stories have been adapted for the screen in *From Beyond the Grave* and *The Monster Club,* and have been translated into numerous languages around the world. In 1989 he was presented with Life Achievement Awards by both the Horror Writers Association and the British Fantasy Society.

————————•▬•————————

I live in a house that was – with three others – built by my great-grandfather back in 1864, but so far as I am aware not one of my family who lived and died in those four houses ever came back as a ghost.

But back in the 1960s I read a book by that master story teller Dennis Wheatley. It was called *Strange Conflict.* In this story, Wheatley's heroes leave their bodies while asleep and journey across this earthly plane and the one immediately above it.

The idea was enthralling and I, with a few thousand others, decided to have a go. I obeyed all the rules, as laid down by Mr Wheatley: go to sleep with a notebook and pen beside you; keep the mind empty until sleep comes; and, most important, touch nothing while asleep or in the sleep state.

Weeks passed, and I found it difficult to fall asleep. And most certainly not a sign did I see of the Hidden World. After giving myself a sick headache, I decided to give up. I reasoned I was not the psychic type. On the other hand, the entire business might well be a load of rubbish.

Then one night, the result maybe of suddenly relaxing, I fell into a deep, restful sleep, and woke up poised over the landing. Or standing on the topmost stair looking down on to the first-floor landing. And that was the point – the only sense left was sight, so far as I could tell. No sound to let me know if hearing was still mine. Certainly no aroma announced the presence of smell.

To my left was the bathroom, to my right my office and workroom. In front the landing window, through which I could see a full moon. Its cold light was almost dazzling (I might be wrong, but it did seem unnaturally bright).

Writing this after ten or fifteen years makes me realize that I should have taken greater notice of my surroundings; tried to decide if I (the essential 'me') was housed in some kind of body. I think I must have been, even though I could not see legs or arms.

But, to be frank, I was scared silly – in constant fear that I was going to lose all contact with my body. The everyday earth body, I mean. Nevertheless, curiosity was beginning to come to terms with fear. Could I move? If so, how? Once again the answer was simple. I thought, Upwards, and found myself (if that is the right term) up under the ceiling. But at the cost of clarity: I was looking down at the landing, but the entire scene appeared to be covered by a faint mist. That mist became more dense even as I watched.

Remembering Alice and her small cake, I thought Upwards again.

I was standing by my bed looking down at my body. It was lying on its right side and I could only see the back of my head. Strangely, the right hand and wrist dangled from under the bedclothes. It was very white and still, making me wonder if I was dead. After all, what I was doing was by no means natural, and my heart (which was not in tip-top condition) could well have decided to call it a day (or night). Then the hand moved, jerked, and something eerie was happening to the 'me' who stood by the bed.

I fell very slowly forward – 'floated' would be an apt description – and found my earthly body fighting some kind of battle with the sheets and blankets . . .

And that was it. I came awake: drenched with perspiration, shaking like a leaf in an autumn gale, heart thudding in no pleasant fashion.

There was no need for the pen and paper; I could remember every second of my sleeping adventure. After all, there wasn't much of it. I lay very still for a long time, rather hoping that I would slip once again into that strange sleep, but this time I would advance with full confidence into the Hidden World.

But let me confess here and now: although quite a few years have passed, and I've tried to find the dark path, the return journey has still to be taken.

And maybe it is for the best: I keep remembering how cold and lonely it is up under the landing ceiling . . .

A. E. COPPARD

The Shock of the Macabre

Alfred Edgar Coppard (1878–1957) was born in Folkestone, Kent. Largely self-tutored, he left school when only nine and pursued his studies diligently while working as an office boy in Brighton. He ultimately became a clerk and then an accountant to an Oxford engineering team. In 1919 Coppard gave up his clerical position to devote his time to writing prose and poetry. Two years later his first book was published, the short-story collection *Adam and Eve and Pinch Me*. Other collections followed, including *Clorinda Walks in Heaven, The Black Dog, Fishmonger's Fiddle, The Field of Mustard, Silver Circus, Count Stefan, The Gollan, Pink Furniture, Nixey's Harlequin, Polly Oliver, Ninepenny Flute, You Never Know Do You?, Ugly Anna* and the author's own selection of *The Collected Tales of A. E. Coppard*. His first book of poems, *Hips and Haws*, appeared in 1922, followed by his *Collected Poems* six years later. In 1946, Arkham House published a collection of Coppard's ghost stories, *Fearful Pleasures*, from the foreword to which the following is taken:

If I should ever see a ghost I should know it was time for me to consult an oculist, or better still sign the pledge; if it hit me I should prefer not to regard that as an insult; if it spoke to me I should want to argue with it until it apologized for making such a blunder; in short, I am a bigoted and dogmatic materialist. All the same I have written a few ghost stories and quite a number of fantastic tales that revolve more or less around the supernatural. And I like doing this, it makes work easy, for with its enchanting aid a writer can ignore problems of time and tide, probability, price, perspicuity and sheer damn sense, and abandon himself to singular freedoms on the aery winds of the Never-was.

And here and now I confess that I am not at all immune to the shock of the macabre or the ghoulishly suggestible, although that doesn't ruffle a feather of my scepticism. For a period of about five years I lived alone in a forest that had real snakes in it and some deer. Well, not a forest exactly – they don't grow in England now – but it was a tidy old wood stretching a mile or more in one direction and half a mile across, with me in the middle of it in a bit of a clearing encircled by brooding beech trees. There were no roads, only paths and tracks through the trees and undergrowth, and at night it could be ghoulish enough if you fancied any ghouls. Unexpected sounds and shadows could startle me, although I knew them for what they were; the rush-away of a rabbit, the horridly silent swoop of the owls, or the clatter of bare boughs in windy winter would set my heart thumping and my sweat glands teeming, but in general this would only be when I was *returning* to my hut at night from the outer world. When I walked at night to the village inn a couple of miles away I wasn't perturbed by such things, and I suppose it was because I was *leaving* the solitude and going *towards* companionship or some human association, whereas in the reverse journey I would be leaving all that and returning through darkness to the unknown, the covert, that encompasses a lone habitation.

I instance these experiences of mine as evidence that a positive unbelief in the supernatural does not divest one of the instinctive leap to fear. I recall too that when I was in my teens my people lived in a street where there were about forty or fifty houses in a line and all exactly alike. On reaching home one winter eve I entered by the usual way. There was no light in the passage, nor, when I got to the sitting-room and pushed open the door, was there any light or sign of life there. I groped my way in and was truly startled to find I was walking on bare boards, no carpet there. I could hear nothing, see nothing, yet it was my home. I tiptoed further into the room. No fire in the grate, no ornaments on the mantelshelf, and apparently no furniture – an empty room. What fearful thing had happened? Our home emptied, my people gone, and I alone in darkness. I rushed out into the street again. Yes, it was our house indeed, but straight away the horror cracked and crumbled into laughter, my parents *were* there – upstairs. Unknown to me the sitting-room had merely been prepared for the visit of a chimney-sweep next morning, a very murky occasion in those far-off days, but for a few minutes I had been gripped by a terrible awe.

Recently I was on holiday in the Lake District and proposed to visit Grasmere, the village where Wordsworth lived and died and was buried. So on a morning I bought a newspaper at ten o'clock and then boarded a bus for Ambleside, eight miles off, where I should have to change to another bus for Grasmere. As I rode along I scanned the newspaper. The day was Thursday, 28 September. At Ambleside I joined a queue waiting for the Grasmere bus, and as Ambleside is a good shopping centre it occurred to me that I might as well buy a few things there when I returned from Grasmere in the afternoon. Now in England there is an Early Closing Act compelling all shopkeepers to close for one afternoon each week (excluding Sunday), and this half-day is fixed by the local authorities and may be any day they choose – Tuesday, Wednesday or Thursday. I turned to a lady standing beside me in the queue, an ordinary pleasant woman, and asked her if it happened to be early closing in Ambleside that day.

She said, 'No, not today.'

I thanked her. 'What day do they close here?'

'On Thursdays,' she said.

Somewhat puzzled, I said, 'But that is today.'

'Oh, no!' she laughed. 'Today is Friday.'

'Friday! No!'

'Yes,' she said, and then a mysterious officer in a foreign uniform just alongside us confirmed it, nodding eagerly. 'Is Friday. Oh ya. Friday.' And he kept on nodding and smiling.

I bethought me of the newspaper I had shoved into my pocket. I drew it out. Yes, it was dated Thursday, 28 September. 'The skunks!' thought I. 'They sold me a yesterday's paper.' But the bus then arrived and we went. I dropped off at Grasmere and having nosed around all the morning I went into Wordsworth's old church. The visitor's book lay open on a desk near the door. I glanced at the signatures. The last three were newly inscribed that morning, names, addresses and the date 29 September.

'Very queer, this. Apparently I've missed a day somehow. One whole day of my life gone, and I have known nothing about it, nothing at all! How can it have happened?'

Well, in this afternoon I returned in the bus to Ambleside and as we drew near that town you may be sure I peered out eagerly to discover one special thing. I soon saw what I wanted to see, despite my desire to make some purchases, and be blowed to the pleasant lady and the mysterious officer: the shops *were* all closed, and it *was* Thursday the 28th!

That's all, but if only somebody near or dear to me had been blasted with some strange affliction what a splurge of speculation would have settled upon me, an enigmatic bee in a bonnet trimmed with dates!

There was another occasion when the spook was invited or invoked. I went to a spiritualist seance. A number of us sat in gloom around a table while a medium, a middle-aged lady much begimped and wearing a huge china brooch, tried to get into touch with some familiar gladiator of ancient Rome. He was not at home, but at length the medium got on to something much better. In a solemn whisper she enjoined the strictest propriety and devoutness upon us, she was in contact – she declared – with the Lord of Heaven himself. For some time exceeding silence possessed the assembly, although buses and cars were hooting by and all the cries of a bustling centre of activity came up to us in that high room overlooking the heart of Oxford city. Being a shocking sceptic I indulged in as much mute blasphemy as I could think of, but if any of Jove's bolts were aimed at me for it they missed. When the china brooch emerged from its trance we were informed that God was very pleased with us but had forbidden to reveal anything else.

In subsequent conversation with the medium I learned that she had been in touch with God once before, many years ago, soon after the birth of her son. 'It was an extraordinary and wonderful experience, and I asked God to give me a message that would be a beacon to my little boy when he grew up.'

'Did He?'

'Oh, yes, a most beautiful message.'

'What was it?'

The medium pondered. 'Humph, I've forgotten it now! But I know it was very, very beautiful.'

It was my turn to ponder.

BASIL COPPER

The Haunted Hotel

Basil Copper (b. 1924) worked as a journalist and editor of
a local newspaper before becoming a full-time writer in
1970. His first story in the horror field was published in 1964
in *The Fifth Pan Book of Horror Stories*, since when his short
fiction has appeared in numerous anthologies, been exten-
sively adapted for radio and television and collected in *Not
After Nightfall, Here Be Daemons, And Afterward the Dark,
From Evil's Pillow, Voices of Doom, When Footsteps Echo* and
Whispers in the Night. Besides publishing two non-fiction
studies of the vampire and werewolf legends, his books
include the novels *The Great White Space, The Curse of the
Fleers, Necropolis, House of the Wolf* and *The Black Death*. He
has also written more than fifty hard-boiled thrillers about
Los Angeles private detective Mike Faraday, and has con-
tinued the adventures of August Derleth's Holmes-like consulting detective in several volumes, the most recent being
The Exploits of Solar Pons and *The Recollections of Solar Pons*.

No, this has nothing to do with Wilkie Collins's famous
macabre tale, but relates to a series of ghostly happenings
experienced by myself and friends. But I should perhaps first
state that I am not, for various obvious reasons, going to
give the actual locations and names of persons involved,
other than myself. I hasten to add that this is not because
the events related are fictitious – far from it – but because
the owners of the hotel would hardly be pleased at such

publicity, nor the present owners of the house concerned. In fact I was a young journalist when these incidents took place and actually wanted to write a series of articles on the happenings, but the hotel chain issued a stern veto with which my then editor concurred.

As befits a writer whose most important fictional output is set firmly in the macabre and Gothic fields, I had long been fascinated by the supernatural and even as a young child gorged myself on the horrors of Edgar Allan Poe, M. R. James, Robert Louis Stevenson and other classic masters of the genre.

Though of a highly sensitive disposition, I always went out of my way to confront potentially fearful situations and, when I was about thirteen or so, devised a system to abate night fears. I occupied a narrow bedroom in my home and there was a gap between a wardrobe and the wall at the foot of my bed. Sometimes, when moonlight penetrated the curtains, this dark gap assumed a sinister aspect and I often felt that something might be stirring within it. So I devised a scheme to dissolve these fears.

I made a hideous mask out of white paper, cutting large sockets for eyes and a leering slit mouth below a paper nose of simian form. I pinned this to the wallpaper where the moonlight would fall on it and it would shine out in the alcove. The effect was extremely disturbing but, as I knew what it was, I was able to face up to it (no pun intended). Within a few days – or nights – I took no further notice of it, and the mask remained there for more than a year until I tired of the game. It was inspired, no doubt, by my reading Hugh Walpole's short story 'The Silver Mask'.

However, these childish escapades were but the prelude to genuine unexplainable happenings.

I once lived in a largish Edwardian house and one winter night I was reading quite late when there came a tapping at the back door. The house was a very long building which had three doors to it, and the kitchen door (from which the

tapping emanated) was situated right at the far end. It was
sheltered by a trellis adjoining a paved walkway. There was
a strip of lawn running along the main garden path to the
back gate, which was about fifty feet away.

A gate at the far side of the house, leading to the front
lawn, was about thirty feet away. I make these points in view
of what subsequently happened. I got up to open the back
door, which was securely locked and bolted. In those days,
the late 1940s, there was little fear in Britain of muggers or
criminals, and I was used to friends dropping in late at night,
up to 1 a.m. on occasion. As I crossed to the door, the
tapping evolved into a tremendous pounding so that the
whole door was beginning to shake.

I called out sharply, 'All right! I'm coming!' As I started
unbolting the door there was a thunderous crescendo of
blows upon it, so that the whole of the panels were shaking.
I was pretty angry by this time and called out again. I had
the kitchen light on, of course, and felt no fear and was
prepared to give the uncouth visitor a piece of my mind. But
the door swung open and there was no one there, although
nothing human could have disappeared so quickly. There
was moonlight and street-lighting nearby. The path to the
back gate was empty and so was its continuation to the front
gate. In any event the back gate, which was about eight or
nine feet high, was securely locked at night.

I was considerably shaken by this and got a powerful torch
and searched every area of the garden, including the garden
shed, but there was nothing there. The only way any person
who had been knocking could have disappeared before I
unbolted the door (which was still shaking from the blows
upon it) was upwards, which was impossible because of the
height of the wall and the steepness of the tiled roof. The
mystery remains. The whole incident reminded me most
uncomfortably of W. W. Jacobs's famous horror story, 'The
Monkey's Paw'.

*

But the most bizarre experiences of my life concerned the haunted hotel. This was a large sixteenth-century building in the middle of a bustling town in urban Kent, which catered for a prosperous family trade. It contained perhaps a dozen or so bedrooms, an elegant dining-room, a coffee lounge and numerous bars where waiters and barmen, soft-footed and courteous, catered for the needs of the guests. It was one of my favourite watering-holes, and I was friendly with the landlord, his wife and sister, who attested to the veracity of the extraordinary happenings at the inn. These included strange slithering noises down the sitting-room walls during the night; and the mad antics of their cat, which would not stay in the room, but rushed about and scratched at the door until it was let out, terrified. More sinister than this were the menacing footsteps over the bedroom of the landlord and his wife, which commenced exactly at midnight every evening and went on for some time.

Investigating, the landlord courageously ascended to the attic after this had been going on for some nights, and found nothing there: merely an empty roof space, no floorboards but just the joists. Even more conclusively, the dust had not been disturbed!

This went on for some years, and eventually the couple became used to it and would laugh and say, 'There he goes again!' as the footsteps began promptly at midnight. In later years a young ex-RAF officer, his attractive wife, young daughter and sister-in-law took over the running of the hotel. This was when I and a few other friends became actively involved. The newcomers soon told me that there were strange things going on and eventually myself, the family and several other regulars formed a sort of ghost hunters' club, and we stayed up all night at weekends waiting for and often experiencing the strange manifestations.

I was in the sitting-room one evening when the newcomers' cat suddenly went mad: it got up from its chair and glared around the room, staring at something invisible to me, as though it were following an unseen person – or thing. Eventually it became so agitated that, howling, it rushed out of the room. I must confess that the hairs on the back of my neck were tingling by this time, and I hastened to follow!

One night, I joined a small party gathered on the hotel's main staircase long after the premises had closed, as we had been told there had been strange happenings in the large kitchens. We had left the lights on there and from the staircase balustrade we could see the half-open kitchen door and the dim hallway below. We had been sitting there for about half an hour, quite silent, when we became aware that the kitchen lights had gone out. Then there came furtive movements from the kitchen beyond: the clinking of dishes; creaking sounds; the rattle of spoons; and then the faint rushing of water as though someone had turned on the taps to wash up.

Though extremely alarmed, a couple of us crept down. Half-way towards the half-open kitchen door all the sounds ceased. I switched on the lights with some trepidation, but there was nothing to be seen and none of the plates, cups and saucers or spoons etc. had been disturbed, so far as we could make out. There was another door to the kitchen, but that had been securely locked and remained so. We crept out, considerably subdued, but this time left the light off. The same thing happened again, but this time the lights went *on* and once again came the same furtive movements and sounds as though someone were washing up crockery and utensils. This time the hair on my scalp did actually rise and there was a young police constable with me who was white-faced when we put the main lights on.

This continued over a period of several weeks of our watching and waiting, with the additional factor of the kitchen door being opened and closed, in contrast to the way we had left it.

But the weirdest happenings were to come. A few friends and the manager and his family were having a late dinner one night after the hotel had closed, when the pictures on the dining-room walls started flapping about. There was great consternation, as can be imagined, as these solid-framed prints stood out horizontally from the walls, held only by their hooks and cords.

We all rushed over, and I shall never forget the weird thrill as I pushed one picture back to the wall and could feel an unseen force vibrating beneath my fingertips. It was like an electric shock and I can only say that I then became convinced that there were such things in reality as supernatural forces. The others, both male and female, felt the same and I am sure these and the other incidents added to the verisimilitude of the details of my work when I launched myself on a career as a professional writer in the macabre field.

Kinetic energy, poltergeists? Most probably, but these are glib explanations for something which is quite unexplainable in human terms. My hair did not go white, but it did definitely rise on my head until (I was told) it resembled a wire brush, and others present experienced the same shock of the unknown. Later still, when we measured rooms and corridors in the hotel, we found there was a large section of wall which did not fit in with the general plan. We bored a large hole in the ancient plaster and, on looking through with the aid of a powerful electric torch, could see a dusty room containing tables and chairs.

My friends who ran the hotel were obviously eager to investigate further, but the brewers who owned the premises were adamant that nothing should be done. Equally obviously, I was keen to run a series of articles for my newspaper but, quite understandably, they vetoed that idea also. It would not have been good for trade and would have put my friends in an awkward position, so I dropped the idea. But I remain convinced that what I and others experienced were very real phenomena and none of them was capable of any logical explanation.

*

Years later, our beloved cat Whisky died at the age of fifteen and a half. For weeks afterwards we were aware of a dull thumping noise from the kitchen downstairs, in the early hours, exactly the same as when Whisky jumped down from a kitchen unit to welcome us every day. Eventually the sounds ceased and some time later I was looking out of the dining-room french windows prior to going to bed when I saw, sitting on the courtyard in the moonlight, a black and white cat surveying his domain.

Whisky taking a last look at the garden he loved and where he lies buried? I would like to think so . . .

PETER CROWTHER

Safe Arrival

———————————— • ━ • ————————————

Peter Crowther (b. 1949) was born in Leeds. Although his short stories enjoyed some success in the early 1970s, for the next sixteen years he concentrated on freelance music and arts journalism and worked for one of the UK's biggest financial institutions. He returned to the literary field via freelance review columns, interviews and articles, and his first fiction for almost twenty years appeared in 1990 in *Fear* magazine. Since then he has become a full-time writer, having sold more than sixty stories to various anthologies and magazines, and his work has been reprinted in *The Year's Best Fantasy and Horror* and *The Year's Best Crime and Mystery*. In 1992 he edited *Narrow Houses*, the first volume in a three-book British and World Fantasy Award-nominated anthology series based around superstitions (*Touch Wood* and *Blue Motel* followed). He went on to edit *Heaven Sent* (with Martin H. Greenberg), *Tombs* and *Dante's Disciples* (both with Ed Kramer) and more recently *Destination: Unknown* and *Tales in Time* (with John Clute). His dark fantasy novel *Escardy Gap* (co-authored with James Lovegrove) was published in 1996, along with *Forest Plains*, a chapbook from Hypatia Press. He currently lives in Harrogate with his wife Nicky and their twin sons Oliver and Timothy.

———————————— • ━ • ————————————

During 1970, my parents embarked on an exciting new project: the purchase of a small shop. The idea was for my

mother to leave her job as an accounting cashier for a large
department store in Leeds and try her hand at the retail
trade, albeit on a small scale.

These, of course, were the halcyon days when such an
undertaking still held the prospect of making a living ...
although the sun was already showing distinct signs of setting
on the concept of the Small Business.

My father, who was really masterminding the whole thing,
looked at several small businesses but each one failed to
ignite even the tiniest spark of enthusiasm or optimism. I
wasn't involved at all, but merely looking on from distant
sidelines as I got on with my own life. I had just left
('survived'?) my teens and was having a thoroughly hedon-
istic time. So they just got on with it.

Early in 1972, a suitable proposition was found: a small
women's- and children's-wear business in a nice double-
fronted shop near Roundhay Park in Leeds. The figures
(four years' worth) seemed encouraging and the asking price
was both reasonable and affordable. My father was convinced: this was the one. Needless to say, my mother was
delighted.

The necessary arrangements were made, documents signed
and the cheque handed over. My mother handed in her
notice and started her new life.

Miss Russell, the shop's previous owner, a pleasant if
matronly spinster, agreed to stay on for a few weeks to
introduce my mother to the various company reps and to
some of the regular customers. One of these was Mrs
Clayton, a large, bustling woman with an easy manner and a
large smile. Always a good customer, Mrs Clayton had taken
to visiting the shop on an even more regular basis following
the death of her husband the previous year, often staying
long enough to take a cup of tea with Miss Russell. It
appeared that she saw no reason to change such an arrangement as a result of the arrival of my mother, and she and
Mum took to each other right from the start.

About three weeks in – this would be around mid-April 1972 – the three of them were in the back room drinking tea. Conversation had drifted to this and that – the price of wool, the closure of the Clock Cinema, which was directly opposite the shop, and the worrying spread of supermarkets – when, somehow, mention was made of Mrs Clayton's 'special skills': she was, according to Miss Russell, a medium.

The idea of this roly-poly Margaret Rutherford lookalike (who, at least in my mother's experience and that of Miss Russell, had never removed her hat – her coat, her scarf and even her cardigan might come off on exceptionally pleasant days, but never the hat) conducting seances struck my mother as quite unbelievable and she said so. The woman smiled and said that such was the usual reaction she got whenever her gift was mentioned but, she went on, she was perfectly prepared to prove it.

My mother has always been superstitious – a trait I have inherited in a big way – and she was both nervous and excited at the prospect. Her initial token refusals having been swept aside, both by Miss Russell and Mrs Clayton herself, Mum agreed to have her tealeaves read.

And so the scene was set.

Miss Russell volunteered to attend to customers while Mrs Clayton, on a buffet tucked away behind the curtain, turned my mother's cup upside-down, muttered something and then turned it over. Peering over the cup's rim, closely watched by my mother, Mrs Clayton then proceeded to tell Mum that, amongst other things, it appeared that she would be buying a hotel or a guest-house at some stage in the future – she had seen, she said, my mother surrounded by lots of tables at which people were eating. My mother was incredulous and sceptical.

Then, frowning, Mrs Clayton said that it also appeared that my mother was going to marry again.

My mother's incredulity turned to out-and-out horror. After all, she and my father were completely devoted to each other, to the extent that they rarely so much as ventured out of the house – with the exception of going to work each day – unless they were together.

Marry again? The idea was preposterous, and my mother, bristling and already on her feet, told Mrs Clayton as much in no uncertain terms.

But Mrs Clayton was adamant. The leaves were fuzzy, she said, but she definitely saw another ring, a wedding ring, coming into my mother's possession. Then, as my mother began to bluster in a mixture of annoyance and distress, Mrs Clayton quickly excused herself – to avoid any further unpleasantness, my mother believed – and went home. She didn't come back at all that week, and Mum was not disappointed.

The following week was my mother's first or second week completely alone in the shop, Miss Russell having 'done her bit' for the new owner and now beginning a life of peace and quiet.

It was Monday, 24 April 1972, around 9.15 a.m. I was on evening shift at work, which meant that I could spend longer in bed.

The telephone rang. It was our doctor, sounding very serious. My father had been taken ill at work, complaining of pains in his leg, and, as the pains worsened, his colleagues had taken him to the doctor. The doctor had diagnosed some kind of heart attack and he had made arrangements for my father to be taken to St James's Hospital. He emphasized the seriousness of the situation. Things did not look good.

Rather than ring my mother at the shop, I dressed quickly and drove the seven or eight miles to pick her up and take her to the hospital.

The rest of the details of that day are unpleasant to recall.

The bottom line is that, despite one very serious operation to remove the clot in his leg – an embolism, I found out later – my father died at a little before 7 p.m. that same day.

All of the intervening time, my mother and I had paraded up and down in the hospital car park, talking of inconsequential things and displaying bravado optimism, as people do in such situations.

Dad returned from the recovery room at about 6.15, groggy but coherent, and Mum and I went immediately to his bedside. He recognized us and smiled a lot, seeming to be in no pain, and said that he hoped the shop went well. Then he told me to take care in the car. It sounded for all the world as though he were mentally checking things off before he moved on to matters of infinitely greater importance ... or, at least, of far greater significance. I'm sure to this day that my father knew he was not going to last the night.

As it turned out, he didn't last the hour.

When he had spoken to us for a few minutes more, he settled back into his pillow, closed his eyes and, seconds later, commenced convulsions. All of the high-falutin' doodads with the flashing lights and bleeps and mini-sirens started up together and my mother and I were hustled away from the bedside while people pulled screens into place and set about trying to do the impossible with the technology that was available. But, for my money, my father – although he was still breathing – was already dead. I like to think he had died just after

... and take care in the car, son ...

he had finished speaking to us.

In the small waiting-room, my mother slipped into a kind of wide-eyed disbelief. We didn't have to wait long.

It must have been only a few minutes later that a doctor came in and, in as calm and considerate a voice as he could muster, told us that my father had died. My mother, who had, I suppose, been expecting it – I know *I* had – slumped back on to a chair and broke down completely. She was fifty-one.

This was when my transmission shifted into gears I didn't

even realize I had. I took hold of the doctor's arm and stepped out of the room with him. I asked him to make sure my father's false teeth were in – they had been removed for the operation – and I asked for his wedding ring. I gave this to my mother as we drove home.

When we got back to the house, still running on pure adrenalin, I set to telephoning relatives. I was between calls when the telephone rang. Mum was in her bedroom. I picked up the phone and immediately heard a distant snivelling ... not a straight-out sob but more like someone recovering from a real weeper. It was Mrs Clayton.

She said for me to tell my mother that she was sorry she couldn't say anything more than she had said the previous week. She hadn't realized the significance of the second ring until she had already mentioned it and, of course, by then it was much too late. I was absolutely stunned. Then she said that, anyway, Mum didn't have to worry. My dad had arrived safely and was already settling in. Then she hung up.

And the rest, as they say, went the way those things go.

The bald facts are these: there was no way for Mrs Clayton to find out my father had died. The relatives I was calling lived at the ends of the country and certainly didn't know her. There was no information on the shop door other than the usual CLOSED sign.

One other thing, though.

The shop was great for my mother, but not great in terms of making her a millionaire. She's still got a little way to go on that score, seventy-five as I write this and as lovely as ever. But the trials of running it did take her mind off her situation for four years until, with a great deal of regret, she let it go. It was 1976.

Mum decided she would try to get some kind of clerical or cashiering job. She didn't particularly need the money, but she – and I – felt that the interest would help her, particularly as I was getting married and leaving home in the October. She got a job as a cashier in a restaurant in Leeds

... where she was surrounded by tables at which people ate their meals.

Mrs Clayton made several more visits to my mother's shop during 1972 and 1973, although she declined to discuss the events of April 1972. She died in the latter part of 1973.

My mother has not remarried.

JACK DANN

A Gift of Eagles

Jack Dann (b. 1945) was born in Johnson City, New York, and now lives in Melbourne, Australia, with his wife Janeen. He is the author or editor of more than forty books, including the novels *Junction*, *Starhiker*, *The Man Who Melted* and *High Steel* (with Jack C. Haldeman II). Dann's work has been compared to that of Jorge Luis Borges, Roald Dahl, Lewis Carroll, Castaneda, J. G. Ballard and Philip K. Dick. His short stories have appeared in *Omni*, *Playboy*, *Penthouse*, *Shadows*, *After Midnight*, *A Gallery of Horror* and other major magazines and anthologies, and have been collected in *Timetripping*. He is the editor of the anthology *Wandering Stars* and several others, including *More Wandering Stars*. He also edits the multi-volume Magic Tales fantasy series with Gardner Dozois, the White Wolf Rediscovery Trios series with Pamela Sargent and George Zebrowski, and is a consulting editor for Tor Books. He has been a finalist for the Nebula Award eleven times and a World Fantasy Award finalist three times. He has also been a finalist for the British Science Fiction Award, and is a co-recipient of the Premios Gilgamés de Narrativa Fantástica Award. Dann's major historical novel about Leonardo da Vinci, *The Memory Cathedral*, was published in 1995; his latest novel, *Counting Coup*, appeared in 1997; and he is currently working on *The Silent*, a new novel about the American Civil War.

Some twenty years ago I was in a sweat-lodge being led by a medicine man who, it was claimed, had the gift of eagles. It was explained to me that that was his medicine, his power. In that sweat-lodge where it was so hot that your skin could suddenly crack, I remember the steam coming up so hot that it actually felt cold; I remember trying to hunker down into my blanket and, in that moment of sensory deprivation, in the intense heat and darkness, in that small space with eight other men – a space that seemed like miles of darkness – I heard a giant bellows working, felt something flapping inside the lodge, felt the touch of feathers, as something very large frantically flew about, trying to get out of that dark.

The bellows was probably my own blood pounding. The medicine man had an eagle's wing, and was slapping it against my thigh, probably waving the wing in the steam-black air. I know that now, knew it then; but I remember that, on one level, it was an eagle loose in the sweat-lodge. I knew it was a trick, but a trick played by the Trickster, one that had resonance on a level beyond the rational. For in that instant I had felt the eagle – not the medicine man's feathers, but the eagle.

It was a shared hallucination. I remember shyly asking someone who had sat next to me if he had felt anything strange in that session. He laughed and said, 'Yeah, you mean the eagle in the sweat-lodge.'

Why was I in that Indian sweat-lodge twenty years ago?

I was researching a novel, of course.

However, traditional Indian religion is not often accessible to non-Indians, and I've been told that most accounts of Indian religion are not entirely accurate. Traditional Indians are wary of 'wannabes', groupies who see Indian life as glamorous and want to be close to it. How did I get in? I got lucky, I wasn't a wannabe, and . . . it's personal.

But those experiences subtly changed the way I experience the world. I recall being at a friend's vision-quest where everyone was 'giving flesh', a ceremony in which the medicine man cuts the supplicant's skin with a razor and drops the tiny pieces of flesh into a coloured square of cloth, which the participant later ties to the branch of a nearby tree as a totem. I asked the medicine man why people were doing this, and he looked at me as if I had just asked the most stupid question imaginable. He laughed and answered, 'Because that's the only thing you've got to give. Your skin is the only thing you really own. So you give a little of it to your friend, to help him. You give a little of yourself. You take a little pain for him.'

And so I gave flesh.

For my son Jody. For my friend Albert. For all of us. And for a little while I lost hold of my ego. There and in the sweat-lodge where I burned for a few minutes, or a few hours, I had the revelation – or aberration, depending on your point of view – that perhaps down deep in the quick of our unconscious our basic impulses are not selfish and self-seeking.

Of course, back then I also felt the wings of eagles beating in the sweat-lodge.

But it's in my fiction and poetry that I come closest to remembering the sight and smell and 'feel' of those experiences. In my road novel *Counting Coup*, you can hear the spirit voices and feel the steam that's so hot it's cold.

If you can dig up a copy of my autobiographical story 'Bad Medicine', you'll find some of the spirits that caught me in the sweat-lodge way back in 1978.

And they are in poems like 'Ceremony', which is probably a fitting end to this piece:

> I burn in the darkness
> with the others. I
> fold into my sweat-stinking
> blanket

My body hot wax my hair
on fire. I look down
at the rock people glowing
before me.

Steam chokes me, spirits
flicker in the round
blackness and I tell myself
I'm not afraid.

Oh, Wakan Tanka, what is
this Jew-boy doing here
burning for a vision
in the sweat lodge?

CHARLES DE LINT

The House on Spadina

---·—·—---

Charles de Lint (b. 1951) was born in Bussum, in The
Netherlands, but as a result of his father's job as a surveyor
he grew up in such places as the Yukon, Turkey, Lebanon
and Canada, where he currently lives. His first two books,
The Riddle of the Wren and *Moonheart*, won him the first
annual William L. Crawford Award for Best New Fantasy
Author in 1984. Since then he has published a number of
acclaimed fantasy novels, including *The Harp of the Grey
Rose, Mulengro, Yarrow, Jack the Giant Killer, Greenmantle,
Wolf Moon, Svaha, Drink Down the Moon, The Dreaming
Place, The Little Country, Into the Green, Memory and Dream*
and *Trader*. He has also written *The Wild Wood* for *Brian
Froud's Faerielands* series and two volumes in *Philip José
Farmer's The Dungeon* series, *The Valley of Thunder* and *The
Hidden City*; he contributed to the three-novella collection
Café Pergatorium, and he has published such horror novels
as *Angel of Darkness, From a Whisper to a Scream* and *I'll Be
Watching You* under the pseudonym 'Samuel M. Key'. De
Lint's short stories have been collected in *Hedgework and
Guessery, Spiritwalk, Dreams Underfoot* and *The Ivory and the
Horn*, while his columns on horror fiction and his book
reviews have appeared in a wide variety of magazines.

---·—·—---

Even though I've had far more life-threatening and traumatic
experiences than the small mystery I'm about to relate, this
incident has stayed with me over the years and, in retrospect,

might even explain why my own work so often deals with intangibles – the movement almost seen, the sound not quite heard.

I was living on the streets when I was fifteen. At one point I was renting a room on Sweetland Avenue in Ottawa, but when I couldn't make the next month's rent, I hitch-hiked to Toronto because ... well, it was the summer of love, after all, and that's where everyone was going, if they weren't making the longer trek to the west coast. Toronto wasn't Haight-Ashbury, or even Granville Street in Vancouver, but it did have Yorkville.

Physically, Yorkville was a very short street running between Avenue Road and Yonge Street, with very little happening the further east you went. Closer to Avenue Road, there was the Riverboat coffee house, a grocery store, lots of scruffy kids hanging about cadging spare change, straight people driving bumper to bumper down the length of the street to gawk at the hippies ... nothing like the fancy boutiques and restaurants you'll find there today. But then, everything changes.

Living on the streets is a lot rougher now than it was in the sixties. Year by year, and at an ever-accelerating pace, the world seems to grow harsher, so perhaps the change in street life should come as no surprise. But homelessness and being hungry is never a picnic and, if random violence wasn't so common that summer, it still existed. Life on the streets, for all its unwritten 'rules', can never fully escape its state of anarchy.

At the point in time we are discussing here, getting knifed or beaten up by those to whom long hair or an earring was a personal affront was not your only worry. There were also the police to contend with: street people made easy victims for bored cops – who were they going to complain to? – and the police were quick to pick up anyone unable to produce an address, holding them for up to three days before either letting them go or charging them with vagrancy, which usually got you thirty days in county. If that kind of a policy were enforced today, the jails would be filled in record time with people whose only crime is that they don't have a home to go to at night.

All of which is to say that it was in one's best interests to find some place to crash for the night – indoors, preferably; out of sight, definitely. You were not escaping the weather (though I doubt that walking all night in the rain, when you don't have a place to stay and the ground is too wet to sleep on, would be high on anyone's list of fun things to do); you were escaping the attention of your fellow-man.

The trouble is, kids – which is all that so many of us were in those days – might think they know everything, but they rarely have much foresight. They live in Zen time, especially when the street is their home, dealing with whatever comes up, when it comes up. They have street smarts, but not a lot of planning skills. So instead of looking for some place during the day, we would wait until it was past midnight when everything had finally died down before we finally left Yorkville. We would walk the streets, keeping one eye out for police cruisers and suburban rednecks in town to break a few hippy heads, the other scanning the area for a likely squat.

Safe squats were few and far between in the downtown core. You were far more likely to crash a party and find a corner to sleep in. Or maybe someone had come into some money and had a room for a few days or a week, so you would squeeze as many people into the space as possible until the money ran out or the landlord got wise and evicted everyone. The Diggers (who took their name from those early socialists/hippies who lived in St George's Hill, England, during the mid-1600s) provided food, medical and legal advice, but they couldn't house what seemed like an endless stream of runaways and drop-outs. Besides, their rambling house on Spadina was one of the first places that private investigators and the police would come looking for runaways.

But because of the Diggers' house, the residents of Spadina were used to having scruffy long-haired boys and barefoot girls in flowered dresses wandering up and down their neighbourhood, day and night. So long as you were quiet and weren't sleeping or urinating in their gardens, they were less likely to call the police than might the residents of some of the other areas.

The night that concerns us here started bad and got worse.

There was a dark side to the summer of love, and I'm not simply referring to drug deals – or, for that matter, drug trips – gone bad. Everybody believed in peace, love and flowers, sure, but the group mentality that could reach for such positive attributes was unfortunately just as capable of turning into a lynch mob, given the right set of circumstances. That night, those circumstances were: a hippy girl was raped by a carload of yahoos from the suburbs.

When word of this got back to Yorkville it was accompanied by the rumour that her assailants were still in the area, partying in a nearby playground. A crowd, some thirty-strong and armed with makeshift weapons like lengths of two-by-four, went to investigate and found that not only were her assailants still present, but they had been joined by twenty or so of their friends.

A brawl ensued and all that stopped it from getting more serious than it did was the approaching sirens of the police. By the time the police arrived, the playground was deserted.

The police maintained a high profile in the area over the next few hours, so it wasn't a good night to be out. But it also wasn't a good idea to stray too far from the neighbourhood because those suburban yahoos were still cruising those streets.

After the business in the playground, I was looking for a

place to crash with a couple of friends, ducking behind hedges or shrubs whenever we saw a car coming. Eventually we found ourselves on Spadina, a few blocks down from the Diggers' house. When I remember Spadina now, I always think of it as a broad, sunny street, lined with old houses and trees. But that night was overcast and everything seemed different, viewed as it was through a high-adrenalin blood count.

We'd been walking for hours and wanted nothing more than to get off the street. So when we saw the uncut lawn of a three-storey house coming up, our hopes rose. An unkempt lawn meant the owners had been away for a while – were probably still away. We went around the back and tried the door – why we expected it to be open I have no idea, but I suppose one always tries a door first. The handle turned and in we went, moving cautiously so as not to awaken anyone if the building was occupied.

We found ourselves in a kitchen that looked as though the family living there had simply gotten up in the middle of a meal and walked out – not that evening, or even that week, but years ago. The table was set, there was still food on the plates, pots on the stove with more food, all of it shrunken and dry, rather than spoiled. I remember thinking how odd that the only smell in the house was that of dust.

Brave or stupid (or perhaps we simply hadn't seen enough horror movies at the time), we went exploring, to find the whole house in the same state. From the lights of the street-lamps outside, we could see that all the furnishings were still intact. The closets were full of dusty, moth-eaten clothes; old magazines and books lay scattered on coffee and night tables. There was dust everywhere. We left trails of it as we wandered from the downstairs up to the second floor.

Then we found one room that was entirely empty except for a mattress on the floor. And there was no dust in that room at all.

We slept there that night, the three of us, and for the next couple of nights, sneaking in through the back door late at night and back out again in the late morning, being careful to make sure we weren't seen, of course.

And we continued to explore the house.

We were never really spooked, but you couldn't escape the eeriness of the place. Because of the thick dust on the floors, we knew that no one had been in the place for years – we would have seen their tracks, for one thing. And except for that one room on the second floor that we had commandeered, the impression remained that its occupants had momentarily stepped out in the middle of that meal still waiting for them in the kitchen and then never came back. Never came back and no one had come looking for them, if only to ask why, on a street where everyone took pride in their yards, they were letting theirs go wild.

We didn't tell anyone about the place in the days we were staying there, but only because we didn't want it turned into a party house and thereby lose our squat. But after a few days one friend hitch-hiked back east, another went west. When I returned that night on my own, I couldn't find the place, though I walked up and down the street dozens of times – that night, and again in the day.

No uncut lawn. No deserted house.

And now, years later, I'm left with the memory of a mild encounter with Mystery and the questions: who lived there, where did they go, and why so suddenly? Why was the house undisturbed for what must have been years? Why that one empty, dust-free room? How can an entire house disappear?

I could have asked people in the neighbourhood at the time, but that would have elicited far too many more questions that I couldn't answer, such as what was I doing going into the house in the first place, and 'What kind of drugs are you on, kid?' The residents of Spadina may have been somewhat tolerant of the hippies wandering down their street, but that tolerance would have quickly disappeared if they had thought that the next time they were out of town a bunch of scruffy kids might try to crash at their place.

So I can only make up fictional answers and, who knows?, one day I might write one of them down.

TERRY DOWLING

Sharing With Strangers

Terry Dowling (b. 1947) was born in Sydney and is one of Australia's most internationally acclaimed writers of science fiction, fantasy and horror. He is author of the Tom Rynosseros saga (*Rynosseros, Blue Tyson* and *Twilight Beach*), *Wormwood, The Man Who Lost Red, An Intimate Knowledge of the Night* and the linked collection of horror stories, *Blackwater Days*, set in a mental hospital in the Hunter Valley. He has edited (with Dr Van Ikin) *Mortal Fire: Best Australian SF* and was senior editor of *The Essential Ellison*. He has had more than sixty stories published in such magazines and anthologies as *Omega Science Digest, Australian Short Stories, Aurealis, Australian Ghost Stories, The Magazine of Fantasy & Science Fiction, Interzone, Strange Plasma, The Year's Best Fantasy and Horror* and *The Best New Horror*. As well as being reviewer of science fiction, fantasy and horror for the *Australian* newspaper, Dowling is also a musician and songwriter, with eight years of appearances on ABC TV's *Mr Squiggle & Friends*, and is a Communications lecturer at a large Sydney college. He has won fourteen awards for his fiction, including nine Ditmars for Best Fiction, one William Atheling for criticism, the inaugural Aurealis Award for Best Horror Novel and two Readercon Awards.

I'm sure we've all been told stories by people who insist they saw something otherworldly, really did have a supernatural experience, or at least know someone who did, just as we've all reached a point when someone's telling us a supposedly true story where we no longer believe it for a minute, when we say to ourselves, Uh-uh, that's it. We've been polite, tried to reserve judgement, then, suddenly, it's gone too far. They've crossed some critical line; now it's checking-the-watch, eye-rolling time.

My encounter is of the other kind. You're sharing a meal with a couple you've just met that afternoon, and suddenly you're being told an incredible story. You act polite and interested, wondering what on earth you've got yourself into, but then find yourself realizing that, even though you don't necessarily believe what they're telling you, you believe that they believe it. The tension in their bodies, the spontaneous, artless way they dart reassuring glances at one another, the evident relief – you see it all. It makes all the difference in the world.

Sure, you tell yourself, being cynical, streetwise, so tired of the old chestnuts and urban myths being served up again and again, it's just a performance piece, a psychodrama. But there's nothing to gain but the telling itself, no larger audience, no other reward than the purging, their getting it out there so they're not alone with it any more. And, sure, sometimes, a lot of the time, it is easier to share things with strangers. You know with certainty that this is the way it's done. But more, you sense the truth of what they're saying.

On 13 January 1984, on our way to a jazz concert at Three Rivers in central California, acclaimed, award-winning SF and fantasy writer Jack Vance, his wife Norma and I met a couple – I'll call them Jeff and Margaret Tate – who knew Jack's body of work and invited us to have dinner with them at a local Basque restaurant. Conversation was easy and relaxed but, as the meal progressed, Jeff and Margaret conferred quietly to one side, then asked if they could tell us about what happened to their family back in 1971 in a quiet suburban house close by. What could we say?

Soon they were telling us how a job transfer for Jeff had brought them to the area in April 1971. Their three children – Melinda, thirteen, Julie, twelve, and Lenny, ten – all liked the eleven-room, two-storeyed house, especially its spacious attic bedroom. The girls won it on the toss of a coin, much to Lenny's disappointment, and they moved their things in.

Several weeks later, over breakfast, Julie told the family how she'd had a frightening dream about a 'green man' sitting on the end of her bed. The announcement astonished Melinda, because she'd had the same dream that very night. A green man had been sitting on the end of her bed too. Like Julie, Melinda remembered no other details.

Daily routines of work and school soon made it all seem an odd and rather unpleasant coincidence; that is, until they both had the same dream again several weeks later. Once again, the Green Man was sitting on the ends of their beds, watching them. Jeff and Margaret came downstairs that morning to find their daughters asleep on sofas in the living-room.

The girls refused to sleep in the room again, much to Lenny's delight.

He promptly moved his things into the attic. For weeks nothing else happened. Then, one sunny afternoon when Lenny was home from school early and coming out of the upstairs bathroom, he glanced along the hall and saw the Green Man running at him in great, impossible, cartoon-figure strides. He rushed back into the bathroom, slammed the door shut and locked it, and went blind in his right eye. He is blind to this day.

His mother found him crying, still locked in the bathroom, when she came home from work a short while later. Lenny was hysterical, calling over and over, 'Is he still out there? Is he still out there?'

Worse still, convinced that the Green Man was impersonating his mother, the boy refused to come out when Margaret told him to. Shrewdly, she phoned the police and paramedics, who finally persuaded the boy to unlock the door. Not surprisingly, the police suspected Margaret of having struck her son, but there was no bruising around the blind eye, no signs of a blow at all. He was later diagnosed as having a detached right retina. Though grudgingly listed by the relevant authorities as being the result of a hysteria-induced trauma, fear is what caused it. A profound and deeply felt terror.

Needless to say, the daughters were blamed for spooking the boy with their talk of a green man and, as so often happens, the boy's partial blindness became just an unfortunate event in otherwise pretty ordinary lives. Lenny's things were moved to a first-floor bedroom and the attic room was used for storage. Again weeks passed, enough time to make any supernatural connection seem foolish. Time seems to dull almost everything.

The next phase of the haunting involved poltergeist activity. One Sunday evening, the family were having dinner in the family room when there was a sudden crash from the living-room adjacent. When they rushed to investigate, they found everything on the mantelpiece – vases, photographs, various ornaments – lying shattered in the middle of the floor.

They discussed moving at last. Several nights later, Jeff and Margaret awoke to thumping from the attic room, the first of many such disturbances. By now, the Tates were keeping a gun in a drawer beside their bed but, whenever Jeff went with gun and flashlight to investigate, he found nothing. The thumping always stopped before he got there.

They put the house on the market, but not soon enough. When Margaret was alone in her bedroom one afternoon, she heard a noise from downstairs and went to investigate. Standing on the first-floor landing, she was picked up from behind and thrown down the stairs. She broke her back and is very lucky to be alive. Naturally the authorities were never given the 'real' story. She tripped and fell, she said. At the time of sharing their story with us these twelve years later, Margaret still used a walking stick and was in constant pain from the incident. Telling us about it, her hand was closed so tightly around the stick's curved handle that the knuckles were white.

Having unburdened themselves at long last, having lived in the fear of being written off as crackpots, Jeff and Margaret asked if we'd mind meeting their now grown-up children so they too could 'purge', be 'debriefed', whatever you could call it. Apparently they all lived close by and had kept their family's story pretty much to themselves. We begged off doing that. We'd driven a long way and were tired, but in truth we'd simply had enough of the incredible intensity, of being prized out of our mundane affairs so dramatically and having to deal with the unacceptable. We needed to scramble back.

Now I regret not following through, of course, and finishing what we'd started, giving what they needed. Absolution of some kind. The comfort of strangers.

And that's the story, one which Jack, Norma and I have never quite known what to do with. On our way back to our motel, we discussed what they had told us, so quietly, so convincingly, in that cheerful, brightly lit restaurant, and on our return journey from Three Rivers even made a detour to see the house in question. It seemed peaceful, ordinary enough. The curtains were drawn.

On the back seat of a car parked out front were a dozen or so crucifixes.

Just a house, just a story, yet, adapted, changed in appropriate ways, brought into southern climes and added to material I already had for a story, ironically, about the true nature of ghosts and hauntings, their tale became the chilling heart of 'The Bullet That Grows in the Gun', a story in my 1995 collection *An Intimate Knowledge of the Night*. I guess, like the Tates, I needed to talk it out too.

LIONEL FANTHORPE

Hands on the Wheel

Lionel Fanthorpe (b. 1935) was born in Dareham, Norfolk. While working as a full-time teacher, he wrote his first published story for John Spencer & Co. in 1952, and until 1966 he produced almost two hundred science fiction, fantasy and horror novels for their Badger Books imprint with titles like *The Macabre Ones, Softly By Moonlight, Valley of the Vampire, The Crawling Fiend, The Loch Ness Terror, Fingers of Darkness* and *Rodent Mutation*. Using a variety of pseudonyms, he also wrote more than half the stories published in Badger's paperback series *Supernatural Stories* (1954–67). In 1987 Fanthorpe was ordained as an Anglican priest, serving part-time in the Church-in-Wales. After taking early retirement as the Headmaster of Glyn Derw Comprehensive High School in Cardiff, he became a self-employed writer, broadcaster and lecturer in 1989. His more recent books (sometimes written in collaboration with his wife Patricia) include *Rennes-le-Château: Its Mysteries and Secrets, The Oak Island Mystery, Thoughts and Prayers for the Bereaved, Thoughts and Prayers for Healing Times*, two volumes of *Thoughts and Prayers with the Bible, Children of the Bible* and *Down the Badger Hole*. He recently hosted the popular television show about extraordinary phenomena, *Fortean TV*.

I met Bill Farrar in 1967 when we both worked at Gamlingay Village in Cambridgeshire. I was Further Education Tutor and Bill was Head of Maths and Science. He was a very talented guy: an expert photographer, a good all-round scientist and a gifted mathematician. He was also an *incredibly* good driver. There is Mr or Ms good average motorist; then there are really expert driving enthusiasts; finally there are nature's wheelmen and -women who seem to have an invisible external nervous system that puts their brains in direct contact with the road wheels. They are the car. They are road magicians. Bill was one of those.

All too rarely, you meet people for whom you have an instant and instinctive natural affinity – Bill was one of them. He was the kind of friend and colleague who was always there when he was needed. We studied together for a College of Preceptors teachers' exam and he also co-authored a textbook with me. We really were like brothers. Sadly, we lost touch for a few years when I moved to London, but we met up again four or five years ago when I heard he'd been seriously ill. He lost a kidney and the transplant didn't last long. Then there was a major heart problem and finally lung cancer. Brilliant medics at Addenbrookes kept him going for a miraculously long time, and he fought it like a Trojan all the way, but the day came when he said simply: 'Lionel, I'd like you to take my funeral service when the time comes.' We both knew it was only a matter of days.

I got a phone call from Father Ian, the Cambridgeshire village priest in whose church the service was to be conducted. Bill had gone. I drove over from Wales the night before the service and around midnight Fr Ian and I were sitting on the couch in his study with Bible and prayer books spread out in front of us, planning Bill's service for the following morning.

Now I must emphasize here that I'm not normally in the least psychic. I'm as solid and down-to-earth as Norfolk clay. I'm an ordinary, simple and basically orthodox Anglican priest. I believe every word of the Christian creed – but mystic visionary I definitely am not.

As Ian and I discussed who was going to do what during Bill's service, I was suddenly very strongly *aware* that Bill was in the room with us. I sensed him quite clearly standing behind us, leaning over the couch with a gigantic smile and resting a hand on each of our shoulders. When I 'heard' him speak, the 'voice' was inside my head. There was nothing that a tape recorder could have picked up, but I knew exactly what he was saying. The phrasing and intonation were undoubtedly Bill's.

'It's really good of you two boys to go to all this trouble for me after a long day's work!' His characteristic humour shone through.

I said to Ian, 'Bill's here, and he's thanking us for getting his service ready.' Then I got a second message. Bill said: 'All shall be well, and all shall be well, and all manner of thing shall be well.' Then that strong sense of his presence slowly faded. I turned to Ian. 'Bill just quoted the words of Lady Juliana of Norwich, you know the bit where she had the mystical vision of heaven, and when the other nuns asked her what it was like all she could say was: "All shall..."' and I repeated Bill's message to Ian.

He went very quiet. 'Say that again, Father.'

I repeated it. Ian drew a deep breath.

'I was actually with Bill in the hospital as he slipped away,' he said, 'and I was holding his hand as he lost consciousness. The very last thing I said to him was "Hold on to this, Bill: 'All shall be well, and all shall be well, and all manner of thing shall be well.'"'

Next morning the funeral service went normally. The church was packed with Bill's family, friends and former students. I said my goodbyes to his people and then set off to drive back to Wales.

About half-way along the M4 I was overtaking a slow-moving juggernaut with a trailer. I was in the middle lane doing about sixty when the juggernaut driver suddenly pulled over to the right and connected with the nearside rear of my Granada. This imparted an irresistible left-hand spin which I couldn't control, and I found myself broadside in front of him being pushed up the M4 like dust in front of a broom. A tyre ripped off sideways. The Granada started to tilt. I guessed it was going to roll at any second and the juggernaut would then be straight over the top. I had a quick mental image of something like human corned beef being cut out by the fire brigade and identified by fingerprints and dental records. Then the artic driver saw me and braked hard. Being jammed up against his front bumper had prevented the left-hand spin from continuing, but as soon as he braked and made space the spin continued ... so I came all the way around and faced him more or less head-on. There was another crash as he hit my nearside front; the Granada took off like a snooker ball at an angle of forty-five degrees: straight over the hard shoulder, and over a ditch. She finally came to rest in long grass with the front bumper up against a hedge. I'd heard the fuel tank scraping the ground ominously on the way over, and my first thought was to get out fast in case the petrol exploded. Fine in theory, but the crash had jammed the doors. Thirty years' weight training and martial arts experience can provide a bonus or two in an emergency. I wriggled out of my safety belt, got lengthways across the front seats, kicked the driver's door open and scrambled out like the Terminator, looking for the lorry driver. *I didn't have a scratch.* I couldn't believe it: no whiplash, nothing at all. I stood on the grass verge, put both hands in the air like an evangelical preacher from Georgia and shouted, 'Thank you, God!'

The driver of the artic duly arrived. He was Swedish. He was volubly apologetic – his left-hand drive and a very high cab had rendered me totally invisible. He had seen a deer in the hedge (there are deer warnings all along that stretch of the M4) and he had swerved out to avoid it. The rest I knew ...

You remember that I described Bill Farrar as one of the

best wheelmen who ever lived. During that half-minute or so while the Granada was performing like a circus acrobat, I *knew* that everything was going to be OK, that all manner of thing would be well. I was totally unafraid, and completely calm, even during the time I was vividly imagining being scraped out of the crushed body shell. I don't consciously know what I did with the wheel, the brakes and the accelerator during those vital seconds. It was all instinctive, *but it worked.*

I firmly believe that Bill had a hand in it somehow, that he was there with me, as he had been in Ian's vicarage the night before. He was the only driver I knew who could have manoeuvred his way out of that one. I also firmly believe that the eternal world which awaits us beyond this life is a world of purposeful activity, that the life to come is infinitely *more* than anything we've experienced here. I think it's highly probable that those we love who've gone there ahead of us are sometimes able to assume the guardian angel role. I believe Bill's hands were on the wheel, guiding mine when I needed him most. When I see him again, I shall ask him.

ESTHER M. FRIESNER

That Old School Spirit

---•◆•---

Esther M. Friesner (b. 1951) was born in Brooklyn, New York, and now lives in Connecticut with her husband, two children, a pair of rambunctious cats and a fluctuating population of hamsters. She was educated at Vassar College, where she completed BAs in both Spanish and Drama. She has published around thirty novels to date, including *New York By Knight*, *Elf Defense*, *Demon Blues*, *Hooray for Hellywood*, *Yesterday We Saw Mermaids*, *The Sherwood Game*, *The Psalms of Herod*, *Child of the Eagle*, *The Sword of Mary* and *Playing With Fire*, and with Martin H. Greenberg she has co-edited the anthologies *Alien Pregnant by Elvis*, *Blood Muse*, *Chicks in Chainmail* and its sequel *Did You Say 'Chicks'?!*. Her own short fiction and poetry have appeared in numerous magazines and anthologies. She won the Romantic Times Award for Best New Fantasy Writer in 1986 and the Skylark Award in 1994. Her short story 'All Vows', took second place in the *Asimov's SF Magazine* Readers' Poll for 1993 and was a finalist for the Nebula Award in 1994, and her story 'A Birthday' was a finalist for the 1996 Hugo Award. Her *Star Trek: Deep Space Nine* novel, *Warchild*, made the *USA Today* bestseller list.

---•◆•---

Engrained prejudices die hard. Say the words 'Vassar College' and for most people they will immediately conjure up images of a swanky all-girls institute of higher education and gracious refinement, of pumps and pearls, with perhaps a few flickers of white wrist-length gloves and teacups. It matters not to them that Vassar has been co-ed for over twenty years, that the only gloves on campus come out for snowball fights, that we don't take tea (although we did chugalug parlous quantities of the school coffee in demitasse cups during lengthy bridge-playing sessions – sort of the caffeine-lover's equivalent of doing tequila shots) and that the sole vestige of pumps and pearls is the perhaps apocryphal story of a certain celebrity undergraduate who was asked to leave because pumps and pearls were *all* she was wearing while entertaining a gentleman caller.

And yet, despite such drab things as facts to the contrary, these images of Vassar still haunt the public mind. The ghosts of Vassar can do no less. After all, this college was begun in the nineteenth century by one Matthew Vassar, brewer. Can a college founded on beer fail to be a nurturing haven for spirits of another sort?

I am a Vassar graduate, class of 1972. I saw the first co-eds arrive. I saw the protests against the war in Vietnam. I saw the black students take over Main Building until their demands were met. And I saw a ghost.

That is, I *think* I saw all that. The fact is, for most of my life I have suffered from severe myopia and astigmatism. James Thurber wrote a delightful article on the joys of being unable to see past the end of one's nose in which he pointed out that, for the profoundly short-sighted, the world loses its harder edges and assumes a romantic haze. I concur.

Sceptics and scientists alike frequently tell ghost spotters: 'You didn't actually see that phantom. Your eyes were playing tricks on you.' Did my eyes ever play tricks on *me*? Don't ask. As far as those two ocular Merry Andrews were concerned, it was April Fool's Day all the year round.

It is precisely *because* my eyes were untrustworthy things that I am so sure of what I saw that night. How can I claim this? That is for you to see for yourself, anon, below, and – I hope – to your satisfaction.

Which brings me to the ghost itself.

I confess: I am a confirmed romantic, and romance and drama go hand in hand. For me, ghosts will always carry with them a fine flourish of the dramatic. What better place to encounter one, then, than in the college theatre? At the time I attended Vassar, the Drama Department was housed exclusively in Avery Hall. Avery was the school riding academy back in the days when a Vassar girl would no more think of coming to school without her horse than a Vassar woman today would dream of attending without her PC.

Times do change, and what was once a riding ring was converted into a theatre. It wasn't a very imaginatively designed theatre, such as the one they have now. The stage had a simple proscenium arch with a small apron, a serviceable backstage area, stairs leading up to the stage from the audience and rows of plush seats of the style that inevitably makes me think 'movie theatre'.

I don't remember the name of the play that they were doing on the night I saw the ghost. I do know that I certainly wasn't alone when I saw him; the theatre was full and I was with my friends. For whatever reason, I was the only one of us who spotted the phantom. (Then again, I've never heard of ghosts and logic keeping company.) I also remember quite clearly that whatever play it was we had come to see, it was *not* set in the eighteenth century. The ghost, however, was.

I think I bear him a grudge to this very day, whoever he was. He appeared so abruptly, so nonchalantly, being simply *there* without benefit of the usual harbingers. I felt no unearthly chills, no stirring of the small hairs at the back of my neck, no premonitory sensation of dread, not even so much as the courtesy of pricking thumbs. It was a very banal entrance, more worthy of a weekend guest than a wandering ghost.

He stood stage left on the apron, the curtains at his back. Although he had offended against my romantic sensibilities, he was otherwise a very considerate phantom, for his figure (which looked quite opaque) did not upstage the play in progress. He was a bit of side business made incarnate – or should I say ectoplasmic? If he hadn't known how to dress, I might never have paid him any mind at all.

But that is where he redeemed himself in my eyes, for he wore the garb of a gentleman of two hundred years past. He reminded me of nothing so much as one of the famed 'gentlemen of the road', a highwayman in cape and tricorn hat and even the poetical requirement of a bunch of spotless white lace at his throat. He stood there with one hand on his hip and the other resting easily on his sword. He seemed to be watching the play with a deep, almost a professional interest. And then, before the play ended, or even the act was out, he strolled off stage left and blurred into oblivion.

Now before I take this story any further, I think I'd best pause and respond to the host of objections I already hear from those people who expend the great barren stretches of their existence seeking the factual flaws in supernatural narratives. Simply because they themselves have never had their tiny cheesebox lives shaken up by the mystery, the romance, even the icy terror of such encounters, it pains them to countenance those of us who have. Their favourite colour is beige, they eat creamed parsnips and they pounce like Furies on a fratricide whenever they spy a detail in a ghost story that they can't manacle to Reality.

'Aha!' they cry, with much triumphal pointing of fingers. 'You said that Vassar was founded in the *nineteenth* century. How, then, could it possibly be haunted by an *eighteenth* century ghost? A highwayman, no less! We are talking about Poughkeepsie here, a city in upstate New York near the Hudson River. We might allow you the ghost of a Vassar girl in days gone by, or an old Dutch farmer, or even Henry Hudson himself, in a pinch, but that wouldn't suit you, oh no! You want to foist off Dick Turpin on us. We think not.'

To these people I reply – Well, never mind what I reply exactly; that sort of language wouldn't reflect well on my *alma mater.* Let's just leave it at 'Pooh-pooh,' or, if I am pushed to it, 'Tchah!' For you see, there is one other thing about being as dreadfully short-sighted as I was: when I actually saw something worth looking at, I made mighty sure I knew it for what it was. And I saw my highwayman. He wasn't as anachronistic or as out of place as all that. He *did* belong. He just might not have been *he.*

How many pre-1960s plays can you name that feature an all-female cast? *The Women*? *The* Trojan *Women* as well, you say? And after that? No, no, come back from the library before you turn into one of those beige-wearing eaters of creamed parsnips. The only answer you need to know for now is: very few indeed.

Given this, what do you think an all-girl school does when they wish to put on a play? I'll give you a hint. The answer is *not* 'They perform *The Women* in repertory with *The Trojan Women* and hope no one notices.' No, what they do – what they did do at Vassar – was they cast a few women in the male parts and got on with it. Shakespeare would have been proud.

(Alas, by my own era the procedure had changed. The Drama Department employed a couple of male resident actors. Between them and the occasional male drama professor who took the men's roles, they pretty much had the bases covered. Why did they make this change? I couldn't say. Perhaps they thought they were saving their fragile charges from suffering any future doubts about their femininity. Oh wasn't that *kind* of them?)

Thus the conclusion to which I came was that my phantom must have been one of those long-vanished young ladies who played the breeches part on that very stage. Perhaps she died at school, perhaps not. Perhaps, for her, her time on the Vassar stage was the high point of her earthly existence. Or – o horrible! – perhaps one of her fellow-students was a theatre critic of the castor-oil-and-vitriol school. They say ghosts walk the earth hard by the spot where they were done to death. Why shouldn't a theatre ghost haunt the place where her performance was murdered?

I did not see the ghost again. No curtain calls, alas. However, on another occasion in the same building, I thought I caught sight of a dark shape whisking across the back of the theatre. I am willing to sacrifice this sighting on the altar of astigmatism, but I refuse to give up on my highwayman.

As a side note, there are other ghosts on the Vassar campus. Rumour claims that the old chemistry building was haunted by the spirit of a turn-of-the-century teacher who committed suicide there by hanging herself from the second-floor banister. Two of my friends decided to test the veracity of these rumours, and so they took a Ouija board into the building at midnight, settled down on the steps that were the purported spot of the suicide, and tried to attract the ghost's interest.

They succeeded. I am sorry to this day that I wasn't there at the interview itself, but I was present at the debriefing. (By the way, let it here be recorded that despite everything you've heard about the sixties there were plenty of college students who never smoked, dropped or otherwise ingested any substance more mind-altering than much too much Constant Comment tea, my friends and myself included. Bear this in mind before you dismiss our experiences as something that crawled out of a pack of Zig-Zag papers.) The ghost freely admitted that she had taken her own life for love. The object of her affections was another woman who in all likelihood never knew of the ghost's passion, for she made a conventional marriage. It was this event that precipitated the suicide.

Having established this, one of my friends now asked the ghost, 'If I were to push my chemistry teacher down the stairs in here and he broke his neck, what would be the first words you'd say to him when he came through to the other side?'

Very slowly the planchette spelled out the words: MAZEL TOV.

A postscript: I am no longer myopic nor astigmatic. During an operation to remove cataracts from both eyes, the surgeon implanted corrective lenses and adjusted the shape of the eyeball. I have yet to see another ghost since the operation. On the other hand I also have yet to see the charm of liver and onions, although plenty of people assure me that it exists. And that it is even tastier when served with creamed parsnips.

GREGORY FROST

Twice Encountered

———————— •—•— ————————

Gregory Frost (b. 1951) was born in Des Moines, Iowa. He is the author of four novels of fantasy and science fiction: *Lyrec, Tain, Remscela* and *The Pure Cold Light*; his short fiction includes horror and dark fantasy as well, and has been published in such major genre magazines and anthologies as *Asimov's, The Magazine of Fantasy & Science Fiction, Twilight Zone, Whispers, Night Cry, Tropical Chills, Cold Shocks, Ripper!* and *The Best New Horror.* His more recent appearances include stories in *Intersections,* edited by John Kessel et al., and *White Swan, Black Raven,* edited by Ellen Datlow and Terri Windling. He is currently Principal Researcher for Grinning Dog Pictures, who oversee the *Science Frontiers* series for the Discovery Global Network, and is at work on a book about spiritualism.

———————— •—•— ————————

The thing about ghosts is, you don't anticipate them. I honestly think that if you go looking for them you'll never encounter one. At least, that's how it's worked in my case.

I'd finished up my first year at the University of Iowa, and the lease I had on an efficiency apartment ran out on the 1st of August, but the lease I'd signed with three other students on a larger apartment didn't take effect until the 15th. For two weeks I was stuck. I stored all my belongings, and went home for a week to see my family; but before I did that, I secured a room at the 'Phi Kap' house. This was an old fraternity house on the main drag at the edge of Iowa City, overlooking Hancher Auditorium and the park.

My buddy Crowley lived there and offered me his room for the week, as he would be in Des Moines (I stuck him in a short story years later by way of revenge). He had a room at the end of the second-floor hall in which he'd constructed a hanging bed – essentially a plywood board suspended by chains. It was a clever arrangement, freeing up almost all the floor space in the small room. I opted to just spread out my orange sleeping-bag on the floor and not even try to negotiate the bed. He'd mastered it, but he was part chimpanzee.

One warm evening I came back from my job at Lind's Art Supply in town, intending to have dinner with friends, some of whom lived in the frat house year-round. But I got back later than planned, and missed them. Everybody was gone, I didn't know where.

So I lay back on my sleeping-bag and continued reading *The French Lieutenant's Woman*. I'd begun it once before, gotten sidetracked half-way through and never finished it. But I liked Fowles so much I meant to finish it.

I don't know how long I lay there reading. Maybe half an hour. Some part of my brain was attuned to the sounds of house, I suppose, for my friends' return; I was hoping that one of them at least would still want to go out and eat.

As I say, after maybe half an hour, the fire door at the far end of the hall opened and someone came walking down the hall. I stuck my bookmark in the book, got up and went to see who'd come back.

The instant I reached the open doorway, the footsteps stopped. I stared down an empty hallway. Nothing moved. The fire door was on a pneumatic arm and closed slowly after being opened. It was shut.

There wasn't a sound. No one had ducked into his room. No one was moving around. All the doors were closed and locked, except the bathroom door, but you could hear when someone pushed that swinging door open and stepped on to the tile floor there. No one had.

Uneasily I resolved that I hadn't really heard the door creak open after all. I'd been reading, and only *thought* I heard it.

Leaving my door open, I went back to my sleeping-bag and picked up the Fowles. Only now I wasn't paying much attention to the book. I had to re-read each paragraph. I was listening. I didn't have to wait long.

Less than five minutes passed before the second-floor door opened again and someone came walking jauntily down the hall. I heard it, as clear as any sound I've ever heard. I got up and went to the door and looked out.

The footsteps stopped instantly. The hallway was empty, the fire door closed.

For the first time in my life, the hair on the back of my neck actually stood up. I'd always believed that to be a literary effect.

I closed the door to Crowley's room and stayed in there until I heard the unmistakable sounds of multiple people in the house. Very different from the sounds I'd heard before. For one thing, I could hear them coming up the stairs from below, hear the murmurs of their voices – the sounds of life.

When they got to the second floor I came out. I'm not sure now whether they could see the look on my face or if I just blurted everything out, but I told everyone what had been happening. One of the Phi Kaps nodded and said something like, 'Wow, the Spook's back.'

The Spook, it turned out, was reputed to be a fraternity pledge from the 1930s who, during some idiot hazing event, had fallen out of a third-storey window and broken his neck on the patio. Over the years he had supposedly turned on showers, flushed toilets and unspun toilet paper rolls for amusement. He only showed up when the house was almost deserted – almost always during holiday breaks. But he hadn't put in an appearance in years; he'd become a legend.

His room, I was informed, had been at the end of the hall, directly across from Crowley's.

That's all that happened to me in that house. I moved into my new apartment a couple of days later. But there was a curious coda to the whole thing. About two weeks later, as the fall semester students came pouring back on to campus, the freshman brother of one of the Phi Kaps was hanging out in his brother's room on the second floor. He was pledging the house and had visited any number of times the previous year. He knew the guys who lived there, but he didn't know a thing about the Spook. He was also all by himself in the house.

As he stood in the room, he caught a glimpse of someone passing the door, and he looked out to see who it was. He saw a figure walk to the end of the hall, turn and go into the room opposite Crowley's. He knew that a character named D.J. occupied that room, and naturally he took off down the hall to welcome D.J. back. He found the door closed and locked. No one answered his rapping. No one was there.

I didn't hear about this for weeks after it happened. By then the semester was in full swing, and the house was noisy and fully occupied. Whether the Spook put in any more appearances after that, I never knew. I never followed it up.

I would argue that one such event should be enough for anyone. But, some eight years later, I had a second experience. I was living at the time in Raleigh, North Carolina. My wife was working for the World Health Organization at their office in the Research Triangle Park, and one British lady who worked there, Gwen Carnelly, had decided that she would buy a house and stay in the US when her stint in the RTP office was up. She was in her sixties and wanted to settle down there. So she started looking for a house in the area.

She found one in Durham for which the realtor was having an open house, and she asked if we would go with her and look it over. We liked her a lot, and so of course agreed.

The house was nothing special to look at, a modest two-storey dwelling, probably built around the turn of the century. I remember that the front door was in the centre, and that it opened on to a hallway that ran straight to the kitchen in the back. Half-way along on the left was the doorway to an enclosed staircase to the second floor. That was as far as I ever made it.

The moment I reached the bottom of the stairs, I was overwhelmed by a sense of absolute physical dread – I mean as steeped in it as any line ever written by Lovecraft. It was formless, unidentifiable and horrible. I backed away, excused myself and went outside. I was sweating and shaky. I quickly lit a cigarette and just stood there, collecting myself. My wife followed me and asked what was wrong. I just shook my head. The whole thing was made weirder by the fact that, behind her, I could see half a dozen people milling around inside, oblivious to whatever had settled upon me. No one else was feeling it.

Gwen came out to see what was the matter. I told her what I'd felt. I said I didn't know what had happened in there, but it was very bad and I couldn't be in that house. She looked at me for a moment, then went inside and spoke to the realtor. I saw the woman shake her head; I knew that Gwen had asked her about the history of the place, and that the woman couldn't tell her anything.

Gwen didn't buy the house. She eventually chose not to stay in the US after all, but returned to her small home on the French–Swiss border. Someone must have bought the place – maybe one of the people who was in there that afternoon. Someone who didn't feel a thing. I sure hope so.

NEIL GAIMAN

The Flints of Memory Lane

———————•—•———————

Neil Gaiman (b. 1960) was born in Porchester, and now lives
just outside Minneapolis, Minnesota, with his wife Mary and
their children Mikey, Holly and Maddy. He is one of the
most acclaimed comics writers of his generation, most
notably for his epic World Fantasy Award-winning *Sandman*
series (collected into various volumes), *Death: The High Cost
of Living* and *The Books of Magic*. His books include *The
Official Hitch-Hiker's Guide to the Galaxy Companion*, *Good
Omens* (with Terry Pratchett), *Ghastly Beyond Belief* (with
Kim Newman), *Now We Are Sick* (with Stephen Jones), *The
Sandman Book of Dreams* (with Ed Kramer), the shared-
world anthology series *Temps*, *The Weerde* and *Villains!*, and
various graphic novel collaborations with artist Dave
McKean: *Black Orchid*, *Violent Cases*, *Signal to Noise*, *Mr
Punch* and *The Day I Swapped My Dad for Two Goldfish*.
Angels & Visitations is a bestselling collection of his short
fiction, and his novel *Neverwhere* is based on the BBC TV
series he created.

———————•—•———————

I like things to be story-shaped.

Reality, however, is not story-shaped, and the eruptions
of the odd into our lives are not story-shaped either. They
do not end in entirely satisfactory ways. Recounting the
strange is like telling one's dreams: one can communicate
the events of a dream, but not the emotional content, the
way that a dream can colour one's entire day.

There were places I believed to be haunted, as a child, abandoned houses and places that scared me. My solution was to avoid them: and so, while my sisters had wholly satisfactory tales of strange figures glimpsed in the windows of empty houses, I had none. I still don't.

This is my ghost story, and an unsatisfactory thing it is too.

I was fifteen.

We lived in a new house, built in the garden of our old house. I still missed the old house: it had been a big old manor house. We had lived in half of it. The people who lived in the other half had sold it to property developers, so my father sold our half-a-house to them as well.

This was in Sussex, in a town that was crossed by the zero meridian: I lived in the Eastern Hemisphere, and went to school in the Western Hemisphere.

The old house had been a treasure trove of strange things: lumps of glittering marble and glass bulbs filled with liquid mercury; doors that opened on to brick walls; forgotten toys; things old and things forgotten.

My own house – a Victorian brick edifice, in the middle of America – is, I am told, haunted. There are few people who will spend the night here alone any more – my assistant tells of her nights on her own here: of the porcelain jester music box which spontaneously began to play in the night, of her utter conviction that someone was watching her. Other people have complained of similar things, following nights alone. I have never had any unsettling experiences here, but then, I have never spent a night here alone. And I am not entirely sure that I would wish to. 'There is no ghost when I am here,' I said once, when asked if my house was haunted. 'Perhaps it is you that haunt it, then,' someone suggested, but truly I doubt it. If we have a ghost here, it is a fearful creature, more afraid of us than we are of it.

But I was telling of our old house, which was sold and

knocked down (and I could not bear to see it empty, could not stand to see it being torn apart and bulldozed: my heart was in that house, and even now, at night, before I sleep, I hear the wind sighing through the rowan tree outside my bedroom window, twenty-five years ago). So we moved into a new house, built, as I said, in the garden of the old one, and some years went by.

Then, the house was half-way down a winding flint road, surrounded by fields and trees, in the middle of nowhere. Now, I am certain, were I to go back, I would find the flint road paved, the fields an endless housing estate. But I do not go back.

As I have said, I was fifteen, skinny and gawky and wanting desperately to be cool. It was night, in autumn.

Outside our house was a lamppost, installed when the house was built, as out-of-place in the lampless countryside as the lamppost in the Narnia stories. It was a sodium light, which burned yellow, and washed out all other colours, turning everything yellow and black.

She was not my girlfriend (my girlfriend lived in Croydon, where I went to school, a grey-eyed blonde of unimaginable beauty who was, as she often complained to me, puzzled, never able to figure out why she was going out with me), but she was a friend, and she lived about a ten-minute walk away from me, beyond the fields, in the older part of the town.

I was going to walk over to her house, to play records, and sit, and talk.

I walked out of our house, ran down the grass slope to the drive, and stopped dead, in front of a woman, standing beneath the street-lamp, staring up at the house.

She was dressed like a gypsy queen in a stage play, or a Moorish princess. She was handsome, not beautiful. She has no colours, in my memory, only shades of yellow and black.

And, startled to find myself standing opposite someone where I had expected no one, I said, 'Hello.'

The woman said nothing. She looked at me.

'Are you looking for anyone?' I said, or something of the sort, and again she said nothing.

And still she looked at me, this unlikely woman, in the middle of nowhere, dressed like something from a dream, and still she said nothing at all. She began to smile, though, and it was not a nice smile.

And suddenly I found myself scared: utterly, profoundly scared, like a character in a dream, and I walked away, down the drive, heart beating in my chest, and around the corner.

I stood there, out of sight of the house, for a moment, and then I looked back, and there was no one standing in the lamplight.

I was fifty paces from the house, but I could not, would not, turn around and go back. I was too scared. Instead I ran up the dark, tree-lined flint lane and into the old town, and up another road and down the road to my friend's house, and got there speechless, breathless, jabbering and scared, as if all the hounds of Hell had chased me there.

I told her my story, and we phoned my parents, who told me there was no one standing under the street-light, and agreed, a little reluctantly, to come and drive me home, as I would not walk home that night.

And that is all there is to my story. I wish there was more: I wish I could tell you about the gypsy encampment that was burned down on that site two hundred years earlier – or anything that would give some sense of closure to the story, anything that would make it story-shaped – but there was no such encampment.

So, like all eruptions of the odd and strange into my world, the event sits there, unexplained. It is not story-shaped.

And, in memory, all I have is the yellow-black of her smile, and a shadow of the fear that followed.

STEPHEN GALLAGHER

In There

Stephen Gallagher (b. 1954) was born in Salford, Lancashire, and currently lives near Blackburn with his wife and daughter. He graduated with joint honours in Drama and English from Hull University in 1975 and worked for a number of British television companies before making his first professional sale as a writer to commercial radio. Gallagher became a full-time freelance writer in 1980, and he went on to work for Yorkshire Television's documentaries department and script two serials for BBC TV's *Doctor Who* series: *Warrior's Gate* and *Terminus* (both of which he subsequently novelized under the pseudonym 'John Lydecker'). His other books include the novelization of *Saturn 3*, *Chimera*, *Follower*, *Valley of Lights*, *Oktober*, *Down River*, *Rain*, *The Boat House*, *Nightmare With Angel*, *Red Red Robin* and *The Painted Bride*. He adapted his own novel for the 1991 television mini-series *Chimera* (a.k.a. *Monkey Boy*); scripted Peter James's *Prophecy* for Yorkshire TV's *Chillers* series; and has worked as a scriptwriter and story and continuity consultant for BBC TV's popular *Bugs* series. Several of his books have been optioned for filming.

It's August 1996, North Carolina. We're up in the rafters of the old Moravian church in Bathabara, preserved site of one of the state's original settlements. It's a modest little place, in green fields and woodland outside Winston-Salem. Not much remains of the village-sized township apart from exposed foundations and a recreated stockade and herb garden, but the church itself is complete and stands overlooking the empty, grassed-over ruin of the community it once served. It's a hot, slow day, the sun outside bright enough to make you squint even behind sunglasses, but here in the attic space it's cool.

Apart from our guide, we have the place to ourselves. Our guide is a fourth-generation Moravian woman in her seventies. She wears the traditional clothing – a plain, full dress that almost reaches the floor, a white apron, white bonnet. We've squeezed through the low door from the organ loft and we've seen the trestle on which the coffin was laid whenever there was a burial. Now she's telling us about the church ghost. According to legend, this is where he's been seen walking.

Suddenly, the Offspring pipes up.

'I saw a ghost in our house, once,' she says.

We all turn to her. It's the first time she's spoken out in the entire building tour. But she has that gleam in her nine-year-old's eye, and my heart begins to sink.

'*Did* you?' says our guide. She's patient, kindly, a little frail-looking. She's taken care to include the Offspring in everything she's been telling us, and to point out anything that might catch a child's imagination: that tiny chair, this wooden doll.

'Yes,' says the Offspring, warming to the attention that she's suddenly getting. 'In my bedroom.'

Our guide is fully focused on her now, eyes wide behind her wire-rimmed glasses, encouraging the Offspring to go on and say her piece.

Encouragement is now the last thing that's needed.

'She looked like me, but she was dressed in Victorian clothes,' the Offspring says, 'and she was very pale. And when she turned around, she had no eyes.'

I daren't even look at the guide now.

'Where her eyes should have been,' the Offspring goes on,

'there were just these two deep holes. And in these holes, I could see worms and maggots.'

My sinking heart hits rock bottom with a thud like a safe, and now I can only wait to see where we go from here. Our guide's eyes are wide and her mouth is a shocked, dark little O.

Then her face screws up into a big, kind, old-lady smile, and she puts her hand on to the Offspring's head and pats it.

'This is why I love children,' she says. 'They'll always surprise you.'

We move on.

'It happened,' the Offspring's whispering furiously at me as we descend the narrow stairway from the organ loft. 'It *did*.'

I'm not a believer in ghosts. But, like everyone else on this entire planet since the dawn of time, I'm a sucker for a good ghost story. This is a contradiction that I've never had any problem with; I don't believe in vampires, either, or werewolves, or the gods of ancient Greece. Heresy for a genre writer, I know, but I've always seen them as concepts whose power lies in their corner-of-the-eye presence. They're echoes from the depths of the human unconscious; to argue for their actual, material existence would be to diminish them. Finding one would be like trying to catch faith in a bottle.

I'm not saying that all those who tell tales of the paranormal are liars or attention seekers. Some most certainly are, but many are sincere; the sense of their awe is almost palpable. In such cases I believe that they've glimpsed something to which their consciousness has given a shape, much as words whispered into the ear of a dreamer will find a form within the context of the dream. How else can we explain how the styling of UFOs has changed with the years,

through the chrome hubcaps of the 1950s all the way back
to those sailing ships in the sky of Elizabethan times?

And if I believe they've glimpsed something, doesn't it
follow that I have to believe that there's something there to
be glimpsed?

Here's why I believe that's so. It's tiny, and it's absurd.
But it's true.

It was fifteen years ago. I know, because before I sat down
to write this I phoned around the family to check. We were
at the house of my wife's parents. Bet, my mother-in-law,
was handed a wrapped and sealed package by Alyson, my
wife's sister. It was a surprise present.

I had no idea what was in it. But in that moment the
strangest-seeming thought dropped, completely unbidden,
into my mind, landing there with such a force that I almost
blurted out the words like a Tourette's sufferer unable to
resist an impulse. In retrospect, I wish I'd done exactly that.
But right then I managed not to.

The thought was, Mind the painted egg doesn't fall out.

Just that, in those exact words.

No sense to it, no reason for it. What could I have been
thinking of? I'd almost gone and said it, and then wouldn't
I have looked an idiot?

Bet undid the packaging. She lifted out a leaded glass case.

Inside the little case was a blown hen's egg, mounted and
painted with a delicate oriental design.

Everyone agreed that they'd never seen anything like it
before. Its unusual nature had attracted Alyson to it; she'd
found it in the shop of an oriental goods dealer on Manchester's Quay Street. I sat there a bit dazed. Somehow, I'd
known what it was before I'd seen it. Known it with a
powerful, unlikely certainty; and it was, let's face it, a deeply
unlikely object for a random prediction.

I told you it was tiny, I told you it was absurd. And since
I'd managed to stop myself from saying anything, I was the

only one to whom it would ever be anything other than just one of those stories.

But.

For me that one authentic, personal moment of precognition was like a slit of light under a door. It tells me nothing of what lies in the room beyond. It doesn't even prove that what's beyond is anything I'd recognize as a room.

But it kills stone dead any argument that there can be nothing there at all.

The painted egg sits on the in-laws' mantelpiece still. It has a crack in it now. I was shocked to be assured that fifteen years had passed; that startling moment of certainty is still as fresh in my mind as the moment when the thought appeared.

Not only is it tiny and absurd, but it's anecdotal. Of no scientific value. No use as proof of anything.

And all I can say in support of my certainty, much as when we were descending the stairs from the organ loft, is: It happened.

It *did*.

RAY GARTON

Haunted in the Head

———————•◆•———————

Ray Garton (b. 1962) was born in Redding, California, and he currently lives in northern California with his wife, Dawn, and their two cats, Murphy and Bob. Since making his writing début in the mid-1980s, his horror novels have included *Seductions*, *Darklings*, the Bram Stoker Award-nominated *Live Girls*, *Crucifix Autumn*, *Trade Secrets*, *The New Neighbor*, *Lot Lizards*, *Dark Channel*, *Shackled* and *Biofire*. His short fiction has been collected in *Methods of Madness* (another Bram Stoker nominee), *Pieces of Hate* and various anthologies, including *Night Visions 6*, *Café Pergatorium* and *Best New Horror 2*, and he has also written the movie novelizations of the *Invaders from Mars* remakes and *Warlock*. He is the author of a number of successful Young Adult horror books and in the early 1990s he wrote the 'nonfiction' study, *In a Dark Place: The Story of a True Haunting*.

———————•◆•———————

Most kids love ghost stories, and as a boy I was no different. I especially enjoyed true ghost stories, which is why I faithfully followed the adventures of Ed and Lorraine Warren, professional ghost chasers, as chronicled in the *National Enquirer*. (Hey, give me a break, I was just a kid . . . how did *I* know it was a rag that specialized in Bigfoot encounters, UFO abductions and tawdry celebrity gossip?) I clipped and saved all the articles about the Warrens and read books about their adventures.

Ed and Lorraine were a middle-aged married couple who travelled around the country investigating reports of hauntings, possessions and other supernatural phenomena. Sometimes, the *Enquirer* articles were accompanied by fuzzy pictures of 'ghosts' – usually spooky lights floating in someone's basement or kitchen. Their stories – usually involving families living in haunted houses – were especially scary because they were 'true'. It was my dream someday to meet Ed and Lorraine, maybe even work with them ... although I knew, deep down inside, that I was much too cowardly to go hunting for ghosts.

As I grew older, I forgot about Ed and Lorraine and their ghostly adventures. I grew up, became a writer (contrary to popular opinion, the two aren't necessarily mutually exclusive, but it usually helps to pick just one and stick with it) and got married. When I was approached to write a book about the latest adventure of Ed and Lorraine Warren, all those childhood memories of haunted houses and *National Enquirer* clippings rushed back, and I couldn't say yes fast enough.

They had just finished a case involving a family tormented by demonic forces in a New England house that used to be a funeral home. I travelled to Connecticut and was given a warm welcome by Ed and Lorraine. I met with the demon-plagued family, the Snedekers, and their children. They had five, but the oldest, a teenage boy, was staying with friends.

The family no longer lived in the demonic house, and the new occupants, who claimed the Snedekers were nutburgers, wanted nothing to do with the book, so we couldn't go inside. But the story had been well publicized, and I looked at several newspaper photos of the interior of the house. Armed with a micro-cassette recorder, I talked at length with the Snedekers and the Warrens, recording all the scattered information I would later organize into a book.

I was given a tour of Ed and Lorraine's home. It was warm and cosy and quaint, thoroughly New England. During the

tour, they told me about their 'museum'. It was in an
extension of the house and contained artefacts and souvenirs
from all the cases they'd investigated. They explained that,
because of the evil associated with so many of the objects on
display, the museum was charged with a great deal of
negative energy and was not a pleasant place. Sometimes,
they said, as they lay in bed late at night, they heard
frightening sounds coming from the museum: tortured
screams, maniacal laughter, the babblings of deep, guttural
voices. Some of their visitors couldn't handle it and didn't
make it all the way through the museum; others weren't
even invited.

I told them how much it would mean to me to take a tour
of the museum (even as the skin on the back of my neck
began to prickle), but they wanted to get to know me better
first, just to make sure I could handle it.

They asked if I was addicted to drugs or had a history of
mental illness. I said no to the drugs, but told them if they
asked around they'd find there were differing schools of
thought on the subject of mental health. They explained that
drug addiction and mental illness made people more vulnerable to the things in the museum.

Vulnerable? To *things*? In my head, I began to backpedal
quickly, thinking maybe I didn't want to see their museum
after all. Eventually, Ed told me they thought I could take it,
but it would just be the two of us, because Lorraine just
didn't 'feel up to the stress'. The stress? Of going into
another part of her own house? I was doomed.

I'm not ashamed to say my palms began to sweat as Ed
led me down the long, dark corridor that led to the museum.
The corridor was lined with Ed's paintings of haunted
houses. Each painting had a story, and each story, at some
point, was interrupted by Ed cocking his head and saying,
'Did you hear that?' Hear what? 'Oh, just something moving
around in the museum.' The first time he said that, I didn't
hear anything. But by the third time, I was hearing noises all

over the place. I was hearing so many noises, the museum was starting to sound like a disco.

After listening to a dozen chilling haunted-house stories on my way down the corridor, we finally arrived at the museum . . . and I was ready to wet my pants. The museum was one enormous room. It was dark and uncomfortably cold. 'We used to run the heaters in here,' Ed said, 'but the temperature never changed, so we decided to save on the electricity bill and just leave 'em off.' For about ninety minutes, Ed showed me all the souvenirs of their investigations of things haunted, possessed and generally creepy.

Before I left Connecticut, Ed and Lorraine asked me if I ever prayed. I said yes, I did. They encouraged me to pray often in the next few months. The evil forces responsible for tormenting the Snedekers would not want the truth to be told, and I would be the most likely target for any hostility. And besides . . . I'd been in the museum. They said several visitors had taken something supernatural home with them upon leaving the museum, and hadn't even known . . . until it was too late.

Very jumpy and desperate for a sedative, I went home to California to start work on the book. I got off to a slow start, though, because I kept hearing noises. At first, I convinced myself it was the house settling. But the noises got louder. Sitting in my office, I was startled by what sounded like furniture being moved around roughly in the living-room. My wife Dawn was at work; I was home alone. I went into the living-room to find nothing amiss. Even our cat Murphy was sound asleep in my recliner.

For a couple of days, I tried to tell myself the sounds were perfectly normal – the old house settling, traffic noises, people in the apartment buildings across the street shooting at each other over video game disputes – and that they were not what they sounded like: people in the living-room stomping their feet, pounding the walls and rattling things

around. I didn't tell Dawn right away. I was afraid she'd
think I'd been sniffing airplane glue or something. But I was
genuinely afraid.

I became even more afraid when the strange activity
moved to the bedroom. On the very edge of sleep, I sat up
suddenly when I thought I felt the mattress move, as if
someone had jarred it intentionally, pushed down on it with
a hand or knee. Dawn was sound asleep and motionless, and
besides ... the movement had been on *my* side of the bed. It
happened a few more times, always when I was just about to
fall asleep. I finally woke Dawn and told her about it, and
about the sounds in the house as well.

Once I'd convinced her I hadn't been sniffing airplane
glue, she wondered if perhaps I was letting the book get to
me. She said, 'I know how impressionable you are, how
susceptible you are to suggestion. Remember last year, when
you were convinced the Earth was going to be struck by an
asteroid? We've still got more canned goods and batteries in
the garage than any three households.'

But I was certain it wasn't just my imagination. I feared
that whatever had caused the frightening activity in the
Snedeker house was trying to keep me from writing the book
... or that something had followed me home from the
Warrens' cold, dark basement of haunted exhibits. Or, worse
yet, *both*.

Dawn heard nothing, felt nothing. The sounds only
occurred while I was alone in the house, and the mattress
only seemed to move while Dawn was asleep. It went on for
a couple of weeks, and my nerves became raw. I continued
to work on the book, but I was so preoccupied that the
pieces of information I was organizing wouldn't fit together.

Then, quite suddenly, I realized why the information
wouldn't fit together ... because the stories I'd gotten from
Ed and Lorraine Warren and Mr and Mrs Snedeker weren't
straight. The 'facts' weren't meshing. I made some phone
calls. First, the Snedekers. I asked some questions, tried to

clear things up. Instead, their incongruent answers only clouded things further. Mr and Mrs Snedeker contradicted one another *and* the Warrens. Their teenage son was home and I had an opportunity to talk with him for the first time. His answers were mostly monosyllabic.

I asked him specifically what he had witnessed in the demonic house. 'Only a few things,' he said. 'It all stopped as soon as I started taking my pills.' Mrs Snedeker snapped at him and suddenly came back on the line. After that, Mrs Snedeker told me, quite reluctantly, that their teenage son had had a drug problem, and that Mr Snedeker had had a 'minor' drinking problem, both around the time of the demon infestation.

When I told her that many details of their story didn't mesh, she asked, 'Are you saying you don't *believe* us?' I ended the conversation promptly and called the Warrens.

Once I told Ed and Lorraine the problem I was having and what I'd learned from Mrs Snedeker, Ed laughed and said, 'Well, sure, kid, they're *crazy*. Hell, *most* of the people we deal with are crazy. Why do you think they call *us*? I mean, we're *ghostbusters*, for cryin' out loud. Normal people would just go to a therapist!' I was stunned, speechless. 'Hey, you write scary books, right, kid? Well, just do what you do. Make it up and make it scary. You're a *writer*.'

Yes, I was a writer, but at the moment I was supposed to be writing a book of *non*-fiction. Suddenly, I wasn't at all worried about the sounds I'd been hearing, because I realized Dawn was right. I *was* impressionable, I *was* susceptible to suggestion. I'd fallen for the Warrens' museum set-up, and I'd fallen for the whole Snedeker story. I'd tapped into my childhood love for a good scary ghost story and got carried away with it.

I made several righteously indignant phone calls to my editor and agent, but it didn't take long for me to read the ghostly handwriting on the wall. The contract had been signed, I was committed to the project and there was no way

I could get out of it unless I could afford a *lot* of legal fees
... and I couldn't. So, I was stuck writing a 'non-fiction'
book that I'd been told to make up, and make scary.

It was not a complete waste, though. I learned what a
sucker I could be, and that the difference between 'fiction'
and 'non-fiction' is not always that great. And for a little
while I remembered what it was like to be a kid who loved
to be scared by a good ghost story, especially if it was 'true'.

JOHN GORDON

The House on the Brink

———————————— •—• ————————————

John Gordon (b. 1925) was born in Jarrow-on-Tyne, but he moved to the fen country of East Anglia with his family at the age of twelve. He is married with two grown-up children. During World War II he joined the Navy and served on minesweepers and destroyers. After the war he became a journalist and worked on various local weekly and daily newspapers in East Anglia and Plymouth. His many books for young adults include such novels as *The Giant Under the Snow, The House on the Brink, The Ghost on the Hill, The Waterfall Box, The Edge of the World, The Quelling Eye, The Grasshopper, Ride the Wind, Secret Corridor, Blood Brothers* and *Gilray's Ghost*, plus the collections *The Spitfire Grave and Other Stories, Catch Your Death and Other Stories* and *The Burning Baby and Other Ghosts* (which was described in *Children's Books of the Year* as 'not for the faint-hearted' and in America gained a recommendation from the Young Adult Library Services Association). His most recent novel, provisionally titled *Voices*, is a horror story set in the Fens of East Anglia. He has also written his autobiography, entitled *Ordinary Seaman*.

———————————— •—• ————————————

Writing, to paraphrase L. P. Hartley, is a foreign country, and no writer ventures further into this strange land than the teller of ghost stories. The words lead deeper and deeper into mists and quagmires where it is impossible to be sure what one is seeing or, more worrying still, what manner of creature may at any moment be reaching from the swamps to place a clammy hand over the fingers that guide the pen.

Long before I wrote *The House on the Brink* I was very familiar with the place where the novel is set, and I knew the house. When I was a schoolboy in Wisbech in the flat Fens of Cambridgeshire I saw Peckover House every day. It stands on the north brink of the River Nene that curves through the centre of the town, and the grammar school faced it on the opposite riverbank. The school has found new premises, but the house remains, its Georgian front overlooking the river as it has done since 1722. I saw it often, but I was never inside it, for in those days it was still a private residence and occupied by a member of the Peckover family.

I used what I knew of the house when I began to plot *The House on the Brink*. The story harks back to the time when King John, travelling through the Fens, lost his baggage train when it was overwhelmed by the incoming tide near Wisbech. The Crown Jewels of England vanished with the wagons that were swallowed by the marshes and they have never been found, although many have searched.

In my story one of the King's servants is also claimed by the marshes, and his body becomes mummified as it sinks into the mud and is carried out to the Wash. It reappears centuries later on the mudflats at the mouth of the River Nene, where it is seen standing like a wooden stump. It has a malign presence, and gradually it works its way upriver to threaten a woman who lives alone in the house on the brink.

I had left Wisbech long before I wrote the story, and Peckover House had become the property of the National Trust and was open to the public, but I preferred to work on what I remembered of it and did no research. But then, some years after the book was published, I was asked to write a piece about the origins of the story, so this time I went with my wife to take a closer look at Peckover House. It was then that I discovered that the garden at the back, the only garden I knew about, led through an archway into another garden, and then another, so that there was a series of linked gardens all belonging to the house – and unknown to me. We explored them.

In the furthest garden, on the far side of a lawn and almost hidden under a tree, stood a stump. It was very much the shape of the stump that, in my story, is the body of a man, so we crossed the lawn to take a closer look. The stump turned out to be a very old and incomplete stone column, but at its top, where the skull of the mummified man would have been, there was a carving of a human face. It had been much worn by time, but it was still visible.

The stump stood on a plinth on which there was an inscription. It read: THE WHITE CROSS OF THE LOW. Not understanding this, we went back to the house and asked the custodian what it meant. She told us that the stump was the shaft of a medieval wayside cross that had once stood in the road that runs behind Peckover House and is called Low Side.

That seemed to say everything that needed to be said, but then she added something that caused me to wonder just what I had been in touch with when I was sitting at my desk and the story was forming in my mind. About a century ago, she said, the stone stump had been discovered in the mud of the river just outside the house, and then it had been brought up the bank at the very spot where the mummified man in my story drags himself on mouldering feet to threaten the woman who lives alone.

ED GORMAN

Riding the Nightwinds

Ed Gorman (b. 1941) was born in Cedar Rapids, Iowa, where he still lives with his wife Carol. After a lengthy career in advertising and politics, he became a full-time writer little more than a decade ago, since when he has been described by *Kirkus* as 'one of the most original crime writers around', and Dean R. Koontz has called his writing 'strong, fast and sleek as a bullet'. Gorman has published more than a dozen novels of mystery, horror and dark suspense, including *Shadow Games, Murder in the Wings, The Autumn Dead, A Cry of Shadows, Night Kills, Blood Red Moon, Cold Blue Midnight, Black River Falls, Hawk Moon* and *Cage of Night*; such collections as *Dark Whispers and Other Stories, Cages* and *Moonchasers and Other Stories*; and written several screenplays. With Martin H. Greenberg he has co-edited a number of anthologies, including *Cat Crimes, Dracula: Prince of Darkness, Stalkers, Predators, Werewolves, Night Screams, Celebrity Vampires* and *White House Horrors*, and collaborated on the non-fiction volumes *The Fine Art of Murder: The Mystery Reader's Indispensable Companion* (with Greenberg, Larry Segriff and Jon L. Breen) and *The Dean Koontz Companion* (with Greenberg and Bill Munster). He has won the Shamus Award of the Private Eye Writers of America and been nominated for the Edgar Award of the Mystery Writers of America.

This was back in the spring of 1974 and I didn't know anything at all about out-of-body experiences.

A brief set-up is required here. I started drinking alcohol when I was fifteen years old. From that time until the spring of '74 I pretty much stayed drunk. I'd ruined a marriage, alienated a son, gone through a number of jobs and found myself spiralling ever downwards.

I was the worst kind of drunk – loud, belligerent, occasionally violent, and given to terrifying blackouts. While I believe that alcoholism is largely genetic, I do think environment plays a role. Some things had happened to me as a boy that I'd never been able to face.

But on 14 April 1974, face them I did. I put down the Scotch bottle and have had nary a drop since.

At the time, I was relatively flush financially, living in a large apartment that overlooked the small city of Cedar Rapids. At night, the view was beautiful – a vast starry stretch of midnight sky enveloping the towers and spires and lights of the cityscape below.

Sobriety was scary. I was afraid I couldn't hold out, that I'd give in and take a drink. Some nights, I'd buy a bottle of Scotch and set it on my dining-room table and just sit there and stare at it. Tempted.

Sobriety was scary for another reason. I had nowhere to hide. The trauma of my childhood was now with me constantly – and so were all the scenes I'd caused in my drinking days. Sometimes, I was ashamed to walk down the street.

This was my mood when, one night, I lay on the couch in my darkened living-room looking at the sky. I knew nothing of the stars. My science background was pathetic. But for five or six nights running I'd been doing this, staring at the stars. I felt some ancient inexplicable kinship with them.

On this particular night, I fell asleep on the couch. When I awoke, I was disorientated. I felt a kind of panic. Something had happened to me, but what? Alcoholic blackouts used to do this to me. I'd try to put together the previous day and night, and couldn't, and really went into a state of terror. What had I done? Where had I been? With whom?

This feeling was not unlike that. Near dawn, I went in and lay down on my bed; and then I began to remember what had happened a few hours ago.

And what I remembered was a kind of ecstasy. I'd ridden the nightwinds above Cedar Rapids, all the way out to the surrounding farmlands where I'd lived for a few years as a boy.

I had no idea how I'd done this. But I had. And it wasn't a dream. I had somehow been separated from my body. I wasn't sure if 'I' was soul or simply consciousness or both, but whatever... I had a memory of travelling through the night and knowing great joy, something I'd known only a few times in my life.

The next afternoon, I went to the library and read several pieces on out-of-body experiences, the most interesting of which were written by Jack London, Guy de Maupassant and Aldous Huxley. The experiences they described were very much like my own. London, too, commented that he was able to remember the incidents only an hour or so after they had happened.

Over the next few weeks, I had the experience four more times. Each time, I clearly remembered the sense of wind and night and joy, of seeing places of my childhood that no longer had the power to hurt me, of feeling a real serenity. I'd always hated myself. While that feeling hadn't gone entirely from me, I felt a kind of compassion for myself I'd never been able to muster before. Maybe I wasn't quite so hateful after all.

Then the experiences stopped, just as mysteriously as they had begun. I sensed that whatever it had been was gone from me now. I'd never ride the nightwinds again. And I never have.

Out-of-body experiences? I don't know, and I mostly don't care. Whatever inspired them, the night flights gave me a pleasure and sense of security I'd rarely known. I'd be happy if they'd come again.

ELIZABETH GOUDGE

ESP

————————•◆•————————

Elizabeth de Beauchamp Goudge (1900–1984) was the only child of the Rev. Dr Henry Leighton Goudge, author of a number of theological works who became Regius Professor of Divinity at Oxford, and Ida de Beauchamp Collenette. The author of more than forty books, including novels, collections and non-fiction on religious themes, she is best known in the fantasy field for her whimsical children's book *The Little White Horse*, which won the Carnegie Medal in 1947. Among her other novels are *Island Magic, A City of Bells, Towers in the Mist, Smoky-House*, the Literary Guild Award-winning *Green Dolphin Country* (a.k.a. *Green Dolphin Street*) which was made into a film after winning a Metro-Goldwyn-Mayer prize of £30,000, *Henrietta's House, Gentian Hill, The Valley of Song, The White Witch, The Dean's Watch* and *Linnets and Valerians*. Goudge's short fiction is collected in *The Fairies' Baby and Other Stories, The Pedlar's Pack and Other Stories, The Golden Skylark and Other Stories, The Ikon on the Wall, Songs and Verses, At the Sign of the Dolphin, The Reward of Faith, White Wings: Collected Short Stories, A Christmas Book, The Ten Gifts* and *The Lost Angel*. She firmly believed in her mother's psychic powers, which included precognition and ESP, and her own ability to sense and occasionally see ghosts, both of which she discussed in her 1974 autobiography, *The Joy of the Snow*.

————————•◆•————————

I am not really qualified to write about what we call extra-
sensory perception since I have not studied it enough, and
have little to go upon but my own slight experience and
what I have learned from my astonishing mother, but
nevertheless I am having a go. What was astonishing about
my mother was not that she had remarkable psychic powers
but that she resolutely refused to use them. The only
explanation she would give me was that once in her youth
she had terrified someone by what she did and had decided
to turn her back on the whole business. I have inherited very
little of my mother's ESP, only enough to be a worry to
myself and not much help to other people. Only twice in my
life has telepathy enabled me to know that someone I loved
was in trouble and come up with the help needed. Sometimes
I know when a friend is suffering or has died, at other times
I do not. Often I am convinced that someone is in trouble
and I write to find out what it is and nothing is the matter. I
cannot trust my intuitions. My dogs have always known far
more than I do; but then the powers of animals are so
exquisite that ours dwindle to nothing beside them.

But meagre though my small shoots of perception were
my mother discouraged them whenever they appeared.
When I tried to tell her about my encounters with our Ely
ghost, whom I disliked intensely, she made no comment.
That she also had her meetings with him I have no doubt,
but she would not say that she did, and when asked if I
might change my haunted bedroom for another she referred
the matter to my father, who from first to last of our time in
that house remained untroubled by our ghost. He was not a
man to see things, hear things or imagine things. He belittled
himself when he said he had nothing of the mystic in him,
and no imagination whatever, but he was a hard-working
intellectual who prayed and toiled from six in the morning
till twelve o'clock at night, when he fell into bed and was
instantly unconscious, and so had no interstices in his life
through which bogles and their like could insert a clammy

finger. Appealed to about my bedroom he had no intention of yielding to teenage bletherings, but being a just man he said he would look into the matter of my ghost. We should exchange bedrooms for the night and he would sleep in my room, and hope to have a personal experience of the phenomenon. To my disappointment he reported in the morning that he had seen nothing, but nevertheless what with the howling of the wind round my attic and the scuttling of the mice he had scarcely slept all night. Never had he experienced a noisier bedroom and I might change it for another.

So, keeping the old schoolroom as a sitting-room only, I moved into a smaller and more sheltered room that looked out on the next-door garden; a peaceful green view, but I missed the sight of the sun rising over the fen. However, the ghost came there just the same, and when later I moved to yet another room he followed. But it was not as bad as it sounds, for as these were my boarding school and college days, I was only at home in the holidays and he was not a very frequent visitor. Nor is he now. For I was not alone in seeing that ghost. Subsequent dwellers in the house have seen him too. I do not know how he appeared to them but to me he appeared as a grey-cowled monk with no face. Where his face should have been there was only darkness. The experience was always the same. I would wake suddenly from sleep as though woken up and alerted, and would find him standing beside me. I would feel fear and revulsion, a sense of struggle as though I fought against something, and then he was gone. He was not a pleasant person, not like the angel figure who haunted the next-door house but one.

This apparition was so unusual that Canon and Mrs Glazebrook, who lived in the house at that time, came to the conclusion that it was not a ghost at all. For what ghost stands still to have its portrait painted? And, Mrs Glazebrook being a painter, that is what this ghost obligingly did. Yet it could inspire fear for it appeared in the spare room, and guests from the outside world were not acclimatized to the unexplainable as we were who lived always in the shadow of history and legend. One of the guests went to bed early in the Glazebrooks' spare room and was later heard frantically tugging at the bell-rope that hung beside her bed. It was answered by the old, serene and saintly housemaid who had been with her master and mistress for some years in that house and did not leave it until she died.

'What is the matter, miss?' she asked mildly.

'I cannot stay in the room with that!' cried the terrified guest, and pointed to the beautiful figure who stood in the moonlight against a blank wall.

'Why, that's nothing to be afraid of,' said the old maid soothingly. 'I can see it in my room and I call it my angel. When the moonlight leaves the wall it will go.'

She fetched her mistress to comfort the girl and when the moon moved on so did the ghost. That was the extraordinary thing about this ghost. It appeared only when the moon shone upon a particular patch of wall, and upon the wall of the old maid's room above it. It was so to speak a double ghost, slightly smaller in the upper room. The portrait that Mrs Glazebrook painted and then showed to my mother portrayed a figure in a long robe, resembling a saint in a stained-glass window. It was as though the reflection of some window was cast upon the wall by the moonlight. But the window that could have cast such a reflection was just not there. Another theory advanced by someone was that the bright moonlight brought out the outlines of some hidden fresco. But that did not seem feasible either. The mystery was not solved while I lived at Ely, and whether that angelic figure can still be seen I do not know.

The house next to our own, on my left as I went out by our back door for evensong on dark nights, had something rather nasty. I never discovered what it was, I only knew that some guest, a male one this time, was reputed to have rushed headlong from the house in terror. The house on the right, also joined to ours, had been relieved of its haunting some years before our arrival. The family who lived there then had seen nothing but had been weighed down with a sense of misery in a certain part of the house. They endured it for a while and then alterations to the house required the pulling-down of an old wall, and the skeleton of a walled-up monk was found behind it. The bones were taken away and buried and the misery went with them, but I could seldom walk down the lane without horrible thoughts of what it must feel like to be walled up. They were walled up in a standing position. The agony must have been hideous.

SIMON R. GREEN

Death is a Lady

───────── • ► • ─────────

Simon R. Green (b. 1955) was born in the picture-postcard
town of Bradford-on-Avon, Wiltshire, where he still lives. A
profile of the author in *Interzone* magazine was headlined
FIFTEEN YEARS OF NOTHING, THEN AN OVERNIGHT SUCCESS.
After years of publishers' rejection letters, he sold an incredible seven novels in 1988, followed in 1989 by two more, and
a commission to write the bestselling novelization of the
Kevin Costner film *Robin Hood, Prince of Thieves*, which has
sold more than six hundred thousand copies to date. *Hawk
& Fisher* was the first book in his series of heroic fantasy
whodunnits featuring the eponymous sword-and-sorcery
detectives, followed by *No Haven for the Guilty, Devil Take
the Hindmost, The God Killer, Vengeance for a Lonely Man,
Guard Against Dishonour* and *Two Kings in Haven*. His other
series novels include *Blue Moon Rising, Blood and Honour*
and *Down Among the Dead Men; Mistworld, Ghostworld* and
*Hellworld; Deathstalker, Deathstalker Rebellion, Deathstalker
War* and *Deathstalker Destiny;* while *Shadows Fall* was a
much darker fantasy, set in a supernatural town stalked by a
serial killer.

───────── • ► • ─────────

I once had a near-death experience. This was back in 1972,
before they became fashionable, and everyone was having
them. Which is probably why mine bears little or no
resemblance to later descriptions. Or perhaps I just need to
be different in everything.

I was on a walking holiday in the Lake District. Seventeen years old, bright and bushy-tailed, hair half-way down my back. Well, it *was* 1972. I walked fifteen miles a day, and spent all evening in the pub. I couldn't do that now; it would kill me.

Half-way through the week, I took a nasty fall, split my head open and woke up in hospital. But while I was out, I had a dream that was not a dream. It did not feel anything like a dream, but it was some years before I was able to put a name to it.

There was darkness, and then I was sitting in a stuffed leather chair before a crackling open fire, in an old Victorian study. Books on the walls, gas lamps, blocky old Victorian furniture. Slow ticking clock. A bit dark, but not gloomy. Peaceful. It was a place I had never seen before or since, but I felt immediately at home there.

Sitting in the chair on the other side of the fire was a tall, dark-haired, pale-faced woman, dressed in black. The height of Victorian fashion. She was beautiful and, although I had never seen her before, I trusted her immediately. I can see her face as clearly now as then, but it is no one I have ever known. I fell in love with her at first sight. She knew, and smiled, understanding.

She was Death. I knew that as clearly as I know my own name.

She told me in a warm, reassuring voice that I had come too soon. It was not my time yet, and I had to go back. I did not want to go, but she was sympathetically insistent. I could not stay. It was not my time. She would see me again, eventually.

And I woke up in hospital with stitches in my head.

The experience was as real to me then as anything else I had ever known. It is real to me now. Every moment of the experience remains clear and distinct to me. And I know that when my time finally comes, she will be waiting to greet me again. As she promised. Death is a lady.

PETER HAINING

The Smoke Ghost

───────────────── •─◆─• ─────────────────

Peter Haining (b. 1940) was born in Middlesex. He has been described as 'the most prolific anthologist of horror fiction in the world', and has edited and written more than two hundred books in his career, which now spans half a century. A former journalist and editorial director of New English Library, he has also written about crime, mystery, fantasy and science fiction as well as editing such anthologies as *The Hell of Mirrors, The Craft of Terror, Dr Caligari's Black Book, The Evil People, The Midnight People, The Hollywood Nightmare, The Ghouls, The Necromancers, Christopher Lee's New Chamber of Horrors, The Fantastic Pulps, The Ghost's Companion, The Black Magic Omnibus, Weird Tales, The Frankenstein File, M. R. James – Book of the Supernatural, The Edgar Allan Poe Bedside Companion, Hallowe'en Hauntings, Supernatural Sleuths, Werewolf: Horror Stories of the Man-Beast, The Television Late Night Horror Omnibus, The Frankenstein Omnibus, The Vampire Omnibus* and *The Vampire Hunter's Casebook*, amongst many others. His 1990 study, *Agatha Christie: Murder in Four Acts*, was an Edgar Award nominee of the Mystery Writers of America. Married with three grown-up children, he lives in Suffolk in a haunted house.

───────────────── •─◆─• ─────────────────

The first sensation was of woodsmoke. A curiously acrid but unmistakable smell that became apparent for a few days in the upper rooms of the house and was experienced by each member of the family. The smoke, which seemed to have no identifiable source and was smelled rather than ever being seen, occurred at a time of the year when there was no longer the need for a fire to be lit in the house. For a while, there seemed to be no logical explanation of the phenomenon – until the night when something quite extraordinary happened to my wife.

Peyton House, where we live, is a sixteenth-century, three-storey timber-frame building which stands in the middle of the picturesque little village of Boxford in Suffolk. It was once the grace and favour home of the chief stewards to the Peyton family, the local landowners who lived about a mile away in their Elizabethan manor house, Peyton Hall. For the last twenty years, though, Peyton House has been home to me, my wife Philippa and our three children, Richard, Sean and Gemma. What has happened to us there would seem to have no other explanation than yet another instance of the supernatural at work.

We had been living in the house for a while before we became fully aware of the manifestation that is repeated each year. This realization came about because of what occurred late one spring evening. It was on a night during the first week of June and Philippa was sitting reading in our bedroom, a high-ceilinged room at the front of the house. On the rear wall of this room there is an interior window which looks out on to the landing. Philippa was engrossed in her book when she was suddenly aware out of the corner of her eye of someone going past the window. She looked up and caught sight of a figure with long hair passing by. A moment later and it was gone.

Philippa's first reaction was that it must have been Gemma going along the landing to the bathroom. Then she realized that our daughter was not in the house. Indeed, the whole place was deserted because everyone *else* had gone out, too. Curiously, though, this realization did not make her feel afraid. Only the strong conviction that the figure – whoever or whatever it was – was quite benign.

It was to be some months later, and as a result of making a number of enquiries in Boxford, that an explanation for my wife's experience was forthcoming. Tales of a strange visitant in Peyton House were, it seemed, known to a number of the older residents in the village whose parents and grandparents had once worked as servants in the house. Several of these men and women had even lived for a time in the attic rooms. All told of experiencing the ethereal smell, and a few had even seen the long-haired wraith. And all at precisely the same time of year. Even stranger, not one of them had felt there was anything of which to be afraid.

The old house, we were informed, had years ago been surrounded by several acres of land – later sold off for farming and a small housing development long before we arrived – but during the early years of the nineteenth century, at the time of the Napoleonic wars with France, something terrible and tragic had occurred there. A group of French soldiers who had been taken prisoner during the conflict had been billeted at Peyton House, where they were kept in the outbuildings and set to earn their keep by working on the land. This was a common practice during this particular war, and a number of property owners in East Anglia benefited from these gangs of enforced labourers – although there is no evidence that they treated the Frenchmen with anything other than kindness as long as they worked conscientiously and did not cause any trouble.

Then, one June day, a fire broke out at Peyton House. Fortunately, the blaze was put out before it could do any serious damage to the building, but one of the PoWs was trapped by the flames and perished in a smoke-filled room. There is no record as to whether the man was buried locally or his body returned to France. Each June thereafter, we were told, a distinct aroma of smoke was evident in the house, growing in intensity until the same specific day when it stopped as dramatically as it had begun.

That day was 6 June – the very day on which Philippa had seen the figure on the landing . . .

JOE HALDEMAN

Never Say Die

———————————————•━•———————————————

Joe Haldeman (b. 1943) was born in Oklahoma City. He took a BS in Physics and Astronomy, doing postgraduate work in Mathematics and Computer Science before being drafted as a combat engineer to Vietnam, where he was severely wounded. He sold his first story to *Galaxy* in 1969 and his début book, *War Year*, was published in 1972. The next novel, *The Forever War*, won the Hugo, Nebula and Ditmar awards, and he followed it with *Mindbridge*, the *Star Trek* novel *Planet of Judgement*, *All My Sins Remembered*, *World Without End* (another *Star Trek* novel), *Worlds*, *Worlds Apart*, *There is No Darkness* (with Jack C. Haldeman II), *Tool of the Trade*, *Buying Time* (a.k.a. *The Long Habit of Living*), the *Worlds* trilogy (*Worlds*, *Worlds Apart* and *Worlds Enough and Time*), *The Hemingway Hoax* (which won the 1991 Hugo and Nebula Awards in its novella version), *1968* and *Forever Peace*. He has also edited the anthologies *Cosmic Laughter*, *Study War No More* and *Nebula Awards 17*, and his short fiction and poetry have been collected in *Infinite Dreams*, *Dealing in Futures*, *Vietnam and Other Alien Worlds*, *None So Blind* and *Saul's Death*, and have appeared in *Playboy*, *Omni*, *Cutting Edge* and *Blood is Not Enough*. He scripted the 1989 movie *Robot Jox* for director Stuart Gordon.

———————————————•━•———————————————

I think of myself as a thoroughgoing rationalist. Nevertheless, for some twenty years after a summer day in 1968, there was a hole in my rationalism. I had to believe in parallel universes, or supernatural intervention, or *something* ... because otherwise, there was no explanation for my continuing existence.

We were on a hill in Vietnam that some genius had dubbed 'Alamo'. After a couple of months of continuing attrition, we were finally being allowed to give it up.

There was a twin hill about a half-kilometre away that belonged to the enemy. We had strafed it and firebombed it and even brought in a B-52 'arclight' strike, which was pretty loud. The hill was as sterile and cratered as the surface of the moon. But the enemy were not *on* the hill; they were underneath, in a complex of tunnels. They were probably completely deaf and very angry with us.

Hidden within the tunnels, behind camouflage, they had weapons pointed at us with telescopic sights. Not just sniper rifles. They had at least one 'scoped .51-calibre machine gun and a bazooka-like recoilless rifle. They were tearing us up. We were in World War I-style trenches, and if you showed your head you were liable to lose it.

But when the high command finally authorized us to leave the hill, there was a slight problem of method. If we tried to walk away, we'd be creamed. The jungle below was thick as a briar patch and belonged totally to Charlie (as we affectionately called the North Vietnamese enemy). We had colonized the hill by helicopter and were more or less constrained to leave the same way.

Of course the helicopters were not enthusiastic about drifting in and hovering around while the enemy could blast away at them with gay abandon. One bazooka round could turn a million-dollar helicopter into a few bucks' worth of malodorous slag. There was only one place they could land out of sight of the enemy, and landing there was like something out of a Charles Bronson movie.

On the leeside of the hill, away from the enemy, there was a sheer cliff that dropped about five hundred metres.

On the cliff, near the top, was a ledge perhaps two metres wide. A helicopter couldn't actually land on it, but it could hover alongside, with one skid lightly touching the edge.

This was the drill: one helicopter at a time would come up and hover. The sarge in charge would yell your name, and you would leap out of your safe trench, and run with enthusiasm over the crest of the hill and leap into the helicopter. When it had eight passengers, it would buzz away and take them to Camp Enari, about twenty minutes distant. The rest of us would wait, and sort of hope our name would be called next, and sort of hope it *wouldn't* be called, because Charlie knew exactly what was going on, and as soon as you ran for the helicopter, he'd start shooting.

It was far too much like a movie. First they kill the black guy who everybody likes. Then they kill the tough Jewish kid from New York. Then they kill the professor.

My code name was Professor, because somewhere along the line I had learned to read and write.

In the fullness of time, whatever the hell that means, he did shout my name, and I did my little try-out for the Olympic try-to-run-without-shitting-yourself event. They actually fired at me with the bazooka, which I suspect was a T21 Czech recoilless. My handbook says it has a maximum effective range of only 450 metres, so they can be forgiven for missing me by a country mile. They may have been firing other weapons at me, but I didn't notice. It's really distracting to have a rather slow bazooka round swish over your head and explode some distance in front of you.

It takes ten seconds to reload a T21. It didn't take me ten seconds to get over the hill.

The helicopter was thud-thud-thudding down there, with seven passengers already gripping this and that and each other. I got aboard the way one normally does, facing away from the open door and hopping aboard butt-first, legs dangling over the edge. I gave the pilot a thumbs-up and he swooped away.

Footnote: I was an 'air-mobile' demolition engineer. Everywhere I went, I went by helicopter. They were like my family car.

But something happened that had never happened before: the helicopter pitched wildly sideways. And I fell out.

It was not a hallucination brought on by stress. Stress was my good buddy by then. It was not an illusion or a dream. I was looking between my knees as the helicopter drifted away from the ledge, and it suddenly pitched sideways and dumped me out. I was looking down through five hundred metres of air at a distant jungle and certain death.

And then I was suddenly back in the helicopter.

There was no sense of a passage of time. I was standing up, hanging on to some guy I didn't know.

In movies, people talk to each other in helicopters. In real life, you don't even try, unless it's to scream a word or two of vital information. Those suckers are loud. So I waited until we landed at Camp Enari, and then I asked, 'Which one of you guys pulled me in?'

They were all puzzled. 'What do you mean? You were with us all the time.'

So for some time I applied Occam's Supernatural TM Razor: Nobody really dies, at least not young. When something happens to kill you, you slip sideways, into some universe where it didn't happen. *Other* people die there, sure. But they just slip into their own alternate universe.

I told this story to people for about twenty years before I happened to tell it to a helicopter pilot. 'Downdraught,' he said. A sudden wind pushed the helicopter down and (let us say) to the left, with an acceleration greater than gravity. So I was falling, but so was the helicopter; from the helicopter's point of view, I was drifting weightless just above it. But 'left' was the direction of the cliff. To keep the blades away from the rock, the pilot automatically twisted it around so that the helicopter tilted to the right. In the blink of an eye,

I fell back inside. Nobody else noticed, because they were all looking in the other direction, the direction of freedom.

Well, OK. My rationalistic sci-fi-guy mind prefers that explanation. But I have to admit that some part of me wants to think that some god or gods thought that maybe it was a little early. Maybe I should be allowed to hang around and write some books.

JAMES HERBERT

Not Very Psychic

———————— • ━ • ————————

James Herbert (b. 1943) was born in London's East End and now lives near Henfield in Sussex with his wife Eileen and their three daughters, Kerry, Emma and Casey. At sixteen he went to Hornsey College of Art, where he studied graphic design, print and photography; this led to him working as an art director in a leading London advertising agency. Inspired by watching the Bela Lugosi version of *Dracula* on television, he made his début as a novelist in 1974 with *The Rats*, which was an instant bestseller. He became a full-time writer in 1978 and is now Britain's top horror author with such novels as *The Fog, The Survivor, Fluke, The Spear, Lair, The Dark, The Jonah, Shrine, Domain, Moon, The Magic Cottage, Sepulchre, Haunted, Creed, Portent, The Ghosts of Sleath* and *'48*. He also scripted the graphic novel *The City*, his short fiction is collected in the book-length study *James Herbert: By Horror Haunted*, and he collaborated with photographer Paul Barkshire on *James Herbert's Dark Places: Locations and Legends*. *The Rats, The Survivor, Fluke* and *Haunted* have all been filmed. Herbert keeps an open mind about the paranormal, as he explained in a series of interviews during the 1980s:

———————— • ━ • ————————

'I'm a Catholic – so naturally I believe in the afterlife,' he said in *Danse Macabre*, later disclosing to interviewer Tony Eyers: 'I do believe in ghosts: life after death is too important to trivialize.'

'A psychic told me it's not me who writes these books,' he explained to journalist Suzanne McDonnell in 1987. 'It's an ancient spirit that possesses me and wills me to write. It's funny because when I do sit down, it's as though I'm taken over. The story flows, it tells itself, like someone else is writing it.'

The author also told Lesley Bendel in another 1987 interview: 'I've talked to a lot of people involved in the occult: psychics, ghost hunters, and psychic researchers . . . When I meet these psychics they always say to me, "You're obviously very psychic," and I always deny it because I'm not. Certain things have happened to me but I can usually explain them.'

'The incidents usually go in threes,' he revealed to journalist Peter Grosvenor, 'graduating in violence. First I was at a conference with a film man when a can of beer I was drinking slid slowly over to the other side of the table. Yet the table was absolutely flat. Then we went for a drink at a Kensington club and the entire bar collapsed. I knew then we shouldn't have gone on holiday. But I did, to the Algarve. And there the entire kitchen blew up because of a gas explosion.'

'Yes, I believe in God,' Herbert said in *Danse Macabre* in 1986. 'I'm not sure that I believe in Heaven, Hell and all that, but I think there's something going on out *there* that we don't know about. I just speculate in my stories.'

BRIAN HODGE

Confessions of a Born-Again Heathen

---•—•---

Brian Hodge (b. 1960) was born in southern Illinois. A two-time nominee for the Bram Stoker Award, he is the author of *Dark Advent, Oasis, Nightlife, Deathgrip, The Darker Saints* and *Prototype*. Hodge has also completed a crime novel, *Miles to Go Before I Weep*, and a dozen of his seventy-some published stories have been collected in *The Convulsion Factory*, themed around the aesthetics of urban decay and offering no easy answers save that cities should perhaps brush after every meal. Out from Bovine Records (motto: 'Destroying Music's Future Today') is a chapbook-and-soundtrack combination titled *Under the Grind* in collaboration with 'sludgecore' band Thug, who previously released a sonic version of the author's 1991 story 'Cancer Causes Rats'.

---•—•---

In early 1996 my sixth novel, *Prototype*, was released, and shortly thereafter I read a favourable review that also noted how grim my finales had become in recent books. 'Ironically,' it said, 'as Hodge's novels have grown bleaker, he has drifted away from the supernatural.'

Well, yes and no. The shorter works are too plentiful and varied to account for neatly, but where novels are concerned the reviewer was correct.

One reason for this evolution may be that, given continued experience with both human nature and what might be termed the paranormal, I find myself growing ever more

jaded on the former, while more predisposed to the validity
– even beneficence – of the latter.

But let us back up a moment.

As rich as the English language is, it strikes me as
inadequate to make clear distinctions between obvious cre-
ations of fantasy, e.g. ambulatory mummies, and occurrences
that are less easily explained away, e.g. the Angel of Mons.
We are handicapping ourselves in terminology by labelling
certain events 'supernatural', for, if they do occur, then they
occur not in defiance of the laws of nature, but in accordance
with codicils of natural law that we have yet to decipher.
They occur as frustratingly unquantifiable evidence that, as
Arthur C. Clarke has said, 'the world is not only stranger
than we imagine, but stranger than we can imagine'. Let's
not forget that, as late as the nineteenth century, something
as tangible as the gorilla was dismissed by western science as
mere myth.

All of which is, I suppose, a roundabout way of saying I
hope you don't think I'm crazy.

No rides hitch-hiked in flaming chariots have I taken, nor
legions of risen dead espied. Many happenings with which I
can claim experience, I suspect most people could report at
one time or another: the heavy mug that shot from its secure
resting place to land half-way across the kitchen; the dream
that felt so much more concrete and unfragmented than
usual, unfolding in vivid real time as I was asked by an old
friend – recently kidnapped and murdered – to tell his
brother that he was fine now.

Staunch rationalists will wield handy explanations, and
that is fine. Certainly I cannot prove that my desire to
furnish my surviving friend comfort after his brother's
murder did not generate that dream. Desire and expectation
undoubtedly affect perception.

But then, what of the autumn afternoon I was running my
customary few miles, and stopped at the sight of a wooden
cabin within a familiar grove of trees. I never knew there

was a cabin in there, I thought, figuring it had escaped notice because the leaves that were now falling had blocked the view. I ran on, not giving it another thought ... until the next afternoon, when I again passed the grove, this time fully expecting to see the cabin. And of course didn't, and never did again.

Those of us who have had religious upbringings as children – overwhelmingly Christian in the west – often find ourselves stymied by paradoxical standards the more we grow into the secular world. We have been raised to accept as historical fact paranormal feats of staggering proportions, only to watch those who have taught us about them hedging when it comes to the modern age. When we grow bold enough to ask why we no longer witness, for example, the bifurcation of the Red Sea, or the holiest among us rising into the clouds, we are told (rather self-consciously) that, well, God does not work that way any more. But could if He wanted to. And He will again some day, wait and see. But not now.

By age nineteen I was entertaining serious doubts about the foundations for the Protestant faith of my fathers. Oh, I'd give it lip service in select company, still nervous with residual indoctrination about Everlasting Torments; and, like countless others, I would periodically rediscover some reservoir of faith during a crisis. Which is how I found myself on my knees in prayer that summer, after the world fell out from beneath me, as it so often does to nineteen-year-old boys who have loved the same girl for the past three years.

I prayed to get her back (but never did), although barring that, asked for some small thing to hold on to while I got over the loss.

Funny things, dreams. As the paranormal goes, they are the most suspect and easily dismissed, yet sleep is also considered the widest gateway through which very real, if unseen, realms can be accessed.

That night I dreamed – again, in sequential real time,

although this preceded my friend's murder by years – of being with someone who knew me well and always had. Who implicitly understood my pain, offered encouragement and, moreover, reassured me by his formidable presence that, whilst I might hurt, I was not alone. Some would say that such qualities characterize guardian angels.

Sixteen years later I remember this dream clearly, long after countless others have been forgotten. I remember the murky light, and the tolerantly bemused yet understanding expression on my encourager's face; I remember his height ... and it was most definitely a 'he', in defiance of those whose orthodoxy mandates strict gender neutrality.

In fact, it was such details that, at the time, led me to reluctantly ascribe the whole episode to my imagination ... but if I had wanted an otherworldly pat on the shoulder, I'd sure let myself down, because the details just didn't fit with what I had been taught. This was no chaste androgyne; rather a very earthy, virile sort who was familiar with physical love. The fact that it was male at all argues against self-creation; I'd have found a Botticelli female far more welcome. Then there was locale to consider: we stood in an empty bar, during daylight hours, with chairs upended on table-tops – hardly someplace I would expect to meet my Watcher.

Because none of this fit predisposed ideals, I dismissed it as a pleasant but insignificant dream, and only years later began to re-evaluate it in a far different light, having by then rejected Christianity altogether, if hardly turning nihilist. After all, Carl Jung wrote, 'You can take away a man's gods, but only to give him others in return.'

This is not the forum to speculate on the nature of what, for lack of any clearer term, I'll call God. Suffice to say that I place much credence in a Japanese metaphor: 'All paths lead to the top of Mount Fuji.' And whatever is atop Mount Fuji is not averse to meeting us half-way, if we pay attention.

Sometimes it takes work, but then shamans have known

that for millennia, along with insights into the nature of existence that are only now being validated by quantum physics, one of these being the interconnectedness of all things.

What has emphasized this to me like little else began with my receiving a letter from a reader on the other side of the globe, in Switzerland. Pure Jungian synchronicity, that: for a new project I needed information on Swiss banking, and here was a prime source, out of the blue.

As we continued to correspond, it became apparent that there was a genuine psychic undercurrent going on, rather like having found a lost sister. But it is quite unnerving to hear someone you have never met face to face tell you, from thousands of miles away, facts about yourself she has no way of knowing, repeating word for word things you have said only to yourself. Her source of information? This reader of mine, while also versed in quantum theory, is a practising witch, and claims periodic visitations from an intelligent, non-physical entity she calls the Bluesman, who told her what I'd said. He also told her that he had once met me face to face.

I wondered – and still do – if it was in my nineteenth summer.

Some months later my correspondence grew lax, which happens sometimes. As I later found out, my friend accurately sensed that I was going through a bout of depression. Nothing terribly unusual there. But out of these weeks of silence came an exhilarating burst of productivity as a contracted novelette I needed to write suddenly emerged in full flower, unlike anything I had written before but every bit as satisfying, and written to a heretofore unheard-of accompaniment of Delta blues. Very little of my *oeuvre* has seemed to write itself, but this one did.

My friend called shortly after the novelette was completed, and without my having uttered a word about it, said, 'I knew you were having a rough time, so I asked the Bluesman to send you some blues.' I asked when she had done this; the timing corresponded perfectly to the genesis of the novelette.

It is tempting to quip how good it is to have friends in high places, but this – assuming they are really there – overlooks their inscrutable work ethic, and why they so often seem silent to the point of abandonment. If indeed I was spoken to by something beyond me at nineteen – and I believe now that I was – I can't help but wonder why it has not intervened since, when periodically the need has been far greater, the stakes higher than a broken heart. Perhaps the enigma does us more good in the long run than absolute certainty and dependence. Perhaps the cry of a lovelorn nineteen-year-old is purer in its naïvety. Perhaps most of us are given but one or two subtle reminders to last us our whole lives.

And perhaps we are expected to do nearly all the work amongst ourselves. In a book by Welsh magus David Conway, he postulates that when one is truly ready to walk a more esoteric path someone more experienced will often appear to help one along. Certainly this was borne out by my Swiss friend, whose unexpected 'arrival' preceded the onset of more unusual events, both psychic and physical, than there is space to document and do them justice.

How to explain, for example, awakening one dawn to the sensation of my mattress sinking first on one side of me, then the other, accompanied by the sound of weeping, far away but seeming to originate within the room, which continued for half a minute before fading away ... then learning it coincided with a crisis in my friend's life? Explain it? I can't, really. But for now the enigma is enough to explore, and I welcome it in all its dimensions.

Rejection of Christianity has informed much of my work and life for several years, as I seek those other gods that Jung spoke of, and traffic in ideas whose publication might have once earned me the heretic's stake. I can't help but feel I have made the proper choice, given a stamp of approval by, yes, another of those incredibly vivid dreams:

I was standing off to one side in the vast sanctuary of a church, deserted but for two Protestant ministers standing by a sturdy pulpit with low, semicircular walls. Across the sanctuary stood a monstrous grandfather clock, towering nearly to ceiling level, as proportionately wide as it was tall ... easily the biggest grandfather clock I had ever seen. For no apparent reason, then, it fell forward, straight on to the pulpit, with a thunderous crash. I went sprinting for cover, dodging chunks of wooden shrapnel, but was hit by none of them. When the dust settled I looked back to see the two clergymen lying half-dead in the pulpit's wreckage. Perhaps most significantly, the clock itself remained intact.

It wasn't until the following evening that the dream's symbolic puzzle pieces clicked together, when I realized that their key lay in the previous afternoon, when I was working on an interview-by-mail for a magazine. I had been asked about my interest in exploring religion and spirituality, and careened off on several tangents. One thing I'd said was that, where personifying God was concerned, I preferred to adopt the Native American manner, as typified by Lakota shaman Black Elk's famous prayer: Grandfather.

Perhaps it meant nothing. Sometimes a cigar, Freud said, is just a cigar.

But one likes to think that Carl Jung, at least, might have been amused.

NANCY HOLDER

To Pine With Fear and Sorrow

———————————— •➤• ————————————

Nancy Holder (b. 1953) was born in Los Altos, California, and currently lives in San Diego with her husband Wayne, their daughter Belle and their three dogs, Mr Ron, Maggie and Dot. She has written fifteen romance novels under a variety of pseudonyms, the mainstream thriller *Rough Cut*, the TV tie-in volume *Highlander: Measure of a Man*, the horror novels *Dead in the Water*, *Making Love* and *Witch-Light* (the latter two in collaboration with Melanie Tem), and she is currently working on a science fiction trilogy. Her short fiction has appeared in a wide range of magazines and anthologies, including *Best of Shadows*, *Love in Vein*, *The Mammoth Book of Vampires*, *Dark Voices 6*, *Narrow Houses* and *The Mammoth Book of Dracula*, and she is the winner of four Horror Writers Association Bram Stoker Awards.

———————————— •➤• ————————————

I never knew my grandfather well, but he was the father of my father, whom I adored. He moved through my life almost silently, leaving no distinct impression on me except that he was, in our family, someone very special. Whenever he spoke to me, I was surprised he knew as much about me as he did.

He was terminally ill when I decided to move to Germany to be a ballet dancer. That my plans troubled him astonished me, as I didn't know he had thought much about it either way. One day he murmured something about there being many different careers in medicine – he and Father were doctors – and that was the first inkling I had that he had harboured some kind of hope or expectation about my future.

Before I left for Europe, my aunt took me to see him in the hospital. He was by then very sick. We had a short conversation about nothing in particular. Then I kissed his cheek.

As my aunt and I prepared to leave, I ran back down the hospital corridor to say goodbye one more time. My grandfather was staring straight up at the ceiling and sobbing. I was so taken aback I didn't let him see me in the doorway, and tiptoed away.

He died while I was in Frankfurt, and no one told me he was gone until well after his funeral. I was devastated, and my new German friends took me to a bar in the Sachsenhausen district and got me drunk on cassis.

Shortly thereafter I saw, to my despair, that I had harboured illusions about life as a dancer – and a mediocre one at that – and returned home. I grieved. I had studied ballet all my life, and the person I thought I was had vanished. I was eighteen, and I thought my life was over.

While I searched for what to become next, I visited my widowed grandmother. She put me in the downstairs guest room, where my grandfather had lain alone, sick and dying, for many months, because he was unable to climb the stairs to their bedroom.

My first night there, I was taking a shower in the adjoining bathroom. The shower door was semi-transparent and, as I washed, I saw a figure near the doorway. I assumed it was my grandmother, and spoke to her. She didn't answer.

The figure disappeared.

Suddenly, my hair stood on end. In the warm water, my teeth chattered. I saw nothing more, and heard nothing, but the sensation of fear was overwhelming. I couldn't get out of the bathroom without going through the doorway, and the only alternative was to stay boxed in the shower.

I called to my grandmother, but she didn't come. Staring at the empty spot, I pushed open the shower door, leaped for a towel, wrapped it around myself and ran through the doorway with my eyes shut and my teeth clenched.

I burst into the downstairs bedroom, shaking as I tried to see a figure, or a shadow, something to explain what I had seen in the bathroom. There was nothing. But I was even more afraid than I had been.

There are cultures who fear their beloved dead. They turn the heads of their corpses backwards or drive stakes through their hearts. They beg or threaten or cajole them into not coming back to haunt the living. This used to perplex me. How could someone believe that the dearly departed would ever wish them harm?

Yet for years I believed that the ghost of my grandfather was in those rooms, and I was terrified of him. Not afraid that a ghost had visited me, but of something deep and profound in my personality, or in his. I never thought, I saw a ghost. I thought, I saw my grandfather. There was a darkness or sorrow there that we had never spoken of, and it struggled now to manifest itself.

Maybe it was the residue of his wishes and hopes and despair, finally communicated directly to me: the fear of dying; the frustration of not having influenced a young granddaughter; the realization that we neither of us knew the heart of the other and that it was too late. Maybe it was my own fear that the life I had dreamed of was over, and that I, in a way, had died too.

Maybe he came to say goodbye one last time, and my soul was staring straight up at the ceiling, sobbing. Maybe the figure I saw was my own dancing ghost.

These are some lines from Spenser:

> Full little knowest thou that hast not tried,
> What hell it is, in suing long to bide:
> To lose good days that might be better spent;

To waste long nights in pensive discontent;
To speed today, to be put back tomorrow;
To feed on hope, to pine with fear and sorrow.

Perhaps this was the root cause of my terror, and in that moment, I was closer to my grandfather than I had ever been in life. I don't know. I like to think that we both went on to better times and happier days. I know I have. I hope he has too.

M. R. JAMES

A Ghostly Cry

---•—•---

Montague Rhodes James (1862–1936) was born at Good-
nestone Parsonage in Kent, where his father was curate. He
developed a life-long interest in medieval books and antiqui-
ties at an early age. Educated at Eton and later at King's
College, Cambridge, in 1905 he became Provost of King's
and Vice-Chancellor of the university from 1913 to 1915,
before returning to Eton as Provost in 1918. Most of his
ghost stories were occasional pieces, written for friends or
college magazines, and were collected in *Ghost Stories of an
Antiquary, More Ghost Stories of an Antiquary, A Thin Ghost
and Others* and *A Warning to the Curious*. Often asked if he
believed in ghosts, he replied in the preface to his *Collected
Ghost Stories* in 1931: 'To which I answer that I am prepared
to consider evidence and accept it if it satisfies me.' In an
article published the same year in the *Evening News*, he
revealed that he was prepared to believe in the existence of
ghosts, and in 1884, while he was still studying at King's
College, James lived in the supposedly haunted Gibbs Buildings. In his 1926 memoirs, *Eton and Kings*, he recalled the
strange atmosphere of the place, made even stranger by an
old man who lived in rooms nearby and kept a coffin beside
his bed:

---•—•---

What first interested me in ghosts? This I can tell you quite
definitely. In my childhood I chanced to see a toy Punch
and Judy set, with figures cut out in cardboard. One of these

was the Ghost. It was a tall figure habited in white with an unnaturally long and narrow head, also surrounded with white, and a dismal visage.

Upon this my conceptions of a ghost were based, and for years it permeated my dreams.

The ghost story can be supremely excellent in its kind, or it may be deplorable. Like other things, it may err by excess or defect. I am speaking of the literary ghost story here. The story that claims to be 'veridical' (in the language of the Society of Psychical Research) is a very different affair. It will probably be quite brief, and will conform to some one of several familiar types. This is but reasonable, for, if there be ghosts – as I am quite prepared to believe – the true ghost story need do no more than illustrate their normal habits (if normal is the right word), and may be as mild as milk.

Ghosts and ghostly phenomena are rare in colleges and highly suspect when they do occur. Yet, on the staircase next to mine was a ghostly cry in the bedroom. Other professors knew of it, and knew whose voice it was believed to be – a man who died in 1878.

PETER JAMES

One Extra for Dinner

Peter James (b. 1948) was born in Brighton and educated at Charterhouse. He lived in North America for a number of years, producing movies (including the award-winning *Dead of Night* (a.k.a. *Deathdream*) and *Children Shouldn't Play With Dead Things*) before returning to England. His novels *Possession*, *Dreamer*, *Sweet Heart*, *Twilight*, *Prophecy*, *Host*, *Alchemist* and *The Truth* all combine his deep interest in medicine, science and the paranormal and have been translated into twenty-two languages. He has also written a children's book, *TechnoTerrors: Getting Wired*. *Host* was the first electronic novel ever published, and both *Prophecy* and *Host* have been filmed for television. He lives with his wife Georgina, their Hungarian sheepdog Bertie and a collection of vintage Jaguars in a reputedly haunted mansion in Sussex.

'You'll love this place, writing the kind of books you do,' the couple we bought our house from said. 'It has three ghosts. A monk, a dead baby and a Roman centurion.'

They lied, it has four. I haven't yet seen one of them, but plenty of people have. The house dates back to 1720. There was a monastery here before that, and a Roman villa before that. Everyone in the village has a story to tell about the place, either something they've seen or noises they've heard, but in six years our otherworldly lodgers have so far kept to themselves. However, I live in hope, and leave the word processor on some nights in case one of them wants to tap out a message, or maybe a chapter or two of my next tome for me; but so far, zilch, not even a crooked picture, or a book mysteriously ejected from a shelf – no, not even one of mine . . .

It's a little ironic, therefore, that the only truly convincing ghostly encounter my wife and I have had was in someone else's house. I saw nothing that evening, but Georgina very definitely did:

About four years ago we were invited to a dinner party in Rodmell, a flinty village in Sussex once inhabited by Virginia Woolf. Our friends, Michael and Rachel, live in a house converted from several artisan cottages knocked into one, and dating back to the sixteenth century.

There were ten of us at the dinner party, on an October night, and we had drinks first in the drawing-room – a warm and inviting *Homes and Gardens* room: chintz curtains, antiques to die for and a log fire blazing in an inglenook so huge it crosses three time zones. We then moved into the dining-room which has a quite different atmosphere: it has a rather baronial-style table and chairs, and is a stark, distinctly cold-feeling room, although very imposing.

I noticed during the course of the dinner that Georgina seemed rather quiet and distracted, and even a little withdrawn – not at all her usual sparky, outgoing, mischievous self. We left the party before the other guests, shortly after midnight, as I had an early start on a book promotion tour in the morning.

In the car I asked Georgina if she was feeling OK. She replied that she had been disturbed during the dinner by the sight of a rather colourless woman, dressed in 1920s clothing, who had been standing in one corner of the room, in the archway through to the entrance hall, watching us.

I suggested that it might have been a nanny, or either Rachel's or Michael's mother, or someone else staying in the house. Georgina responded that she had asked Rachel if there was anyone else in the house and had been told, categorically, that there was not.

I dismissed the whole thing, in my mind. Georgina had been tired that night and I figured she must have been mistaken and simply been looking at some trick of the light – this was in spite of her insistence that she could see all the details of the woman's face and dress very clearly. The following day I had forgotten about it and Georgina said no more. In retrospect, I'm not sure quite why I was so dismissive at that time, in view of my deep interest in the subject, and I rather suspect it was because Georgina was playing it down, and had perhaps not wanted to believe it herself.

About five months later, we went to the Theatre Royal in Brighton with Michael and Rachel – the first time we had seen them since the dinner party – and saw a play so forgettable that I've forgotten everything about it except for the cost of the seats, which was about the same as the gross national debt of Mexico. After the theatre we went to an Italian restaurant nearby. Then Rachel stunned us.

She asked me if I knew an exorcist. When I asked why, she replied that they had had a number of dinner parties during the past five years, at which one of the guests had later said they had seen a woman, in a corner of the room, watching them. The description of the woman each of them had given matched Georgina's description exactly.

The guests who had seen this woman could not in any way be described as flaky, nor would they have had anything to gain other than ridicule by making the story up. They included a British Airways pilot, a senior medical consultant, a barrister and a vet.

Michael then went on to say that their two daughters were terrified of using the downstairs lavatory, claiming this woman sometimes appeared when they were in there. And he said that one night, as he was going up to bed, she had venomously chased him down the landing!

I did speak to an exorcist, Canon Dominic Walker, who is a personal friend and is also the chief exorcist of the Church of England. His advice was, in the first instance, for Michael and Rachel to tell the woman, very firmly, that she should leave and stop bothering them.

They subsequently tried this. To their amazement, and mine, it seemed to work. Eighteen months have now elapsed and there have been no more sightings of this woman.

During my research for my novels I have encountered numerous people with convincing stories to tell about their experiences. Always, I wonder whether each experience is a product of their imagination, and always I am drawn back to Georgina's experience that night in Rodmell. I don't believe that was a figment of her imagination, nor do I believe she is alone in what she has seen.

I believe that ghost stories revive in an adult way our childhood fears. They free our imagination from the rational drummed into us in modern life. But it is more than that: I think that if I had to make one definitive statement to explain the enduring appeal of the ghost story it would be this: out of the millions – probably billions – of ghost stories that have ever been told, it only needs one demonstrably to prove intelligent existence beyond the grave. Just one, and life for many people on this planet would be changed for ever.

MIKE JEFFERIES

A Face in the Crowd

Mike Jefferies (b. 1943) was born in Kent but spent his early years in Australia. He attended the Goldsmiths School of Arts and then taught art in schools and prisons. A keen rider, he was selected to ride for Britain in the Belgian Three Day Event in 1980. He now lives in Great Massingham, Norfolk, with his wife, working as a writer, illustrator and occasional wood-carver. His books include the how-to volume *Learn to Draw Fantasy Art*, plus the 'Loremasters of Elundium' trilogy (*The Road to Underfall, Palace of Kings* and *Shadowlight*), the 'Heirs to Gnarlsmyre' series (*Glitterspike Hall* and *Hall of Whispers*), two more Elundium books (*Knights of Cawdor* and *Citadel of Shadows*) and such stand-alone novels as *Shadows in the Watchgate, Hidden Echoes, Children of the Flame* and *Stone Angels*, the latter inspired by the events described below.

Most ideas start as a tiny thought, a what if? that gets tossed around between my wife, Sheila, and me until it gradually takes hold of our dreams and builds slowly into a story. From then on it just takes hard work to put the story into words, the words into paragraphs, and finish up with a book. But there was one time when the idea for a book came in one afternoon.

It was late summer. We had handed a finished manuscript in to our publishers and were preparing to write our next book. The ideas had been written down and accepted by our editor; all we had to do was present a proper synopsis and then get on with it. In the mean time, we were having a few days off work to take an American friend around Norfolk.

Having spent the first day or two playing darts and drinking beer, we set off to Norwich to see, among other things, Elm Hill, where we had set a previous story, and the nearby cathedral. You always imagine that a strange and supernatural story should involve storms, cold draughts and spooky atmospheres, but there was nothing strange about this day at all; it was warm, there were plenty of people around, the sun was shining. We had visited the cathedral dozens of times, and there was no suggestion that this visit would be any different from any of the previous ones.

It is always illuminating taking friends to your favourite places: they see different things, draw your attention to them and make you look again with altered understanding. It builds up the picture until it is no longer just a familiar place but a collection of many different dreams, fears and comprehensions; this grows until you can walk through and feel the strength of countless visions.

And so it was that once we were walking around, and our friend was standing in awe at the thought of how they knew the names of the bishops for hundreds of years before anyone in England knew that America existed, the place seemed no longer ordinary. But in truth it never was.

There was a display of paintings in one of the chapels and the three of us had split up slightly to look at the pictures when Sheila found herself standing beside a man, not quite a boy, probably in his late twenties. He was slightly scruffy, with wild hair, and was holding a bundle of notebooks and papers – clearly a mature student from the university, somebody you would never normally give a second glance to in a place like that.

He appeared to be talking to himself, mumbling and muttering softly and consulting his notes as if trying to come to some conclusion, and then he quite abruptly turned his

attention to Sheila. The one-sided conversation became more
urgent and he tried to thrust his untidy bundle of papers
towards her.

Sheila, embarrassed, tried to move away from him but he
persisted, following her through the exhibition, becoming
more and more animated, repeatedly trying to show her the
pieces of paper and scribbled drawings he was holding.
Eventually our friend and I felt we had to intervene.
However, moving away from him didn't defuse the situation
– he followed us and, wherever we went in the cathedral, he
was only a footstep behind, becoming increasingly agitated
until we felt forced to leave.

Our trip to the cathedral was thus unfortunately cut short,
and our American friend made some disparaging remarks
about the crazy English before we continued out into the old
part of the city and set off towards Elm Hill, laughing,
tensely, at our experiences. But before we had even reached
Norris Court, half-way up Elm Hill, Sheila and I agreed that
those wild, almost inarticulate babblings of the young man
in the cathedral had sown the germ of an idea for a story.
Exactly what it was, beyond a veiled warning of impending
disaster, neither of us knew; but it was a feeling strong
enough to make us scrap the synopsis our editor was waiting
for, as the new idea about the cathedral and the strange
character began to take shape.

Over the next week or two we visited the cathedral two or
three more times, in the hope of seeing the young man and
perhaps questioning him, but we hardly needed to look for
him – he was there each time, suddenly emerging from the
crowds of visitors, thrusting the papers and drawings of his
at Sheila and yet never actually letting us talk.

Eventually we gave him a name: Jarvin Mandrake, who
was to become the hero of the book, although now I am not
sure he didn't utter it himself – he spoke so quickly that
most of what he said became an agitated babble. Each time
we came away, the image of what he was trying to tell us

about became clearer in our heads. There was something hidden, something dangerous, lurking in the cathedral that we felt sure he was desperately trying to warn us about, but what was it?

He was always in the cathedral – we never once saw him in the grounds – and he was always reading from his papers, making those agitated gestures. We began to notice that he kept trying to draw us towards a huge empty stone plinth where, the small notice fixed to it said, a medieval stone angel had once stood but had been taken away for cleaning and restoration.

Something we had noticed from the very beginning was that he never seemed to bother other people; although, at times, he would stop and stare hard at somebody, almost looking directly into their face, but with a shrug he would dismiss them and return his attention to us, although during these weird meetings he focused his attention mainly on Sheila. At times he seemed quite mad, almost frightening in his intensity, barely seeming to notice if we tried to interrupt. In an odd way it was as though he was behind glass. We could hear him and see him but he didn't seem to be able to hear us, or didn't want to. Invariably his intensity and determination drove us out of the cathedral. But still the story was forming and we had started taking notes.

We imagined that he was trying to warn us about what sounded like a blood sacrifice that had been taking place in the cathedral for almost a thousand years and was still going on. Crazy ... impossible ... the ravings of a lunatic ... but a brilliant idea for a story.

We had our camera with us on that last day, and we had been standing in the aisle when we noticed Jarvin. He was talking to himself near that empty stone plinth. We still can't decide what made that visit different, but he didn't come hurrying across to us; instead he turned his back and ignored us. We both felt slightly deflated – there was still so much missing from the story, so much he had to tell us. The atmosphere in the cathedral seemed stilted; the noisy echo of footsteps and voices from a large group of foreign visitors with their guides filled the building.

After a short while we decided to leave and have a last walk around the square outside before going home. Perhaps, after all, we had enough for the book. As we were heading towards the south transept we noticed Jarvin sitting down between two elderly ladies, reading his notes and looking as though he was almost in tears.

'Take a photograph!' Sheila said.

'He'll see me.' There was something about Jarvin that made us reluctant to cross him in any way. There was a menacing feeling, as though he were not quite rational.

'Pretend you're taking a picture of the stained-glass window behind him – he need never realize he's the subject.'

So I took out the camera and focused it very carefully. It was never going to be an easy photograph with the low sun streaming through the window almost directly into the lens, but we had to give it a go. As soon as the shutter clicked we left the cathedral, slightly ashamed that we had not had the courage to go up to him. After all, he had pestered us on every visit, but in taking that photograph it almost felt as though we had taken something that didn't belong to us.

Over the next few weeks we visited the cathedral frequently, but Jarvin was never to be seen. The story he had put into our heads built so quickly that we had a synopsis written and posted and were started on the first chapter before the photographs came through the post.

We quickly rifled through them, eager to see how the picture of our hero came out. There it was. The sun through the stained-glass window had made the figures into silhouettes, but shapes were clear – the two old ladies were there but between them was nothing, just an empty chair.

NANCY KILPATRICK

Raggedy Ann

———————•◆•———————

Nancy Kilpatrick (b. 1946) was born in Philadelphia, but is now a resident of Montreal. She has published several novels, including the *Darker Passions* series of erotic reworkings of classic horror themes under the pseudonym 'Amarantha Knight', and the vampire volumes *Child of the Night, Near Death* and *As One Dead,* the latter a collaboration with Don Bassingthwaite. Her short fiction has appeared in numerous anthologies and magazines; *Sex & the Single Vampire* and *The Vampire Stories of Nancy Kilpatrick* are collections of her stories; *Endorphins* contains two vampire novellas; and she has also edited a number of erotic horror anthologies, including *Love Bites, Flesh Fantastic* and *Sex Macabre.* A finalist for the Bram Stoker Award and the Aurora Award, she is a winner of Canada's Arthur Ellis Award for best mystery story.

———————•◆•———————

My second husband's mother and I did not have a close relationship. She was a sweet but timid and private woman, fearful of her own shadow, very quiet and incapable of expressing an opinion. I didn't get to 'know' her over the ten years that she was my mother-in-law, but then nobody else seemed to get close to her either. Still, I liked her sweetness – she seemed to have a good heart, and I had the feeling that she was thrilled to have a writer in the family. From what I'd been told of her background, I realized that we had several things in common: we had both been excruciatingly shy little girls, had both come from very poor households, and our primary female caregivers had died before we were eight years old. This made us *simpático*, if not in an overt manner then in a kind of subterranean way. We had a sort of unconscious, psychic connection, yet on the surface I couldn't have told you whether she preferred coffee or tea.

When my mother-in-law was diagnosed with colon cancer she underwent surgery, then chemotherapy, but the cancer metastasized to her liver. My then-husband went to be with his mother for several weeks. During the death watch, I received daily phone calls updating me on her condition. For several days before the following incident, his mother appeared to be improving. She was coherent, eating a bit and could walk around a little each day. Everyone was encouraged.

I had in my office at that time a collection of about two thousand books in bookcases that surrounded my desk on three sides. The bookcases were so tall, the tops almost touched the high ceiling. Along the tops I had put about a dozen things I wanted around but didn't need handy, like the Arthur Ellis Award of the hanged man, a ceramic Bela Lugosi as Dracula, a winged horse and, on the case directly behind me, a Raggedy Ann doll that a friend had given to me many years ago. I could not reach the top of the bookcases and rarely cleaned up there. In fact, I know it had been several years since the last time I'd borrowed a ladder and climbed to 'the vaults', as I liked to call them, and disturbed any of the items along the tops of the bookcases. So, poor little Raggedy Ann had perched up there, collecting dust and viewing my writing efforts for quite some time without me paying any attention to her.

I like to work at night, and one evening I sat at my computer writing a ghost story. Since I like the night, I don't often get creepy feelings after dark. This time, however, I did. All evening I felt a presence in the room with me, directly behind me. This caused me to turn around frequently as I continued writing. As midnight approached, the feeling of not being alone intensified – I felt I was being watched. I wrote it off to the fact that I had been alone for a couple of weeks and that I was working on a ghost story, but my logical mind wasn't having it, and the part of me that connects to the fantastical had cranked into high gear.

I had just glanced at the clock – it was 12.14 a.m. Suddenly, I heard a loud crash behind me. I nearly hit that high ceiling myself! Heart pounding, I turned. Raggedy Ann had toppled from her lofty post on to a table below, breaking shells and glass objects, and had landed in such a way that she was on her head.

The next morning my husband phoned to report that the in-home nurse had awakened him around midnight: his mother had gone into a coma (from which she never recovered, and she died two days later). 'You wouldn't know the time she went into the coma, would you?' I asked, as an eerie feeling rippled along my spine. He asked the nurse, who told him: 'Twelve-fourteen. I checked my watch so I could record it on the chart.'

By the way, did I mention that my mother-in-law's name was Ann ...?

STEPHEN KING

Uncle Clayton

Stephen King (b. 1947) is one of the most popular novelists in the history of American fiction and is indisputably the most successful horror writer of all time. His first novel, *Carrie*, appeared in 1974, since when he has published a phenomenal string of bestsellers, the most recent being *Insomnia, Rose Madder, The Green Mile, Desperation* and *The Regulators* (the latter under his 'Richard Bachman' pseudonym). His short fiction and novellas have been collected in *Night Shift, Different Seasons, Skeleton Crew, Four Past Midnight* and *Nightmares and Dreamscapes*, and he wrote a nonfiction volume, *Danse Macabre*. Many of King's books and stories have been adapted for movies and television, and he wrote and directed *Maximum Overdrive* in 1986. The winner of numerous awards, King was born in Portland, Maine, and currently lives with his wife, novelist Tabitha King, in Bangor, in a house that is supposedly haunted by an old man: 'I've never seen this old duffer,' he explains, 'but sometimes when I'm working late at night, I get a distinctly uneasy feeling that I'm not alone.' As a youngster he would often listen to ghost stories and local legends spun by his uncle, who had some peculiar talents of his own, as the author revealed in a 1983 *Playboy* interview with Eric Norden:

Uncle Clayton was a great spinner of tales. He was an original, Clayt. I'd listen spellbound to that slow down-eastern drawl of his on the porch of a summer night, and I'd be in another world. He could 'line' bees, you know. That's a quirky rural talent that enables you to trail a honey-bee all the way from a flower back to its hive – for miles, sometimes, through woods and brambles and bogs, but he never lost one. I sometimes wonder if more than good eyesight was involved.

Uncle Clayt had another talent, too: he was a dowser. He could find water with a piece of forked wood. How and why I'm not sure, but he did it. I was sceptical about dowsing at first, until I actually saw it and experienced it – when Uncle Clayt defied all the experts and found a well in our front yard. I was bone-sceptical. I think it's far more likely that there's a perfectly logical and non-supernatural explanation for dowsing – merely one science doesn't understand yet.

It's easy to scoff at such things, but don't forget Haldane's law, a maxim coined by the famous British scientist J. B. S. Haldane: 'The universe is not only queerer than we suppose, but it is queerer than we *can* suppose.'

HUGH LAMB

Go On, Open Your Eyes . . .

Hugh Lamb (b. 1946) was born in Sutton, Surrey. One of Britain's most acclaimed anthologists of ghosts and gaslight terrors, he is renowned for unearthing many obscure tales by Victorian and Edwardian writers, including a lost M. R. James story for his 1975 compilation *The Thrill of Horror*. Since his first anthology, *A Tide of Terror*, appeared in 1972, his books have included *Victorian Tales of Terror*, two volumes of *The Star Book of Horror*, *Terror By Gaslight* (1975), *The Taste of Fear, Cold Fear, Forgotten Tales of Terror, The Man Wolf and Other Horrors, New Tales of Terror, Stories in the Dark, Terror By Gaslight* (1992), two volumes of *Gaslit Nightmares*, plus collections by such authors of the macabre as Erckmann-Chatrian, E. Nesbit, Jerome K. Jerome, Bernard Capes, A. C. and R. H. Benson and Robert W. Chambers.

At the end of 'Thurnley Abbey', one of the scariest ghost stories ever written, the narrator cannot find the courage to look at the ghostly nun when it comes back for its bone. I'd always thought this very unlikely – well, you would have a peep, wouldn't you?

Since 1981, I've thought differently.

We moved into our present house in 1979 and I have to say that nothing spooky happened before the event I'm writing about, nor has anything happened since. There were one or two odd things about the place: the bath was very scratched and dirty, and I discovered that the previous occupier but one had used to keep coal in it. Yes, the old insult has some truth in it after all. And I found under a floorboard in the front bedroom an airmail envelope containing a mass of human hair; this was never explained. But of ghosts, not a sign. However...

Some layout information will be useful. The upstairs landing runs from front to back and you can see straight down it from the back bedroom into the front, and vice versa. The stairs come up parallel to the landing, entailing a sharp right turn at the top to get onto the landing (in fact, there is nowhere else to go when you do get up the stairs). In those days we slept in the back bedroom, the children in the front, and the bed faced the door so that you could see straight down the landing, to the front bedroom (the main reason why we moved the bed around eventually).

It was a summer night, and the window and curtains were open; plenty of light (mainly yellow street-lamp). I woke up with a bang about 3 a.m.; my wife was fast asleep and stayed that way throughout. The noise I heard didn't wake me up; in the same way that you often wake up and then hear the alarm go off, I was wide awake before it happened. The bedroom door was open, as usual, and I could see all the way down the landing. I rolled over, intending to go back to sleep, and then it began.

I heard – clearly and plainly – someone run up the stairs, very fast, and then stop dead at the top. If it was possible to run in divers' lead boots, then that is what it would have sounded like – every step on every stair like that of an extraordinarily heavy person. After the footsteps up the stairs, it was suddenly quiet, as though the runner were standing there, stock still.

All my remembered life, I've been fascinated by ghosts. I've read more books of ghost stories, true and fictional, than I care to remember. I've given myself the horrors with M. R. James and umpteen horror films. Like many others,

I've been in spooky places at night, but not seen a thing. I used to think that I would like to see a ghost.

So there I was, waiting for another sound, and all I had to do was open my eyes and look down the landing at where whatever it was that had crashed up the stairs must have been standing. And what did this gallant editor of ghostly anthologies do? You bet. I kept my eyes tight shut, stayed absolutely still and waited ... and waited ... and waited ... and the next thing I knew it was morning and I was awake again.

In the daylight, I cursed myself for not looking. But I do know that were it to happen again – which it hasn't – I would almost certainly chicken out once more. Well, what would you have done?

TERRY LAMSLEY

Moving Houses

———— •◄• ————

Terry Lamsley (b. 1941) was born in the south of England but has lived in the north for most of his life. The stories in his first collection of supernatural tales, *Under the Crust*, were set in and around Buxton, in the heart of the Peak District, where he lives with his family. Although originally intended to appeal to local readers and tourists to the area, *Under the Crust* reached the hands of the late Karl Edward Wagner, who was instrumental in the book being nominated for three World Fantasy Awards in 1994, and ultimately winning the Best Novella award for the title story of the collection. In 1996, Ash-Tree Press published his second collection of tales, *Conference With the Dead*, and his atmospheric ghost stories have also recently appeared in such anthologies as *The Best New Horror*, *The Year's Best Fantasy and Horror*, *The Year's Best Horror Stories*, *Dark Terrors*, *Lethal Kisses* and *The Mammoth Book of Dracula*.

———— •◄• ————

For various reasons, mostly to do with my father's work, my parents moved home a number of times during my childhood. This must have disrupted my education somewhat, and it certainly meant that I had no long-term friendships with people my own age, but I had no objection to that at the time, and used to look forward to being uprooted from one area and plonked down in another every few years.

I was in the habit of setting out to explore each new place pretty thoroughly as soon as I could, to familiarize myself with my surroundings, because having a map of each new terrain inside my head made me feel more secure there. When I was fairly familiar with every street and field for miles around I felt that, metaphorically, I had subjugated the territory and could plant the flag and claim the land as my own. These compulsive explorations were essentially solitary affairs, done before I had had the chance to get to know other children in the area who could have shown me around, but this just made all my discoveries more exciting.

The last move my parents made while I was still living with them, when I was about thirteen, was to Castleton, a tiny mill town near Rochdale, in Lancashire, where my father then worked. The house on Manchester Road had a very inviting view from the back, overlooking fields, a length of canal and more fields beyond, stretching away as far as could be seen. True to form, as soon as I could, before most of my belongings were even unpacked, I walked out to try to get the measure of this landscape. It must have been early evening when I set off on my initial investigation, if my memories of the quality of the light are correct.

To begin my brief reconnaissance I climbed over a low fence into the nearest field and walked straight ahead to the canal, wandered some way along it, then crossed over a bridge and continued on for a short distance. Walking alongside a stretch of water is always enjoyable, but I soon came to a path leading away at right angles to the canal that looked more interesting, for some now forgotten reason, so I followed that. Behind me, my new home was still visible, so I had not gone very far at all. Certainly less than a mile.

Almost as soon as I stepped on to the path I heard something banging irregularly in the distance. The sound grew louder as I progressed, so I knew I was heading towards its source. I guessed someone up ahead was beating a large, empty metal container with a hammer. It was an ugly noise that echoed slightly, and jarred uncomfortably with the otherwise peaceful scene all around me. I didn't take much

notice of it though, because everything I could see was novel
and absorbed most of my attention.

After following the path for some minutes I came to a row
of small houses to the left of me, built along the crest of a
slight slope, about three yards above the level of the canal.
They looked old, but by no means ancient. I was walking
along past the back of these buildings. Thin gardens
stretched towards me down the slope, containing a number
of tiny outhouses and sheds, rabbit hutches and wire com-
pounds for the chickens I could hear clucking away somewhere. As with gardens everywhere, some were better cared
for than others, although my general impression was that
they were mostly rather dilapidated and untidy.

In one of them I saw a stooping man, his right arm
swinging up and down from time to time as he hit something
I could not see with slow, even lazy, motions. Here was the
origin of the sounds I had heard. The only other person in
sight was a woman in a floral frock who emerged from a
house a couple of doors away and began to put out or take
in washing from a line. She was facing my way, and I thought
she glanced at me once in some surprise, but I looked away
from her myself then, and continued on past the last of the
houses (there could not have been more than six or seven of
them).

When I had gone beyond the range of the beating sounds
that continued spasmodically behind me, I forgot about the
encounter, if such a trivial incident could be so described.
Half an hour later I found myself at a point I recognized,
where the canal ran under the Manchester Road, and
returned home.

A couple of weeks later I set out in the same direction,
taking the same path away from the canal, intending to
extend my exploration much further. It was not until I had
gone beyond the farthest point I had reached on my previous
walk that I realized I had not noticed the row of houses –
but I assumed I had been preoccupied with something else

for the few moments it would have taken to pass them, and had walked by without seeing them. This seemed odd, since – then, at least – I was normally quite observant, but I did not think too much about it at the time. Nevertheless, some seed of doubt must have taken root in my mind, because the next occasion I had reason to go that way, I was on the lookout for the houses – but they were not where I expected them to be. Nor were they anywhere else. I searched hundreds of yards in all directions but there was no sign of them at all. The land in the area was fairly flat and open, and I didn't even locate a small hillock anything like the one they had been built on.

It's hard to believe now, but I took their absence very matter-of-factly, and wasn't the least bit disturbed or alarmed. I guess at first I must have thought I had made some sort of mistake, and wandered off in the wrong direction. Vague unease persisted at some level, however, and over the next months I made frequent returns to the path leading away from the canal (there were no others anything like it in that stretch of the waterway in either direction, by the way) and searched around, but without any success at all. There were no houses, no patch of sloping land and not even, as there would perhaps have been if this was a ghost story, the remains of ancient house-platforms.

I never said anything to anyone about the experience at the time, and soon gave up looking. At that age, the world is full enough of mysteries of a more personal and urgently demanding kind and, like any healthy child, I turned my full attention on them.

I never quite forgot the vanished houses though: they and their enigma slowly grew in significance the older I got. Many years later I made some effort to search through old maps of the district, but got no answers from them, and even, feeling appropriately sheepish, returned to the spot and took another investigative walk through the fields. That made things worse, because my mature self was only able to confirm the absence of any evidence for the buildings' existence. But I knew then, and continue to believe, I hadn't been dreaming or hallucinating when I walked down that path that day: I remain convinced that I walked by those houses once, somehow, somewhere.

The experience began, right from the start and very subtly, to subvert my assumptions about the nature of reality. I knew the world was a place where rows of perfectly normal-looking houses can disappear without trace, along with their occupants, and was well aware most people would not have agreed with me about that. I became distrustful of received opinion of all kinds, tested everything out, and soon found that, if you shake hard enough, everything comes apart in your hands.

Later, more powerful experiences convinced me I was right and everybody else (almost) was wrong, but I kept quiet about that too. Wouldn't you? I adapted accordingly, and learned to live insecurely in chaos without any faith in anything.

Where has that got me now? Well, it gave me a pretty good training to become a writer of a certain kind of fiction: morbid tales of supernatural terror, that is.

And, it has to be said, not much else.

JOHN LANDIS

Inspiration

—————————— •◆• ——————————

John Landis (b. 1950) was born in Chicago and raised in Los Angeles. Although he never went to film school, he started working in the mail room at Twentieth Century-Fox in 1968. Three years later, after various jobs as a stuntman, actor, writer, extra and gofer, he took his life savings of $30,000, raised another $30,000, and wrote and directed his first feature film in 1972: *Schlock* was a comedy about a revived prehistoric ape man. After bit-parts in such films as *Battle for the Planet of the Apes* and *Death Race 2000*, he had his first success as a director with *The Kentucky Fried Movie*, a low-budget spoof which led to such hits as *National Lampoon's Animal House* and *The Blues Brothers*. Since then his many credits have included *An American Werewolf in London*, the ill-fated *Twilight Zone The Movie*, Michael Jackson's *Thriller* video, *Trading Places*, *Into the Night*, *Amazon Women on the Moon*, *Coming to America*, *Innocent Blood*, *Beverly Hills Cop III* and *The Stupids*. When asked about his encounters with the paranormal, he admits that 'Working in the film industry is weird enough.'

—————————— •◆• ——————————

There are those who think that angels are real. Intelligent, educated, thoughtful people who sincerely believe in the Holy Ghost. Adults still seriously consider Satan a very real threat.

Politicians calmly send troops to kill and be killed. Businessmen constantly choose profit over the general welfare. Why look to the supernatural for evidence of something 'other', when mankind will never disappoint the true cynic?

Well, for one thing, the supernatural is extremely entertaining.

I keep an open mind. I personally have not yet been given enough information to believe or disbelieve. This is all prelude to the actual event that inspired *An American Werewolf in London.*

In 1969 Woodstock took place, Ted Kennedy had an accident in Chappaquiddick, Charles Manson murdered in L.A. and man walked on the moon.

I was behind the Iron Curtain working as a 'go-fer' on the Brian Hutton film *Kelly's Heroes* in what is now referred to as 'the former Yugoslavia'. This was an MGM World War II action comedy, starring Clint Eastwood, Telly Savalas, Donald Sutherland and Don Rickles.

I was being driven down a long single-lane road by a young man named Sasha. Sasha spoke excellent English and talked non-stop, recounting his many sexual conquests. After an hour or so, these tales seemed to melt into one another and it was hard to remain awake in the back seat of the shabby old Mercedes.

I was dozing off when we stopped. Sasha was swearing as he got out of the car. After a few moments I roused myself too. 'Where are we? Still in the countryside? Why have we stopped?' I climbed out to see.

A crossroads, around thirty people milling about. Sasha standing to one side. I went to stand by him. 'What is that?' It's a body wrapped in canvas with garlic strung around it and, yes, those are rosaries. Two men digging in the road at the crux of the crossroads as a Greek Orthodox priest waits. Tall hat, long beard, yes, I'm sure he's a priest. The others are gypsies. I know this because they look and dress like gypsies. The whole scene was straight off the Universal back-lot.

'What's going on?' I asked Sasha.

'Peasants,' he answered, 'stupid superstitious peasants.'

The men put down their shovels and lifted the body. Yes, it is a body all right. They placed it in the hole feet-first, and let go. It fell over with a dull thud. The priest said something and threw holy water into the grave. The men started to shovel the dirt on top of the body. The people all crossed themselves, even Sasha.

It took some time for them to fill the hole. Sasha smoked a cigarette, the priest mumbled on. When it was full, the men stamped on the mound with their boots and pounded it with their shovels. More holy water, more words. That was it.

Once back in the car, back on the road, Sasha was both contemptuous and amused by the burial we had witnessed. The dead man had committed some crime. He was buried this way so that he would not cause any more trouble.

That was all the information I could get.

That night there was a brilliant full moon. I could picture fingers desperately clawing their way through the earth, hands straining, the corpse pulling himself up and out of the ground on to the road. Illuminated by the glow of the full moon, the dead man would turn slowly and start to walk down the road. To where? Revenge? A shower?

It is true that all mental institutions put on more staff, give out more medication, on nights of the full moon. Hospital emergency rooms and police all over the world will tell you that acts of violence increase during the full moon. Lunacy?

Well anyway, it got me thinking . . .

The closest I ever came to a supernatural experience was in the early 1970s. I had a girlfriend who lived in the Hollywood Hills. She shared a house with four friends, two other girls and two boys. There was one couple in the group who shared a room, but the others had their own bedrooms. All were students.

By pooling their resources they were able to lease quite a big house with a garden and a maid. It was the maid who first saw Andy.

Coming home one day, one of the girls heard screams from the kitchen. She ran downstairs to discover the maid shaking with fear. The maid described how a man with a mop of shaggy blond hair, a pale complexion, dark sunglasses and wearing a blue bathrobe had walked into the kitchen, passed her and disappeared through the wall!

Once she had calmed down, the maid was absolutely positive that she had seen a ghost, and announced that she was quitting that day.

That night, upon hearing the maid's description, we named the ghost Andy, after Andy Warhol.

A new maid was found, and much discussion of ghosts and strange noises began. Everyone but me heard bumps in the night. Everyone but me heard footfalls on the stairs. I was amazed to discover that even my girlfriend took Andy's presence seriously.

Over the following weeks one of the girls caught a glimpse of Andy in the yard, still wearing his bathrobe. She called for the others to come quickly, but by the time someone had arrived Andy had vanished.

We tried to contact Andy with a Ouija board, but, of course, the seance was diminished by all the giggling.

Bottom line, everyone in the house eventually saw at least a flash of Andy but me.

One Sunday morning my girlfriend and I were sleeping late when we heard the front door open and close. We listened to someone coming down the stairs. We called out to see who it was and no one replied. So I got up to see who was there. We were alone in the house.

STEPHEN LAWS

Norfolk Nightmare

———————— •—•— ————————

Stephen Laws (b. 1952) was born in Newcastle upon Tyne, where he continues to live and work as a full-time writer. He began writing fiction at the age of eight and worked as a committee administrator in local government before making his novel début in 1985 with *Ghost Train* (which had a publicity campaign banned by British Rail, who were concerned it might alarm their passengers). He followed it with *Spectre, The Wyrm, The Frighteners, Darkfall, Gideon* (winner of the Count Dracula Society's Children of the Night Award for Best Vampire Novel), *Macabre, Daemonic* and *Somewhere South of Midnight*. A shared collection of stories with Mark Morris was published in chapbook form as *Voyages Into Darkness*. His books have been widely translated around the world, and among his research highlights he includes being dropped down an elevator shaft for *Darkfall*, almost drowned in a Stockport canal on a so-called 'controlled' scuba-dive for *Macabre*, and nearly demolishing a three-bedroom, semi-detached house while behind the wheel of a runaway bulldozer for *Daemonic*.

———————— •—•— ————————

I've had two real supernatural experiences in my life. I don't talk about the most important one, since it's too personal and turned my life around. But I'll gladly tell you about the other one, which was deeply disturbing and was most definitely not faked by the two other people involved.

Back in the 1970s, two pals and I hired a boat for a week

cruising on the Norfolk Broads. It was the usual sort of thing for three single guys: puttering down the waterways at a leisurely ten miles an hour, tying up outside a pub or nightspot, getting legless on the local beer and failing to understand why none of the women we approached seemed to be at all taken with our chat-up lines. Next day, it was off to the next venue, nursing hangovers. At one stage, we tied up too tight to the quay and by the time we came back from the pub the tide had gone out and our boat was left hanging on the quay wall. We had to sit there, sobering up, until the tide came back in again. Not cool.

Towards the end of the week, we didn't read our maps very well. Instead of tying up outside a pub, we found that the waterway we'd taken had led us deep into the Fens. It was very late, very dark, and there was no sign of habitation anywhere. For that night, we decided just to tie up at the bank and drink the cans we'd stocked up on in case of emergencies. To this day, I don't know where we were. Perhaps a part of me still doesn't want to know where it is. I remember that there was a ruined windmill not far from us: skeletal sails silhouetted by the moon. It looked sort of romantic when we arrived. It had taken on a completely different look when we left.

Sometime in the early hours, and on the outside of several cans, Keith suggested that we make an improvised Ouija board and see what we could pick up. I'd heard about Ouija, of course. It was a popular 'game' back then, although I'd never tried it. There'd been warnings about trying it out, from various religious groups. Maybe that all added to the spice of it. Tony and I assented, and Keith set about writing out the letters of the alphabet on a scrap of paper, together with the words YES and NO. He cut them out, added some written numbers and then laid them out in the usual formation. Then he upended a glass tumbler on to the table and started on his spiel of 'Is there anyone there? Do you wish to contact us?' etc. Clearly, he'd done all this sort of stuff before.

Something started to happen. Keith told us to keep our fingers on the upended bottom of the tumbler and not break contact. The glass started to move. No one was pushing it. The first message came through, first for Tony – and then for his father.

TELL HIM ... TELL HIM ... And then some garbled words that didn't make sense.

Tony looked a little troubled. 'Are you having trouble with English?' he asked, it's motivation unclear.

The tumbler slid quickly to YES. To and fro then: YES, YES, YES, YES, YES.

'Take your time,' continued Tony. 'What's the message?'

124, came the reply. TELL HIM ... TELL HIM ... ONE HUNDRED AND TWENTY FOUR DEAD IN KOBLENZ. JUNE 1941.

Tony snatched his hand away and the tumbler stopped. Suddenly, things weren't funny any more. His father was Polish. He'd been living here in England ever since the end of the war. During the conflict, he had been forced to work as slave labour for the Germans. Tony had never told anyone about this, until now. And there was something else about this message that obviously meant something to him, but he wasn't going to let us in on it. White-faced, he refused to have anything else to do with the 'game'. Keith coerced me into trying again, insisting that it would still work with only two. Slightly troubled by Tony's reaction, but not wanting to give in to anyone's trickery, I continued. Keith pointed out that his mother (or perhaps his grandmother, I forget which) was a medium, and he started his introduction again. Was there another message for someone else?

YES.

'Who?'

STEPHEN. I eyed Keith warily. Either he was the greatest actor in the world, or he was equally baffled. What was the message? No answer. Again, what was the message?

ASK.

'Ask? Ask what?'

'It wants you to test it out,' said Keith.

'How do you know, unless you're doing all this?'

'It's not me, honest. Look, we'll stop if you want.'

'All right, I'll ask.'

So I did. I asked questions that neither Keith nor Tony could possibly give answers for. I asked it to give me the address of the woman I was currently 'seeing', and whom the other two did not know about for reasons that were too complicated and too personal to go into here. It gave me the address. I asked for her initials. It gave them. There were other questions, too personal to reveal; all unknown by Keith and Tony (and deliberately chosen by me because I knew that they didn't know). It even gave me facts that I'd forgotten about. Would I get married? The same message came back again and again: NO, NO, NO, NO, NO, NO, NO (that's one it most definitely got wrong. My first marriage ended in divorce. Melanie is my second wife). Then the bloody thing became agitated, jetting about all over the table. It was then that I got a bad feeling about this whole business. There was a malicious intent about whatever was sending these messages. It was palpable in the air. Suddenly, the cabin of our boat was claustrophobic, and the night was pressing heavily on all sides.

'What are you trying to say?' asked Keith. 'Who is your message for?'

The tumbler began to move back and forward to two letters.

S . . . L . . . S . . . L . . . S . . . L . . .

OK, the messages were still for me. I became aware of the fact that I was physically having to keep up with the movement of the glass. I looked at Keith's finger. He wasn't pushing. He was having the same trouble keeping up with the tumbler's impetus.

'What are you trying to tell him?' asked Keith.

The tumbler moved again. This time, it didn't glide across the table. It moved with a sure and steady purpose that was not only methodical, but horribly malicious. It began to spell out one word.

D . . . E . . . A . . . T . . .

And before it could reach H, I snatched my hand away.

Keith took his hand away too.

And the tumbler span and rattled by itself, slid to the edge of the table and fell off.

We were, all three, very shaken.

We finished off the rest of the beer, while dark water lapped at the boat and Keith tried without success to convince us that it was all just rubbish. I still remember the phrase he used over and over again. 'Just think about it as a bad joke.' He didn't mean that *he'd* been joking, that he'd somehow fixed the whole thing. What he meant was that whatever had sent the messages was playing a bad joke. His choice of phrase just served to unsettle me further. During the long hours ahead, we subjected him to a serious interrogation about whether he'd been fixing it all. It would have been a lot easier if he'd just admitted to something. But his face remained as white and drawn as Tony's and mine.

It was a long, long night.

When morning came, we got out of there just as quickly as we could. The whole 'game' had cast a pall over the holiday that the consumption of alcohol couldn't fade.

So there you go. A trick? No, I don't think so. Something was going on then. I researched the subject quite considerably, since the event had badly shaken me up. There's one view that messages transmitted via Ouija are from deceased relatives or acquaintances. Another that the messages come, quite literally, from ourselves. No one else knew the answers to the questions I asked; so perhaps I was somehow unconsciously manipulating that glass myself, answering my own questions on some deep telepathic level that we'd been able to tap into. Perhaps even providing the answers to questions

I'd forgotten, as I mentioned earlier. There's another theory: that the Ouija contact is with elemental spirits, not human in any way, some of them extremely malicious. Maybe that's what we were talking to: something that could draw on our subconscious minds and find the answers to the questions.

I know a few people who've been foolish enough to mess around with Ouija boards. Whether the contact is made with the dead, with inhuman spirits or is merely some kind of reflective telepathic condition, I wouldn't be tempted to try it again. And I think that anyone who does should have their head examined. So there you go, a true experience.

Now I'm beginning to wonder whether I shouldn't have told you about the day I was walking past the Imperial Cinema in Byker. It was the setting for my second novel, *Spectre*, and had been boarded up ever since its closure in the early sixties. On that morning, the steel-shuttered doors had been literally torn out and thrown in the street. Here was my chance to have a look inside the building that had meant so much to me when I was a kid, before the bulldozers moved in to flatten it. There was a storm coming. I hesitated for a moment, then stepped through into the darkness. Inside, there were no seats, but there was still a torn projection screen there. Over there were the old balcony and projection booth. And didn't the place look so much *smaller* now? As I stood in the middle of the cinema, looking around in wonder, something utterly terrifying began to happen. Just as in the climax of the novel, the walls began to shake and shudder, and plaster-dust started to drift down from the roof. The whole building seemed to be falling apart around me. I whirled in terror and saw that –

Ah, but that's another tale. Which is also, I swear, absolutely true. Maybe next time.

Pleasant dreams.

SAMANTHA LEE

Not Funny

—•—

Samantha Lee (b. 1940) was born in County Londonderry, but currently lives in London. Her short stories have appeared in a number of anthologies and magazines, including *The Pan Book of Horror Stories*, *The Fourth Armada Monster Book*, *Fantasy Tales*, *The Anthology of Fantasy & the Supernatural*, *Final Shadows* and *Cold Cuts III*, and several of her tales have been broadcast on BRMB, Radio Eirean and London's Capital Radio, plus Thames TV's *Rainbow* series for children. Lee's novels include the 'Lightbringer' Trilogy (*The Quest for the Sword of Infinity*, *The Land Where Serpents Rule* and *The Path Through the Circle of Time*), *Childe Rolande*, and a retelling of *Dr Jekyll and Mr Hyde* for younger readers. She has written two lifestyle books, *Fit to be 50* and *All By Myself*.

—•—

August 1986.

Formentera. A small island off the coast of Ibiza, Spain. Four miles by thirteen. Almost totally flat. Salt marshes, crystal seas, bone-white beaches untrammelled by tourists or trannies.

No airport. Access by ferry.

No traffic. Bicycles the favoured mode of transport.

No buildings over two storeys. It's the law.

The apparition strikes without warning half-way through the four-week holiday. One minute I am fast asleep. The next I am bolt upright, eyes on stalks, heart drowning the sound of the sea-surge below the balcony.

There is a light at the end of the bed. Man-sized but not a man. A presence, bringing with it a sense of desolation, a deathly bone-chilling cold. In the middle of the sweltering Mediterranean night, my teeth chatter like castanets.

The vision flares across my retina for no more than an instant. Then slowly it implodes, folding back on itself like dragon's breath dissolving into a vacuum.

I am rigid with terror. The heat comes back with a rush. Sweat runs down my face, dripping from the end of my nose and on to the rumpled sheet. It is pitch dark.

Beside me, my other half snores gently, oblivious. I don't wake him. He'll only laugh. But I can't stay in this room, in the dark, a moment longer.

I slide out of bed and move to the kitchen where I turn on the light. The wall clock tells me it is 3 a.m. I pour myself a large drink and sit down at the Formica table.

My friend Maurice, newly diagnosed with multiple sclerosis, is dead. I am sure of it. I tell Peter as much when he emerges, tousle-haired, five long hours later. As anticipated, he laughs, tells me I'm weird, asks if I couldn't come up with something a bit more original? Lights at the end of the bed have been done to death.

The doorbell makes us both jump. Peter goes to answer it, comes back, minutes later, ash white under his tan.

His father, a man in his prime, in hospital for routine tests, has unexpectedly died of blood poisoning. The message has just been relayed to the police station. Time of death: 3 a.m.

So it wasn't Maurice after all.

'Why did *you* see him?' Peter accuses. 'Why didn't he come to me?'

'Maybe he thought you'd laugh,' I tell him.

That's when he begins to cry.

BARRY B. LONGYEAR

The Gray Ghost

———————————— • ◆ • ————————————

Barry B. Longyear (b. 1942) was born in Harrisburg, Pennsylvania, and currently resides in New Sharon, Maine, with his wife Jean and a used dog. In 1977 he sold his printing company and went into writing full-time. He made his first sale to *Isaac Asimov's Science Fiction Magazine* the next year. Following that he sold numerous short works, with stories appearing in *Analog, Amazing, Omni, Alfred Hitchcock's Mystery Magazine* and *Twilight Zone*, and non-fiction pieces in *Writer's Digest*. His stories include the award-winning novella 'Enemy Mine', later made into a major motion picture by Twentieth Century-Fox. In his first year of publication he sold his first three books, *Manifest Destiny, Circus World* and *City of Baraboo*, and a year later became the first writer to win the Nebula Award, Hugo Award and John W. Campbell Award for best new writer in the same year. His subsequent books have included two sequels to 'Enemy Mine': *The Tomorrow Testament* and *The Last Enemy*, plus *Elephant Song, Saint Mary Blue, Sea of Glass, Naked Came the Robot, The God Box, Infinity Hold, The Homecoming, It Came From Schenectady* and two *Alien Nation* novels, *The Change* and *Slag Like Me*. He has also published a how-to volume entitled *Science Fiction Writer's Workshop*.

———————————— • ◆ • ————————————

My wife, Jean, and I were in southern Connecticut on the turnpike driving home to Maine. It was in 1985 in early autumn, late at night. The highway was almost deserted. As usual, I was driving on autopilot – over the speed limit and my mind elsewhere – when I heard Jean scream. There was the body of a woman stretched across my lane. I jammed on my brakes and turned, and as the car went up on two wheels and we flashed by, I managed to see that the body was a fully dressed home-made dummy such as New Englanders make to put on their front porches for the Hallowe'en season.

By the time I had regained control of the car and commented at length upon the prankster's lineage and biological configuration, I was shaking rather badly. We got off the turnpike at the next exit, stopped at the golden arches and had some coffee. After we had calmed down, we continued our journey. I kept it down to the speed limit and, to keep us both awake, we began 'novelling'. Often when we have a long stretch of driving to do, Jean and I make up stories, kick around titles and ideas, and even plot out novels. It fills in the time, and at least two of these rolling workshops have been published.

This time we began with the dummy in the road. Who made it? Who put it on the turnpike? Why?

Jean said, 'I don't think it was put on the road. I think it fell out of an overloaded pick-up truck. The driver probably doesn't even know that it's missing.'

I nodded. 'Maybe by now he does know it's missing and that means he's in big trouble. Fear is choking him because he really needs that big doll.'

'Is it because it's stuffed with money, or is this going to be some kind of perverse sexual thing?' she asked.

'Maybe both,' I offered. 'Maybe something worse. Inside that dummy, behind that mask, underneath those rags, there might have been a man or a woman.'

'Murder?' Jean almost squealed with glee. She is a murder mystery fan and had been after me for some time to take a detour from science fiction and fantasy and try my word processor out on some homicide. 'A murder, how?'

'Oh, old Malachi couldn't bear to do in his wealthy granny

with his own hands, so he drugged her, dressed her up to look like a Hallowe'en dummy and dragged her out on the highway for me to run over.'

'Do you suppose that might really be true?'

'Why not? New England is full of weirdos.' I continued with my renewed recollection of one of the dummy's arms. Instead of a glove, I thought I remembered a hand, and so on. We continued in this vein until, hours later, we were on the Maine Turnpike approaching the town of Gray, and were pretty well talked out. As we passed the Gray exit, I saw what appeared to be a man walking from the grassy median across the inner lane. Since that was the lane in which I was driving, I began slowing down.

The figure was walking very slowly and seemed completely oblivious to my car's approach. I slowed some more and was now close enough to see it. The figure was a filled outline, almost an animated cut-out, of a man wearing a coat, long trousers and a wide-brimmed hat. The entire surface facing me was flat and coloured an iridescent grey. As it moved across the road, it did not reflect the beams from my car's headlights, but had a source of illumination from within. The car was no more than twenty feet from it and I had slowed almost to a stop.

'Why are you slowing down?' asked Jean.

'Can't you see it?'

'See what?' She looked through the windshield, frowned and looked back at me. 'I don't see anything.'

I looked again and the apparition was in the next lane, taking another step. As it did so, the grey faded until I could see through the thing. It was less than ten feet away. In its partly transparent state, it took another step, faded some more and then vanished.

'You didn't see that?'

'No,' Jean answered. 'What was it?'

I speeded up and began describing what I had seen. By the time I was finished, we were both rather spooked. That was when I passed another car and Jean screamed. While I was nurturing a cardiac arrest, she began laughing.

'When we passed that car I thought I saw a skeleton driving it. I think we both need some sleep.'

I passed the whole thing off as a hallucination prompted by too little sleep and too much imagination. I had experienced something of the sort when I was in the Army twenty-three years earlier. I was standing watch on one of the decks of the troop-ship that was taking us all to Okinawa. The army guards were standing watches four hours on and eight hours off, and I spent my eight hours off playing poker below decks. So there I was, after three days without sleep, in the middle of the Pacific Ocean at two in the morning on a dimly lit deck trying to keep from falling asleep and going over the rail into the drink.

Stacked amidships were some life-rafts covered by a tarpaulin. On top of the tarp was an enormous black panther. I knew what I was seeing was the wind moving the tarp, causing the shadow cast by the lone deck-light to move, but it looked like a black panther to me, down to the yellow eyes and gleaming white fangs. I watched it for a long time, then turned away with promises to myself to skip the poker game at the end of my watch and get some sleep. As I turned I was faced with a triple-headed hydra that was attacking me. When I finished screaming, I saw that there was a fire hydrant mounted on the bulkhead with three brass connectors for hoses. After my watch, I went to bed.

Especially since Jean hadn't seen the ghost, and with my shadow black panther in mind, I tried to write off the Gray ghost experience as a hallucination. Still, every time I was on the Maine Turnpike and passed the Gray exit, I'd remember what I saw that night and that there was no way that it could have been caused by any sort of shadow. I would also remember where I saw the Gray ghost and the direction in which it was walking. It piqued my curiosity.

About three years later I was looking for a suitable spot in which to set a horror story, and I used this as an excuse to make the more than an hour drive to Gray. When Jean and I got off at the Gray exit, we had facing us the place where the Gray ghost had been heading: the town cemetery. We toured the town, and also toured the cemetery. There we found a curious headstone. The name on it was STRANGER. At the town library we found the story of the headstone.

From George T. Hill's *History, Records, and Recollections of Gray, Maine* (1978) is this tale of the American Civil War:

On August 2, 1862, Lieutenant Charles H. Colley of Gray was wounded in the battle of Cedar Mountain. Three weeks later he died while hospitalized in Alexandria, Virginia. At that time, families, by paying expenses, could have the bodies of soldiers returned to their homes for burial, and arrangements were made for the return of the Lieutenant's remains. When the casket, supposedly with the soldier's body, arrived, it was opened, and there was the body of a stranger in Confederate uniform. An attempt was made to correct the mistake, but communications were slow, and, after waiting several days without receiving any word, the stranger was buried on a vacant lot.

About three weeks later the body of Lieutenant Colley arrived and was buried with the usual services. Some time after this, a ladies' organization had an appropriate stone erected on the Confederate soldier's grave.

The outline of the thing I saw crossing the turnpike heading for the Gray cemetery was entirely consistent with the uniform used by some of the Confederate forces during the rebellion. Hallucination? Ghost? Which was it?

I believe that the town of Gray, far north in Yankeeland, has in its cemetery a rebel soldier who is buried a long way from home and rests uneasily for it.

H. P. LOVECRAFT

Witch House

───────────── ◆ ─────────────

Howard Phillips Lovecraft (1890–1937) is one of the most important and influential authors of the supernatural in the twentieth century. Born in Providence, Rhode Island, he lived there for most of his life as a studious antiquarian. Lovecraft's fiction, poems and essays appeared in the amateur press and such pulp magazines as *Weird Tales*. In 1939, August Derleth and Donald Wandrei founded Arkham House, a publishing imprint initially created to keep all Lovecraft's work in print. Beginning with *The Outsider and Others*, his stories were collected in such volumes as *Beyond the Wall of Sleep, Marginalia, Something About Cats and Other Pieces, Dreams and Fancies, The Dunwich Horror and Others, At the Mountains of Madness and Other Novels, Dagon and Other Macabre Tales, 3 Tales of Horror* and *The Horror in the Museum and Other Revisions*, along with several volumes of 'collaborations' with Derleth and others, including *The Lurker at the Threshold, The Survivor and Others, The Shuttered Room and Other Pieces, The Dark Brotherhood and Other Pieces, The Watchers Out of Time and Others* and *Tales of the Cthulhu Mythos*. Although he was a total disbeliever in the supernatural, Lovecraft was a voluminous correspondent, and in a 1923 letter to Frank Belknap Long and Alfred Galpin he gave an atmospheric account of his visit to the home of a convicted witch in Salem:

───────────── ◆ ─────────────

I struck out along the roads and across the fields toward the lone farmhouse built by Townsend Bishop in 1636, and in 1692 inhabited by the worthy and inoffensive old widow Rebekah Nurse, who was seventy years of age and wished no one harm. Accused by the superstitious West Indian slave woman Tituba (who belonged to the Reverend Samuel Parris and who caused the entire wave of delusion) of bewitching children, and denounced blindly by some of the hysterical children in question, Goodwife Nurse was arrested and brought to trial. Thirty-nine persons signed a paper attesting to her blameless conduct, and a jury rendered a verdict of 'not guilty'; but popular clamour led the judges to reverse the verdict (as was then possible), and on 19 July 1692 the poor grandam was hanged on Gallows Hill in Salem for a mythological crime. Her remains were brought back from Salem and interred in the family burying-ground – a ghoulish place shadowed by huge pines and at some distance from the house. In 1885 a monument was erected to her memory, bearing an inscription by the poet Whittier.

As I approached the spot to which I had been directed, after passing through the hamlet of Tapleyville, the afternoon sun was very low. Soon the houses thinned out; so that on my right were only the hilly fields of stubble, and occasional crooked trees clawing at the sky. Beyond a low crest a thick group of spectral boughs bespoke some kind of grove or orchard – and in the midst of this group I suddenly descried the rising outline of a massive and ancient chimney. Presently, as I advanced, I saw the top of a grey, drear, sloping roof – sinister in its distant setting of bleak hillside and leafless grove, and unmistakably belonging to the haunted edifice I sought. Another turn – a gradual ascent – and I beheld in full view the sprawling, tree-shadowed house which had for nearly three hundred years brooded over those hills and held such secrets as men may only guess. Like all old farmhouses of the region, the Nurse cottage faces the warm south and slopes low toward the north. It fronts on an ancient garden, where in their season gay blossoms flaunt themselves against the grim, nail-studded door and the vertical sundial above it. That sundial was long concealed by the overlaid clapboards of Gothic generations, but came to light when the house was restored to original form by the memorial society which owns it. Everything about the place is ancient – even to the tiny-paned lattice windows which open outwards on hinges. The atmosphere of witchcraft days broods heavily upon that low hilltop.

My rap at the ancient door brought the caretaker's wife, an elderly unimaginative person with no appreciation of the dark glamour of the ancient scene. This family live in a lean-to west of the main structure – an addition probably one hundred years less ancient than the parent edifice. I was the first visitor of the 1923 season, and took pride in signing my name at the top of the register. Entering, I found myself in a low, dark passage whose massive beams almost touched my head; and passing on, I traversed the two immense rooms on the ground floor – sombre, barren, panelled apartments with colossal fireplaces in the vast central chimney, and with occasional pieces of the plain, heavy furniture and primitive farm and domestic utensils of the ancient yeomanry. In these wide, low-pitched rooms a spectral menace broods – for to my imagination the seventeenth century is as full of macabre mystery, repression and ghoulish adumbrations as the eighteenth century is full of taste, gaiety, grace and beauty. This was a typical Puritan abode; where amidst the bare, ugly necessities of life, and without learning, beauty, culture, freedom or ornament, terrible stern-faced folk in conical hats or poke-bonnets dwelt 250 and more years ago – close to the soil and all its hideous whisperings; warped in mentality by isolation and unnatural thoughts, and shivering in fear of the Devil on autumn nights when the wind howled through the twisted orchard trees or rustled the hideous corpse-nourished pines in the graveyard at the foot of the hill. There is eldritch fascination – horrible buried evil – in these archaic farmhouses. After seeing them, and smelling the odour of centuries in their walls, one hesitates to read certain passages in Cotton Mather's strange old *Magnalia* after dark. After exploring the ground floor I crept up the black crooked stairs and examined the bleak chambers above. The furniture was as ugly as that below, and included a small trundle-bed in which infant Puritans were lulled to sleep with meaningless prayers and morbid hints of daemons riding the nightwind outside the small-paned lattice windows. I saw old Rebekah's favourite chair, where she used to sit and spin before the Salem magistrates dragged her to the gallows. And the sunset wind whistled in the colossal chimney, and the ghouls rattled ghastly skeletons from unseen attic rafters overhead. Though it was not supposed to be open to the public, I persuaded the caretaker to let me ascend to that hideous garret of centuried secrets. Thick dust covered everything, and unnatural shapes loomed on every hand as the evening twilight oozed through the little bleared panes of the ancient windows. I saw something hanging from the wormy ridge-pole – something that swayed as if in unison with the vesper breeze outside, though that breeze had no access to this funereal and forgotten place – shadows ... shadows ... shadows ... And I descended from that accursed garret of palaeogene arcana, and left that portentous abode of antiquity; left it and went down the hill to the graveyard under the shocking pines, where twilight showed sinister slabs and rusty bits of fallen iron fence, and where something squatted in shadow on a monument – something that made me climb the hill again, hurry shudderingly past the venerable house and descend the opposite slope to Tapleyville as night came.

BRIAN LUMLEY

The Challenge

Brian Lumley (b. 1937) was born in Horden, on England's north-east coast. He joined the Army when he was twenty-one and, after discovering the stories of H. P. Lovecraft, he decided to try his own hand at writing horror fiction, initially set in Lovecraft's famed Cthulhu Mythos. In the 1970s Arkham House published two collections of his short stories, *The Caller of the Black* and *The Horror at Oakdene*, plus the novel *Beneath the Moors*. He continued Lovecraft's themes in a series of books: *The Burrowers Beneath, The Transition of Titus Crow, Spawn of the Winds, The Clock of Dreams, In the Moons of Borea, Elysia* and *The Compleat Crow*. More recently, his vampiric 'Necroscope' series has made him a bestseller on both sides of the Atlantic with such titles as *Necroscope, Wamphyri!, The Source, Deadspeak* and *Deadspawn*; a follow-up trilogy, *Blood Brothers, The Last Aerie* and *Bloodwars*; plus the two-volume *Necroscope: The Lost Years*. Other novels include *Khai of Ancient Khem, Psychomech, Psychosphere, Psychamok, The House of Doors* and *Demogorgon*, while his short fiction can be found in *The House of Cthulhu and Other Tales of the Primal Land, The Last Rite, Fruiting Bodies and Other Fungi* (which includes the British Fantasy Award-winning title story), *Dagon's Bell and Other Discords, Return of the Deep Ones and Other Mythos Tales* and *The Second Wish and Other Exhalations*.

It was 1974, and I don't remember it too well. Not because of all the time that's passed between, but just because. You'll see what I mean. And you'll perhaps learn from it. I did.

I was in the Army, just posted to Edinburgh Castle as the Company Quartermaster. So they sent me on a Qs' course to Aldershot. In the barracks at Aldershot, I had a nine-by-six room (or cubicle, or broom closet) on the third floor at a corner of the building looking out on thin air. My room had a window half as wide as the room itself that opened outwards: good. For of a night, even a cold night, I like to breathe fresh air. The room also had a six-foot steel locker for my uniform, kit and personal valuables or other lockup-able stuff, and an indestructible steel-framed army bed, a chair, and a small table for my typewriter. Ceiling height was about eight feet. And that's it. Throw in my mattress and bedding, and that sets the scene.

The typewriter was for any homework during the course, and if I got any spare time I would work on a story Ramsey Campbell had requested for his upcoming anthology *Superhorror*. In fact I didn't have much homework and so got on with my story. It was called 'The Viaduct' – and it wasn't supernatural. I mention this in order to confirm that my thinking wasn't as yet under threat from ghoulies and ghosties. Not as yet.

So far so good. I *think* all of this is fact. I *believe* I'm telling it the way it was . . .

The course lasted two weeks, so right in the middle came a weekend. Time to do a little writing, studying, relaxing. There was this movie going the rounds, and I wanted to see it. It was showing in Aldershot. *The Exorcist* – my kind of picture, obviously.

Well of course it was a stunner. It didn't 'frighten' me; I'm not the sort (the first and last time a film frightened me it was George Zucco in *The Flying Serpent*, when I was eight or nine years old. And I got a kick out of *Night of the Demon*: the twittering ball of lights in the trees, like something out of Lovecraft, and the nameless whistling in the shimmery corridor). So *The Exorcist* didn't scare *me*, but the three senior ranks I was with were a little bit twitchy, oh yes . . .

Back in the mess we had a couple of drinks, and I told a handful of 'true' spooky stories. (Hey, it's my business . . . I was testing out some stuff, that's all.) OK, so maybe those stories weren't true – but this one is.

Anyway, the point I make is that we had a *couple* of drinks. No one was drunk, and certainly not me. As a military policeman there are things you do and things you don't. If you are intent on getting drunk you do it in your own mess, not while visiting someone else's. '*Exemplo ducemus*', and all that . . .

My colleagues and fellow-students – mature students, you understand, for no one on the course was younger than thirty or so years – were accommodated on the same floor as myself. About midnight we trooped upstairs, showered, sacked. And in my room I threw open the windows, lay on my back on my bed, looked out at the stars. They were very bright against a darkness that was very dark. I could hear one of my friends in the next room bumping about a bit, and more faintly the door next to his slamming as another friend went to bed.

Which was when the practical joker in me whispered: 'Well, why not?'

So I let them get settled down for the night, then crept out into the corridor and stood between their doors, spread my arms and put my nails on the door panels . . . and *scraaaatched*!

Oh-so-slowly scraaaatched – then paused and did it again, before fleeing back to my room, closing the door quietly behind me, slipping between my sheets and commencing to snore. A count of ten and they were there. Door bursting open, light switched on, a pair of irate faces glaring into my blinking, astonished, oh-so-innocent eyes.

'Geordie bastard!' said one.

'Fucking redcap!' said the other.

'Eh? Wha –?' said I.

Maybe I convinced them of my innocence, maybe not. Anyway, they went back to bed, and I got up and *locked* my door. That's important – this is a 'locked room story'. And I took the key out of the lock and put it on the table with my typewriter. At least I think I did, but everything is vague.

Then, in bed, I lay on my back and grinned, and looked out of the window at the night and the stars. The supernatural? *The Exorcist?* The Great Big Horrid Unknown? Me, I don't believe. In fact I was ... what, contemptuous? Yes, I suppose I was. And I was very secure in my contempt, my disbelief.

So looking out at the night I said to myself, *and to anyone else who might be listening,* Hey, you! You out there – if you are out there – why don't you come on in and try it on me? What are you, a stray thought? A wisp of smoke? A beam of moonlight? A niggle in the night? A shiver that fell off someone's back and lost its way? A ghostie, ghoulie or nasty smelly demon? Oh dear me! I'm really scared! Well, I'm just flesh and blood. But I'm big and I'm solid while you're just so much wind. So by all means go and rustle some leaves or moan in the eaves, but whatever you do don't fuck with me!

I said something like that to myself, anyway. And although I said it silently, I said it very firmly, very 'loudly'. Do you know what I mean? Like a challenge.

And then I fell asleep . . .

And dreamed. But the only thing that I remember about the dream is one *very* frightening scene.

Something came. Something big. Awesome strength. It stank. It burned. It crouched on the sill of my open window. Its outline blocked out the stars. Big and black, it came in. And it looked at me, cocked its head on one side, and said, 'Unbeliever?' Or if it didn't actually say it, it wondered. And I sort of heard it wondering.

Which is why I said, 'Please, don't . . .'

And I *think* it smiled.

Next morning, it was like waking up into a different world. Thank God it was the weekend. I had forgotten about the dream (just *think* about that); or rather, I wasn't bothered (think about that, too). But God, the state of my room!

As I have said, a room like that is tiny as a nest, with space for just one bird at a time. That's why you keep it neat and tidy. Get something out of place, there's no room left for you. And that morning, *many* things were out of place.

The bed was sideways. The steel locker was standing on its head. All my sheets and blankets were knotted together in a big ball. A pillow had been shredded and feathers were everywhere, and there were fist-sized lumps of gum, or black jelly, or shit? – but never *human* shit – all over the place. Only the small table was where it should be, but it wasn't *how* it should be. Because someone had pissed on my typewriter. Drenched it. Well, God help his insides, whoever he was, because his piss had dried like so much glue. Later, I got it off with alcohol (and you're probably thinking I'd got it *on* with alcohol, too, and I don't blame you), and disguised the nasty smell with many a liberal splash of Old Spice.

I did nothing. Well, I *did*; I cleaned the mess up. Tossed the large gumballs out of the window, untied the incredibly *intricate* knots in my bedding, emptied my locker – it really was *that* heavy – so that I could turn it the right way up. Oh, and I put my bed back the right way, too, because now it was *across* the room: a six-foot bed fitting snug in a space that only just accommodated it. And I had been *on* that bed; I had woken up on that mattress, with no sheet on me and no sheet under me!

And all of this had been done in absolute silence, in darkness, while I slept. And the door still locked, and the sticky key to my room still on the sticky table beside my sticky typewriter. But apart from cleaning everything up I did nothing at all, said nothing to anyone . . .

And that, my friends, is the frightening bit. I didn't give

any of this a thought – not a single *thought* – except to put it right and so return to my own mundane universe, the world with which I was familiar. I didn't accuse anyone, probably because I suspected that no one had done it, or that I'd done it to myself. Oh really? I had made water on my beloved typewriter . . .?

Four days went by and it was the middle of the week. My work hadn't suffered; I was going to get an 'A' on this course, no problem. Then one morning I woke up and noticed that my window was closed – noticed it for the first time since the incident: the fact that I now kept the window closed. And I smelled the stale air . . . and I suddenly remembered. I remembered *something* of all this, anyway, but can't honestly say if it was the same story I've just told. For I've never been able to fix it in my mind.

It's as if I wasn't *supposed* to think about, talk about, or worry about it. As if I wasn't supposed to blow my top immediately this thing happened, but that the message should be allowed to get through to me in its own sweet time. As if someone had said to me: 'Hey, take this as a warning. You did something wrong. You *invited* a confrontation. So don't do it again, OK?'

That day at lunchtime, I walked the lawns around the outside of the accommodation block. I couldn't find any snotballs. It had rained and they'd melted or been washed away. Or they'd never been there. I could never get my typewriter to work right from that time on, and I soon scrapped it. Ramsey Campbell used my *un*supernatural story, 'The Viaduct', in *Superhorror*.

And six or seven years later I wrote another story, 'The Unbeliever', which gives a fictional and far more horrific account of the 'facts' of the thing. By which I mean 'The Unbeliever' is a fictional development of this *true* story . . .

Of course there's an explanation, perhaps more than one. Maybe my mind was more susceptible to suggestion than I used to think it was. Maybe it was the booze. (What booze? Two or three shots of brandy, when I might easily have sunk half a bottle?) Or maybe it was *The Exorcist*? What, without George Zucco or the Twitterer in the Trees? Or someone(s) had got into my room ... wreaking all that havoc and leaving alien crap behind without waking me? Let me tell you that I've always slept light. All it takes is a creaking floorboard and I wake up.

And over the years, more than twenty of them, it has faded away until I can't any longer be sure of anything. But like the grin on the face of the Cheshire cat in *Alice*, a certain smile remains where almost everything else has vanished. That darkest of dark smiles that something smiled at me on the night I said, 'Please, don't ...'

Oh, I still meet things head-on; an ex-soldier, I'm still into confrontation, certainly on a mundane level. But then I'm a Geordie after all, and a Sagittarian to boot ... not that I *believe* in any of that stuff. And yet you won't catch me denying it, either. Not any longer. Or if I do, it'll be because I think I've found an explanation for it. A scientific reason.

But until then I won't be messing with Ouija boards, tarot cards, fortune-telling or anything of that nature. And you can believe me when I tell you I don't even feel tempted to experiment. Not me. I won't be putting out challenges to anything I don't understand. No sir. You've got to be kidding.

I'll tell you something: I've even had to find a way, when I'm lying in my bed at night just about to go to sleep, to put it right out of my mind. So that I don't do anything inadvertently, as it were. It's not a pleasant thought, but I'm fairly sure I *could* do it again – in error, of course. That I *could* say the wrong things to the wrong Thing.

And I feel sure, too, that whoever he is he'd be listening ...

ARTHUR MACHEN

The World of the Senses

————————•◆•————————

Arthur Machen (1863–1947) was born Arthur Llewellyn Jones in Caerleon-on-Usk, Wales, which according to legend was the site of King Arthur's Camelot. He occasionally worked as a clerk, teacher, travelling actor and journalist, although he always regarded himself as a writer. After he moved to London in 1883, two short novels were published as *The Great God Pan & The Inmost Light* in 1894, followed by the collections *The Three Impostors or The Transmutations* and *The House of Souls*, and the autobiographical novel *The Hill of Dreams*. When his short story 'The Bowmen' was published in the *Evening News* in 1914, this tale about how British troops were saved by ghostly archers at the Battle of Mons was widely accepted as fact and was followed by claims of many similar sightings. It was reprinted the following year in *The Angels of Mons: The Bowmen and Other Legends of the War*, and his later books include *The Great Return, The Terror: A Fantasy, The Green Round* and such collections as *The Shining Pyramid, The Children of the Pool and Other Stories, The Cosy Room, Dreads and Drolls, Holy Terrors* and *Tales of Horror and the Supernatural*. Machen made little money from his fiction, and in later life he described himself as 'a man who has worked hard for forty years and has received as his reward insult, cruelty, beggary'.

————————•◆•————————

It was somewhere about the autumn of 1899 that I began to be conscious that the world was being presented to me at a new angle. I find now an extreme difficulty in the choice of words to convey my meaning; 'a new angle' is clumsy enough, 'here in this world he changed his life' is far too high in its associations; but there certainly came to be a strangeness in the proportion of things, both in things exterior and interior. And it is in these latter that I held and still hold that the true wonder, the true mystery, the true miracle reside. There is the old proverb, of course: 'Seeing is believing' and, for once, the old proverb is widely astray. All phenomenal perception is apt to be deceitful, and very often is deceitful.

I had a curious instance of this in the midst of the famous 'Angel of Mons' controversy. An officer of very high distinction wrote to me from the front, and described a most remarkable experience which had been vouchsafed to him and to others during the retreat of August 1914. The battle of Le Cateau was fought on 26 August. My correspondent's division, as he writes – his letter is quoted at length in the Introduction to the second edition of *The Bowmen* – was heavily shelled, 'had a bad time of it', but retired in good order. It was on the march all the night of the 26th, and throughout 27th August, with only about two hours' rest.

By the night of the 27th we were all absolutely worn out with fatigue – both bodily and mental fatigue. No doubt we also suffered to a certain extent from shock; but the retirement still continued in excellent order, and I feel sure that our mental faculties were still quite sound and in good working condition. On the night of the 27th I was riding along in the column with two other officers. We had been talking and doing our best to keep from falling asleep on our horses. As we rode along I became conscious of the fact that, in the fields on both sides of the road along which we were marching, I could see a very large body of horsemen. These horsemen had the appearance of squadrons of cavalry, and they seemed to be riding across the fields and going in the same direction as we were going, and keeping level with us. The night was not very dark, and I fancied that I could see squadron upon squadron of these cavalrymen quite distinctly. I did not say a word about it at first, but I watched them for about twenty minutes. The other two officers had stopped talking. At least one of them asked me if I saw anything in the fields. I told him what I had seen. The third officer then confessed that he too had been watching these horsemen for the past twenty minutes. So convinced were we that they were really cavalry that, at the next halt, one of the officers took a party of men out to reconnoitre, and found no one there ... The same phenomenon was seen by many men in our column ... I myself am absolutely convinced that I saw these horsemen; and I feel sure that they did not exist only in my imagination.

Now I have not the faintest notion what really happened to the Colonel, to the two officers and to many of the men in the column. What concerns us for the moment is that these people were at first perfectly certain that they saw sensible objects, that is, cavalrymen, and then were perfectly certain that there were no sensible objects to see; and therefore it may be concluded from this instance and from many instances, of like sort, that the senses are deceptive; that the world of the senses is very largely a world of illusion and delusion.

GRAHAM MASTERTON

My Grandfather's House

Graham Masterton (b. 1946) was born in Edinburgh and currently lives in Epsom Downs, Surrey, with his wife Wiescka and their sons. He was a newspaper reporter and Editor of *Mayfair* and *Penthouse* before becoming a full-time novelist with his 1976 book *The Manitou* (filmed two years later). Since then he has written more than thirty horror novels and dozens of short stories, as well as historical sagas, thrillers and bestselling sex manuals. In 1989 he edited *Scare Care*, an anthology of horror stories, to benefit abused and needy children, and he is currently writing a new series of supernatural novels for young adults, *Rook*, set in a community college in Los Angeles. Masterton's horror novels have explored all kinds of alternative existences. *Mirror* was based on the looking-glass world of Lewis Carroll, while the climax of *Family Portrait* took place inside a painted landscape. In *Walkers* a host of lunatics were imprisoned within the solid walls of their asylum, and in *Burial* a Native American shaman tried to drag the whole of civilization into the upside-down world that exists beneath our feet. 'The whole business of horror is turning the world inside-out, both physically and intellectually,' he says.

Thomas Thorne Baker was my grandfather. He was born in 1888, when Queen Victoria was still on the throne and London's buses were still drawn by horses. He grew up to be eccentric but prolifically inventive, one of the great research chemists of the twentieth century.

In the 1930s, he invented Day-Glo, the fluorescent paint that you can still see today on life-vests and motorway workers' jackets. In collaboration with Sir William Stephenson, he was the first man to transmit news photographs by wireless – a project financed by the *Daily Mail*, which then enjoyed the largest circulation of any newspaper in the world. He was also deeply involved in the early days of television.

For amusement and scientific interest, he kept bees on the roof of the *Daily Mirror* building which stung any reporter who came up for a breath of fresh air.

During World War II, in a requisitioned apartment on Regent Street, he painted the entire wall with light-sensitive emulsion, so that RAF photographs of bombing raids over Germany could be enlarged, developed and fixed at hundreds of times their actual size, and examined in minute detail.

I knew him as a balding, bespectacled man who treated me with great affection. He would take me down to his laboratory and let me play with his chemical balance, and try to explain to me the complexities of a 'plastic wood' that he was trying to invent (he posted a sample to a furniture company in Birmingham and it arrived as a small pile of dust). As he worked in the red-lit dark-room, he told me stories about a planet where people had bread rolls for heads, and whenever they were hungry they would cut a slice out of their own head and butter it.

Back home, in his dining-room, in a reverential hush interrupted only by the Westminster chimes of the wall clock, he would give me sample sips of Châteauneuf-du-Pape (at the age of seven) to 'educate my palate', at a time when most families couldn't even afford Tizer. I think he spent most of his money on good wine.

He died in 1962 and I badly missed him, but I never

thought that I would hear from him again. I read his books and his diaries, but all of his books were so technical that they contained no trace of the warm, humorous man who called a bearded friend of his 'the Coconut', and who brought home a small model of a woman whose breasts were exposed by the squeeze of a rubber bulb.

I had no sense at all that he was still there, or that he had left behind anything except his desk with its Lalique lamp and its old-fashioned portable typewriter. In his garage his chocolate-brown Austin stayed musty and unpolished, undriven for years.

It wasn't until 1972 that I began to feel his presence again, and even then I didn't immediately realize what was happening. I was visiting Manhattan on business, and I was walking up Third Avenue in the lower East 80s in a light, windy rain-shower. Discarded umbrellas were strewn everywhere, like a flock of fallen pterodactyls. I was passing a large apartment building when I saw a pink-frosted cake lying on the basement steps. It was broken and pock-marked with rain. I could just make out the word IRTHDAY on it.

I wouldn't have thought any more about it, except that three months later, when she was making a cake for my children, my mother almost dropped it on the kitchen floor. I mentioned the cake that I'd seen in New York, and she gave me the most peculiar stare. My grandfather had lived and worked in New York in the 1930s, developing a new film for Dufay Color, a now-defunct rival to Technicolor. The family had kept an apartment at the Croydon Hotel, on East 86th Street, where they had a maid who thought that my grandfather was adorable – so much so that she had baked him a huge pink-frosted birthday cake.

My grandfather disliked frosted cake with a passion, but to spare his maid's feelings he smuggled the cake out of the apartment and took it for a walk. A few blocks away from the hotel, he tossed it into a basement, thinking that nobody would notice. But an enraged tenant came after him, threatening him with a broom handle, and one of the world's leading scientists had been forced to run four blocks through the afternoon crowds before his pursuer gave up the chase.

Two broken pink birthday cakes, thirty-five years apart in time, but in almost exactly the same place? Perhaps it was a coincidence, but it was less than three weeks later that something occurred which led me to believe that the appearance of the cake wasn't entirely accidental. I took my children to London Zoo, and just inside the entrance a Chinese man was waiting. It was a grey foggy November day and he was wearing a brown hat and a brown gaberdine raincoat. His whole appearance was oddly dated, and he gave me an extraordinary sensation of *déjà-vu*, as if I were back in the London of the early 1950s.

The Chinese man saw me looking at him and lifted his hand, as if he had been waiting especially for me. He came up and said, 'Excuse me, can you tell me the time? I think my watch has stopped.' I told him it was just after eleven, and he said, 'Thank you. I'm looking for a friend. I have to go back to China and this is going to be my last chance to see him.'

The incident didn't seem at all significant, but for some reason I had the strongest urge to see who his friend was. I waited for a while, but then my sons started to grow impatient, and I had to follow them. I turned around just once, and I saw the man talking to another, older man, wearing a grey hat and a black overcoat. I couldn't have sworn to it, but it looked as if the Chinese man was sobbing.

The feeling that I had seen all this before was so overwhelming that I called my mother again and asked her about it. She confirmed that in the early 1950s my grandfather had employed a Chinese research assistant at his laboratory in Baker Street. The assistant had been happy and inspired. But threats had been made against his family if he didn't return to China, and so he had been forced to leave. The last time my grandfather had seen him was when my mother had taken me to London Zoo in 1952. A November day, foggy. My grandfather and the Chinese man had embraced each other, and wept.

I had no doubt then that I had re-experienced an event that had happened over twenty years before. And I had no doubt then about the identity of the slightly stooped man in the grey hat and the black overcoat. Thomas Thorne Baker.

I saw him twice more after that. Once, in Kew Gardens, close to the Pagoda, on a summer's day so bright that I had to shade my eyes. He wasn't doing anything at all, just standing on the path watching me. I didn't approach him – not because I was frightened, but because I felt that he didn't belong to me any longer. I walked quickly away and a cloud came over the sun.

The last time was one of the most hair-raising experiences I've ever had. I was back in Manhattan, window-shopping along Fifth Avenue, on a clear spring morning. I stopped to look into Bergdorf Goodman and suddenly I became conscious that somebody was standing a little way behind me, perfectly still. In the window, my grandfather was reflected, with utter clarity. He was wearing a light-grey coat and a trilby hat. He wasn't looking directly back at me: his head was turned slightly as if he were waiting for somebody to come walking up Fifth Avenue towards him.

My scalp prickled, but I thought: This time I'm going to speak to him ... if he keeps appearing, there must be a reason, and I need to know what it is.

I turned around and there was nobody standing within thirty feet of me. He simply wasn't there.

It was these experiences that led me to explore the possibilities of parallel existences – similar but different worlds that we can glimpse only in mirrors, or in the reflections in windows or rain-puddles. In my novel *The House That Jack Built*, one time overlaps another, so that different lives are lived out simultaneously.

As one of my characters says:

It is not time which moves forward from minute to minute, but only our perception of it. The events of what we consider to be 'the past' and the events of what we consider to be 'the present' exist coincidentally with the events of what we consider to be 'now'. History is like a house with an infinite number of rooms. Just because we have passed from one room to the other, that doesn't mean that the previous room ceases to exist.

I have no explanation for my grandfather's appearances. I don't understand the significance of the birthday cake or the encounter in Kew Gardens. But I do believe that the past is still with us and that, if there is a possibility of life after death, it's the possibility of living your life all over again, right from the moment you opened your eyes.

In a hushed dining-room somewhere, an elderly man is still handing a small glass of Châteauneuf-du-Pape to a seven-year-old schoolboy, or hugging a distraught Chinese man in the fog at London Zoo.

Somewhere, all the people we have loved and lost are still among us, in the house that we call history.

RICHARD MATHESON

More Than We Appear to Be

––––––––––––––––––– • ►• –––––––––––––––––––

Richard Burton Matheson (b. 1926) was born in Allendale, New Jersey. In 1950 he sold his story 'Born of Man and Woman' at the first attempt, and it became the title of his first collection (a.k.a. *Third from the Sun*) in 1954. Having moved to California, he began to blur the boundaries between horror, fantasy and science fiction with his modern treatment of vampires, *I Am Legend* (filmed twice). He followed it with *A Stir of Echoes* and numerous short stories (collected in *The Shores of Space* and four volumes of *Shock*). He scripted his Hugo Award-winning 1956 novel *The Shrinking Man* for the movies, and worked for many years adapting his own and other authors' work for film and television. Among his numerous credits are *The Fall of the House of Usher, Pit and the Pendulum, Tales of Terror, The Raven, The Comedy of Terrors, The Devil Rides Out, The Night Stalker, Dracula, Trilogy of Terror* (with William F. Nolan), *Twilight Zone The Movie, Jaws 3-D, Trilogy of Terror II* (with William F. Nolan and Dan Curtis), and various episodes of *The Twilight Zone, Thriller, Star Trek* and *Night Gallery*. His later novels include *Hell House* and the World Fantasy Award-winning *Bid Time Return* (both filmed), *What Dreams May Come, Earthbound* (as 'Logan Swanson'), *7 Steps to Midnight* and *Now You See It*. In a 1985 interview, he explained to Douglas E. Winter about his belief in a psychic energy field that surrounds each of us:

––––––––––––––––––– • ►• –––––––––––––––––––

We are more than we appear to be. The world is more than
it appears to be. Mankind, generally speaking, is very limited
in its awareness of what's really going on. Parapsychology is
an attempt to work at the edges of it, to find out more about
what we are.

I believe that every human being is surrounded by some
bioenergy field – what they refer to as the 'aura' – that
creates psychic phenomena, that can affect healing and is
responsible for telepathy, telekinesis, precognition. This field
is connected to the body during this lifetime, disconnects
itself at death, and is eternal. Our body is just the vehicle it
uses during this particular phase of its existence. And then it
comes back and attaches itself to another vehicle – which is,
of course, reincarnation.

There is an overall meaning to everyone's existence, which
is this constant cycle of living, dying, coming back. We are
headed somewhere – back to where we came from initially,
when we were perfect in a very real sense.

I am sure that you and your wife read each other's minds
all of the time. This is psychic experience. When people are
married a long time, this energy field I speak of, which they
both have, becomes so strongly intertwined that, when one
of them dies, it's like having a huge living chunk taken out
of each other. It's not just grief that survivors are feeling. I
think that explains why people who are so close sometimes
die within minutes of each other.

RICHARD CHRISTIAN MATHESON

Visit to a Psychic Surgeon

————————•◆•————————

Richard Christian Matheson (b. 1953) was born in Santa
Monica, California, the son of famed horror and fantasy
writer Richard Matheson. He left school to become an advertising copywriter, wrote material for stand-up comedians,
became a professional studio musician (drums), taught creative
writing at university level, worked as a researcher/investigator
at the parapsychology labs at UCLA and became the young-
est TV writer ever put under contract by Universal Studios.
He has written, produced and executive-produced more than
five hundred episodes of over thirty primetime series such as
Hill Street Blues, *Magnum*, *Amazing Stories*, *Tales from the
Crypt*, *Wiseguy* and is now one of the hottest young pro-
ducers in Hollywood. He recently sold his fifteenth original
million-dollar screenplay (considered a record) and has had
four feature films made including the dark satire *Three O'Clock
High* and the 1994 werewolf movie he wrote and executive-
produced, *Full Eclipse*, which was HBO's highest-rated film
of the year and their biggest video release. His short fiction
has appeared in numerous magazines and anthologies, thirty
stories were collected in *Scars and Other Distinguishing Marks*
and a new collection of fifty more, *Dystopia*, is scheduled for
release in 1998. He is at work on the follow-up to his acclaimed 1993 début novel *Created By* which was a Bram Stoker
Award finalist for best first novel, a Book-of-the-Month
Club selection, and has been translated into six languages.

————————•◆•————————

I don't like to admit it but sometimes I feel there's no way out. I stare at life like a tropical specimen, waiting for someone to kick over the bowl.

Maybe that's why I agreed to go.

I think it's why Patrick did, too.

We were looking for magic, though we didn't realize it. But since it's said magic eludes when initiates seek it directly, maybe we were better off. Keep reading, you may disagree.

Patrick is a very interesting guy. He grew up in Buffalo, New York, where it gets bitterly cold; it's even said people freeze to death in their cars there and enter the afterworld as Fudgesicles. But for Patrick it was always sunny and he grew up a torrid optimist in a volatile Irish Catholic family. When he was nineteen he finally left Buffalo, as all people who want more in life eventually leave somewhere or something, and with his congenial anarchy as companion, joked westward, across America, taking odd jobs as a truck driver, ski instructor or whatever he could charm someone into.

But he couldn't always hear how much he made others laugh because he has a hearing problem. Where you and I hear children laughing in a park, Patrick hears bad bearings in an overheating engine, and these disparities occasionally drive him insane.

Maybe that's why he eventually came to Hollywood to become a writer and succeeded beyond his wildest dreams.

That's how we met.

On the writing staff of a television show Patrick had co-created with a prime-time pharaoh named Stephen J. Cannell. It was a funny show filled with warmth and humour and conflict. Just like my relationship with Patrick. And though the two leads never said anything close to affectionate, Patrick and I often tried. It's one key reason that as people who should visit those claiming to perform miracles go, we were perfectly cast.

We'd heard about a woman who opened up human bodies with her empty hands, from a friend who'd been to see her. The procedure was called psychic surgery and Patrick and I were enthralled by its exotic details. So much so, that on a guarded whim, we decided to go; Patrick wanted to hear right again and I wanted to see magic up close. Not coins hidden in knuckles or fluttering capes. *Real* magic. Like in South American jungles when the dead walk again after potions are dripped on their foreheads.

That's how we ended up riding together, in his black Porsche, to a friendly house near the ocean in L.A., laughing the whole way, nervous beyond our capacity to admit it.

Remember what I said about being afraid there's no way out? It's an important feeling to recognize in yourself so you can change whatever you must to live a better life. And I think Patrick and I both knew we needed to change our lives, each for different reasons. I won't go into those reasons because everyone has their own and each is as valid as the next. But it seems, now and then, that we all need to abandon certain ideas; to do things which disagree with our ease. I've met otherwise pleasant people who didn't and they worried me; enough to see I didn't want to end up as they had; untested, dozing in habit.

As we sped towards the inexplicable, though Patrick and I were laughing, anxieties seeped. When you're within an hour of having your body scissored by a woman from some weird, snake-filled country where death-squads and toucons are normal as 7-11s, irony befriends you. And by the time we'd finally found the house and went inside to face our scheduled innards, we were on a macabre roll.

The house wasn't important. Just a place for the psychic surgeon to stay while she was in town, since she travelled the globe, year-round, roaming flesh; exterminating the unwanted or malignant. Many regarded it a regal honor to have her hands within them and had come from other states to be here.

After Patrick and I signed in with one of her assistants
and gave him seventy-five bucks each (no cheques or credit
cards accepted), we sat and read magazines with a handful
of others who waited. The money was called an 'offering'
because, as the release form we signed clearly stated, she
wasn't a doctor. Just a 'spiritual guide'. A 'counsellor'.
Basically, a jigsaw in a dress.

We sat and waited.

And though we said much, we said little. Patrick and I
easily fell into that sort of armoured sharing; sardonic, film-
critic glances around the room, and shared observations that
stole attention from our often uneasy relationship. Wide,
alarmed eyes staring at some absurdity we alone observed,
yet done so covertly no one noticed but us. The little bullets
we fired around the room ... bullets of curious superiority
... bullets of polite interest; obligatory and low-calibre.
Bullets fired by two guys who thought they needed to go
through life armed. We were funny. But we didn't realize we
had the choice not to be. We needed the magic more than
we understood.

We looked up with wordless dread when the first person
in this living room filled with five or six other 'patients' was
summoned. She was a *Vogue*-faced, Hollywood actress,
suffering colitis, who'd come with her boyfriend, a temperamental, narcissitic actor, who was starring in his own TV
series about a temperamental, narcissistic detective.

She was led down the dim hallway and taken to one of
the small bedrooms which we couldn't spy from our living
room vantage. We saw only the hallway and a second
bedroom. A bathroom separated the two, as if the common
membrane between two heart chambers. I use an organ
analogy here because body parts were very much on my
mind.

From where we all sat, we had a perfect view of the
bathroom and Patrick and I split a look, apprehensions
clouding. We all tried to calm our nerves, each imagining in

our own mind what the actress would look like with the hands of the healer sunk to the wrists in her body. And though none said it, we were grateful for the company; relieved not to be here alone.

There were faint murmurs from the bedroom, as if lovers were trying not to awaken children. There was also muted laughter, like what Rosemary heard through the vents when the coven burned candles and celebrated the evil infant. It was so dulled by wall, it seemed all the more far away and unsettling, like we weren't supposed to hear it and if we could, we'd be very sorry.

I suppose for Patrick the faintness of it was nothing special. I felt badly for him.

Within minutes he nudged me, discreetly pointing to the assistant with the glass bowl who was coming out of the bedroom where the actress was undergoing surgery. The bowl was clear, big enough to hold tortellini for a family of four. But it wasn't full of pasta; rather what looked like pink lemonade. Floating in the pastel slosh were pieces of what appeared to be tissue. They weren't big; had no exact shape, but we all winced. If nothing else, it was first-rate theatre.

As they were carried by, the assistant who carted the bowl walked into the bathroom and poured the contents into the toilet where they splashed loudly. He flushed the pulpy evidence and began to rinse blood-stained towels which also soaked in the bowl. Patrick leaned to me, whispering that he thought the best parts the actress would ever have may have just been flushed. I felt queasy and he offered to get me a glass of water.

I was sorry to see him disappear into the kitchen, but continued to wait patiently, watching the tortellini bowl go by several more times, red contents resembling a tiny sea after a shark attack. As Patrick handed me my water, I wondered how much of the actress might remain when surgery was completed.

She finally came out from the bedroom operating theatre

looking pale and exhausted, sat heavily beside her boyfriend, on the couch, and promptly fell asleep before we could ask questions.

Patrick and I were called next.

I was led into one bedroom, Patrick the other, and we waved farewell to one another. In my room, I was told she'd be in shortly by her surgical assistant, a sedate MD who was on the faculty of UCLA Medical School. He asked that I undress, try to relax, then left. I disrobed and wrapped my waist in a towel; a pre-op jungle boy. Per his instructions, I laid on the portable examination table and stared at the roof, feeling very alone. Around me, sunlight branded restless shapes on the wallpaper; cute sailboats rocking on dragon-filled sea. Its whimsy failed to lift my worry.

As I tried to relax, the door finally opened.

She was fifty, maybe sixty. Short, stocky. Tobacco skin, black hair. She wore a simple cotton dress and other than a heavy crucifix, no jewellery. Her gentle smile tried to reassure as her warm palm felt my forehead and face, searching; a primitive scanning device, stalking deformations. Objects that had no place within my body. She spoke almost no English.

'You have pain?' I didn't. 'You are scared?' I said nothing.

Her soothing hands glided slowly down my bare chest; twin gulls skimming skin sea, searching for what hid behind bone rocks, nerve kelp. She moved with serene focus, the way people who paint religious art do; calmed by holy task.

She stopped. Felt more carefully. One spot. Above and to the right of my abdomen.

'What is it?' I asked.

The assistant looked calm. 'A blockage.'

A faucet inside me turned slightly and fear began to drip. I started to perspire and as he dabbed at my forehead with a cloth, she placed hands on my heart and stomach. She said something to him in her language and the assistant told me she'd asked if I wanted to continue.

Though perhaps driven by a misguided sense of scientific enquiry or adventure, I said yes and, to this day, am not sure exactly why. Maybe it was knowing this odd appointment might represent other pivotal choices to come in my life and somehow measured my depth of engagement. That if I bailed now, I always would; that this moment, in a way I couldn't totally measure, was indicative; essential. Or maybe I understood in a subconscious wisdom that her question and my reply were mirror versions of the same personal affliction: faith gone to zero.

But I don't really buy any of that.

I now think I agreed because I was afraid. A bit convinced there might truly be bad things lurking within me; not rooting malaises, but contaminations more difficult to rid oneself of. Imbalances not of health but belief; irreversible, self-poisoning. Jealousies, intolerances, self-pity. The list seemed endless; hard to face.

I'd long suspected a host of such flaws, however great their actual presence, and knew any had the power, over time, to defeat me. In my darkest theory, they'd all gathered, undetectable to orthodox medicine, somewhere in my body where I hoped she could corner them and manage removal; save me.

I also think I chose without equivocation, despite unknown risk, because in my own ways, like Patrick, I'd become partially deafened. Not to sound but feeling. Not melody but compassion. Not voices but to the people who spoke.

When I gave the go-ahead, she instantly pressed harder on the spot and I heard a popping sound, like a small suction cup pried off a refrigerator door. In seconds, four, then five fingers were buried to the knuckle and swimming within me, hunting for trouble.

There was blood. Not Tarantino litres of it ... but enough to trickle down my sides, into my navel. I felt absolutely no pain, only pressure, and, from what I could see, she wasn't faking it. I asked her assistant what was happening and after a moment of doubt he told me she'd found it.

The invader.

I wondered what it was; how long it had been in silent residence? Would it regard eviction as antagonistic? Chilling images of combat between her and it filled my mind.

After a bit of struggle, she tweezed two fingers tightly and withdrew what looked like a bloody shoelace, nearly a foot long. She showed it to me quickly, nodded to the assistant with significance and he asked if I'd like to keep it. I should have said yes; I know that now. But I declined, too shaken by the moment to think clearly. She understood and within seconds I was unceremoniously resealed, wiped of spillage. She stared into my eyes with soulful closure, then left.

The assistant told me I could dress and dropped the strand into his glass bowl where it floated freely; a toxic eel. It was taken away and flushed as I buttoned my shirt; a small aspect of me forever edited; to be replaced, over time, I hoped, with something better.

Patrick went next and though the mystic pruning took longer with him, forty minutes later we drove away in silence.

We were both tired, haunted by the experience; its unlikely braid of suburbia and primitivism. Patrick kept asking me if I thought his hearing was improved and we experimented with his Alpine system. It was hard to be certain, though he was hungry to be convinced.

As the Porsche pawed up Sunset Boulevard aside moon-washed Pacific, Patrick asked me if I believed we'd encountered something miraculous. I told him I didn't really know and we rolled down our windows. Wind blew our hair and he told me he'd been scared; I said I hadn't been at all. We smiled at each other and I admitted how frightened I'd actually been. Minutes passed and we talked more, making fewer and fewer jokes.

Because we were naturally on the subject, Patrick began

to talk about other things in life that scared him. I countered with my list. We spoke about what made us insecure, feel alone, lose faith. As the curves held us, we talked about triumphs we'd had in our lives. Big. Small. Admitted heart-aches. Dreams.

Our secret selves.

Sea glittered beyond guard-rails and we heard ourselves say things to each other we never had before. Something in her touch had severed restriction and we were becoming best friends; perilously intimate, no longer wishing to disguise wounds or truths; sharing precious cargo.

After that night, it never happened again. I guess everything heals sooner or later ... even things that seemed better before.

Remember, I told you that sometimes I feel there's no way out? I was right. But I missed the point. The magic is finding the way in. And though I never talk to Patrick any more, for one night in our lives, the way in found us.

PAUL J. McAULEY

The Fall of the Wires

Paul J. McAuley (b. 1955) was born in Stroud, Gloucester-shire. His first major success as a writer was in 1988, when he won the Philip K. Dick Award for his début novel, *Four Hundred Billion Stars*. Later books include *Secret Harmonies*, *Eternal Light* (shortlisted for the Arthur C. Clarke Award), *Red Dust* and *Pasquale's Angel* (winner of the Sidewise Award for best long-form alternate history), the short-story collec-tions *The King of the Hill* and *The Invisible Country*, and the anthology *In Dreams* (co-edited with Kim Newman). He won the 1995 British Fantasy Award for his short story 'The Temptation of Dr Stein', and also the 1996 Arthur C. Clarke Award for his novel *Fairyland*. The same year the author quit his job as a professor at St Andrews University in Scotland and moved to north London to write full-time.

Every family has its store of myths. My grandfather was declared officially dead in the Great War, and my grand-mother thought herself a widow until he turned up three years later, pale and thin as a ghost, having been released from a German prisoner-of-war camp soon after the Armis-tice. My uncle, who was as rational as it is possible to be, who worked as a supervisor in a chemical plant and had built his own television, once saw a real ghost: visiting my great-aunt's boarding-house just after my great-grandfather died, he went into the kitchen and saw the old man sitting in his accustomed chair by the range. He rushed out to fetch

Auntie Bea, and of course the apparition was gone when they returned, but it badly shook my uncle, who said that the old man sat there 'as plain as daylight'.

As a little boy I saw no reason to disbelieve my uncle's story. I had never seen a ghost, but I supposed that it was only a matter of time.

The Elizabethan cottage where we lived, in a village on the outskirts of Stroud, in the Cotswolds, was one of a row of four. It was rented from the neighbouring iron foundry, and across the road were two factories, but despite the looming industrial presence (we marked time not by church tower chimes, but by the clock which adorned the water tank of one of the factories) my childhood was extraordinarily bucolic. We had an acre of gardens to roam in, with an orchard and neat vegetable plots bounded on one side by a brook (with the foundry on the other side) and the remains of a canal lock at the bottom, where pike and roach and trout could be caught; there was a railway branch line beyond, where steam trains ran until the late sixties. There were woods, and a common with a walled-off field called Dead Man's Acre in which none of us children dared to trespass, and an old quarry with a finger of rock left halfway up one side that locals called the Devil's Pulpit, and which *was* spooky late in the day, when the sky still shone blue but the quarry was in shadow. But no ghosts.

Instead, my contribution to my family's myth store involved an industrial accident.

It was a hot summer's day, in June or July. I was supervising my sister, who was learning to ride her bicycle. I was seven or eight, so my sister would have been five or six. I was wearing a short-sleeved Aertex shirt, and khaki shorts fastened with an elastic belt with a snake buckle. I had blond hair then, and it was always in a crewcut. I can't remember what my sister was wearing, but she certainly had sandals and white knee-high socks, and probably a cotton dress with a flower print. The bicycle had a blue frame and a yellow

mudguard, with training-wheels either side of the rear wheel
to keep it steady. Even so, my sister had trouble steering and
pedalling at the same time, so I trotted behind as she
wobbled along the pavement, to make sure that she didn't
stray into the road. There was far less traffic then, in 1962 or
1963, but because of the factories there was always the
danger of lorries or vans.

We went along the left side of the road, past the village
shop, past the tiny terrace of three brick cottages with their
neat front gardens, past the high wall of a larger house,
towards the corner with its red telephone kiosk and the
basket weaver's workshop. We stopped to watch a mobile
crane rumble past in the other direction, the catenary of its
jib neatly tucked behind its cab, and then my sister started
pedalling again. Seconds later, seized by a moment of
complete certainty, I grabbed the back of the bicycle's saddle
and brought it to a halt. Before my sister could protest,
astonishingly, cables fell all around us. One landed just in
front of the bicycle; another fell right behind me; others
landed in the road, laying a skewed criss-cross grid. I stood
behind my sister on her bicycle in a little patch no more
than three feet square defined by fallen cables, as neatly as a
magician's trick. I remember the noise they made, like whips
snapping on the tarmac.

The explanation was simple. The mobile crane had taken
the corner too fast, and the jib had swung out and knocked
over a telegraph pole; because of the factories, there were
many cables above the road, and they had all come down, a
hundred yards in either direction. Some were six inches in
diameter, and I remember how difficult it was to carry the
bicycle back without touching them; I knew about electricity,
and treated the fallen cables with the utmost respect, as if
they might suddenly strike like snakes. I felt mildly dizzy,
but very calm.

I do not know what made me stop the bicycle. With
hindsight, I can suppose that I heard the crane's jib hitting

the telegraph pole, but I do not remember it, and I certainly
did not see the cables falling towards us: if I had, I do not
doubt that I would not have been able to move. I simply
acted, as if I knew without thinking what was about to
happen. It was my own personal miracle of premonition.

Over the next few days, I began to imagine that I had
somehow deflected the falling cables, so that they had landed
around us but not on us, and came to believe that I might
have some kind of magical powers. It did not seem unreason-
able. How else could the dense web of falling cables have
missed us? I remember practising my imaginary powers,
although with rather modest ambitions. I did not try to
make the sun stand still, or predict the outcome of horse
races, but instead tried to change traffic lights from red to
green, or to influence the dipping flight of swallows, or the
erratic buzzing path of a housefly, or the fall of dust motes
in a sunbeam.

At the same time, I continued with my experiments with
the chemistry set I had been given that Christmas, and with
the little microscope from the Christmas before, and avidly
read about the new space rockets.

It did not occur to me that the two kinds of activities
required incompatible world views; or rather, as a child, I
was capable of holding both in my head at the same time.
After all, like cats, children are only partly domesticated, and
are able to inhabit two worlds: the ordered world of their
parents and of school; and the world of their own tribal
culture, of fierce loyalties and territorial disputes more
complicated than any in former Yugoslavia, of rites and
rituals as complex and important as those of any Stone Age
tribe. Or at least, that is how it was when I was a child; these
days, children are ferried everywhere by car, like prisoners,
and drugged by television's blue hypnotic light.

The cottages where I grew up are gone now; where they
stood is a mini-roundabout that regulates the constant flow
around the Stroud bypass. The gardens are gone, too, except

for a clump of willows at the bend of the brook; and the village shop and the basket maker's. Gone, razed like Troy, or Carthage. I grew up, and chose the world of science, where every successful experiment adds to what is already known, building a city of knowledge that can predict the composition of the farthest star, and explain the beginnings and intimate secrets of life, and the history of time from the first picoseconds after the Big Bang. That human minds are capable of this seems to me a larger miracle than the parting of the Red Sea, or the Burning Bush.

Only once did the feeling that I had after the fall of the cables come back to me. It was in a casino in Las Vegas in the early 1980s. I was playing roulette. For spin after spin of the wheel I bet with utter certainty, and won on every bet, parleying my minuscule pile of chips into several hundred dollars (the man who started following my bets won much more, but he was playing to win, not for fun). I stopped after half an hour, with a mild headache and a dizzy sensation, cashed in my chips and bought my friends cocktails.

ANNE McCAFFREY

Unto the Third Generation

———————— •◄► •————————

Anne McCaffrey (b. 1926) was born in Cambridge, Massachusetts, but is now an Irish citizen and lives in County Wicklow, Ireland. The most successful woman writing fantasy today, with more than eighteen million copies of her books in print, she started publishing her stories in the early 1950s and was the first woman to receive both a Hugo Award (in 1967) and a Nebula Award (in 1968). Best known for blending elements of science fiction, fantasy, romance and adventure in her books, she began publishing her interwoven novels of Pern in 1968 with *Dragonflight*, followed by *Dragonquest, Dragonsong, Dragonsinger*, the Hugo-winning *White Dragon, Dragondrums, Moreta: Dragonlady of Pern, Nerilka's Song, Dragonsdawn, The Renegades of Pern, All the Weyrs of Pern, The Dolphins of Pern* and *Red Star Rising* (a.k.a. *Dragonseye*). Her numerous other novels, many aimed at young adults, include *Restoree, Decision at Doona, The Ship Who Sang, To Ride Pegasus, Pegasus in Flight, Dinosaur Planet, Dinosaur Planet Survivors, The Crystal Singer, Killashandra, Crystal Line, The Rowan, Damia, Black Horses for the King, Catteni's Choice, An Exchange of Gifts, No One Noticed the Cat, Freedom's Landing, Freedom's Choice* and *Pegasus in Space*. Her short fiction has been collected in *A Time When, Get Off the Unicorn, The Worlds of Anne McCaffrey* and *The Girl Who Heard Dragons*.

———————— •◄► •————————

It was known that my grandmother had the second sight, which she was loath to use as it went against her very strong Catholic sense of ethics. After all, precognition is pagan and not respectable. But my mother and I inherited it from her. I think I got more aspects than Mother did but we'd both home in on the same event, even if we were far apart, as I shall tell you.

I was at a boarding-school in Virginia and Mother some forty miles away in Charlottesville when I woke up about three in the morning, very restless, certain something was wrong, and I wandered about the corridors of the dormitory (avoiding the night watchman, for I would have been reported for being out of my room). Almost an hour and a half later, suddenly the restlessness and fear went away and I was so sleepy I could scarcely make it back to my room.

The next day I was called into the Dean's office and told there was a personal call which I would be allowed to take – this once – because of my situation. (The Dean knew that both my father and my brother had been sent overseas and my mother urgently needed to speak to me.)

Mother got right to the point. Had I had any problems sleeping last night?

It turned out we were both awake for the same period of time. Neither of us could pin the anxiety on either Hugh or my father. But we did know that what had happened had turned out well.

It was nearly four months before we found out what prompted the event. Mail from overseas, those little V-mail types, was very slow at first. So we weren't surprised to get a whole batch from my father and sat down to read, in order, what had been happening to him. The night we had been apprehensive, he had been in a lifeboat in the middle of a convoy during a German submarine attack that had lasted an hour and a half.

*

I also have had the ability to 'find' things, though it's never been an especially useful or reliable ability. Just when I most need it, it usually declines to perform. However, I do remember an occasion when it worked just fine.

My husband had a pair of very fine cufflinks, rough lumps of gold nugget with a small peridot set in them: very attractive, and he used them for special occasions. One day he could only find the one and was furious. He had me searching high, low and in between. I vowed I would find it by evening. After he left for work, I took myself upstairs and into my older son's room, opening his top drawer and going through the rolled-up socks. And found the missing cufflink folded into one sock toe. Probably it had fallen into the dirty clothes basket which my husband kept beside his chest of drawers. It had got into a sock and been put away. Harmony was restored, although my husband never did believe my tale of how I found it.

I have also had several experiences with telepathy, generally involving persons previously unknown to me. The best one occurred here in Ireland when I was seeking a mortgage. I had just received news that Bantam had bought the paper-back rights to the *Harper Hall* books from Atheneum: half that money would come to me. I had enough to use as a down-payment on a house in Ireland! So I went to see my then bank manager and showed him the letter.

'A woman shouldn't have this much money,' was what I heard – although, as I was watching his reaction to the letter, his mouth had not moved.

This being Ireland, I could well believe he had thought just that. After he had hemmed and hawed, I thanked him for his time, took back my letter and changed banks.

Back to my grandmother. Her favourite sister, Annie, for whom both I and my mother were named, had died before my grandmother could see her one last time. And Grand-

mother was very worried about how Heaven was pleasing
Annie. So one night, in an extreme of anxiety for her sister's
well-being, she called up her spirit. According to what she
told my mother, Aunt Annie appeared, shawl over her
shoulders, hands folded over the ends at her waist, a very
characteristic pose.

Grandmother summoned enough courage to ask her sister
if she was happy.

'Well, it's not bad,' Annie said in a less than enthusiastic
tone which was also characteristic of her.

Terrified to have done so un-Catholic a thing, Grandmother dismissed the spirit and prayed all night in expiation
of this sin. She never again made use of her power. Which
may be why Mother and I never had any of it. Just as well.
What we did get has been both a trial as well as a revelation,
generally when it was least needed.

THOMAS F. MONTELEONE

Talkin' Them Marble Orchard Blues

Thomas F. Monteleone (b. 1946) was born in Baltimore, Maryland. He has been a professional writer since 1972 and has published nearly one hundred short stories in various magazines and anthologies. His novels have ranged from explicit horror, to fantasy, to more recent mainstream thrillers with supernatural elements. These have included *Night Things*, *Night Train*, *Lyrica*, *The Magnificent Gallery*, *Crooked House*, *Fantasma*, *The Black Net*, the Bram Stoker Award-winning *The Blood of the Lamb*, *The Resurrectionist* and *Night of Broken Souls*. He began editing the *Borderlands* series of non-themed anthologies in 1990, with four volumes published to date (the most recent co-edited with his wife, Elizabeth), and took its name for his own small press publishing imprint. His short fiction has been collected in *Dark Stars and Other Illuminations* and *Fearful Symmetries*. Monteleone has also written for the stage and television, including *Mister Magister* for American Playhouse, which won the Bronze Award at the International TV and Film Festival of New York and the Gabriel Award, and his story 'The Cutty Black Sow' was adapted for television's *Tales from the Darkside*. His often controversial opinion column, 'The Mothers and Fathers Italian Association', has appeared in various small-press magazines.

Several years back, one of my 'Mothers and Fathers Italian Association' columns posed the question: how does one write stories and novels about the supernatural without actually believing in it? Good question, I thought, and my final conclusion in the essay was that, for me, the jury was still out. I simply was not certain whether or not I believed in the paranormal/supernatural. I *wanted* to believe in such things (and the attendant UFOs and lake monsters...) but I wanted my own personal proof, and, as yet in my life, had witnessed none.

Now oddly enough, about three months after I published that column, in the early autumn of 1991, I received a call from a woman I knew in Baltimore. Her name was Ann, a friend and freelance journalist writing for the *Baltimore Sun* newspaper and many regional magazines. She had once written an article about me and one of my upcoming novels for the *Sun*, and knew of my interest in horror, the supernatural and the bizarre. Ann had called to invite me along on an experimental ghost hunt (of a sort). She was working on a piece about a group of paranormal investigators in the Maryland/Pennsylvania area called the Enigma Society, and she had arranged to go on a field trip with members of the society to a graveyard in the outskirts of the rural town of Glyndon, Maryland. Did I want to go along?

Sure, I said. Why not?

Ann filled me in on the particulars: local legend claimed the graveyard in question was filled with restive spirits and that, on any given night, visitors to the spot may hear the conflux of their voices calling out, perhaps speaking to us or each other. The Enigma Society was going to investigate by hauling in a panoply of sensitive recording instruments and other equipment to detect the slightest electromagnetic field disturbances.

On hearing this, I decided I'd bring my portable battery-powered Sony tape recorder and a brand-new, unopened cassette of Maxell Ultra tape. Just in case everybody else was in on some kind of rigged-up stunt, I would have my own gear serving as a personal verification.

And so I met Ann at one of the local pubs in Fells Point –
the bohemian district of Baltimore – and we drove in her
car out of the city, to state road 140, heading north-west
into a cool, early-autumn night. The star-filled sky was
almost completely clear, the air crisp, and there wasn't even
the slightest breeze. We drove through a town called Westminster, then took Route 32 through some gently rolling
pastureland, through a very small town called Glyndon, and
into a field next to a tiny country church. Beyond the
churchyard, up a slight hill and surrounded by old maples,
oaks and a few evergreens, lay the target graveyard, already
invaded by ten or so Enigma Society people, mostly in their
twenties and thirties, all in jeans, sweaters and light jackets.

Some had set up a folding metal table, and stacked it with
some industrial-looking electronic gear. If you have seen any
number of cheesy SF movies, you know what the equipment
looked like. The society folks had also run a power line from
the table, out of the graveyard to the open rear door of a
Dodge van where a small gasoline-powered generator chud-
dered along. When they closed the door to the van, the
sound of the generator was minimal.

OK, so Ann made some quick introductions, and everyone
went back to their stations, either seated in front of the
electronics gear or at strategically selected points around the
graveyard. While Ann spent some time interviewing members of the society and taking notes, I did some reconnoit-
ring, and picked out a headstone that was thick enough to
accommodate my Sony recorder on its flat, upper edge. I
placed it there and waited for the signal from the society
that the experiment was officially in progress.

While standing there, I tried to absorb the atmosphere of
the place, to pick up on any vibrations that may or may not
be there. The cassette contained ninety minutes' worth of
tape – more than enough time to catch any ethereal
conversations – and I sent it spinning as I depressed the red
button marked RECORD.

Then I sat down on the grassy earth, leaned against one of the weathered, granite gravemarkers and waited to hear something. The atmosphere in the graveyard changed dramatically as the society tech-heads signalled they were also recording. Everyone settled as they do on a movie set when the sound man yells, 'Speed!'

An almost palpable silence held everyone. No one even moved, much less spoke, for the next several hours. Each of us just sat there in the dark, several feet above a scattering of rotting caskets and bones, several generations away from a similar fate. It was a time when your mind can get real weird on you; and believe me, when you are sitting there with the express purpose of trying hear the dead speak, the time comes when you are not sure what you have heard and what you have not heard.

Like me, for example.

After about an hour of hearing nothing, and having been totally silent and immobile (other than to flip over my cassette), I *thought* I may have heard something. No wailing, no *wooo-wooo* kind of thing – just a very soft murmuring. It truly sounded like human speech, but unintelligible. As though you were standing in the foyer of a house and people were talking softly in an adjoining room. I thought I may have detected the rhythm of speech, rather than speech itself. Looking around the graveyard for any sign of recognition from my friend Ann or any of the Enigma Society folks proved fruitless. Nobody seemed to be hearing anything; at least that was the message of their body language and facial expressions.

And that is about the way it went for the remainder of the experiment. On and off I thought I *may* have heard something, but . . . well, you know.

Once in Ann's car, on the drive home, we compared notes and she was in agreement with me: totally inconclusive. When we admitted it to each other, neither one of us could honestly say we had heard a damned thing. I held my Sony tape recorder with both hands and said something like: 'OK, so let's see if we got anything on here . . .'

I pushed the PLAY button and we started listening, but the combined sounds of Ann's car engine and wind noise around her less than hermetically sealed windows effectively masked anything we might hear on the tape.

Back at Ann's apartment, it was very quiet when I pushed the PLAY button. She had turned off all the lights and fired up a few candles to promote an atmosphere of focused and silent attention from both of us.

It worked. We both sat there for about a half-hour just staring at the little Sony tape recorder like people used to do with their enormous radios while listening to a thirties drama starring Lamont Cranston.

What we listened to for that first thirty minutes was a kind of low-register whisper that was equal parts soft breezes activating the mike and indigenous tape-hiss from single-head recording technology. In other words, nothing. The muscles in my back and neck had been starting to cramp up, and my throat was dry. I was ready to call the whole evening a complete bust and chalk up another one for the sceptics in the audience.

And of course that's when Ann grabbed my arm and whispered 'What's that?'

I had heard it too – very soft voices carrying on a conversation. I could even make out a few of the words, although sporadically enough as to make no sense in the context of a sentence or even a phrase. But it was definitely human speech. I'd swear to that.

And you know how people say they felt the hair on the back of their neck raise up? Well I felt it too, at that moment, and the hair on my arms and practically everywhere else. My eyes started to water and I had a hell of a time trying to swallow. All these atavistic responses to the sound of those voices on that damned tape.

Ann and I sat there, silent and kind of chilled, listening to the whole thing. There was definitely a collection of different people talking, and there was no way it was ambient conversation from the Enigma Society folks, because I was there with them and everybody (every *live* body, anyway) was completely quiet.

There was no hoaxing going on – I would swear to it.

We replayed the tape several times that night, and Ann took it to a couple of different sound technicians who checked it for veracity, and both guys said the sounds were really there and not phoneyed up in any way. It was real. Voices.

So what did we capture on that tape?

I don't know, but I want to believe it was voices of the dead. In a way, if you've been the agnostic empiricist I've been for so many years, it was very comforting.

If you know what I mean.

MARK MORRIS

A Shadow of Tomorrow

———————————————•◆•———————————————

Mark Morris (b. 1963) was born in the mining town of
Bolsover and spent his childhood in Tewkesbury, Hong
Kong, Newark and Huddersfield. After university he moved
to Leeds and he now lives near Wetherby with his wife Nel
and their two children, David and Polly. He became a full-
time writer in 1988, with the help of the government's
Enterprise Allowance Scheme. His first novel, *Toady*,
appeared the following year. Since then he has published
*Stitch, The Immaculate, The Secret of Anatomy, Mr Bad Face,
Longbarrow* and the *Doctor Who* novel *The Bodysnatchers*.
His stories have been collected in the chapbook *Voyages Into
Darkness* (with Stephen Laws) and *Close to the Bone*, and
many have appeared in such anthologies and magazines as
*Final Shadows, Dark Voices 3, Blue Motel: Narrow Houses
Volume Three, Darklands* and *Darklands 2, The Mammoth
Book of Werewolves, Dark Terrors, Cold Cuts II, Fear, Skeleton
Crew, Interzone* and *Beyond*. He has been nominated for
seven British Fantasy Awards.

———————————————•◆•———————————————

In early 1988 a number of odd incidents occurred in my life
which could perhaps be termed 'supernatural'. I relate them
here as I perceived them, and leave possible explanations up
to you, the reader.

It started on 30 January, when my dad went out to play
golf as he did most Saturday mornings. The friend that he
was playing with that day said that he seemed his normal

self all the way around the course. However, at the final hole, completely without warning, my dad dropped dead of a massive heart attack. He was exactly four weeks short of his fiftieth birthday, and the night before he and my mum had been making arrangements for the big family party he was planning to throw.

It goes without saying that it was a dreadful time for us all. For the best part of six months I moved back home to help my mum through her grief. On the Monday morning after his death, I woke suddenly, my eyes springing open. I found myself lying on my side, facing the wall. The house was absolutely silent, and the light was a pearly grey, as though dawn had only recently broken. Immediately I had the incredibly intense impression that someone was standing behind me, leaning over the bed. I felt a hand touch my shoulder and a voice murmured, 'Mark.' Then I felt myself being pulled gently but firmly on to my back. At this point, although the presence seemed benign, terror flooded through me, and I rolled on to my back, panting for breath, my heart pummelling. I stared up at the place where the figure's face would have been had there been somebody there – but of course there was nobody. Afterwards, though I couldn't stop trembling for several minutes, I felt regretful and ashamed that I had been so scared.

My dad's funeral took place on Friday, 5 February at 11 a.m. When he died, I was three-quarters of the way through writing a book called *Toady*, which would later become my first published novel. When I returned to the book several weeks after his death, I realized that the day before he died I had written a scene involving a funeral that took place on exactly the same date and at exactly the same time as my dad's. I was so spooked by this that I took out all references to specific dates in the book, and also removed the line which stated that the funeral took place at 11 a.m. Now, to anyone reading the book, the funeral will simply take place on a Friday during the winter sometime after Christmas.

One other, perhaps unrelated, incident took place a couple of months later. After finishing *Toady* in record time (a combination of the novel gaining natural momentum as it raced towards its climax, coupled with my own need to immerse myself in my work to make me forget how awful I was feeling), I stayed on at my mum's for a few weeks to type it up. I estimated that if I typed for sixteen hours a day I could finish the book in three weeks – it was a very long novel and I was a very slow typist. About half-way through the book there is a sequence where one of the human antagonists meets the far more deadly supernatural antagonist, who is a kind of shape-shifting entity with a multitude of names. I was sitting in my mum's back room, which faces on to the back yard, typing up the following paragraph:

> The man grinned, revealing teeth like piano keys. His eyes glittered, making Rusty think muzzily of the fairground, of the blinking lights atop a carousel. When he spoke Rusty heard music behind his voice, gaudy candyfloss music, sinister and tinkling. 'I,' the man whispered, and leaned closer, bringing a smell like toffee apples, 'am your friend.'

It was spring by this time, a warm day, and the windows were open. Suddenly I was overwhelmed by the sweet and very distinctive smell of candyfloss. At first I thought I must be imagining things, that I must be becoming so involved in what I was typing that my senses were somehow attuning themselves to the contents of the book.

However, the smell refused to go away, and it wasn't just a faint odour; it was strong, and easily identifiable. I got up off my chair and went into the kitchen, thinking my mum must be cooking something. She wasn't. I then went into the back yard, sure that the smell would be drifting over the fence from a neighbour's house; but outside I couldn't catch even the faintest whiff of candyfloss. Puzzled and a little disturbed, I went back into my typing-room. I expected the smell to have gone, but as soon as I walked into the room it hit me again, as sweet and as strong as before. Unable to think of anything else to do, I sat down and continued typing, and little by little, over the space of perhaps five minutes, the smell gradually faded and finally disappeared altogether.

And that's it. Like most things in life, there was no follow-up to these events, no neat conclusions. I keep an open mind as to what these incidents meant, if anything. All I know is that in 1988 my dad died, and soon afterwards these things happened.

YVONNE NAVARRO

The House on Chadwell Drive

———————————•◆•———————————

Yvonne Navarro (b. 1957) was born in Chicago, and has lived in that area most of her life. Her first story appeared in *Horror Show* magazine in 1984, since when her short fiction (and an occasional dark fantasy illustration) have appeared in nearly fifty magazines and anthologies, among them *Darkside: Horror for the Next Millennium*, *The Hot Blood Series: Stranger By Night*, *Touch Wood: Narrow Houses Volume Two* and *Freaks*. She is the author of the novels *AfterAge, Species* (based on the screenplay by Dennis Feldman), *Deadrush, Aliens: Music of the Spears* and *Final Impact*, and of a reference book for writers and parents-to-be, *The First Name Reverse Dictionary*.

———————————•◆•———————————

Eighteen years ago, and I can close my eyes and easily, *too* easily, relive it all again:

It's 1979, and I'm asleep in the house on Chadwell Drive in Madison, Tennessee, a suburb just north of Nashville. My husband, barely into his twenties, sleeps soundly beside me. It is a cool Southern spring night; the window on the south side of the room is open and through it comes a soft breeze and the muted sounds of traffic from the interstate that borders the far side of the property.

Sleeping, dreaming of nothing, until something dark and unspeakable finds me in the night, brushes against me, and tries to steal everything that I am.

I wake abruptly, dragging open eyelids that suddenly

weigh a hundred pounds. The room is dark as oil and only the window looms over me, skewed at an impossible angle, stretching into a curve from the foot of the bed where it should be to a point a good forty-five degrees over my head where it shouldn't; light rims its outer woodwork like the doorway to damnation. My heartbeat thuds in my ears, ponderous and strained, as if the next beat may be just too much effort.

I open my mouth to speak, or scream, *something* ... but nothing comes out and nothing goes in, I have no air any more. Something unseen is in the room, paralysing me with terror, strangling my voice and suffocating me with its malevolent presence. I do the only thing I can think of, and beneath a high-pitched whine heard only by me the Lord's Prayer starts running through my mind at a frantic pace, garbled but sincere, and my own mental recitation is the last thing I hear as my eyes close unwillingly and blackness sinks over me.

A nightmare, I thought in the morning, and said as much over coffee and southern-fried potatoes and sausage. In the wash of bright morning sunlight it is easy to dismiss something as far away as last night, but my husband looks at me and says nothing. His accusing eyes remind me of something I'd forgotten, a night last week when my tiny indoor mutt, shaking with fear, inexplicably tried to claw her way beneath the blanket at my feet.

But terror needs belief to fuel it, and night-time memories easily bleed away in the light. The world revolves, my husband goes to work, and as the days go by the story is told and retold. Soon it becomes more an interesting tale than a truism, repeated again and again while the soul-deep fear fades away at the edges like chalk drawings on a sidewalk.

Life goes on, time passes; I continue my efforts to fix up this small rental house whose owner, I am told, was an ancient, mean-spirited woman who drew her last breath in it several years previously and is rumoured to have hidden a valuable German pistol somewhere within its depths. Slowly the downstairs is cleaned and painted, and it begins to take on the look of a comfortable if not exactly wealthy home. The upstairs awaits, two rooms with high, peaked ceilings and an empty storage area that runs the length of the house, accessible only through an opening in a tiny closet. The first room has built-in bookshelves and nooks and will make a fine reading room; the second will be nothing more elaborate than an empty extra bedroom. Still, they beckon to receive the same attention and facelift as the downstairs, and one cloudless morning I move my paint cans, brushes and rollers up the stairs and begin the task.

An hour later, I am shuddering at the bottom of the narrow stairway downstairs, loath to go back up, knowing I must do so, at least to retrieve the paint materials I abandoned. But I am young, healthy and intensely stubborn; over the next week I try again and again to give the first of the rooms an initial coat of paint, convinced that, if I can only do this, it will cover whatever malignant presence exists in that upper level and banish it for ever.

But youth and stubbornness are no match for whatever awaits, and I fail. Every time I grit my teeth and heft a brush or roller, ball my fist and bite my own knuckles against the feeling, I cannot resist the urge to whirl in an effort to see what dark thing watches me from behind, to stop the abomination I become convinced is only an inch away from stroking the back of my neck. And it is not just me; no one, it seems, can bear to be alone upstairs for more than a few minutes.

The final project for the downstairs is undertaken. A portion of the master bedroom ceiling is damaged and must be replaced; my husband, the property's caretaker and two helpers traipse upstairs, ready to cut out the damaged sheetrock and install the new. The only way to reach the ceiling is through the closet entrance into the attic, and they stop in surprise: just beyond the doorway into what had been, two months previously, the long and empty storage area lies a twin mattress covered with at least a decade's worth of dust and cobwebs. Coughing and choking and covered with the grime of years, they drag it out of the house, but no one can explain where it came from.

The ceiling is fixed and the work on the upstairs is permanently abandoned. The basement is something that no one mentions or explores; it is too dark and too filled with a seeping, unnameable hatred to contemplate. At night I lie and stare at the master bedroom ceiling next to my oblivious mate, seeing nothing in the lightless room but listening to footsteps crossing the floor above in an area far too small for a person to walk upright.

The marriage begins to disintegrate. My husband, who is wild and AWOL from the Navy, and I are separated as he is apprehended and returned to a federal detention centre some five hundred miles distant. Now I am alone in the house on Chadwell Drive, my tiny dog lost by a careless in-law and my only company within its walls the occasional mouse that skitters along the freshly coated baseboards, too swift for the awkward slap of my old broom. Unemployed and broke, my health begins to slip and nightmares move easily into the dark, doubting thoughts in my mind, shadowy cousins to the pain that inexplicably twists through my stomach at all hours. I cower in the bedroom night after night, afraid to move and catch the attention of whatever demon follows me through the echoing, brightly decorated rooms.

Things begin to get misplaced, objects are found on the floor when I return to a room. The midnight noises upstairs are loud enough to make me sit on the side of the bed and shake, and I can no longer sleep without light – lots of it. My mother, owner of a small security business, provides me with a dog to keep in the house with me temporarily. A Belgian Trahern trained in Spanish, Poz sleeps fitfully on the bed at my feet ... but no command or tug of the leash will make him go up the stairs to investigate the first floor and its constant unexplained clamour. Maternal instincts rising, the next night my mother brings her personal dog to the house; while Mother sleeps on the couch and is beset with nightmares of a scowling old woman who tries to force her into the basement, her dog, more vicious than most, growls deep in his throat and spends the night hours restlessly prowling the confines of the small living-room around her.

The next morning, her own dog joins Poz in instinctively refusing to investigate the upstairs. Out of options, both guard dogs are returned to the van and I reluctantly release my own German shepherd from his chain in the back yard and bring him inside. A prime guard dog in his younger years, now King is old and gentled, blind in both eyes; his other senses, however, are overdeveloped from years of sightlessness. His courage and loyalty to me far exceed even the meticulous training of the other animals: when the door to the upstairs is opened and he is commanded to 'Watch!', he is up the stairs immediately, if not cautiously. Along the still-strong ridge of his back, his fur stands erect and his mouth pulls back in a fierce display of aged and yellow teeth as he picks his way up the stairs and explores the two rooms. His search leads him, finally, to stand poised on the edge of the opening into the bare storage space and snarl and snap at nothing we can see.

There is no courageous, flashy end to this story, no thrilling weekend seance or 'Oh – so *that's* why!' explanation to end it all and finally put some wandering spirit to rest. Amid the fear and night sweats, reality still pressed. As another first of the month reared its monetary head, I seized at the excuse it gave me. Despite the caretaker's assurances that he could wait for the rent and his pleas for me to stay, I was packed and gone, furniture included, within two days. Left behind was a lovingly decorated little house, a now time-worn dwelling that to this day still stands but has never been rented for more than half a year at a time.

WILLIAM F. NOLAN

The Floating Table and the Jumping Violet

William F. Nolan (b. 1928) was born in Kansas City and moved to Los Angeles when he was nineteen. He has been a commercial artist, a racing-car driver, publisher of the *Ray Bradbury Review*, managing editor of *Gamma* magazine, and active as a scriptwriter in television and films since the 1970s. He is also a prolific prose writer with sixty published books to his credit as well as more than seven hundred magazine pieces. Twice winner of the Edgar Allan Poe Special Award Scroll from the Mystery Writers of America, his work has been collected in over 250 anthologies and textbooks worldwide. Since selling his first story to *If* in 1954, his many books include *Logan's Run* (co-written with George Clayton Johnson) and its two sequels; *Space for Hire, Helltracks, The Demon Within*, and such collections as *Wonderworlds, Things Beyond Midnight* and *Nightshapes*. Nolan has worked on five movie screenplays and some twenty network Movies of the Week, including such titles as *The Norliss Tapes, Trilogy of Terror* (with Richard Matheson), *Burnt Offerings, Bridge Across Time* (a.k.a. *Terror at London Bridge/The Arizona Ripper*) and Henry James's *The Turn of the Screw*, which he adapted as a two-part mini-series in 1974. *Trilogy of Terror II* (co-scripted with Richard Matheson and Dan Curtis) premièred as a Hallowe'en special in 1996.

My direct experiences with what I think of as 'the world of the supernormal' are quite limited. Although I have a long-standing friendship with novelist Sanora Babb, who has described in precise detail her many encounters with ghosts, I have never personally met one. I do believe in their existence, however, and a short story of mine, 'Gibbler's Ghost', is based on a phantom encounter related to me by a noted film actor.

During my lifetime I've had just two personal experiences that defy logic, both of which mystify me to this day.

The first took place at a friend's house in Beverly Hills. She owned a massive oak table and after dinner one evening she suggested that we all conduct an experiment involving 'psychic force'. Her guests gathered around the oak table, placed the tips of their fingers against the grained top and began chanting, 'Up, table, up!' in unison. Over and over again. I thought the whole scene was ridiculous; it would have taken three or four husky men, exerting prime muscle power, to lift that heavy table into the air.

I was wrong. As the guests kept chanting, the table began to waver under their touch. Slowly it levitated from the floor. Convinced of a trick, I ducked beneath to see what was really going on. Wires? Someone under there, pushing upward?

No, nothing. The massive oak table floated on the air without any visible support.

Psychic force in action!

My second encounter with the supernormal was even more bizarre. It involves an African violet I gave to my mother for her eighty-third birthday. Although not a 'plant person', she loved this gift. Living alone in her apartment, she often talked to her potted friend, telling it how much she appreciated having it in her life. She especially loved its velvet-purple flowers. Indeed, it continued to bloom all year round and I was amazed at this out-of-season performance.

'Maybe it loves you,' I remarked lightly. 'Plants are alive, and they do respond to affection. Or so I've heard.' I didn't know; I was just repeating what I'd read somewhere. But the damn violet *did* seem to be responding to her.

Late that same year Mother became ill. She was taken to the hospital and died there.

My wife, writer Cameron Nolan, and I then had to deal with clearing out Mom's apartment, and in the course of going through her possessions (an emotionally shattering experience for me) Cam noticed the still-blooming African violet.

She picked it up from the shelf, shaking her head. 'It doesn't know she's dead.'

At these words, abruptly, the potted plant uprooted itself, jumped two inches into the air, and fell over on its side.

Incredible! My wife was still holding the now lifeless violet and we exchanged baffled looks. This couldn't happen.

But it had. We both witnessed the plant's convulsive death spasm.

I've thought a lot since then about just how evolved plants actually are. A century ago, scientists did not believe that animals could think. Maybe today we need to learn that plants can feel. The late genius Itzhak Bentov said that all matter is 'alive' and sentient, located somewhere on an upward arc of rising consciousness.

Mom's African violet taught me that Bentov just may be right.

EDGAR ALLAN POE

Mesmeric Revelation

———————— •▬• ————————

Edgar Allan Poe (1809–1849) has been described as 'the father of modern horror' (as well as of scientific and detective fiction). Born in Boston, Massachusetts, the death of his mother and the desertion of his father resulted in Poe, aged three, being made the ward of a Virginia merchant who later disowned him. In 1836 he married his thirteen-year-old cousin Virginia Clemm, who died of tuberculosis eleven years later. Suffering from bouts of depression and alcoholism, Poe attempted suicide in 1848 and, the following year, he vanished for three days before inexplicably turning up in a delirious condition in Baltimore, where he died a few days later. Poe published a volume of poetry, *Tamerlane and Other Poems*, in 1827, and his first short story, 'Metzengerstein', appeared in 1832. His tales of madness and premature burial never gained him wealth nor recognition during his lifetime, but among his best stories and poems are 'The Fall of the House of Usher', 'The Murders in the Rue Morgue', 'The Pit and the Pendulum', 'The Black Cat', 'The Tell-Tale Heart', 'The Premature Burial' and 'The Raven'. The following piece is excerpted from an article that originally appeared in New York's *Columbian* magazine, and it shares certain similarities with Poe's classic story 'The Facts in the Case of M. Valdemar', which was published around the same time:

———————— •▬• ————————

Whatever doubt may still envelop the *rationale* of mesmerism, its startling *facts* are now almost universally admitted. Of these latter, those who doubt are your mere doubters by profession – an unprofitable and disreputable tribe. There can be no more absolute waste of time than the attempt to prove, at the present day, that man, by mere exercise of will, can so impress his fellow, as to cast him into an abnormal condition, of which the phenomena resemble very closely those of *death*, or at least resemble them more nearly than they do the phenomena of any other normal condition within our cognizance; that, while in this state, the person so impressed employs only with effort, and then feebly, the external organs of sense, yet perceives, with keenly refined perception, and through channels supposed unknown, matters beyond the scope of the physical organs; that, moreover, his intellectual faculties are wonderfully exalted and invigorated; that his sympathies with the person so impressing him are profound; and, finally, that his susceptibility to the impression increases with its frequency, while, in the same proportion, the peculiar phenomena elicited are more extended and more *pronounced*.

I say that these – which are the laws of mesmerism in its general features – it would be supererogation to demonstrate; nor shall I inflict upon my readers so needless a demonstration today. My purpose at present is a very different one indeed. I am impelled, even in the teeth of a world of prejudice, to detail without comment the very remarkable substance of a colloquy, occurring between a sleep-waker and myself.

I had been long in the habit of mesmerizing the person in question (Mr Vankirk), and the usual acute susceptibility and exaltation of the mesmeric perception had supervened. For many months he had been labouring under confirmed phthisis, the more distressing effects of which had been relieved by my manipulations; and on the night of Wednesday, the 15th instant, I was summoned to his bedside.

The invalid was suffering with acute pain in the region of the heart, and breathed with great difficulty, having all the ordinary symptoms of asthma. In spasms such as these he had usually found relief from the application of mustard to the nervous centres, but tonight this had been attempted in vain.

As I entered his room he greeted me with a cheerful smile, and although evidently in much bodily pain, appeared to be, mentally, quite at ease.

'I sent for you tonight,' he said, 'not so much to administer to my bodily ailment, as to satisfy me concerning certain psychal impressions which, of late, have occasioned me much anxiety and surprise. I need not tell you how sceptical I have hitherto been on the topic of the soul's immortality. I cannot deny that there has always existed, as if in that very soul which I have been denying, a vague half-sentiment of its own existence. But this half-sentiment at no time amounted to conviction. With it my reason had nothing to do. All attempts at logical inquiry resulted, indeed, in leaving me more sceptical than before.

'I repeat, then, that I only half felt, and never intellectually believed. But latterly there has been a certain deepening of the feeling, until it has come so nearly to resemble the acquiescence of reason, that I find it difficult to distinguish between the two. I am enabled, too, plainly to trace this effect to the mesmeric influence. I cannot better explain my meaning than by the hypothesis that the mesmeric exaltation enables me to perceive a train of ratiocination which, in my abnormal existence, convinces, but which, in full accordance with the mesmeric phenomena, does not extend, except through its *effect*, into my normal condition. In sleep-waking, the reasoning and its conclusion – the cause and its effect – are present together. In my natural state, the cause vanishing, the effect only, and perhaps only partially, remains.

'These considerations have led me to think that some good results might ensue from a series of well-directed questions propounded to me while mesmerized. You have often observed the profound self-cognizance evinced by the sleep-waker – the extensive knowledge he displays upon all points relating to the mesmeric condition itself; and from this self-cognizance may be deduced hints for the proper conduct of a catechism.'

I consented of course to make this experiment. A few passes threw Mr Vankirk into the mesmeric sleep. His breathing became immediately more easy, and he seemed to suffer no physical uneasiness. The following conversation then ensued – V. in the dialogue representing the patient, and P. myself.

P. Are you asleep?

V. Yes – no; I would rather sleep more soundly.

P. (After a few more passes) Do you sleep now?

V. Yes.

P. How do you think your present illness will result?

V. (After a long hesitation and speaking as if with effort) I must die.

P. Does the idea of death afflict you?

V. (Very quickly) No – no!

P. Are you pleased with the prospect?

V. If I were awake I should like to die, but now it is no matter. The mesmeric condition is so near death as to content me.

P. I wish you would explain yourself, Mr Vankirk.

V. I am willing to do so, but it requires more effort than I feel able to make. You do not question me properly.

P. Then what shall I ask?

V. You must begin at the beginning.

P. The beginning! But where is the beginning?

V. You know that the beginning is GOD. *(This was said in a low, fluctuating tone, and with every sign of the most profound veneration)*

P. What then is God?

V. (Hesitating for many minutes) I cannot tell.

P. Is not God spirit?

V. While I was awake I knew what you meant by 'spirit', but now it seems only a word – such for instance as truth, beauty – quality, I mean.

P. Is not God immaterial?

V. There is no immateriality – it is a mere word. That which is not matter, is not at all – unless qualities are things.

P. Is God, then, material?

V. No. *(This reply startled me very much)*

P. What then is he?

V. *(After a long pause, and mutteringly)* I see – but it is a thing difficult to tell. *(Another long pause)* His is not spirit, for he exists. Nor is he matter, *as you understand it*. But there are *gradations* of matter of which man knows nothing; the grosser impelling the finer, the finer pervading the grosser. The atmosphere, for example, impels the electric principle, while the electric principle permeates the atmosphere. These gradations of matter increase in rarity or fineness, until we arrive at a matter *unparticled* – without particles – indivisible – *one*; and here the law of impulsion and permeation is modified. The ultimate, or unparticled matter, not only permeates all things but impels all things – and thus *is* all things within itself. This matter is God. What men attempt to embody in the word 'thought' is this matter of motion.

P. You assert, then, that the unparticled matter, in motion, is thought?

V. In general, this motion is the universal thought of the universal mind. This thought creates. All created things are but the thoughts of God.

P. You say, 'in general'.

V. Yes. The universal mind is God. For new individuals, *matter* is necessary.

P. But you now speak of 'mind' and 'matter' as do the metaphysicians.

V. Yes – to avoid confusion. When I say 'mind', I mean

the unparticled or ultimate matter; by 'matter', I intend all else.

P. You have often said that the mesmeric state very nearly resembles death. How is this?

V. When I say that it resembles death, I mean that it resembles the ultimate life; for when I am entranced the senses of my rudimental life are in abeyance, and I perceive external things directly, without organs, through a medium which I shall employ in the ultimate, unorganized life.

P. Unorganized?

V. Yes; organs are contrivances by which the individual is brought into sensible relation with particular classes and forms of matter, to the exclusion of other classes and forms. The organs of man are adapted to his rudimental condition, and to that only; his ultimate condition, being unorganized, is of unlimited comprehension in all points but one – the nature of the volition of God, that is to say, the motion of the unparticled matter. You will have a distinct idea of the ultimate body by conceiving it to be entire brain. This it is *not*; but a conception of this nature will bring you near a comprehension of what it *is*. In the ultimate, unorganized life, the external world reaches the whole body (which is of a substance having affinity to brain, as I have said), with no other intervention than that of an infinitely rarer ether than even the luminiferous; and to this ether – in unison with it – the whole body vibrates, setting in motion the unparticled matter which permeates it. It is to the absence of idiosyncratic organs, therefore, that we must attribute the nearly unlimited perception of the ultimate life. To rudimental beings, organs are the cages necessary to confine them until fledged.

P. You speak of rudimental 'beings'. Are there other rudimental thinking beings than man?

V. The multitudinous conglomeration of rare matter into nebulae, suns, or planets, is for the sole purpose of supplying *pabulum* for the idiosyncrasy of the organs of an infinity of rudimental beings. But for the necessity of the rudimental, prior to the ultimate life, there would have been no bodies such as these. Each of these is tenanted by a distinct variety of organic, rudimental, thinking creatures. In all, the organs vary with the features of the place tenanted. At death, or metamorphosis, these creatures, enjoying the ultimate life – immortality – and cognizant of all secrets but *the one*, act all things and pass everywhere by mere volition – indwelling, not the stars, which to us seem the sole palpabilities, and for the accommodation of which we blindly deem space created – but that SPACE itself – that infinity of which the truly substantive vastness swallows up the star-shadows, blotting them out as non-entities from the perception of the angels.

P. Still, there is one of your expressions which I find it impossible to comprehend – 'the truly *substantive* vastness of infinity'.

V. This, probably, is because you have no sufficiently generic conception of the term '*substance*' itself. We must not regard it as a quality, but as a sentiment: it is the perception, in thinking beings, of the adaptation of matter to their organization. There are many things on the Earth which would be nihility to the inhabitants of Venus – many things visible and tangible in Venus which we could not be brought to appreciate as existing at all. But to the inorganic beings – to the angels – the whole of the unparticled matter is substance; that is to say, the whole of what we term 'space' is to them the truest substantiality; the stars, meantime, through what we consider their materiality, escaping the angelic sense, just in proportion as the unparticled matter, through what we consider its immateriality, eludes the organic.

As the sleep-waker pronounced these latter words, in a feeble tone, I observed on his countenance a singular expression, which somewhat alarmed me, and induced me to awake him at once. No sooner had I done this than, with a bright smile irradiating all his features, he fell back upon his pillow and expired. I noticed that in less than a minute afterward his corpse had all the stern rigidity of stone. His brow was of the coldness of ice. Thus, ordinarily, should it have appeared, only after long pressure from Azrael's hand. Had the sleep-waker, indeed, during the latter portion of his discourse, been addressing me from the region of the shadows?

VINCENT PRICE

In the Clouds

———————————————•‣•———————————————

Vincent Price (1911–1993) was perhaps the screen's most suave merchant of menace. Born in St Louis, Missouri, he appeared in more than one hundred movies, seventy-five stage plays and numerous television shows. After making his début in the screwball comedy *Service de Luxe* in 1938, his films included *Tower of London*, *The Invisible Man Returns*, *The House of the Seven Gables*, *Shock* and *Drogonwyck*, before the 1953 3-D movie *House of Wax* turned him into a horror-film star. For the next four decades he was typecast in such classics as William Castle's *House on Haunted Hill* and *The Tingler*, Roger Corman's Edgar Allan Poe series – *The Fall of the House of Usher*, *Pit and the Pendulum*, *Tales of Terror*, *The Raven*, *The Masque of the Red Death* and *The Tomb of Ligeia* – and Robert Fuest's *The Abominable Dr Phibes* and *Dr Phibes Rises Again*. Also among his best films are *The Fly*, *Witchfinder General* (a.k.a. *The Conqueror Worm*) and *Theatre of Blood*. His final feature film role was as the kindly inventor in Tim Burton's *Edward Scissorhands*. Some years ago, Price revealed to journalist and author Michael Munn how he learned through a bizarre psychic experience that his friend and fellow-actor Tyrone Power had died:

———————————————•‣•———————————————

I was on a plane flying from Hollywood to New York, and I was reading a classic French novel. This was 15 November 1958. I know it was the date because of what happened on that day. I glanced up to look out of the window and – I swear this is true – I saw huge letters emblazoned across a cloudbank which said TYRONE POWER IS DEAD.

It was a tremendous shock of course, and I thought that I was seeing things at first. I looked around and couldn't see anybody else acting as though they'd seen the words. But I had definitely seen these words which were like giant teletype that were lit up with brilliant light that came from within the clouds.

It was only when I landed in New York that I learned that my friend Tyrone Power had died in Spain where he was making *Solomon and Sheba*. He'd had a heart attack on the set while I was in the clouds. There was no way I could have known he was going to die so I didn't just imagine the words. Yet I think the words were somehow formed only for me, perhaps in my mind, like a message sent by Ty.

ALAN RODGERS

Clinic-Modern

Alan Rodgers (b. 1959) was born in Montclair, New Jersey, but he grew up mostly in the South. He currently lives in Eugene, Oregon, with his wife, Amy Stout, and their three children. His first novelette, 'The Boy Who Came Back From the Dead', won a Bram Stoker Award in 1988. Since then he has published such novels as *Bone Music* and *Light* (the first two volumes in a proposed themed trilogy), *Pandora, Fire, Night, Blood of the Children* and *New Life for the Dead*. During the mid-1980s he also edited the horror digest magazine *Night Cry*.

My father died slowly and horribly in the fall of 1989.

My wife was pregnant with our first child that fall, and even before my dad went in for the operation that killed him (murdered him, I say sometimes, and that may be exactly true: in retrospect the doctors were criminally stupid to perform a coronary bypass on a man so given to spontaneous surges of blood pressure that he haemorrhaged in the hospital two days before the operation, during a catheterization) we had decided to name the nascent child for him. It's a family tradition: I'm named for my grandfather, and my daughter is named for my dad.

The operation came up suddenly, two days after I told my father that my wife was expecting – he was switching insurance providers, and went in to his doctor to see if there was anything that needed tending before he went across the gap between two policies. The doctor found a blockage in one of the arteries that fed his heart.

Two days later, on that Friday, he went into the hospital for the disastrous catheterization; the next day, Saturday, I flew down from Connecticut to see him.

Early Monday morning, he went in for the murderous operation.

The surgery itself went well enough – but thirty minutes after the doctors sewed him up, Dad's blood pressure surged, bursting the sutures that bound the veins that fed his heart. For ten long minutes Dad had no blood pressure to speak of while they hauled him back down into the operating room, opened him up and sewed him back together . . .

He was as good as dead when those ten minutes were over. Not because of his heart, oddly enough, but because those ten minutes had starved his brain of oxygen, strangling him from the inside out.

The hospital's specialist in morbidity came around to see us almost immediately. Even then, before anyone knew for certain how grave the damage was, the doctor of morbidity tried to persuade us to pull the plug on Dad. Sweet people ran that hospital. Do I need to mention that this was University Community Hospital in Tampa, the Stygian pit that later made headlines for doing things like sawing the wrong legs off cancer patients? I didn't think so.

We didn't shut Dad off, of course. He spent three long days decaying in the intensive-care unit, and all that while the doctors and eventually my relatives maintained the pressure to effect my father's euthanasia: the hospital had motives of its own, intentions that I can't claim to know but can't imagine charitably; my relatives could not bear the pain that gripped them while they watched my father dying breath by breath for days.

It was a terrible, terrible week. I was not about to consent to euthanasia while there was the remotest chance my father might recover, and the hospital could neither relent in its pressure for euthanasia nor offer proof that no one had ever recovered from my father's state. (There have been cases, I gather, but precious few, and those may have been the work of miracles.)

I do not want to live a week like that again.

Ever.

I remember the sight of my father in the intensive-care bed, packed in ice, his chest shaved bare, broken and rebound with stitches; there was a pallor to his skin that made me think of Frankenstein's monster in some clinic-modern remake.

I've seen that chest many times since then. It haunts me, sometimes.

On Thursday morning Dad's collapse overcame the remedial appliances and medical phylactery that worked to keep him breathing, and he died.

And he was gone.

Or seemed to be.

There were days of mourning, then, and sometime later my wife (who had flown down in the heat of things, I don't remember when) and I went home to Connecticut.

You need to know this about Connecticut: I'm allergic to the place. Literally, so far as I can tell. All the years we lived there I had terrible breathing problems, day and night – and most especially at night. Nearly every night we spent there I'd wake the next day dizzy and unsteady, half strangled by the swelling in my respiratory tract. Lots of nights I'd wake gasping for air, often from dreams of suffocation and enclosure.

I didn't understand this in the weeks after my father's death. I'd hardly got acquainted with the problem then – we had only lived in Connecticut a month or two when my father passed away. Which is to say that the nightmares I had in the weeks following my father's death came to me from many causes, roots of one affliction and another twisting around themselves till it becomes impossible to tell one from the other . . . And I had an awful lot of nightmares in those weeks, no matter where they came from. The worst of them were frightful stuff that ran and re-ran the moments at my father's deathbed, but there were other dreams, too – dreams of my father's ghost.

When I saw Dad's ghost in those dreams it was a joy to me, because he was my father and I loved him and I missed him.

'Why do people fear a haunting by the people that they love?' I asked the ghost in one dream. 'Stay,' I said.

In the dream the ghost of my father smiled, and he seemed pleased, just as we all are pleased to hear that those we love still want our company. But he did not answer.

I had that dream a dozen times or more in the weeks after my father's death. And then, in December, something else entirely came to me.

I woke that night to the sound of running water in the bathroom down the hall. It was the shower, I realized – someone was taking a shower in our bathroom in the middle of the night, and my pregnant wife was there in bed beside me, sleeping peacefully. I pushed out of bed, stumbled towards the bathroom as dizzily as I always stumbled when I woke nights in Connecticut. What had I done, I wondered, left the water running in the shower? Had my wife? And it was the shower, too, the shower and not the tap. Listening to the sound, it was much louder and more intense than water when it rushes through a sink . . .

If I'd had an ounce of sense I would have gone more warily. It could have been a burglar. But I never think that clearly when I wake at night, and nights in Connecticut my thoughts were more bewildered still. It didn't even occur to me to think there might be an intruder in our shower.

But there was.

An intruder – or an invited guest, perhaps.

I stumbled down the hallway to the bathroom door, where I saw light creeping out around the doorjamb, and there was steam in the air, drifting with the sifted light like tiny lazy puffs of cloud . . .

Someone was singing in there – no, it was humming, soft, pretty humming, a tune I recognized but could not name, and I knew that voice.

I opened the door without thinking I should hesitate – though now I know I should have waited – to see my dead father, fresh and naked from the shower, towelling himself dry.

His chest was shaved bare, just as it had been in the hospital, and there were the throat-to-gullet wound and the great bloody black-and-blue stitches that sealed it, fine red-brown bits of drying blood along the centre of Dad's chest, all the detritus of the operation that had killed him.

'Son,' my father said, greeting me, opening his arms to embrace me – And part of me wanted to cry for joy, it wanted to embrace the ghost. Because he was my father and I loved him, and I mourned the loss of him, and I wanted him to see his granddaughter, and I wanted him to see her grow and thrive –

But another, bigger, louder part of me recoiled in horror, terrified of that horrific apparition. I screamed, and backed away.

And my father was gone. Vanished as though he'd never been there, as though my fear had driven him away.

It isn't clear to me if that vision was a dream or a real haunt-ing: I know that later I sat on the edge of my bed, rocking back and forth, trying to breathe; I know I slept and woke and slept again many times that night. It may be that I dreamed that moment and the apparition of my father; it may be I imagined him awake, hallucinating because I could not breathe.

And it may be that I saw the ghost I think I saw, and drove him from my home.

I can tell you this: I have never dreamed my father's ghost again. And that makes me sad, because I loved my father, and I miss him even now.

NICHOLAS ROYLE

Magical Thinking

—————————————— • ❯ • ——————————————

Nicholas Royle (b. 1963) was born in Sale, Cheshire. He is
the author of more than seventy horror tales, several of
which have been reguarly selected for such anthologies as
The Best New Horror, The Year's Best Fantasy and Horror and
The Year's Best Horror Stories. Other recent appearances have
included *Dark Terrors* and *Dark Terrors 2, Twist in the Tail:
Cat Horror Stories, Love in Vein II* and *The Mammoth Book
of Dracula,* while anthologies he has edited include the
award-winning *Darklands* and *Darklands 2, A Book of Two
Halves* and *The Tiger Garden: A Book of Writers' Dreams.* He
is also the author of three novels, *Counterparts, Saxophone
Dreams* and *The Matter of the Heart.*

—————————————— • ❯ • ——————————————

The distance, as the crow flies, from the Lanesborough Hotel
at Hyde Park Corner in central London to St George's
Hospital in Tooting, south London, is 5.3 miles. The distance
from the Lanesborough Hotel to another hospital, the
Central Middlesex in west London, is also 5.3 miles. St
George's has been based exclusively at the Tooting site since
1979. Before that the main site, incorporating the medical
school, was located at Hyde Park Corner, in the exact spot
where the Lanesborough now stands. The hotel was built
within the existing structure of the old hospital.

In August 1994, an old and dear friend of mine, Dell,
introduced me to a doctor called Kate. Dell and Kate had
worked together as doctors. Kate and I got on and we started

to see a lot of each other. On 30 August 1996, two years to the day since our first date (and forty-four years to the day since my parents' wedding), Kate and I got married. We chose the day for these reasons – but when I had asked Kate out to dinner for the first time two years earlier, I hadn't realized the date fell on my parents' wedding anniversary. The dates and the echoes resounding down the years please me; they suggest the potential for a pattern, which offers some kind of appeal, some strange comfort. But it's not supernatural.

Kate and I had not met before Dell introduced us, but we had both attended the same Jim Whiting art event in the Old Pumping Station, Wapping, in the early 1990s. And our paths had crossed – literally, possibly – several years before that.

In the summer of 1984, I worked as a cashier and waiter at Pizza on the Park, a branch of Pizza Express which was located at Hyde Park Corner, right next to an abandoned hospital – St George's. Because I am fascinated by derelict institutions – and thanks to Zoran Petrović, the Yugoslav kitchen hand, who showed me how to do it – I broke into the old hospital one evening. Access was round the back, on the second or third floor, gained by jumping off the tiny triangle of roofspace where the waiters would go to eat their pizzas. You landed on part of the old hospital roof and climbed in through an open window.

I spent what now seem like hours patrolling the empty corridors and smashed laboratories, accompanied by the constant sound of broken glass crunching underfoot and the drip-drip-drip of leaky ceilings. I was moved by the thrill of being inside a forbidden place (notices warned that security guards would treat intruders as if they were terrorists) and excited by the resonances I sensed in the fabric of the walls – the dramas which had begun here and which would still start and finish here in the future. I walked for what seemed like miles, travelling up and down floors and reaching the far side of the hospital, where the windows looked out on to the Wellington Arch. It was always with reluctance that I crept back out of St George's to resume my shift in the restaurant.

In 1985, when I was back working at Pizza on the Park, they started redeveloping St George's, eventually to turn it into the Lanesborough Hotel.

Ten years after my explorations of the abandoned hospital, I met Kate. She was a consultant haematologist at Central Middlesex Hospital. She had studied, however, at St George's. Most of her lectures and tutorials were given at the new site in Tooting, but for some teaching she had had to travel to Hyde Park Corner.

Our paths may well have crossed. Kate was there in 1979 and with some fellow-medics she explored little-used corridors and short cuts which led them out on to the roof; five years later I was doing much the same thing.

Kate later told me that her Aunt Maureen had been a sister at St George's during the war and a colleague of hers had claimed to have seen a ghost there. Others had spoken of seeing the same phantom. I was not that lucky. My only genuine experience of the supernatural – unless you count the above, which in a way I do – happened when I was about eleven.

We were sitting in the lounge of our house at 33 Ellesmere Road, Altrincham – my mum, my two sisters and I. It was late at night, around eleven or midnight. My dad was at work, on a night shift (he was a customs officer at Manchester docks). My grandmother, whom we called Nana, had died some months earlier. She used to spend her days in an annexe room which my dad had built on to the side of the house, and she slept in her own bedroom on the first floor of the main part of the house. It was quite a big house, four bedrooms, detached, and lots of dark wood, purple walls in the hall – quite scary at night if you were the last one up, which I often was.

The four of us were sitting on the floor in the lounge in front of the sofa. We hadn't got up after the programme we'd been watching had finished and the channel had closed down for the night. The door to the hall, which was behind us and behind the sofa, was closed. Suddenly we all became aware simultaneously of footsteps coming down the stairs. We looked at each other, petrified. We knew Dad was at work. There was no one else in the house.

I don't know how long we sat there whispering to each other before my elder sister plucked up the courage to lead us out of the lounge, through the hall and the dining-room and into the kitchen, where she armed herself with a carving-knife. As a group we checked the back door. It was locked, as it had been. We tiptoed upstairs and gingerly checked in all the rooms, including no doubt the airing-cupboard. None of the windows was open. Nowhere was there any sign of entry. The front door was locked.

We never explained it. Or we never explained it satisfactorily. My mum's theory was that it was the ghost of Nana. I came to believe this as well, as the only possible explanation. Whether or not it was Nana, I think it must have been someone's ghost. We didn't hallucinate the sound of the footsteps. I've had plenty of hallucinations over the years – visual and aural – and I have always been able to tell the difference between what's real and what's not.

At the time I was frightened, terrified. Now I find the implications of the experience strangely comforting. Forced by my dad's death in September 1994 to confront human mortality, I long for there to be something, anything – some form of consciousness, some meagre kind of survival after death. For his sake and for my sake. For the sake of all of us. The patterns, the criss-crossing paths we take during our lives, provide some comfort as well. A form of what psychologists call magical thinking, they offer a glimmer of hope that there might be some shape to our existence – rather than meaningless chaos followed by eternal nothingness.

JAY RUSSELL

De Cold, Cold *Décolletage*

———————————— •►• ————————————

Jay Russell (b. 1961) is a native of New York City. He attended Cornell University and the University of Southern California, from which he received a PhD in Communications. He has worked for a private investigation agency in Los Angeles and as a media researcher and editor. His short stories have been published in various anthologies and magazines, including *Splatterpunks*, *The King is Dead: Tales of Elvis Post-Mortem*, *Dark Terrors 2* and *3*, *The Year's Best Fantasy and Horror* and *Midnight Graffiti*. He moved to England in 1993 with his wife Jane, since when he has published the novels *Celestial Dogs*, *Blood* and *Burning Bright*.

———————————— •►• ————————————

Weird happenings in New York City are as common as roaches in restaurant kitchens – hell, anyone can have their very own otherworldly experience for the buck and a half it costs to ride the subway – but this is something that happened to me.

There's a neat little bar down in Greenwich Village, tucked away inside what looks like a residential courtyard, so that you sort of have to know which wrought-iron gate to walk through to find your way in. Apparently there's also a more visible entrance to the place, but the quirky, vaguely spooky doorway is the only one that I know. I haven't been there in many years – I don't even know if it's still in business – but I later learned that the place is fairly well known. Apparently, it's been there since the days when the bums on the Bowery were spitting on horse-drawn carriages instead of wind-shields for their two-bit handouts.

I was never a regular at this particular drinks emporium, but it was an OK enough place to go for a short beer before dinner or a nice conversation after. The house was great about buying drinks back for customers, and you could nurse a glass and sit and chat all evening without being assaulted by 120 decibels of whatever was top of the pops that week.

And that goofy entryway really was pretty cool.

This all happened right after I graduated from college and was working in the city as a slave labourer for a horrid little video firm. Most every Friday night I'd meet up with a couple of buddies for some beers and a nice dinner. None of us had girlfriends at the time and we all hated our jobs, so Fridays were pretty well the highlight of the week.

One particular Friday, smack dab in the middle of a cold January – every city has its own brand of cold, you know; Chicago's may be windier and Boston's snowier, but there's something about a New York winter that freezes your guts no matter *how* many layers of clothing you're wearing – I got lucky. I was supposed to take the afternoon to run some errand for my pharaoh's taskmaster of a boss and then head home, but, *mirabile dictu*, the job only took half as long as it should have. The afternoon was *mine*!

I tried spending the time fruitfully. Honest I did. I poked around the Strand and Barnes & Noble book stores, hit a few record shops (Christ, this is so long ago that they still sold recorded music on vinyl), grabbed a quick slice of pizza at Ray's Famous.

Did I mention that a New York winter will turn your backside into a buttsicle? Right, sorry.

So there I was, cold as the proverbial Wiccan's hooter, with a good couple of hours to kill before my buddies showed up for a pitcher or three of Molson and a burger-all-the-way at the old Jimmy Day's on West 4th Street, when

I realized I was no more than a pebble's throw from the neat little bar with the cool entrance.

What was a boy to do?

I walked, briskly, the couple of blocks to the bar just as dusk was taking serious hold and the January wind grew that extra little vampire's incisor of a fang. It was almost normal Friday quitting time and the sidewalks were getting busy, but the bar is off on a little nowhere street and there was nobody else in sight. As always, I got a little confused about which gate opened on to the path to the bar – there's no sign, of course – but I managed to find it while I still had feeling left in six of my toes.

The big gate swung open and I passed through the familiar, if gloomy, little passage that led on to the courtyard. It was getting pretty dark now, with just a trace of fading daylight left to illuminate the courtyard from above the five-storey buildings surrounding it. There were lights set along the path, but for some reason they hadn't been turned on yet.

As I came out into the courtyard, I saw a couple dancing in the middle of the square. Nothing too weird, you might think, except that the couple were dressed in costumes like something out of the eighteenth century, powdered wigs and all. The man was tall and stocky with puffy, chipmunk cheeks, wearing a silk brocade jacket and knee-length pants with high stockings. The woman wore some fancy, floor-length silvery ball gown, cut low on her considerable chest. Not to sound like a perv or a sexist, but I believe it was precisely this look for which the word '*décolletage*' was coined. We're talking Wonderbra-plus here, no fooling.

You get used to strange shit in New York. There was the Viking dude who used to bongo on the manhole covers up around 57th Street, and some grimy cat named Poet O who'd regale you with his epic verse in Washington Square. There are bag ladies and bums and goofballs by the score practically begging for a sliver of attention if you're fool enough to let it stray.

But it's not every day you see a couple dancing in a dark courtyard, in the bitter January cold, dressed like George and Martha Washington.

I watched them for a minute – there was no music, by the by – but neither of them so much as glanced at me. They were pretty good, I thought, and though the outfits didn't look any too warm, neither dancer seemed bothered by the weather.

Finally, *I* got cold and dashed across the courtyard and into the bar. I stole a last glance at the couple before I went in, but they just waltzed on.

The place was empty inside. I sat at the bar, but it was a couple of minutes before the bartender wandered over. I ordered a beer and asked the obvious question.

'They shooting a movie here today?'

New York's not as bad as L.A. (what is?), but at times it seems you can't swing a dead actor on a Manhattan sidewalk without hitting a film crew at work. I just assumed that's what was happening here.

The bartender shook his head.

I described for him what I'd seen in the courtyard and he looked at me like I had a weasel on my head. He came back out from behind the bar and walked to the door. He stuck his head out, then beckoned me over.

The lights had come on outside, but the courtyard was as quiet as a schoolhouse on Sunday. No sign of George or Martha. A couple of women in business suits were coming up the path, though, so the bartender scooted back inside. I stood there for a moment, holding the door open, but it was cold and there was nothing out there to see.

I sat in a corner for a while, doing the *New York Times* crossword and sipping my beer. It was almost time to brave the elements again and go meet my buddies when I noticed a painting on the wall on my way to the men's room. It was a ballroom scene, with many people dancing and a band playing. A bald fiddler was highlighted in the foreground.

It was one of the painted dancers that caught my eye. Her partner had been depicted half turned away from the viewer, but the artist had caught the woman full-on. I have to admit that the faces of all the women in the painting looked pretty much alike – there was a reason this old piece of crap was hanging in a bar near the toilet – but I'd swear on a stack of Arkham House first editions that I'd seen that *décolletage* before.

Outside. In the courtyard.

I stared at the painting for a while, trying to connect further the painted couple to the ones I'd seen dancing. Crazy as soap on a rope, I know, but it seriously freaked me out. I thought about saying something to the bartender, but I simply didn't have the nerve.

I don't believe in the supernatural, even if I do sometimes write about it. Certainly there are obvious and easy explanations for what I saw. Like I say, they shoot a lot of movies in New York, and it *was* a crap painting. But I've never had another experience quite like it.

I also haven't been back to that bar.

ADAM SIMON

The Darkness Between the Frames

Adam Simon (b. 1962) was born in Chicago, and currently lives in a house perched precariously on a hill above Malibu. He attended Harvard University from 1980 to 1984 and won the Student Academy Award for his thesis film, *Swamp Song*. After studying at the University of Paris for a year, his short film for the University of Southern California, *The Blue*, was selected by the Movie Channel's *First Take* and distributed internationally on video in the *New American Shorts* series. He wrote three plays for Tim Robbins and the Actor's Gang which were produced in Los Angeles, New York and at the Edinburgh Festival, before making his feature-directing début in 1990 with *Brain Dead* for Roger Corman, based on an uproduced screenplay by Charles Beaumont. The film won the Academy of Horror and Science Fiction's Golden Scroll Award and the Drive-In Movie of the Year and Best Director awards in Joe Bob Briggs's Drive-In Academy Awards, as well as making the *New York Daily News'* Year's Ten Best list. He followed it with *Body Chemistry II: The Voice of a Stranger* and *Carnosaur*, which also received the Academy of Horror and Science Fiction's Golden Scroll Award and became Corman's highest-grossing film to date. His recent television film about director Sam Fuller, *The Typewriter, the Rifle and the Movie Camera*, won the 1996 Cable Ace Award for Best Cultural/Arts Documentary.

> Meaning is invisible. But the invisible is not the contra-
> diction of the visible: the visible itself has an invisible
> inner framework. The invisible is the secret face of the
> visible.
>
>   M. Merleau-Ponty

Movies have always had some fundamental relation to the supernatural. There have been horror films almost from the moment the medium was invented. And much of the apparatus and form of film goes back not only to the magicians' magic lantern, but further, to the strange apparatuses of Athanasius Kircher.

Kircher, one of the towering figures of that lost renaissance of the sixteenth and seventeenth centuries, on the very borders of ancient magic and modern science, created projected phantasms of the beyond (in between making very exact drawings of the structure of Noah's Ark, mapping the secret interior of the Earth and developing a kind of slide-rule for calculating the name of God in every language).

So cinema, not only from its origins, but from its phantasmagoric pre-history, has always been allied with the greater mysteries. As if the real mission of film were, from the start, not simply to record the visible, but the invisible.

Within the filmic apparatus itself lies a buried clue not only to its own internal mysteries, but perhaps to the greater ones that surround us. When we see a series of still frames projected, why do we perceive a single, complete illusion of reality? Every scientific attempt at explanation has failed. It might as well be magic. We simply don't know. But one simple fact remains. When you sit through a two-hour movie, for fully one of those hours you have sat in total darkness. For each $\frac{1}{24}$ of a second of image, we also see $\frac{1}{24}$ of a second of blackness. But we don't see the blackness. Instead we misperceive a continuous illusion of reality. Remove that blackness, show it all and you would see nothing but a blur. Indeed, as Merleau-Ponty said, the visible does have an invisible secret face.

Perhaps then, when we 'encounter', when we experience a glimpse of the strange, whether it be a ghost, a clairvoyant dream, coincidence or synchronicity, we are encountering not an intrusion into normal reality but rather a glimpse of the baroque, often grotesque clockwork that runs reality; a deep glance into the darkness between the frames. A blackness whose very presence creates the illusion of normal reality.

There was a time when thinking and speaking the invisible parts of reality was itself normal. No tale, no philosophy, no image did not seek also to depict the invisible. But over time such thoughts were banished, first to the realms of Romantic art, and then even within the realms of art they were squeezed into the narrow cramped confines of the genres. We who work in and around the genres have in a way allowed this. We conspire with the small-minded realists to lock the truth away into scary closets. In a world where the knowledge of the invisible is repressed or left to the religiously fanatic, the lunatic or, worse yet, the drippy New Ager, the intimations of the invisible would of course appear as monstrous. But real encounters with the invisible are not always, or even usually, moments of horror, but are often moments of love.

My grandmother died when I was about four years old. She had been born in a *shtetl* in Poland that, either despite or because of the grey mud and blood of poverty and pogroms, was awash in a kind of magic, particularly of the cabalistic and Hasidic variety. She was rumoured to have powers. She was a respected woman, a kind of matriarch, sought after for advice, match-making, conflict resolution. Also tealeaf-reading. My grandfather was a tailor. He could guess your size. But she could see your soul. I don't really remember her much. I only remember her eyes, and the dark rings around them, and the fat folds of her freckled face creased with wrinkles. And I remember her in a dream years after her death, floating down a staircase towards me. On her deathbed my grandmother swore to my mother that she would return from the dead to save me from some danger that she foresaw. Six months after she died I was diagnosed with spinal meningitis. My mother refused to allow a spinal tap. She insisted on waiting twenty-four hours. The next day, after a night of horrible pain and fever dreams, I had only a mild ear infection. The doctors were baffled enough to write it up in the Indiana State Medical Association records. A short, dry case-study. Unexplained. Every sign and symptom of spinal meningitis, dangerously high fever and semi-paralysis; brought back to the hospital less than twenty-four hours later with no fever, no pain, just a small localized infection of the inner ear.

There are no such things as scientific explanations; only descriptions. Science substitutes 'how' for 'why' every time. Yes, the disease was gone. How? By moving from my spine to my ear. But why? No, it's not impossible. It just hadn't ever been recorded before, at least not in the state of Indiana, up to the year 1967.

The ancient Greeks (and for that matter most other peoples at some time) saw almost every encounter with nature as a sign. Every bird who flew carried a message. I'm not sure they were wrong. How many times a day do we move through nature, signs all around us, but are deaf to them, trained not to respond? The Cabalists believed that the world itself was constructed out of the names of God, that the very fabric of reality was God's signature and that knowing the formulae of its construction would allow one not only to see the face of the Creator, but to become a mini-creator, a kind of demiurge, oneself, and to be able to alter and work upon nature. This is not opposed to science. This *is* science. But science has forgotten that this is where it came from. That it was born from the very parts of religion, the mystical and magical portions of it, which were as repressed by the orthodox as the nascent sciences were.

I grew up reading horror fiction and literature of the supernatural. But as I get older, though I still read it, think it, dream it, film it, I tend more and more to wonder if there is another way. Is there a way of telling stories, making images of this world, this other part of the world, which could escape from the Gothic, escape from the dark fantastic, and do justice to the strangeness of a world that is sometimes, but not always, in shadow? Maybe it's not possible. Maybe it is simply true, as Melville says, 'though the visible world seems formed in love, the invisible spheres were formed in fright'. I often read works on and from the history of religion now. I find much of the same *frisson* in an old gnostic text, a Jewish description of the ascent through the spheres, a Sufi love poem or a mystic nun's hypnagogic visions as I once did from Lovecraft.

I am not suggesting we abandon for ever the field of horror and all become spiritual writers or artists. But I do think we need to start to recognize the ways in which horror and the supernatural have always been a kind of spiritual literature. An attempt to grapple with the reality of the invisible. There are horror writers of our time, dead and alive, who afford us brilliant glimpses of the invisible world: I think not only of Lovecraft but of Machen, Aickman, Campbell, of Etchison and King and Barker. But we must sometimes wonder what would it read like if we wrote of the invisible world without automatic recourse to the emotion of fear. John Crowley has achieved this lately. Both *Aegypt* and *Love and Sleep* are windows into the invisible, filled with light, with life, with love, and some deep terrors too. And Tarkovsky did it. He might be the only film-maker yet who has really achieved it. Though sometimes tedious, his work remains the closest any of us has come to filming the invisible. And he did it without Industrial Light and Magic.

I remain convinced that the real encounters are all around us. I believe we live in a world filled with them. I know a man who has watched the storms come in off the Pacific Ocean side by side with the ghost of his cousin.

Once, when a foetus was aborted, its little spirit escaped into a mouse and ran up the father's pant leg.

And there is a man who carries a watch which is oddly connected to the life of his heart: every time the old watch stops or breaks down, so does his relationship.

Two twins saw a perfect formation of twelve white geese, followed by one black one. Within weeks, one of them slipped from this world through the veil into the painful light of a temporary psychosis.

A few houses away from me the owners often see a man rocking in a chair. A man who died twenty years ago.

A friend once made protective spells around my home. Two weeks later a firestorm blasted the area – flames surrounded the old wooden house stuffed to the rafters with books, surrounded it on all sides. My neighbour, who was on his roof at the time watering his house, says he saw the fire simply leap over, leaving my home intact.

But the real encounters might well not be these dramatic meetings with the dead, or moments of clairvoyance, but the constant waves of little truths, little coincidences, little fates that make up our lives. Each of us could count hundreds of such events. But recounting the synchronicities and encounters of our life must inevitably be boring to anyone else. Boring in the way that the recounting of dreams is boring.

We began with film and end with dreams. Call the lighted images 'waking life', call the black frames 'sleep' or 'dream'. The average person spends something like one-third of their life asleep. Just think, over an eighty-five-year life one might have spent twenty-eight years in another world. Years and years of unavoidable confrontation with strangeness, with the invisible. Even the most hard-headed analytical philosopher, the rationalist, the pragmatist, the scientist who denies all but the visible and explainable, must sleep. And in his sleep he betrays all his philosophies by flying, by becoming a tree, by eating a window, by dreaming.

We could not live without dreaming, any more than the

film could be seen without the black spaces in between. And yet we say, 'It was only a dream,' and dismiss one-third of our lives as simply unreal. But I say: Realism is only another genre, and a narrow one at that. The literature of the imagination might some day be liberated from the Gothic chains the rationalists bound it with.

They say: Write what you know.

I say: The imagination is a sense organ for knowing the invisible.

GUY N. SMITH

The Mist People

Guy N. Smith (b. 1939) was born in Tamworth, Shropshire. His mother was the historical novelist E. M. Weale, and even as a schoolboy it was evident that he would follow in her footsteps. He was first published at the age of twelve in a local newspaper, but his father insisted that he pursue a career in banking, which he did from 1956 to 1975. After contributing stories to such periodicals as *Dixon Hawke* and the *London Mystery Selection*, his first novel, *Werewolf By Moonlight*, appeared in 1974. Since then he has published nearly ninety books in all genres, although he is still best known for such horror novels as the bestselling *Night of the Crabs* (and its five sequels), *The Sucking Pit*, *The Slime Beast*, *Bats Out of Hell*, *Satan's Snowdrop*, *Abomination*, *The Festering*, *Carnivore*, *Witch Spell*, *The Knighton Vampires*, *The Dark One* and *Dead End*. He has also written a number of non-fiction books on countryside matters; westerns; crime and mystery thrillers; and a series of children's animal novels under the pseudonym of 'Jonathan Guy'. His *Writing Horror Fiction* is a recent manual for aspiring authors. Smith is the UFO co-ordinator for South Shropshire and Powys and is also involved in the on-going Loch Ness project.

I have used a pendulum for more years than I care to remember. My initial experiments were directed at ascertaining whether or not foods contained any additives which were harmful to me. Surprisingly, the results were very accurate and I progressed further. One of my 'party tricks' was to ask guests to place some objects beneath an upturned cup or mug in a row of several. Invariably, and much to my audience's amazement, the pendulum discovered the hidden object every time.

In effect, it is a very simple procedure akin to divining. In fact, using the pendulum, I located an underground spring when we were contemplating drilling a borehole for our water supply. There was water in that exact spot, sure enough – 128 feet below ground.

The method whereby the pendulum is used varies from individual to individual, and I have read of other ways which are in direct contrast to my own. But, if they work for you, you don't confuse the issue by using other methods. Virtually any object can be used; my wife uses her pendant and I began with a piece of tapered sealing wax on a length of string. However, my own pendulum is a metallic one purchased from a specialist shop.

I hold it perfectly still at its fullest extent directly above the object which I am investigating. I need to be perfectly relaxed and keep an open mind; I think that on one or two occasions when I have been tense I have influenced the answers which I am seeking. The pendulum will only give a negative or positive answer to the question asked, it cannot elaborate. If the answer is 'No' it rotates in an anti-clockwise direction, for 'Yes' it moves clockwise. If it is unsure it either moves hesitantly to and fro or remains stationary.

Having exhausted my repertoire of party tricks and established which foods did not suit me, I decided to experiment with the supernatural. My theory was that if the pendulum could 'tune in' to inanimate objects then perhaps it could make contact with something much more interesting.

A friend had a resident ghost; a friendly enough haunting, but at times the spirit became very active within the house and nobody got any peace and quiet for hours on end. Val had actually seen her once: a beautiful woman in her mid-twenties, seemingly of South American origin. So, what was this lovely spook doing in mid-Wales? I was invited to go along and find out.

The house in question was a terraced one in a narrow street and the ghost was most active in the spare bedroom. There were four of us that evening, the lady of the house and a friend, my wife and myself. I must confess that as we all made our way upstairs I was secretly sceptical. It would all be a big let-down, an anti-climax, and I wouldn't bother to try to contact anything on the other side again. How wrong I was! It turned out to be the most spectacular of all my experiments.

I positioned the pendulum and enquired of the beautiful female ghost whether or not she was around tonight. Within seconds the pendulum was spinning in a clockwise direction; I could feel it pulling as though it were trying to jerk itself out of my grasp. In addition, there was a prickling right up my spine and into my scalp. *She* was at home tonight, all right!

Everybody in the room confessed to a prickling of their flesh. I moved from question to question; some she answered positively, others she either ignored or did not understand. I went through several of the South American countries until she told me that she came from Brazil. How had she died? The pendulum remained rock steady – because ghosts are not aware that they are dead, something which I learned on that first night.

We moved to the adjacent bedroom. She was stubborn, she didn't want to follow us. So we went back into the spare bedroom.

Before long the other three became excited because they could see a kind of mist rising from the pendulum. I was unable to discern it. Then this mist formed into a mass like dense drizzle in the far corner, but again it was invisible to myself. My companions on that night claimed that at times the 'mist' almost assumed human shape. I can only conclude that our ghost was trying to materialize (as she had done on the previous occasion when Val had seen her), but for some reason was unable to accomplish it. This resulted in her going into a sulk: the mist faded away and the pendulum refused to move at all. So we packed up and left our haunting in peace.

Some weeks later Val phoned and asked me to try again. My wife had a prior appointment, so this time there were just the two women and myself present. And our ghost was exceedingly active! She clearly became bored with being asked the same questions as last time and, as there are only so many things you can enquire of a supernatural entity, I changed my approach. This time I was really going to put her to the test.

Yes, she very much liked being here.

'Good. Would you like to come back to my house?'

I gave the invitation on impulse, held my breath. What a damned stupid thing to ask. Suppose she said –

The pendulum almost flew out of my hand in a clockwise direction. Oh, Gawd, I had gone and done it now! Still, maybe she was only teasing and, anyway, spooks don't usually change their favourite hauntings. Do they?

My companions were intrigued. I asked them to go downstairs, open the front door and stand in the hallway. Then we'd see if this Brazilian woman really did want to accompany me back home. If so, then I'd think up some explanation for my wife on the way.

'She's right behind you!' Val was staring beyond me as I slowly descended the narrow stairs. Her friend's eyes were bulging, her mouth was open; she was lost for words. 'The mist . . .' Val gasped, 'she's trying to form.'

I glanced briefly behind me but, as before and as on so many occasions in the future, I could see nothing at all. So I just kept on walking, down the hallway and through the open door, right out on to the street.

I unlocked my car and got in. There was no sign of anything untoward. I breathed a sigh of relief. Whatever the others had seen, it had obviously changed its mind and stayed at Val's house. Another game of teasing. I had thrown down the gauntlet but our Brazilian ghost had backed down at the last moment.

I had a drive of some eight miles along lonely country roads to reach my home. I had gone about three miles when that familiar prickling began and, at one stage, I thought my hair was going to stand upright. The spiritual being had accepted my invitation. *She was right there in the car with me.*

How does one explain to one's wife that you have brought a beautiful young woman back home with you and that she might be staying indefinitely? I didn't even try. Jean was busy baking when I walked into the house, so I went straight through to the lounge. Maybe it was all in the mind, mine and Val's and her friend's.

A few minutes later I heard Jean give a cry of surprise and annoyance. She came through from the kitchen to check where I was. Somebody (or something) had prodded her playfully. Well, it wasn't me, but I decided that I'd better come clean. She wasn't convinced ... until some time later she was poked in the back again!

We agreed to say nothing about our 'guest', neither to our teenage sons nor to our cleaner, who admits to having a somewhat nervous disposition. Perhaps Makita (I don't know where I got the name from, but I decided our Brazilian lodger had better have a name) would decide to go back to Val's.

The following day our cleaner came downstairs from dusting my upper office and seemed slightly puzzled. Nothing specific, she told me, but she got the idea that there was somebody standing behind her. However, every time she looked around there was nobody there. Ah well, it was time to be honest again. Fortunately, Brenda was not frightened, just intrigued.

We didn't tell our sons; they wouldn't have believed us, anyway. Far better that they found out about Makita for themselves. A few days later our younger son, Angus, brought a friend home. They sat on the sofa in the lounge watching television. I was working in my upstairs office.

Angus's bedroom is adjacent to my office. At some stage in the evening I heard footsteps in his room. That was not unusual: he often comes upstairs to fetch videos. Then I heard the footsteps go back along the corridor and into our daughter's room at the far end, immediately above the lounge. That wasn't altogether unusual, either, for our family often borrowed tapes from each other and went looking for them. Except that my flesh began to prickle again . . .

I went downstairs to the lounge. Angus and his friend were sprawled on the sofa watching a film. They denied having come upstairs and I believed them. Furthermore, they accused me of walking around noisily in the bedroom directly above!

After the first week Makita's activities grew less. In fact, I almost forgot about her and one day I realized that I hadn't heard or sensed her for some days. I telephoned Val. Yes, Makita was back home and as active as ever!

I've accepted many invitations to take my pendulum along to haunted places. Responses vary. I find that in the case of a very old haunting, particularly if the ghost is that of an uneducated person, then the response is very poor. They either don't understand or they don't want to be disturbed. Sometimes a ghost becomes angry at my interference and then the pendulum goes crazy.

One interesting factor in every case where mist has either come from the pendulum or else shimmered like drizzle in the room is that others have seen it and remarked upon it but I have never witnessed it personally. In any case, I prefer witnesses to recount what they have seen, or else I might stand accused of manipulating the pendulum by some means. I have nothing to gain by perpetrating a trick.

Unfortunately, my efforts have been sensationalized and the press treats it all as a big joke. Worse, those who have invited me to contact a ghost on their premises have sometimes phoned and asked me to return – so that they can invite other members of the family to come along and see if they can see the 'mist people'. So, nowadays, I'm very discerning about where I go to swing the pendulum.

It has all been an interesting and exciting experiment and I've enjoyed every minute of it. Material for research is an added bonus.

MICHAEL MARSHALL SMITH

Mr Cat

Michael Marshall Smith (b. 1965) was born in Knutsford, Cheshire, and grew up in the United States, South Africa and Australia before moving to north London. After earning a degree in Philosophy from Cambridge University, he spent some time as a comedy writer and performer for BBC Radio. After being presented with the British Fantasy Award for Best Newcomer in 1991, his short stories 'The Man Who Drew Cats' and 'The Dark Land' won two consecutive British Fantasy Awards in 1991 and 1992, and he received another in 1996 for 'More Tomorrow' (which was also nominated for a World Fantasy Award). His fiction has appeared in *The Best New Horror* and *The Year's Best Fantasy and Horror* series, *Dark Terrors* and *Dark Terrors 2* and *3*, *Dark Voices 2, 4, 5* and *6*, *Darklands* and *Darklands 2*, *Touch Wood: Narrow Houses Volume Two*, *The Mammoth Book of Zombies*, *The Mammoth Book of Werewolves*, *The Mammoth Book of Frankenstein*, *The Mammoth Book of Dracula*, *Lethal Kisses*, *A Book of Two Halves*, *Twists of the Tale: Cat Horror Stories*, *The Anthology of Fantasy & the Supernatural*, *Shadows Over Innsmouth* and *Omni*. His début novel, *Only Forward*, won the British Fantasy Society's August Derleth Award for Best Novel in 1995, and he has followed it with *Spares* (which was optioned by Steven Spielberg's DreamWorks SKG) and *One of Us*.

I don't know what the following is. It's not a ghostly encounter, but it is inexplicable. To me, anyway. Probably to anyone else it will just sound like a couple of coincidences, with a dash of wishful thinking thrown in. All I can say is that I don't believe it is, and I had to think hard about whether I wanted to write about it or not. Maybe, like dreams and coincidences, it is a personal event, which only really means something to the person to whom it happened. But if so, then perhaps, like dreams and coincidences, it's a glimpse of what the world is really like. Either way, here it is.

Our family had a cat for many years. When we got him as a kitten from the RSPCA we christened him Whiskers, in a blinding spasm of originality, but gradually he became known as Fred, and finally just as Mr Cat. It was as if our attempts to name him fell short of trying to capture him. In the end his name became as irrelevant to us as our own.

I was about nine when we got him, and Mr Cat was there every step of my childhood and adolescence. He slept on my bed; perched on my windowsill watching the wildlife; and, when I started to go out in the evenings and come back the worse for wear, he'd be sitting behind the door in a house full of sleeping people, waiting to welcome me home. He grew from a kitten full of ludicrous energy into a stately elder of regal grace, and quickly became so central to my family's life that it was impossible to imagine what it had been like without him. Though perfectly capable of batting birds out of the air, he was the most affable cat imaginable, and would often sit at a particular point in the driveway conversing in some silent, catty way with the black cat from next door. They'd meet up, peer together at nothing in particular for a while and then go their separate ways.

When I went away to college he was already getting old, and by the time I was back and living in London he was fifteen, and his health was patchy. At that time I was working for a company which, pointlessly enough, was the trade association for corporate video makers. One of my main tasks was to organize and administrate an annual convention in Bournemouth in the middle of summer. The Sunday before I was due to go down to set things up I got a call from my mother. Mr Cat had become very ill, and I was advised to go home and see him before he died.

I did, and found him hiding on my windowsill, panting and barely able to move. He had very severe flu, and the vet said he had a day or so left, at most.

I sat with him for a while, listening to his laboured breathing. He tried to respond to stroking as he always had, but he was really very ill. The intermittent croak which came from his chest sounded more like a rattle than a purr. Sitting with him in the room where I'd spent my childhood, I realized that for the first time in my life I wanted something badly enough to pray for it.

Feeling more than a little stupid, I whispered the following – not to God, because I don't especially believe in Him, but just to Whom It Might Concern.

'He's only little,' I said. 'He can't hack this flu. Give it to me. I'm much bigger, and I'll be all right. Take his flu and give it to me.'

Nothing happened, of course. I spent a couple more hours at home, brightly agreeing with the rest of the family that he'd had a good life, then took the tube back into London.

On Tuesday I drove a van full of convention-orientated crap down to Bournemouth, and set about marshalling three hundred guests, irritable speakers, turbulent hotel staff and losers of every other stripe and description. A hectic task, but I'd done it before, and didn't expect it to be difficult.

It wasn't, except that on Tuesday afternoon I started feeling a bit strange. Rather ill, in fact. By eight o'clock I had a cracking headache, and my arms and back felt so tired I could barely lift them. I rang my parents in the evening, as a matter of course. Mr Cat was still alive. Barely.

I woke up on Wednesday feeling like death. Perhaps it

was a combination of Vitamin C overdose and a mild hangover, but by the afternoon I felt so ill I was delirious. There was no one else who could do my job so I had to soldier on, but I felt like one of the shambling dead with a head full of hot, wet sand. The only time I've felt worse was having pharyngitis a few years before.

Thursday I can barely remember. But in the evening I called home again, and heard that Mr Cat had eaten some food for the first time in five days.

Friday was the last day of the convention, and on Saturday I came back to London. The flu, cold, whatever it was, lasted a couple more days, and then it was gone.

Mr Cat got completely better, and lived for another two years.

Maybe it was just a coincidence. It didn't feel like it. I didn't tell anyone about what had happened in my bedroom. I think I believed that something had taken place there, some favour been granted, and that if I blabbed about it the magic would be taken away.

There are two small postscripts to this story.

I went home again on the day that he did eventually die. We all knew he wasn't going to get better this time, and the vet was called for 3.15 p.m., to help him on his way. Mr Cat died at 3.10, just as the vet's car was pulling into the drive. Almost, we felt, as if he wanted to go under his own steam, to leave in his own good time.

He was buried in the front garden, near where he used to sit in the drive. It's been about six years now, and sometimes the black cat from next door still comes and sits in the driveway, just in front of Mr Cat's grave. He stays there for a little while, looking at nothing in particular, and then gets up and walks away.

S. P. SOMTOW

In the Realm of the Spirits

S. P. Somtow (b. 1952) was born Somtow Papinian Suchar-itkul in Bangkok, Thailand. He grew up in Japan and Europe and was educated at Eton and St Catherine's College, Cambridge. His grandfather, whose two sisters were both married to King Rama VI of Siam, was the proud possessor of a small harem. He began a career as a post-serialist composer in south-east Asia, but turned to writing short stories in the late 1970s, winning the 1981 John W. Campbell Award for best new writer and the Locus Award for his first novel, *Starship and Haiku*. Since then he has published more than twenty books, including a trilogy about twelve-year-old vampire rock star Timmy Valentine: *Valentine*, *Vampire Junction* and *Vanitas*; plus *The Fallen Country*, *The Wizard's Apprentice*, *The Aquiliad*, *Armorica*, *Riverrun*, *Mallworld*, *The Shattered Horse*, *Forgetting Places*, *Moondance* and the semi-autobiographical *Jasmine Nights*. His short fiction is collected in *Fire from the Wine-Dark Sea*, *Chui Chai*, *Nova*, *My Cold Mad Father* and *The Pavilion of Frozen Women* (which takes its title from his World Fantasy Award-nominated novella). More recently, he has directed the low-budget genre movies *The Laughing Dead* and *Ill Met By Moonlight*. Somtow currently commutes between his homes in Los Angeles and Bangkok.

In my semi-autobiographical novel *Jasmine Nights*, a young boy is growing up on a huge, baroquely fantastical family estate in Bangkok, surrounded by eccentric relatives and weird architecture. There are servants, a polygamous patriarch, dangerous liaisons galore – and the odd supernatural event.

The fictional estate is actually a conflation of two different estates: my grandfather's in the city of Thonburi, where he actually did live, surrounded by wives, concubines and mistresses much as described in my novel; the other estate was part of my mother's inheritance. It was there that I actually lived. There was a huge mango orchard, a small artificial lake with a pavilion, a ruined house where I played, and the main house, also known as The Blue House – one of those rambling wooden structures that are often seen in historical movies about the British Raj.

Thailand is a country with more ghosts than people. The belief in the omnipresence of spirits comes from animism, the dominant tribal religion in the region in the days before the inhabitants of the peninsula were converted to Buddhism by the missionary zeal of King Ashoka.

Today, the house I grew up in is a multi-storey condominium, and across the street is a techno-rave establishment frequented by teenagers. But the spirit population hasn't gone down.

Recently, for instance, a woman threw herself off the top floor of my aunt's office building. My aunt immediately engaged an exorcist to appease the *phii tai hong* – that is, the vengeful ghost of someone who has died violently. It was as normal a thing to do as hiring a new secretary or putting in new filing cabinets.

I wrote a short story about a Thai boy and an American boy who spend the night in a cemetery in order to get a winning lottery number from the spirits. Since it's the night before the results are announced, there's a whole convention's worth of people in the graveyard all camped out. The boys encounter a *phii grasue*, which is a monster consisting of a decapitated head with trailing guts, slithering around using its tongue as a pseudopod. They are briefly transported into Heaven for an encounter with the Thai boy's dead great-aunt. Now, here's the point I'm making. A friend of mine was teaching a course in modern fantastic literature in Arizona, and he had a Thai student in the class. This is one of the stories he had the students read.

The young man from Thailand couldn't figure out why he had to read my story. 'There is', he said to my friend, 'no fantasy element in it.'

This, you must understand, is the prevailing atmosphere in the land where I grew up, so any real-life incidents I relate here must be understood in that context.

Everybody knew that The Blue House was haunted. That it was a magical place where the rules were somewhat fuzzier than elsewhere. Ghosts were common. Everyone sees ghosts all the time in Thailand anyway, but they loved to congregate at The Blue House, especially at the veranda which over-looked the garden and which was always permeated with the sickly-sweet odour of *phuttachat*, a night-blooming jasmine.

My bedroom looked out over this veranda, and shortly after my great-grandmother's death (the servants having gossiped for days about a black cat having leaped out of her funeral pyre) I did have occasion to see her, hovering in mid-air, at the window, gibbering about her will. I was always terrified of my great-grandmother when I was little. She had a skeletal face, and her teeth were completely black from chewing betelnut. Her hair was wispy and white. In death, she was even more frightening. I woke up the maid (Thai children of upper-class families tend to have a maid sleeping at the foot of their beds) and I screamed, pointed and shouted; she saw nothing.

The will was never found, and to this day the finances of my late grandparents and step-grandparents are a matter of controversy and conjecture.

Most of the events were less terrifying, though. For instance, I woke up one night to see a winged horse in my room. Not a full-size one – this one was about the size of my palm. It fluttered about. The night was all softly back-lit, and blue and hazy, very Spielbergian in fact; and I was not at all afraid. I got out of bed and followed the mini-Pegasus all over the house until it reached the bedroom of my little sister.

The horse hovered over her pillow, pointing with a foreleg, waiting for something ... I don't know. Well, I looked under the pillow and discovered, to my delight, a bright red hundred-*baht* note. That's only about £2, but this was, you understand, 1961 or so. A fortune. In 1961, a servant's wages were about fifty pence – excuse me, ten bob – a week.

I was amazed at this supernatural largesse. I took the money to school (a British school, mind you) and showed it to all my friends. Around lunchtime, one of the maids came marching into the school yard. Everyone had been accused of stealing, and the house was in an uproar. I gave the money back, but my explanation of how I had obtained it never seemed to convince anyone.

But how else could I have known that it was there?

Back at the British school, the kids a year ahead of me were putting on a production of *A Midsummer Night's Dream*. For a couple of weeks, I had dreams that impelled me to memorize the part of Bottom, even though I had nothing to do with this production.

That day, my friend Kwonping Ho – now a big Singapore tycoon – mysteriously fell ill, and I just 'happened' to know the part. And did it, too. Rather badly, as I recall.

It's this childhood incident that compelled me, thirty years later, to make a film of *A Midsummer Night's Dream*, so obviously it has haunted me.

The Blue House, indeed, has haunted me all my life. Shortly after my tenth birthday, we moved away to a modern, split-level American-style home. Since then, I have never experienced any supernatural events whatsoever. Oh, perhaps a slight *frisson* now and then – but never the real thing.

BRIAN STABLEFORD

Chacun sa Goule

Brian Stableford (b. 1948) lectured in Sociology at the University of Reading until 1988, wrote full-time from 1989 to 1995, and is currently employed as a part-time lecturer at the University of the West of England teaching courses in 'The Development of Science in a Cultural Context'. He has published more than forty science fiction and fantasy novels, including *The Empire of Fear, The Werewolves of London, The Angel of Pain, Young Blood, Serpent's Blood, Salamander's Fire, Chimera's Cradle, The Hunger and Ecstasy of Vampires* and its sequel *The Black Blood of the Dead*. A prolific writer about the history of imaginative fiction, he was a leading contributor to the award-winning *Encyclopedia of Science Fiction* edited by John Clute and Peter Nicholls, and contributed numerous articles to Clute and John Grant's *Encyclopedia of Fantasy*. He has also published a number of anthologies and volumes of translations relating to the French and English Decadent movements of the late nineteenth century.

We are all haunted. The dead are all around us, in substance and in spirit. Every breath we take draws in carbon atoms that were once incorporated into the bodies of other men; with every mouthful of food we engulf the remains of our ancestors. As we devour them they devour us, fuelling the slow fire of life – the fire whose ashes are absorbed, in the end, into the earth and her fruits, or lost on the wings of the wind.

Our inescapable fate is to be eaten and breathed in our turn.

Once we are conscious of the ever-presence of the dead we can easily feel their nearness. To see them, and to hear their voices, is only a little more difficult – but that is not the essence of being haunted. We are not haunted because we sometimes see invisible ghosts, or hear their inaudible words; we are haunted because, in our imagination, *they see us*. In seeing us, even though their sight is imaginary, they know our inmost thoughts.

We have no secrets from the dead.

Those of us who seek to avoid our ghosts cannot win free of them by mere denial. We may narrow our field of view to brute facts and causal explanations, refusing the commitment of belief to everything save evidence and natural law, but our experience of the world remains stubbornly magical. Fear and desire colour everything we see and hear; we cannot observe things as they are without knowing what they might be. Meaning is everywhere in the human world, and meaning is a heritage: the gift of ghosts.

Those of us who hope that we are wise do not try to avoid our ghosts. We try, instead, to choose them: to select from the infinite mazes of shadow those precious shades with which we would like to become more intimately acquainted.

Novelists and historians are no more haunted than anyone else, in the passive sense, but by taking an active part in their own haunting they may make better contact with individual phantoms. The characters which novelists and historians create – and historians *do* create their characters, albeit in imitation of people who once lived and breathed – are not ghosts themselves but they are very like ghosts in certain significant ways. They are seen too clearly and heard too plainly, but they have the same facility that ghosts have for being there when they are not, for seeing and hearing us without the need of eyes and ears. Most importantly of all, characters are built out of materials borrowed from the world of ghosts.

All fictions are ghouls, fed according to the cannibal habit on the icons of the dead.

I cannot name all the ghosts which I have welcomed across my inner threshold, although I recognize most of them. Nor can I tell you where I met them all – although I am happy to agree with the common opinion that they are most often met by night, in lonely places. I do not frequent graveyards at midnight, but I am sure that if I did I would find ghosts therein, and would feel their nearness much more sharply than I feel it when I am surrounded by the glamour of artificial light and the clamour of the living. I do frequent libraries, at all hours, and that might account for the fact that my most intimate relationships are with the ghosts of writers.

I dare say that H. P. Lovecraft was right when he said that the most fearful and powerful ghosts lurk between the lines of *forbidden* books, the most ominous of which would be the *Book of the Names of the Dead* (although I fear that the names in question must have lost at least some of their force in being translated from the Arabic to the Latin). I, like most of us, have had to be content with permitted books, but I have found them to be not without a certain power. I have been fascinated by the shade of Lovecraft, but far more deeply enraptured by the spirit of his friend, Clark Ashton Smith. For wit and world view there is no ghost more eloquent to me than Oscar Wilde; but for intensity and intrigue I put the highest value on visitations from further afield. The ghosts which haunt me most efficiently and most effusively are French. I have no idea why this is, but an element of the unknown and the unknowable is indispensable to any half-way decent haunting.

I wish that Charles Baudelaire had once appeared in my study – wearing no colours but black, as he did in life – to fix me with his stern and disapproving glare. I wish that in some careless reverie I had once been swept aside in time and space to the rue des Saints-Pères at the turn of the century, there to confront the lupus-scarred face of Rémy de Gourmont. I wish that Anatole France had once dropped a skeletal hand on my shoulder as I negotiated some narrow corridor steeped in Stygian shadow. But if any of these things had ever happened, I would not write about it here. It would be irreverent to turn such an experience into a mere anecdote. I am, however, prepared to offer one absolutely true example of the supernatural at work.

On 4 May 1996 I delivered the last batch of entries that I had done for John Clute's *Encyclopedia of Fantasy*. It included an entry on Maurice Maeterlinck. In the course of writing that entry I had come across a reference to a fantasy play called *Joyzelle* (1903), of which I had never heard, although I thought I knew the author's work tolerably well. On 17 May I was visiting a couple of second-hand bookshops in Bristol when I came across a temporary AA road sign pointing the way to an antiquarian book fair, of whose staging I had been entirely ignorant. One of the stalls therein had a shelf of books in French, which I naturally examined with care. There I found a copy of *Joyzelle* – which actually should not have been there, because it was the English translation by Alexander Texeira de Mattos (who was, of course, the second husband of Oscar Wilde's brother's widow).

There are people in the world who would flatly refuse to consider this incident supernatural, dismissing it as mere coincidence. Within the calculus of rationality they would doubtless be deemed correct, but we writers are experts in the business of coincidence. We know that, in terms of their literary functions, there is no difference at all between the impossible and the unlikely; they are invoked at exactly the same points in a narrative for exactly the same purposes.

When the machine of a plot has stalled and requires kick-starting, we writers use coincidence or the supernatural without conscience or discrimination, and when we need a climax that will excite, inspire and astonish we reach with equal alacrity for the spectacular million-to-one shot or the flamboyant miracle. Mundane existence is, of course, full to overflowing with 'mere coincidences', but within the context of a plot no coincidence is *mere*; each and every one of them is significant, meaningful and supernatural. Within the narrative of my life – which I am composing day by day as carefully as I can – there can be no doubt that I have not only met the ghost of Maurice Maeterlinck but have received a little kindly guidance therefrom.

Some readers, I suppose, will regret that my ghostly encounter was not scarier, or (at the very least) funnier. As I have already said, though, haunting is something that goes on all the time; life as we know it would not be possible without it. If meaning is the gift of ghosts – as it is – we ought to hesitate before giving too free a rein to the corrosive ingratitude which insists that all ghosts are horrid. All ghosts are, admittedly, *ghoulish* – but we are ghoulish ourselves if we are honest enough to see and say it; the carefully cooked food on which we dine every day is compounded from the remnant atoms of the legions of the dead.

The French historian Jules Michelet, of whom it was said that no other historian ever cared as little for accuracy, was scrupulously correct in his estimation of himself. 'I have drunk too deep', he wrote – sadly, one presumes – 'of the black blood of the dead.'

I have drunk of that black blood too, and so have you – but I wonder if either of us has truly *tasted* it, savouring its implications to the full. Perhaps we should both try harder.

You will not choose the same ghosts as I from the multitude which passes you by; you will doubtless claim your own, for your own reasons. It is not for me to ask who they are, or where you meet them, or what appearances they offer to you. Such things are private, and perhaps best kept

so. But if I may presume to offer you a little advice, I beg
you to let your chosen ghosts take their proper roles within
the narratives of your lives. Neither deny nor diminish them;
do not say that they do not exist, and do not dismiss their
manifestations as mere hallucinations and coincidences.
They are precious, both as levers to move the plot of your
existence whenever it is stalled, and as aspects of the climax
which your life will inevitably require.

Listen to your ghosts; learn from your ghosts; devour your
ghosts as they devour you, with unashamed ghoulishness.

Every time I dream about Charles Baudelaire or Oscar
Wilde, I awake hopeful that I might find beside my pillow a
tear-stained copy of *Les Fleurs du Mal* or a fresh green
carnation. Were any such thing to happen I would never tell
a soul; too many stories have already ended that way and we
should all do our level best to transcend the limits of cliché
– but if it *were* to happen, I would be grateful.

I feel that I have not yet drunk deep enough of the black
blood of the dead, nor tasted every flavour it has to offer.

LAURENCE STAIG

The Spirit of M. R. James

———————— • ► • ————————

Laurence Staig (b. 1950) was born in Bristol and currently lives near Newmarket in Suffolk. Educated at Manchester and London Universities, he is a former arts administrator and co-director of John Calder Publishers; served as an adviser on the Arts Council's Literature Panel; and was a judge for the Angel Literary Award. He was a community artist in America for seven years with the Piccolo Spoleto Festival before embarking on a career as an author in the mid-1980s. His novels include *The Network*, *The Glimpses*, *Digital Vampires*, *Shapeshifter*, *Fear of the Dark* and *The Dog Walker* (the latter two published under the pseudonym 'Christopher Carr'). His short fiction has appeared in a number of anthologies, including *The Puffin Book of Horror Stories*, *Best New Horror* and *Point Horror: 13 Again*, and has been collected in *Dark Toys and Other Consumer Goods*, *Technofear* and *Beasts*. As well as writing a number of novels for younger children, he is also working on a 'very dark' five-novel saga under the title *The Nightside*.

———————— • ► • ————————

I don't believe that I've ever seen a ghost, although many times in my life I have taken a double glance at flickering images, spied out of the corner of my eye. Glimpses of things, inexplicable movements, strange shapes and some-times sounds. But, that is all they may have been – randomly observed movements in space. Disappointing, really, because I am so fond of ghost stories as a genre of fiction and of course there is some comfort in believing that there is, perhaps, an afterlife.

However, I believe I may have brushed against the unknown in other ways. In particular, during my lifetime I seem to have encountered an extraordinary number of coincidences, some of which begger belief. But chance and the hazard of certainty are fascinating, measurable phenomena – they are, after all, possible. It is the probability that makes certain coincidences interesting. Some more than others.

I first discovered M. R. James's work when I was ten years old. My parents worked in showbusiness and often travelled the country. This meant that I was educated at dozens of different schools. The dreaded eleven-plus grammar school entry exam was looming, and my parents decided that I should spend at least one term in a boarding-school, I suppose to be crammed for the exam. I hated the place. The school was called St Bede's and was in Eastbourne, close to the cliffs. At night the wind would howl and it was easy to be hypnotized by the crashing of the waves on the rocks. The building itself was Gothic in appearance: straddling ivy, towers, and pointed windows lit like sleepy eyes.

On the day of my arrival we went down to the beach. An older boy who had placed his clothes beside me had gone off swimming, leaving me to ponder what life was going to be like here. He had left behind a book he had just bought from a newsagent's. It was a Penguin edition of M. R. James's *Ghost Stories of an Antiquary*. I had never heard of it, but picked up the book and began to read the first story, 'Canon Alberic's Scrap-book'. Despite afternoon sunshine, it scared the hell out of me.

That night, after lights had been turned out, I was told that I would have to tell the other boys in the dormitory a selection of jokes. It was customary apparently. To this day I have never been very good at remembering jokes, but offered instead to tell a ghost story. This idea went down very well and I proceeded to tell the Jamesian tale I had read that afternoon. It scared the other kids so much that one boy had an awful asthma attack and had to be taken away by the school matron, and the light had to remain on for the rest of the night.

The next day word went round that I could tell ghost stories so scary as to almost kill! It was decreed that I had to come up with another story. I went in search of the book, borrowed it and read another story in preparation for the next ghost-story-telling session. And so it went on. Of course, I had to obtain the collected stories, read them all – and like Scheherazade I spent the school term telling the ghost stories of M. R. James. When I ran out of the James canon, as you may have guessed, I had to make them up. This incident may well have been one of the seeds in my becoming a writer and admirer of fantastic fiction. It definitely marked the start of a life-long fascination with James and similar authors.

In 1980, five years before I started to write fiction seriously and professionally, I moved to Cambridge to take up the job of Literature Officer for Eastern Arts. I was so inspired by Cambridge and access to King's College that I embarked on something I had long wanted to do and wrote an academic study of James's work – basically a psychological interpretation (I have always felt that his stories were his catharsis). I failed to find a publisher and, as they say, put it away in a drawer.

I began to write for publication around 1985 and my first efforts were more science fiction than supernatural. However, after several novels I decided to write a book that was a homage to James as well as being a self-confessed reworking of some of his themes. I wrote the first draft of a novel called *The Companion* which featured a shape-shifting monk called Mr Damp. I decided to resurrect my old James manuscript and, since I now worked on a computer, paid a typist to copy it into a word processor, where it remained as a file on my hard disk.

The Companion was published as *Shapeshifter* by Harper-Collins; sadly it is now out of print, but it received great reviews and I enjoyed my first dip into the Jamesian ghost-story world. I didn't write any more James-styled ghost stories for the time being.

My story now moves to the summer of 1995. I was contacted by an East Anglian film-maker, Clive Dunn, who was proposing to make an hour-long documentary about M. R. James. This would involve some dramatized sections but also a lot of interviews with authors and other individuals who had been influenced by James. The list was impressive – Ruth Rendell, actor Christopher Lee, Jonathan Miller and Daniel Easterman, amongst others. I have a small collection of original James editions and Clive wanted to pay me a visit to talk to me about my views on the author's work, plus to generally 'shoot the breeze' about ghost stories. He made an appointment.

That night I had a dream which was directly out of James's story 'Oh, Whistle, and I'll Come to You, My Lad'. A voice whispered in my ear, 'Who is this who is coming?' I sat bolt upright in bed, cold and clammy and feeling a bit like Michael Hordern in Jonathan Miller's film version.

I paid it no attention. The next morning in my office I found myself whistling whilst tidying some papers. I am not a whistler and suddenly became self-conscious and slightly nervous. I did not know why, but there was no tune to my whistle – it was a hollow, faraway train-type whistle. Suddenly, the telephone rang and a fax began to emerge from the machine. It was from a publisher who knew I wrote fantasy and horror fiction and they invited me to write a short novel for a new series they were to launch; this was Henderson Publishing, and the stories were to be written by British authors for their new horror series for teenagers.

I suddenly felt in the mood to revisit James territory and

worked up a proposal for a ghost story using James's themes
in 'Oh, Whistle, and I'll Come to You, My Lad', about
summoning.

They accepted the synopsis I sent and I began work on
Fear of the Dark. My one proviso to Henderson was that I
should write the piece under a pseudonym, as I had now
decided that I would like to do the odd ghost story in a
Jamesian mode. For days I wrestled with what to call myself.
Whilst musing on this I picked up a pile of letters and found
amongst them a leaflet from a local trader named 'Christopher Carr'. He was a hearing-aid consultant in Cambridge! I
decided to borrow his name – it sounded snappy and
different.

A couple of weeks later I prepared for Clive Dunn's visit
by turning out all of my James bits and pieces: articles I had
collected, books and prints and whatever. I also loaded my
long-forgotten text about James on the hard disc so that, if
necessary, I could call it up on the computer during our
conversation, for quotes or whatever. It was a warm summer
day and I had left the garden doors open that led to my
office.

I got on well with Clive and he wanted me in the
programme, explaining that he was interested in my views
about the semi-subliminal aspects of James's writing, sym-
bolism and so on. He had read *Shapeshifter* and I explained
that I was working on another ghost story using another
name, borrowed from a leaflet.

During our conversation we spoke of a letter which James
had been sent from a fellow-don. The letter explained that
'Oh, Whistle, and I'll Come to You, My Lad' had had a
profound effect upon the don after reading it in bed the
previous night. He had awakened feeling strange and mel-
ancholy. I sat at the computer and loaded the text of my
unpublished book about James's work. While I waited for
the file to open and a word search to locate the section for
me, I found that Clive was reading the essay written by

James at the end of his collected short stories. The essay is called 'Stories I Have Tried to Write', and in it he mentions some of his views on ghosts. We discussed his views for a moment or two. James concludes his essay with the following:

> Late on Monday night a toad came into my study: and, though nothing has so far seemed to link itself with this appearance, I feel that it may not be quite prudent to brood over topics which may open the interior eye to the presence of more formidable visitants. Enough said.

Clive chuckled. The James text on the word processor had loaded and strangely a central passage was highlighted, all of its own accord. I read the text and my jaw fell open. I had written how James's good friend, A. C. Benson, had told him that he had just finished writing a book – a novel – and that he had decided to use a pseudonym for publication. The pseudonym was . . . Christopher Carr!

I turned to Clive, crying out that I could hardly believe my eyes. Clive had gone very quiet. He stood a little way away from me and quietly said, 'Stay still. Look down by your desk. Who'd have ever thought . . .'

I looked in the direction of his stare. A large toad had come in from the garden. It was sitting beside the desk looking up at me. *Late on Monday night a toad came into my study.* It was a Jamesian hat-trick: Christopher Carr, 'Oh, Whistle . . .' and the toad.

For a long time I wondered what were the chances of that happening. *Fear of the Dark* was published the following year – as by 'Christopher Carr'. Clive made the documentary, *A Pleasant Terror*, and it was shown on television that Christmas. But no mention was made of the extraordinary series of coincidences.

PETER TREMAYNE

The Family Curse

———————————•◆•———————————

Peter Tremayne (b. 1943) is the pseudonym of an acclaimed Celtic scholar and historian. Born in Coventry and of Irish descent on his father's side, he travelled widely in Ireland, studying its history, politics, language and mythology. As 'Peter Tremayne' he made his début with the short horror novel *Hound of Frankenstein* in 1977, since when he has published such books as *The Vengeance of She*, *Dracula Unborn* (a.k.a. *Bloodright*), *The Ants*, *The Curse of Loch Ness*, *Dracula My Love*, *Zombie!*, *The Morgow Rises*, *Kiss of the Cobra*, *Swamp!*, *Angelus!*, *Nicor!*, *Trollnight*, *Bloodmist*, *Ravenmoon*, *Island of Shadows* and *Snowbeast*. He has edited *Masters of Terror: William Hope Hodgson* and *Irish Masters of Fantasy*, and his short stories are collected in *My Lady of Hy-Brasil and Other Stories* and *Aisling and Other Irish Tales of Terror*.

———————————•◆•———————————

Back in August 1995 I was in Dublin. I was giving a lecture on some aspect of Irish history. Perhaps it is necessary to explain that 'Peter Tremayne' is a fiction-writing pseudonym and under my own name, Peter Berresford Ellis, I am considered something of an authority on Celtic history and culture.

As my lecture proceeded, I became aware of an elderly man sitting in the front row, fixing me with bright, unblinking eyes.

My lecture ended and the time came for questions from

the audience. As I instinctively knew he would, the old man rose and addressed me. 'You are aware', he intoned sibilantly, 'that the name you bear stinks in the nostrils of the people of Waterford to this day? Your family is cursed for seven generations!' With that the old man sat down abruptly and said no more. I turned the taut atmosphere with a smile. 'I know the story. But I am of the eighth generation,' I joked feebly.

But I did know what the old man meant. You see, the 'Beresford curse' is one of the most famous in Ireland. It originated in the eighteenth century. The Beresfords of Curraghmore, Portlaw, Waterford, were big landowners then. They are still in residence at the beautiful demesne of Curraghmore. John Beresford, the 8th Marquess of Waterford, still lives in Curraghmore House amidst family portraits by Sir Joshua Reynolds and Thomas Gainsborough. Today, Curraghmore is a strange, crumbling relic of the Ascendancy days, trying to survive in a country which has long passed the Anglo-Irish gentry by to become a modern republic. To make ends meet, the stately pile is partially opened to the public on afternoons, Thursdays, and Bank Holidays for those who can make the one and a half miles from the gates along the drive to the house.

But to return to the curse. It is said that an old widow woman had approached the lord of Curraghmore one day to complain that her only son was getting a little out of hand. The young man was becoming a womanizer and lazy. She asked whether the lord of Curraghmore would spare the time to remonstrate with her son so that he would no longer neglect his filial duties. The testy lord announced that he had a way of curing indolent fellows on his estate. He promptly had the widow's only son hanged.

Ask anyone today at Seskin, near Carrick-on-Suir, close to Curraghmore, about the affair and they will remember it as if it were yesterday and not an event of 250 years ago.

Well, the old widow cursed Beresford for what he had

done; she cursed all his direct descendants for seven generations. Historically, it is true that over the years the heirs of that particular Beresford died violent deaths, in war, accidents, murder and suicide. Seven generations of Beresfords did not have happy endings to their lives.

Not that I am a believer in curses, and my family connection to that branch is rather distant. *Very* distant indeed! It is a curiosity of the Ellis family in Ireland that, whenever they intermarry with another family, they adopt that family's name as a middle name. Hence, looking through the rolls of Trinity College, Dublin, where scions of the Irish Ellis family have pursued their educations, you will find Brabazon Ellis, Coyningham Ellis, Grattan Ellis and so on. Some ancestor of mine linked up to the Beresfords and, it is my belief, inserted the double R in the name (Berresford) just to be on the safe side from the curse.

Not, as I have said, that I believe in curses. Or so I tell myself.

Yet I remember one particularly odd occurrence. I *am* sensitive to atmospheres. It happened in Dublin one winter evening. By one of those curious coincidences, I was walking down Beresford Street, making my way south towards the River Liffey to keep an appointment in a drinking club on Ellis Quay. It was only later that I suddenly realized the significance of the names. It was late evening and it had been raining so the streets were deserted. There was hardly any sound but my footsteps slapping hollowly on the pavement. I was thinking of nothing in particular save, perhaps, meeting up with my friend and having a drink in the little club I was heading for.

Then I heard a curious sound. It was almost impossible to describe. A sound like something being drawn across the paving, something like a hollow metal object. Not an object like a box, for the sound was smoother than the jerking movements which a box would make, nor was the sound

like anything on wheels. I halted and peered around. The
street was still deserted. I gazed suspiciously at the darkened
doorways along it. Nothing.

I turned and walked on. Again came that rasping sound
of metal upon stone. It seemed nearer and I wheeled around
without warning. The street was still deserted. But the sound
had been so near. So close. There was no place, no dark
nook nor cranny, which could mask the maker of such a
sound anywhere near me.

Intellectual disbelief or not, emotion is a stronger compul-
sion. I turned and began to hurry. The sound continued to
draw nearer. I began to run. The sound was swifter now.
Almost on my heels. I threw caution to the wind and
positively flew down Beresford Street and skidded around
the corner into Mary's Lane leading towards Ellis Quay.

As I reached the corner, the scraping sound suddenly
ceased and I do not know what compelled me except it be
that sudden silence, but I slid to a halt and stood listening to
my panting breath against the abrupt quiet. Then, and I am
sure of it, I heard the distinct sound of a sigh. It came from
close by, yet there was no one in sight. It was a slow, deep
sigh of ... of regret? I took a few tentative steps along the
way but there was now no accompanying metal noise across
the paving stones.

In the noisy little club on Ellis Quay I met my friend and
ordered a large Power's whiskey. My friend simply laughed
when I told him of my experience. His reaction came in a
flinty Dublin vernacular: 'Will ye ever get away out of that?
Who d'ye think ye'r coddin'?' I tried to persuade him that I
was not kidding but in earnest, yet he was still dubious. 'But
everyone knows the story of Billy the Bowl. You don't have
to prove that you are a good story teller to me! Don't I read
your stories?'

I insisted that I could not be classed among the 'everyone'.
I did not know what he was talking about. It took him a
long time to be convinced that I was serious.

'Billy was known as "the legless strangler",' he began. 'Are you sure that you are not coddin' me when you say that you have never heard of him?' I averred that I was not kidding. My friend went on, still anticipating some joke on my part. 'His name was Billy Davis. He was born without legs. But he would sit in an iron bowl and pushed himself along the streets with the use of his powerful arms. He used to live on Stoneybatter.' Stoneybatter was a thoroughfare just north of Ellis Quay and running parallel to Beresford Street. 'Billy had surprising speed and agility. He would propel himself up to his unsuspecting victims and was able to use his powerful arms to drag them to the ground in seconds and relieve them of their valuables. He used to operate around this area, particularly down Beresford Street.'

'When was this?' I demanded. 'What happened to him?'

'Oh, this was back in early Victorian times. He was caught and hanged, of course.' My friend suddenly looked at me sideways with a cynical smile. 'That's why I am thinking that you are coddin' me, when you say you've never heard the tale.'

I frowned. 'Just what is that supposed to mean?'

'Well, one day, at the corner of Beresford Street, he tried to rob a young gentleman and in the struggle he strangled him. The young man's family had powerful connections. They ensured Billy met the public hangman. The young man was named Charles Beresford.'

H. R. WAKEFIELD

The Red Lodge

Herbert Russell Wakefield (1888–1964) was born in Elham, Kent. The son of Bishop Wakefield of Birmingham, he was educated at Marlborough College and Oxford University. For two years immediately preceding World War I, he served as Secretary to Lord Northcliffe, and he saw service in both world wars. For ten years Wakefield was a publisher, before he turned to writing full-time in 1930. He became a script-writer for the BBC, but is best remembered for his collections of supernatural stories: *They Return at Evening, Old Man's Beard: Fifteen Disturbing Tales* (a.k.a. *Others Who Returned*), *Imagine a Man in a Box, Ghost Stories, A Ghostly Company: A Book of Ghost Stories, The Clock Strikes Twelve: Tales of the Supernatural* and *Best Ghost Stories of H. R. Wakefield*. He also published novels of mystery and criminology such as *Hearken to the Evidence, Hostess to Death, Belt of Suspicion, Landru* and *The Green Bicycle Case*. Although never a religious man, Wakefield believed that there are many phenomena loosely called 'psychic' which do occur, however unable mankind is able to explain them rationally. 'I am convinced there are perfectly authenticated cases of most versatile psychic phenomena,' he wrote in 1946. He detailed the inspiration for his first story, 'The Red Lodge', in the introduction to his 1961 Arkham House volume *Strayers from Sheol*:

I must have read several million words on psychic research, most unremunerative words. Masses of alleged evidence, a welter of eager discordant theories – but the key to the maze remains perennially elusive. I doubt that the question, Which phenomena are supernatural? has been answered. Is telepathy supernormal? Is it not merely an extension of an old mystery – that of communication between man and man, though its modes are more flagrantly puzzling? Fooling about with marked cards seems to me the essence of futility. I've no doubt that some people are lucky with telepathic cards, just as some are 'lucky' at bridge.

Why was I persuaded into this arduous (ghost stories are very difficult to write) and unremunerative game? I am a sceptic by temperament, though not, I hope, a wooden one, and the sceptical temperament is essentially a fair, open-spirited one, ever avid to examine and, if necessary, to accept evidence adverse to its creed. And I received such evidence during two weekends spent in a superficially charming and harmonious Queen Anne house about a mile and a half from Richmond Bridge. I mustn't locate it more precisely because – and it is a significant fact – even the most rampant unbelievers often refuse to live in a reputedly haunted house.

And I can assure them they are very wise.

I visited this house in 1917, and during the previous thirty years it had known five suicides – the old gardener, strictly against orders, blurted out this ominous record in his cups, and it was verified. One had hanged herself in a powder-closet. One shot himself in the tool-shed. The others had drowned themselves in the river about a hundred yards away, always, it was said, at dawn. And now mark this! About a year after I went there, the valet of a famous nobleman also drowned himself in the river at first light. He was seen running down the path as though a fearful fiend were hard upon his heels and plunging in to his death. I think you'll agree that gives one somewhat sombrely to think.

Someone who entered this house on a lovely summer day,

knowing nothing of its record, remarked in astonishment, 'How dark it is in here!' And that was so. Always it seemed unnaturally dim, as though seen through those 'reducing' glasses artists use for toning bright light.

The moment I passed the threshold, I knew a general feeling of devitalization and psychic malaise, which remained with me till I left. The household were affected in varying degrees. Remember, some people simply *cannot* see or sense ghosts. The cook was one of them; she couldn't begin to understand what the trouble was. But one of the maids twice encountered a stranger, once in the room with the powder-closet, and once on the stairs. She couldn't 'take it' and left. The lady of the house had one of those rare temperaments which are not frightened by ghosts, and yet she was always seeing and hearing something; for, particularly after dark, that house was sparking with venom, an obscure mode of energy, call it what you will.

My own particular bother consisted of a petrified insomnia. I lay awake till dawn, oppressed by a fear without a name. Call it just ghostly fear, if you like. I felt a craven and a worm, but I was utterly unable to snap out of it. Only those who have experienced something like it will sympathize. I had only one visual bother. I was sitting in the garden one afternoon under the mulberry tree and happened to glance up at the first-floor windows. There was a blurred face at one of them. It was a man's face, but there was no man in the house. I wrote my first story about that house and called it 'The Red Lodge'. Last year, a quarter of a century later, it was republished for the sixth time in America, and a play based on it was done on the radio. It also appeared in a Dutch anthology of ghost stories. No credit to me – it must all be given to the *permanent residents* of the Red Lodge.

That's why I disagree with James. Before you can scare others, you must be scared yourself. Ghostly fear is transmitted, not concocted.

LAWRENCE WATT-EVANS

My Haunted Home

———————————◆━◆———————————

Lawrence Watt-Evans (b. 1954) was born in Arlington, Massachusetts. A full-time writer, he lives with his wife, daughter, son, parakeet and cat in Gaithersburg, Maryland. His novels of fantasy, science fiction and horror include the Lord of Dûs quartet (*The Lure of the Basilisk, The Seven Altars of Dûsarra, The Sword of Bheleu* and *The Book of Silence*), the War Surplus series (*The Cyborg and the Sorcerers* and *The Wizard and the War Machine*), the Legend of Ethshar series (*A Misenchanted Sword, With a Single Spell, The Unwilling Warlord, The Blood of a Dragon, Taking Flight* and *The Spell of the Black Dagger*) and the Three Worlds trilogy (*Out of This World, In the Empire of Shadow* and *The Reign of the Brown Magician*). Among his other books are *The Chromosomal Code, Shining Steel, Denner's Wreck, The Nightmare People, Split Heirs* (with Esther Friesner) and *Touched By the Gods.* His short fiction has been published in numerous magazines and anthologies and collected in *Crosstime Traffic.* In 1988 he was nominated for a Nebula and won the Hugo Award and the *Asimov's* Readers' Poll Award for his story 'Why I Left Harry's All-Night Hamburgers'; he won the *Asimov's* Award again two years later for 'Windwagon Smith and the Martians'.

———————————◆━◆———————————

I was born at midnight between two days in July 1954, and grew up in a small New England town – the sort of place H. P. Lovecraft wrote about. There was, in this town, a house the local kids thought was haunted – it was a big old Victorian monstrosity, with a long, ornate porch, bay windows, tall shutters, stone steps, stained glass in the front doors, a tower on the front, overgrown with assorted greenery, usually in need of paint.

That was *my* house.

My parents had six kids. My father was an associate professor of chemistry and my mother a church secretary – respectable occupations, but not all that lucrative. The only way they could afford a house big enough to accommodate us all comfortably was to buy something very out of style and in visibly poor repair. Which they did, and which they lived in comfortably for the rest of their lives.

It made my childhood interesting. I grew up hearing, 'You live *there*?' And, 'Is it haunted?' Or, 'I heard it's haunted.' Or, 'Are there any secret passages or anything?' (Alas, there weren't, though there were some odd corners.)

Hallowe'en was glorious there. We accumulated props – as a boy I built a coffin out of scrap lumber, and we used that to hold the candy we handed out. A nearby building that had been a butcher's shop a hundred years before was bulldozed, and a cache of old beef bones was turned up underneath it; we appropriated several, mostly leg bones, and used them for our décor. In two of them the marrow had dried out in just the right way to create a candle-sized socket, so we would light the front hall with candles, some in wrought-iron candelabra and some in improvised bone sconces. (The jack o' lanterns were in the other rooms.)

When you actually live in such a place it's easy to play with spooky imagery, hard to take it seriously – but many of the neighbours really *did* think our place was haunted.

What was interesting was that the families who had lived in the area the longest didn't say the *house* was haunted; they said our *barn* was haunted. Allegedly, at some point in the 1890s, a pair of sailors jumped ship in Boston and wandered the twenty miles out to our neighbourhood, drinking heavily the whole way. They chose our barn to hole up in and sleep it off, but got into a fight, and one of them fatally stabbed the other, then fled and was never caught. The ghost of the murdered sailor was said to haunt the place still.

There's absolutely no documentary evidence for any of this, but some of the neighbours swore to every word of it. I heard the stories, of course, but never took them very seriously.

The house, which I've already described, was built in 1851; the barn was added much later, possibly in 1881 (major renovations were done that year), and was comparatively nondescript. No towers, no gingerbread, no stained glass, no carved granite steps. It wasn't particularly traditionally barn-like, either – no multi-angled roof, no red paint anywhere. It looked more like an overgrown garage, with peeling white-painted clapboards and dark green sliding doors on rusted metal tracks; I suppose it was a carriage barn, really.

It was a wonderful place to play, haunted or not – it held a century of clutter. Old doors, off their hinges for decades, made great ramparts for forts; an antique trunk could serve as a space-ship or lifeboat. We jumped out of the hay loft and somehow never injured anyone. We once assembled a full-scale ship's deck in the hay loft out of junk, using the rafters as spars. At one point I teamed up with two of my sisters and some of the neighbours to turn one back section into a full-fledged funhouse; we charged a dime admission and turned a tidy profit.

We never saw any spooks.

Until one fall afternoon I went out to the barn, looking for something to do, mulling over possibilities for some other major project we could undertake there, like the ship or the funhouse. I think I was twelve or thirteen. I climbed the stairs to the hay loft (yes, stairs, not a ladder; I said it wasn't very barn-like) and looked around.

The loft was virtually empty at that point; my father had noticed the floor sagging, and had removed all unnecessary

weight from it until repairs could be made. The two big
trapdoors through which hay could be flung down, and the
two outside doors where bales would be hauled in, were all
closed. It looked like a big empty attic, dimly lit by two
windows high at either end. Dust was dancing in the sunlight
from the south window. I stood in the centre and looked
around.

Something white was moving in the shadows in the south-
west corner, something four or five feet tall and indistinct. It
moved from the corner over towards the stairs in the south-
east corner, and then vanished.

I don't know what it was. It looked like a patch of fog,
really – but how could there be a patch of fog inside a
closed-up barn? Why would it be shaped like that, roughly
four feet tall and one foot wide? And why did it move in
utterly still air? How did it vanish?

So maybe I saw a ghost. At the time I didn't even think of
that – I saw something mysterious, but a ghost? After
spending my life in a 'haunted house', I didn't believe in
ghosts. The whole murdered sailor story sounded stupid to
me.

But what the hell *was* it?

I didn't play in the barn much after that. Maybe I just
outgrew it.

CHERRY WILDER

The Ghost Hunters

———————————•◆•———————————

Cherry Wilder (b. 1930) was born in Auckland, New Zealand, and she currently lives in Wiesbaden, Germany. She published poetry, short stories and criticism before turning to science fiction, fantasy and horror in 1974. Her short fiction has appeared in many magazines and anthologies, including *Isaac Asimov's Science Fiction Magazine*, *Omni*, *Interzone*, *New Terrors*, *Millennial Women*, *Alien Worlds*, *Twenty Houses of the Zodiac*, *Strange Attractors*, *Dark Voices 2*, *Skin of the Soul*, *Asimov's Ghosts*, *Obsession*, *Strange Fruit: Tales of the Unexpected* and *The Best New Horror*, and has been collected in *Dealers in Light and Darkness*. Among her novels are the 'Torin' Trilogy (*The Luck of Brin's Five*, *The Nearest Fire* and *The Tapestry Warriors*), the 'Rulers of Hylor' Trilogy (*A Princess of the Chemeln*, *Yorath the Wolf* and *The Summer's King*), the Planet Rhomary Land series (*Second Nature* and *Signs of Life*) and the horror novel *Cruel Designs*.

———————————•◆•———————————

Stephen King in his indispensable non-fiction work *Danse Macabre* (1981) writes of Shirley Jackson's eloquent and accomplished novel *The Haunting of Hill House* (1959). He quotes Jackson's biographer, Lenemaja Friedman, who states:

> The inspiration to write a ghost story came to Miss Jackson ... as she was reading a book of nineteenth century psychic researchers who rented a haunted house

in order to study it and record their impressions of
what they had seen and heard for the purpose of
presenting a treatise to the Society for Psychical
Research.

Shirley Jackson was struck by the story behind the investigation and the 'differing motivations and backgrounds' of
the ghost hunters. There follows an account of Shirley
Jackson finding two grotesque and striking old houses, on
which she based her sinister portrait of Hill House – and the
striking coincidence that one of the houses was built by her
own grandfather.

I believe I know which classic account of the investigation
of a haunted house this was. It seems to me that Shirley
Jackson read *The Haunting of B. House*, an investigation
undertaken for the Society of Psychical Research at Ballechin
House in Scotland in 1897. The investigation caused scandal
and controversy, not only because of the phenomena allegedly observed, but because the leader of the expedition
arranged to rent the house for hunting and fishing without
mentioning that he and his party would be hunting ghosts.

The Society for Psychical Research was founded in 1882
by Professor Henry Sidgwick of Cambridge and F. W. H.
Myers (inventor of the word 'telepathy'). The society relied
on many voluntary assistants. The ghost hunt at Ballechin
House was led by a trusted and capable investigator – he
had, for instance, been sent to Canada to interview the
medium Mrs Piper. This was, of course, none other than
Colonel George Lee Le Mesurier Taylor, of Cheltenham –
my great-uncle.

In 1978, with the aid of Robert Aickman, I presented to
the society a small packet of letters from Great-Uncle George
to my grandfather, Major Colin McKenzie Taylor of Nelson,
New Zealand. The letters were unexciting – brief information
concerning testaments, family matters – but Great-Uncle
George made one important confession to his brother. He

did enjoy, he said, while referring to his investigative activities, the company of these emancipated women . . .

This sheds some light – not entirely unexpected by Shirley Jackson or myself – upon the fun of ghost-hunting, with intrepid females.

CHET WILLIAMSON

A Place Where a Head Would Rest

———————————— •—• ————————————

Chet Williamson (b. 1948) was born in Lancaster, Pennsylvania. His first short story was published in 1981, since when his fiction has appeared in such magazines and anthologies as *Playboy*, the *New Yorker*, *Esquire*, *Twilight Zone*, *The Magazine of Fantasy & Science Fiction*, *Alfred Hitchcock's Mystery Magazine*, *Blood is Not Enough*, *Monsters in Our Midst*, *Diagnosis Terminal: An Anthology of Medical Terror* and *The Best New Horror*, among many others. His novels include *Soulstorm*, *Ash Wednesday* (nominated for the Horror Writers Association's Bram Stoker Award), *Lowland Rider*, *Dreamthorp*, *McKain's Dilemma*, *Reign*, *Second Chance*, *Ravenloft: Mordenheim* and *Murder in Cormyr* for TSR, and the movie novelization *The Crow: City of Angels*. *Shadow Ops: Blood and Iron* is the first in a new series of books about paranormal investigators.

———————————— •—• ————————————

There was a time, over a quarter of a century ago, one dark summer night away from my home, when something happened to me that was subtle, yet disquieting enough to make me leave that house and never go back.

I had just graduated from high school, and had gotten an apprenticeship at a summer theatre connected with a college in New Jersey. My parents had helped me find lodgings in a house across the river in Bucks County, Pennsylvania. The house was a large, three-storey dwelling, the oldest parts of which were built before the Revolutionary War. It had a barn, a duck pond, a great many trees and a name, which I will not print here, but the fact that it had a single appellation rather than a boring address impressed me greatly.

I was given a room on the third floor. Supposedly there was another roomer on that floor, but I did not meet him when I moved in, nor at any time thereafter, though in the week I lived there I did once or twice hear his footsteps as they came up the stairs to the third floor, and then moved into his room, into the shared bathroom, and back again.

My room was located in the front right corner of the house, and, though large, was furnished spartanly. There was a bed against one of the inner walls, with a small table and lamp next to it, a high-backed easy chair, a chest of drawers, and a hall tree near the door. Several throw carpets were placed over the rough-hewn boards of the floor. The two windows, one looking out on the front of the house and the other giving a view of the side, were recessed so that, with the tall, encroaching trees all about, the room was fairly dark even with the sun shining.

Several nights after my tenancy began, I went downstairs to the kitchen to write a letter home, since there was no desk in my room. I fell into a conversation with the woman who owned the house, and she told me about its history, including the interesting fact that money for the revolution's arms had been hidden under the wooden floorboards. When I said, chuckling, that a house this old must surely have a ghost, she smiled and said, 'Yes, it does.'

'Really? Where?' I asked.

'Right next to you.'

I turned, filled with a delightful *frisson*, to find a small, hand-painted wooden chair standing against the wall.

'That was Mr Picard's chair,' the woman told me, and went on to explain that Mr Picard was the man who had owned the house before she and her husband had moved in. He had done a great deal of restoration, and had bought period furniture for the house as well, but when he died, nearly everything was auctioned. When the woman and her husband moved in, they found that this chair had been overlooked in a back room, and brought it into the kitchen.

The first week they were living in the house, a neighbour brought over some groceries and set the bag on the chair. It fell over almost immediately, and my landlady swore that the bag had not *tipped* over, but had slid sideways and fallen straight down. After that, they dubbed it Mr Picard's Chair, and never sat in it nor set anything on it. She told me that I might hear Mr Picard moving through the house at night, but that he was a very kind and gentle ghost, and would do no harm. They even, she added, got him a present every Christmas. I neglected to ask how he went about opening it.

Naturally I felt a little creepy when I went to bed that night. I was also uncomfortable about my theatre apprenticeship, since I had been told that I would be able to act in small parts, but instead found myself manning the ticket-booth phones. I comforted myself with Jules Verne's *Carpathian Castle*, and finally turned out the light around 11.30 p.m.

I drifted between sleep and wakefulness for some time, and remember looking over towards the easy chair. Though I had not heard the door to my room open – indeed, it could not have, since I bolted it at night – I thought I saw a shape in the chair. Naturally, I looked for the easiest explanation, which was that I had tossed my bathrobe on to the chair and it had landed there in such a way that it approximated a human figure, nothing more. I did not even feel alarmed enough to switch on the light and reassure myself, but simply rolled over and went to sleep, wishing my bathrobe pleasant dreams.

When I awoke the next morning, I lay in bed for a while before recalling the shape in the chair the previous night. When I glanced towards it, I was surprised to discover that there was nothing whatsoever in the chair, and that my bathrobe was hanging on the hall tree. At first I put it down to imagination and got out of bed, but then I noticed something on the grey fabric of the easy chair.

It was a dark, round spot, and it was on the high back of the chair where a sitter might have rested his head. It was not wet, merely damp, for when I pressed my fingers to it they came away with hardly any trace of moisture.

I looked up at the ceiling, but saw no signs of a leak, and a glance out of the window told me that it had not rained the night before. The thought occurred to me that perhaps my mysterious fellow-boarder might have come into my room after his shower, and sat in my chair, either by mistake or through a dark design, but the fact that the small bolt on the door of my room was still thrown shut demolished that theory.

I showered quickly and headed over to Jersey, feeling slightly sick and very confused. At the theatre, the situation had worsened, and I realized that I had been gulled. Neither I nor any of the apprentices would even be able to audition for the plays – we were nothing more than free help, and that realization led me to turn in my resignation.

After a less than amicable parting, I drove back to the house, where I met my landlady in the kitchen. I had simply intended to tell her that I would be leaving the next day, but I did not. To this day, I don't know why I asked her, but after saying hello, the next words out of my mouth were the question of how Mr Picard had died.

She looked at me oddly, but answered quickly enough. 'It was a heart attack,' she said, and I relaxed a bit, only to feel the tension come surging back as she added, 'They found him at the edge of the pond, partly in the water.'

That was enough. I didn't need to ask if his head was in the pond or not. I immediately gave up my idea of staying another night, and told her that things hadn't worked out at the theatre and I would be leaving for home as soon as I could pack. Needless to say, I packed in record time. The spot on the chair had now vanished, the cloth bone dry. I said goodbye and drove home, never having seen the woman's husband nor the other roomer during the week that I stayed there.

So was it a ghost? I think not. I regret not. There must have been some other explanation. Perhaps I had somehow caused the spot myself, and imagined the shape in the chair. In all honesty, I would like to think that it *was* Mr Picard's ghost come to pay me a visit. The logical conclusion to that visitation – that life exists after death – would be a great comfort.

But rationality persists, whispering its dry and sandy explanations in my ear, turning me from beloved and kindly superstition. Sadly, this experience is the closest I have ever come to breathing the sweet air of eternity. So far.

Still, there are times when I silently beg Mr Picard to come again, and this time to let me see the other side of the wall through his ghostly face. I wait, and I hope, for some glimpse of light before the darkness.

F. PAUL WILSON

The Glowing Hand

———————————— •◆• ————————————

F. Paul Wilson (b. 1946) was born and raised in New Jersey. His first short story was published in 1971 in *Startling Mystery Stories 18*, while he was studying to become a doctor, and since then he has also become a bestselling novelist. His books include the science fiction novels *Healer, Wheels Within Wheels, An Enemy of the State, Dydeetown World, The Tery*; such horror titles as *The Keep* (filmed in 1983), *The Tomb, Reborn, Reprisal, Sibs* (a.k.a. *Sister Night*), *Nightworld* and *Mirage* (with Matt Costello); the medical thrillers *The Touch, The Select, Implant* and *Deep as the Marrow* (the latter three as by 'Colin Andrews' in the UK); and the historical horror novel *Black Wind*. His short fiction is collected in *Night Visions 6, Soft and Others* and *Ad Statum Perspicuum*, and he has edited the Horror Writers Association anthology *Freak Show*, and *Diagnosis Terminal: An Anthology of Medical Terror*.

———————————— •◆• ————————————

This is a third-hand supernatural experience. It happened to my aunt, and as a child I heard it from my mother.

Ours was an Irish Catholic household. My father may have been born in Glasgow and raised in Liverpool, but my mother was Mary Elizabeth Sullivan from rural New England. Trust me, it was an Irish Catholic home, where we believed that prayer worked, that statues of the Virgin could weep real tears, that holy people could develop the stigmata, and that a miracle could be just around the corner.

So I was well primed at the age of five to experience my first true *frisson* during my mother's recounting of Aunt Margaret's vision of the glowing hand.

Aunt Margaret had been sleeping peacefully when she awoke in the dead of night. She opened her eyes and noticed a glow from the hall outside her bedroom door. At first she thought her husband had left the living-room light on, but it wasn't that kind of light. This was much paler ... almost white.

And it seemed to be growing brighter.

No ... not brighter. Closer.

The light was coming down the hall ... towards their bedroom door. She was just reaching for Uncle Bill, to wake him, when she saw it: a hand, glowing as white and pale as the moon, floating down the hall outside her bedroom. The sight of it, and the possibility that it was going to float into the bedroom, paralysed her.

But the hand didn't turn. Instead, it continued its slow pace down the hall and, soon after passing from sight, the glow faded, leaving the house in darkness.

Margaret woke Bill and together they searched the house, waking twelve-year-old Billy in the process. He'd seen nothing either, and the apparition was laid off as a nightmare.

But the next night Margaret awoke and once again saw the glowing hand making its way down the hall. This time, after it passed her door, she leaped from bed and ran out into the hall just in time to see it fading from view ... outside Billy's door. She looked in on her son and found him sleeping peacefully. Still, the sight of that hand hovering outside his door had filled her with a terrible foreboding.

The next night she didn't have to wake up because she hadn't been able to sleep a wink. And then it happened again. Shortly after 2 a.m., the glow began at the far end of the hall. But this time Margaret wasn't going to sit in bed and wait for it. She got up and went to the bedroom door.

And there, drifting through the air not two feet from her, was the hand, glowing brighter than ever. But this time – saints preserve us – *clutched in its glowing fingers was a long, sharp knife!*

Margaret almost fainted, but she hung on and stumbled after the apparition as it continued down the hall, *and passed right through the door to Billy's room!*

She lunged forward, burst into the room, just in time to see the hand plunge its knife into Billy's abdomen!

Billy didn't stir. He seemed completely unaware that anything was happening – until he and his father were awakened by Margaret's scream.

But the hand and its knife were gone, and once again the whole experience was written off as a nightmare.

But not for long. Billy doubled over with acute abdominal pain the next day and had to have an emergency appendectomy.

No one ever offered an explanation, or even a supernatural rationale for these 'warnings' that Billy would soon be going 'under the knife'. It was one of those things that just happen. And that's probably why the story chilled me so. Something like that could *just happen.*

Of course I had my mother tell it and retell it until she was sick of the story. But every time she came to the part where the ghostly knife plunged into Cousin Billy's belly . . . Brrr!

I never forgot the story, and even had a character retell it in one of my novels.

DOUGLAS E. WINTER

Finding My Religion

———————•-•-•———————

Douglas E. Winter (b. 1950) was born in St Louis, Missouri, and now lives in Oakton, Virginia, with his wife Lynne. A partner in the international law firm of Bryan Cave LLP and a member of the National Book Critics Circle, he is the author or editor of eleven books (including *Stephen King: The Art of Darkness*, *Faces of Fear*, *Prime Evil* and the epic anthology of apocalyptic fiction, *Millennium* (a.k.a. *Revelations*)). He has published more than two hundred articles and short stories in such major metropolitan newspapers as the *Washington Post*, *Washington Times*, *Philadelphia Inquirer*, *Atlanta Journal-Constitution* and *Cleveland Plain Dealer*; in magazines as diverse as *Harper's Bazaar*, *Saturday Review*, *Gallery* and *Twilight Zone*; and in publications in fourteen languages on four continents. He is book columnist for *The Magazine of Fantasy & Science Fiction* and music columnist for *Video Watchdog*; he also acted as a contributing editor of *Fantasy Review* and *The Penguin Encyclopedia of Horror and the Supernatural*. He is a winner of the World Fantasy Award, and a multiple nominee for that award as well as for the Hugo and Bram Stoker Awards. His short fiction has been selected six times for inclusion in 'best of the year' anthologies. His forthcoming books include a critical biography of Clive Barker.

———————•-•-•———————

Paranormal encounters? It's intriguing to think that someone who is compelled to write fiction evoking the fine emotion of horror has had, or ought to have had, an experience with the supernatural. Sometimes I wish for a simple story to share: oh, yes, that was the night I saw the woman in white descend the stairs, power drill in hand. That would explain everything, wouldn't it?

Certainly it would make for better cocktail conversation. The truth, as always, is less sensational.

I've seen some strange things. When I was young, I found an eerie snake or tentacle of gel growing out of the base of a tree; but when I brought my brother and friends to look, it was gone. I looked up from a basement window to see a man outside, staring down at me. I have even, with the assistance of gin, seen a flight of bats descend over my automobile. These experiences, and others, have explanations, or contexts so mundane that it's impossible to consider them worthy of a supernatural encounter.

It's what I haven't seen that haunts me.

I grew up in a grey and gloomy place called Granite City, a steel-town in south-western Illinois. My parents attended the church that their parents had attended, a Southern Baptist blockhouse of blue-collar conservatism and blood-and-damnation rhetoric. I was told repeatedly that its dour sanctuary was the house of God, and to that sanctuary my family would travel each Sunday morning, Sunday night and Wednesday night to hear sermons that ended in tears and pleas for forgiveness, and to sing hymns that asked Jesus, the sacrificial lamb of God, to wash us in His blood – or implored His father to end this world and call us home.

So it was that on a certain Sunday night, after the evening service had concluded and the remaining members of the congregation chatted in the parking lot, my father asked me to find my brother. When I went back inside the church, something changed me for ever.

A small boy, perhaps seven years of age, found himself alone in the sanctuary of the First Baptist Church ... and as he stood in the centre aisle, the lights clicked out around him. He knew that someone had simply turned the switches, preparing to close and lock the building for the night, but he wasn't in a time or place for knowing – he was experiencing. He stood in the sudden darkness as the vague light of distant street-lamps bred shadows and more shadows in that silent interior. He felt the familiar career into the unknown, and in that moment he felt the most profound emotion, one that uplifted his heart even as it crippled him with fear.

He stood in the presence of the Beyond. The darkness, not the light, brought a message more profound than that of any sermon, any hymn. The darkness taught him the pleasure and the peril of uncertainty – of stepping out on that tightrope where we can neither believe nor disbelieve, know nor not know, where the promise of the supernatural urges us to risk another step.

If I stood in that aisle for much longer, I might have taken that step, touched some untouchable wisdom.

Instead, I ran away.

Although I've searched long and hard, I've found that place again only a few times, almost always in invocations of my imagination – in novels, in films and, on occasion, in my own writing. I treasure those visits, especially the unexpected ones, and I dare say that they are the jewels to be found amongst the muck of horror. Which is another way of saying that great horror is rarely about the supernatural, but instead finds transcendent power in evoking its possibility.

GENE WOLFE

Kid Sister

Gene Wolfe (b. 1931) was born in Brooklyn, and raised mainly in Houston, Texas. He has written more than a hundred science fiction and fantasy stories, and he made his début with a supernatural thriller, 'The Dead Man', published in a 1965 edition of *Sir* magazine. His first book, *Operation Ares*, appeared in 1970, and was followed by *The Fifth Head of Cerberus* (a collection of three linked novellas), *Peace, The Devil in a Forest, Free Live Free, Soldier of the Mist, Soldier of Arete, There Are Doors, Castleview, Pandora By Holly Hollander, Nightside the Long Sun, Castle of Days, Exodus From the Long Sun* and the non-fiction volume *Letters Home*. In 1980 the first volume in Wolfe's 'Book of the New Sun,' *The Shadow of the Torturer*, was published to major acclaim, winning both the World Fantasy Award and the British Science Fiction Award. It was followed by *The Claw of the Conciliator* (winner of the 1982 Nebula Award), *The Sword of the Lictor, The Citadel of the Autarch* and *The Urth of the New Sun*. His short fiction has been collected in *The Island of Doctor Death and Other Stories, and Other Stories, Gene Wolfe's Book of Days, Storeys from the Old Hotel* (winner of the 1989 World Fantasy Award) and *Endangered Species*.

Not long before my mother's death, I took her and a trailer filled with her belongings from Virginia Beach, Virginia, back to Logan, Ohio, where my father had grown up and where she had lived with him from his retirement until his death in 1973.

But before I tell you about that trip through the mountains of West Virginia, a long drive over steep and narrow black-topped roads slippery with snow, I must tell you a little about my mother and her family. Although what I will tell you about them is true to the best of my knowledge (everything in this account is true), I will omit surnames for reasons that will soon become obvious.

When I trace my mother to the end of memory, I find a beautiful young woman bending over the little bed she has made for me on a seat in a railway chaircar. Her eyes are blue, and a strand of auburn hair peeps from under her cloche. A friend of mine jokes about 'sharp-nosed English redheads'; I heard her use the phrase for years before it struck me that my mother had been one of them.

We were going from New Jersey to North Carolina, supposedly to visit her family but in fact to visit her father. As if by magic we were there, and he was an old man who sat on the porch grasping the cane with which he threatened me each time I came too near, a large old man with a jug of corn whisky beside him and a wooden leg stretched stiffly before him. I admired him for the pit dog chained to a tree across the road and the fighting cocks cooped behind the house; I did not know then that he had begun life as a sailor, or that he had fought Indians and Mexican bandits as a cavalryman, or that he had been a circus performer.

Nor did I know that he was a hard and violent man who had lost his leg when a gang of workmen he bossed had tried to murder him; or that he beat his wife and all but one of his children. The one he never struck had been Mary, his favourite. Mary was my mother.

We returned home and he died. Because her father had favoured her, my mother was not well liked by her numerous brothers and sisters. For her and for me, her family virtually ceased to exist for about fifty years.

My father died. My wife and children and I went to Logan for his funeral; and his sister's son, urging me to put on my overcoat before we went to the grave, said something so obvious and so obviously many-sided that I have never used it in fiction: 'It'll be cold out there on the hill.'

After half a year, perhaps, my mother wrote asking us to help her move. When she was a young woman courted by many young men, it had been customary for such suitors to bring candy or flowers. When they went home, she had quietly put the boxes of candy beside the bed of her younger sister, Emily. Both of them were old now, but Emily remembered. Emily had invited her sister to live with her.

My wife, Rosemary, drove my mother in my mother's car. I drove ours, chock-full of our luggage and various possessions of my mother's. We became separated, and thus I came alone, a middle-aged man, to the home of one of the aunts I had never seen. With some trepidation, I knocked on her door; she opened it, and I knew her at once – she looked exactly like my mother. (She talked, however, precisely like Carol Channing.) She was witty and charming, delighted, or at least very willing to pretend to be delighted, to meet her previously unknown nephew.

Another year, and she was dead. I flew to Virginia Beach and rented a U-Haul trailer in which to carry my mother's few belongings back to Logan. The man at the rental agency did not seem to know much about hooking up his trailers to cars like my father's veteran Mercury, but the two of us did our best.

Back at the weathered frame house that had been my aunt's, my mother told me I would have to sleep in Emily's bedroom – there was no other bed except her own. I lugged my suitcase in, and found the bedspread stiff with blood. Emily had lain on it, my mother explained, and the chemotherapy treatments that had not cured her cancer had given her hives. She had scratched them raw.

I threw the bedspread into a corner, turned up a book (a

biography of F. Scott Fitzgerald's wife Zelda) and settled down to read by the frilly little lamp on the nightstand. The switch clicked futilely. I unscrewed the bulb, which tinkled musically as burnt-out bulbs often do. It had been a hundred-watt bulb, I noticed, which seemed very powerful for such a small lamp.

Next morning, as we loaded the rented trailer, my mother told me she had tripped and nearly fallen during the night just past, and I said casually that she and Emily should have had some night-lights. They had not needed them, my mother said, because Emily had kept the lamp beside her bed switched on all night.

I thought about that as we drove away – the frilly little bedside lamp that had kept Death at bay, and Death's coming quietly through the night when the little lamp's brilliant light failed at last.

Soon, however, my mother and I fell to talking as we had when I was a boy; my mother, my father and I had all been great talkers. Now talk cheered our way through the mountains, the snow and the dark, talk of all that had happened to her that I had not seen or heard, and all that had happened to me since I had left the little house in Texas. Among many other things, I told her about a man I had interviewed the week before. He had owned a new and very expensive car, and had been furiously angry with it. There had been something wrong with the locks, so that his own door was the only one that could be opened from inside. To let out a passenger, he had been forced to leave the car and open the passenger's door with the key.

Shortly after that, we stopped at a filling station; it was about ten o'clock at night. My mother wanted to get out of the car, but the passenger-side door of the old Mercury would not open.

My father had bought that car ten years before. He had driven my mother on a thousand little trips and errands in it. Later, Rosemary had driven her in it, and she had driven

Emily around Virginia Beach. There had never been any sort of trouble with the doors.

There was now. My mother pulled up on the lock button again, pulled the handle up and pushed against the door with all her slight strength. I reached across her, jerked up the handle and pounded the door with the heel of my hand. It might as well have been welded shut.

We looked at each other. And then – very slowly – looked into the back seat. There was nothing to see there and nothing to hear, no shadowy figure, no ghostly laughter. But the sensation was overwhelming: a third person was sitting there, an impish passenger who found our efforts with the door very amusing indeed.

I think I muttered, 'All right.' Certainly I got out (just like the man I had interviewed) and opened my mother's door with the key.

That was the end of it, or almost the end. The door opened and closed without difficulty for the rest of the trip.

When we reached Logan and I had unloaded the trailer, I towed it to the U-Haul franchise there to turn it in. The attendant looked at it and the way it was fastened to my father's old Mercury and shook his head. 'You hauled it like this clear from Virginia?'

I said I had.

'The way it's hitched up, you shouldn't have got ten miles.'

Acknowledgements

Special thanks for all their help and support in compiling this book to Mandy Slater, Mike Ashley, Ramsey Campbell, Peter Cannon, Douglas E. Winter, Jo Fletcher, Kim Newman, Mareia Terrones, the Society of Authors, Scott Edelman, my understanding editor Faith Brooker and, especially, Dot Lumley.

'One-Way Trip' copyright © 1997 by R. Chetwynd-Hayes

'The Shock of the Macabre' copyright © 1946 by A. E. Coppard. Extracted from *Fearful Pleasures*, published by Arkham House; reprinted by permission of the agent for the author's estate

'The Haunted Hotel' copyright © 1997 by Basil Copper

'Safe Arrival' copyright © 1997 by Peter Crowther

'A Gift of Eagles' copyright © 1997 by Jack Dann. Some material originally published in different form in *Rod Serling's The Twilight Zone Magazine*, August 1987

'The House on Spadina' copyright © 1997 by Charles de Lint

'Sharing With Strangers' copyright © 1997 by Terry Dowling

'Hands on the Wheel' copyright © 1997 by Lionel Fanthorpe

'That Old School Spirit' copyright © 1997 by Esther M. Friesner

'Twice Encountered' copyright © 1997 by Gregory Frost

'The Flints of Memory Lane' copyright © 1997 by Neil Gaiman

'Haunted in the Head' copyright © 1997 by Ray Garton

'In There' copyright © 1997 by Stephen Gallagher

'The House on the Brink' copyright © 1997 by John Gordon

'Riding the Nightwinds' copyright © 1997 by Ed Gorman

'ESP' copyright © 1974 by Elizabeth Goudge. Extracted from *The Joy of the Snow: An Autobiography*, published by Hodder and Stoughton; reprinted by permission of the agent for the author's estate

'Death is a Lady' copyright © 1997 by Simon R. Green

'The Smoke Ghost' copyright © 1997 by Peter Haining

'Never Say Die' copyright © 1997 by Joe Haldeman

'Not Very Psychic' copyright © 1992, 1997. Extracted from *Danse Macabre*, January 1986; 'Heavy Stuff' by Tony Eyers, *Isis*, March 1989; 'Meeting With a Man of Horror' by Suzanne McDonnell, *Melbourne Sun*, 31 October 1987; 'Oh Rats! It's Herbert's Horrors' by Lesley Bendel, *Writer's*

Monthly, October 1987; and 'James Herbert – The Devil of a Chiller' by Peter Grosvenor, *Daily Express,* 16 May 1980

'Confessions of a Born-Again Heathen' copyright © 1997 by Brian Hodge

'To Pine With Fear and Sorrow' copyright © 1997 by Nancy Holder

'A Ghostly Cry' copyright © 1931 by M. R. James. Extracted from 'Ghosts – Treat Them Gently!', *Evening News,* 17 April 1931. Copyright © 1926 by M. R. James. Extracted from *Eton and Kings* by M. R. James; reprinted by permission of the author's estate

'One Extra for Dinner' copyright © 1997 by Peter James/ Really Scary Books Ltd

'A Face in the Crowd' copyright © 1997 by Mike Jefferies

'Rageddy Ann' copyright © 1997 by Nancy Kilpatrick

'Uncle Clayton' copyright © 1983 by *Playboy* magazine. Extracted from 'Playboy Interview: Stephen King' by Eric Norden, *Playboy,* June 1983; reprinted by special permission of *Playboy* magazine

'Go On, Open Your Eyes...' copyright © 1997 by Hugh Lamb

'Moving Houses' copyright © 1997 by Terry Lamsley

'Inspiration' copyright © 1997 by John Landis

'Norfolk Nightmare' copyright © 1997 by Stephen Laws

'Not Funny' copyright © 1997 by Samantha Lee

'The Gray Ghost' copyright © 1997 by Barry B. Longyear

'Witch House' copyright © 1965 by August Derleth and Donald Wandrei. Extracted from *H. P. Lovecraft: Selected Letters 1911–1924*; reprinted by permission of Arkham House Publishers, c/o Ralph M. Vicinanza Ltd

'The Challenge' copyright © 1997 by Brian Lumley

'The World of the Senses' copyright © 1923 by Arthur Machen. Extracted from *Things Near and Far*; reprinted by permission of the agent for the author's estate

'My Grandfather's House' copyright © 1997 by Graham Masterton